Brent Meersman
HOMO ODYSSEY

This book is a work of fiction. Any resemblance
to real persons, living or dead, is purely coincidental.

The story set in Morocco was first published as
Stranger in Marrakech in *What Love Is*
(Arcadia Books; London, 2011)
© Brent Meersman.

© 2018 Salzgeber Buchverlage GmbH
Prinzessinnenstraße 29, 10969 Berlin
buch@salzgeber.de

Cover design: Robert Schulze
Cover photo: shutterstock.com/everst
Printed in Germany

ISBN: 978-3-95985-341-5

HOMO ODYSSEY

Adventures of a World Traveler

BRENT MEERSMAN

BRUNO GMÜNDER

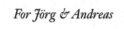
For Jörg & Andreas

INTRODUCTION

Sex between men is not the sole preserve of those who see themselves as 'gay'

In coming to terms with my own sexuality, I developed an almost anthropological obsession with what it means to find yourself inexplicably and irreversibly attracted to the same sex. I wanted to understand homosexual life in all its diversity. How, I wondered, do men sexually attracted to other men live in different parts of the world? How do they see themselves? How have they survived over the centuries, mostly in places hostile to them?

I set out to immerse myself in every part of the world I could reach. Through 60 countries and seven continents, it has been a journey that has fundamentally changed my conception of myself, and along the way my view of so-called 'gay' identity.

As a reader, it used to irk me how sex, such an integral part of most people's lives (which doesn't suddenly stop when traveling) is usually deliberately written out of travelogues; swashbuckling adventurers suddenly become awfully coy. Such intimate contact with someone who has their roots where the traveler is merely passing through often leads to revelation; the unexpected romance with a beautiful stranger that transforms a dingy destination into a brief paradise; a mysterious man who turns exotic fantasy into reality; a dishonest rent boy who poisons a whole city for one.

The stories in this collection are spun from my uncensored travel diaries. I have included accounts of sex and non-sex and no sex, some events of which I am now somewhat ashamed, together with stories of love, and some of violence. They are not in chronological order.

In my short life, I have seen my society make some profound shifts in how it views homosexuality. For most of my childhood, I believed I was the only one *like that* in the world. When I grew up in Cape Town, South Africa, homosexuality was illegal and punishable with imprisonment. The social stigma was even worse than the law. There were no queers on television – unthinkable today. Even heterosexual sex was made into something dirty by the hypocritical, puritanical bigots that ruled my country.

Before the 1990s, you didn't see genitals in South Africa, apart from the breasts of black women, who the authorities thought of as wildlife. Magazines and newspapers redacted white peoples' private parts with big black stripes and put stars over nipples. Even art programs were censored. On state television, when the camera panned down the body of Michelangelo's *David*, the screen would go blank at the navel, and the picture only recover around the knees. The only nude male you ever saw was a Nuba tribesman in a *National Geographic* magazine. No wonder sex was something dirty or unspeakable, something to be sniggered at.

Society had defined me as a pervert. God, I was told, wanted me dead. So it seemed did the government. When I went to university, my country was militarily occupying Namibia, at war in Angola, and on the brink of a civil war at home. Nearly all my close friends skipped the country to avoid conscription into the hated army.

I was in two minds about fleeing. I spent several months on the backpacking circuit with a Eurail Pass crisscrossing the ten countries that at that time made up Western Europe. Coming from parochial, culturally isolated and backward apartheid South Africa, I had an insatiable appetite for the bookstores, the architectural wonders, the galleries and museums of Europe. I sought out all those paintings and great works I had only ever seen as feeble facsimiles in counterfeit color in encyclopedias.

With my nascent sexuality, still unfolding, heuristically, Cellini's Perseus, Moreau's unpierced Saint Sebastian, the men from Picasso's rose period, and all of Géricault's male nudes, came to define a sexual ideal. I began to yearn for male bodies that resembled those palpitating sculptures and paintings; I'd go weak at the knees when seeing a face that appeared like an El Greco saint; my heart skipping when I met a young man who looked as if he had just stepped out of a painting by Botticelli.

Western Europe gave one a bittersweet taste of freedom and the dream of self-actualization. You could dress as you pleased, and you could say what you liked. And in Europe, finally, we could love who we wanted, whatever their sex or race.

Not unlike South African backpackers, British aristocrats of the eighteenth century also took to escaping the rigidity of their society. They embarked on what became known as the Grand Tour. It was meant to broaden, edify and cultivate the mind. Inevitably, the body received educating as well, usually in the form of paid sex in Paris.

At the start of the nineteenth century, the most famous of these travelers was probably Lord Byron, who made a bisexual sweep of the continent. Other homosexuals followed, sometimes discovering their 'true identity', liberating their sexual inclinations suppressed in prudish England, and feverishly indulging their passions in the relatively easy virtues of the continent, where the rustic Italian *ragazzi*, with their swarthy complexions, gazelle eyes and curly locks, were the equivalent of today's rent boys in Pattaya.

Some of those gay travelers are homosexual luminaries to this day, such as E.M. Forster, W.H. Auden and Christopher Isherwood.

However, most of these travels went unrecorded, and the men they encountered have passed into the unknown, much as a page fades to blackout during a Bruce Chatwin travel narrative. I think we can – and we must – guess what happened in the dark.

In my early 20s, I concluded that homosexuality, although not the norm, is perfectly natural. I had slept with girls, but I had never slept with another boy, so on that first trip to Europe it became a priority among other civilizing attractions.

My traveling companion was Simon, a straight boy from school days, my age, at the time living in exile in London.

In Paris, he accompanied me on my pilgrimage to Père-Lachaise to seek out the resting place of Oscar Wilde. We found a stone tomb vandalized with graffiti by fans expressing their undying love for Oscar. I skipped lunch so I could afford to place a red rose on the grave. Then I told Simon, "I think I might be gay". I said I wanted to go to a gay bar to see what it was like.

When we reached Vienna, which was hardly known for its gay life back then, somehow I located a gay spot on my city map, appropriately called The Why Not.

Cherub-faced Simon agreed to go with me as my protector.

We arrived to find a dark entranceway with a heavy wooden door firmly shut. We rang. A slot opened in the middle of the door. A set of narrowed eyes peered at us through an iron grid.

Simon, stammering, asked if we could come in for a drink.

"Sorry," a voice said emphatically in a thick Austrian accent, "this is a gay bar." The slot closed.

I pressed the buzzer again. This time the door opened, but only a crack. "It is a *gay* bar," the man hissed. "It is for men only, understand? For homosexual men."

"Yes," I said, "I know, I know, that's why I want *you* to let me in!"

The man in the doorway looked at us. We were dressed like backpackers; quite unconscious of our appearance those days; hiking boots, jeans with knees worn through, lumberjack checked shirt clashing with a Palestinian keffiyeh, unkempt hair, unshaven. With hindsight, Simon probably looked like a pretty boy for rent and I looked like a gay basher. The man, baring a set of yellow teeth, hesitatingly allowed us to pass.

Inside, there were three single, elderly men sitting on high stools, evenly spaced for equal opportunity along the dimly lit bar, nursing drinks and looking sour. My heart sank; the only open space for two of us was on the corner of the bar counter, where we were in full view of the men.

I ordered two draft beers, which came in embarrassingly large glasses. Simon was looking a little nervous. The men all focused on him. How typical, I thought; what is it with gay men that the straight guy always gets the most attention, even when he looks more gay than you do? But Simon was quite safe; nobody made a move on us.

We left with my virginity intact, Simon relieved, and I despondent. Those men exiled in a dark bar, always waiting, not speaking to each other, haunted me. Understand, that from the 1950s to the late 80s, we were constantly told by society in one way or another that this was how being gay would end – in tragedy without witness.

But then, apartheid croaked its last and Nelson Mandela made homosexuality legal. We went wild. During our Prague Spring, after years under the jackboot, people partied. Gay bars and clubs sprang up, crammed to bursting with patrons spilling into the streets, and backrooms for sex. I remember some revelers openly smoked pot in front of the police. Nobody it seemed was sure anymore what was and wasn't legal.

It wasn't all plain sailing. I narrowly missed a bomb planted in a gay bar on Green Point's Main Road. Nine people were badly injured. That particular bar never reopened.

But in time, Cape Town became a gay mecca, a pink paradise, a rainbow village. Apparently, we middle class gays had won our freedom without even having to fight much for it.

Now in South Africa in the 21st century, we have extensive 'gay rights', including marriage. On Clifton Third, Cape Town's gay beach, muscular bodies of all hues, from deep ebony to blinding white, from chemically bronzed to natural beige and sunburnt pink, lie side by side. At the height of summer, the vast majority of sun-worshippers here are gay males, though scattered between them are always a few umbrellas with families and children, who seem quite unperturbed by the occasional kiss, body rubs and other demonstrative physical affection between the men. It is a postcard for the country's human rights-based Constitution; black and white, straight and gay, young and old, male and female, all peacefully luxuriating in natural beauty. We are celebrating and no longer protesting.

Yet there is another side; the majority of queer men in South Africa are black and living below the poverty line. Victimized by ignorance, cultural chauvinism and religious prejudice as bad as the naked racism of apartheid, they are unable to assert their rights. Sometimes subject to extreme homophobic violence, they nonetheless survive in their communities by forging other ways of expressing their sexuality and hopefully gaining acceptance. Street-smarts, fashion and bling are some of the strategies they employ. Others have even managed to "recruit" local gangsters as their protectors, because it's cool to have gay friends.

Reflecting on their lives during the course of my journey around the world, compelled me to question the very concept of 'gay' identity.

Like Gore Vidal, whenever I hear the words 'gay culture', I too reach for my revolver. When I grew up, gay life was a politically subversive subculture. That was a big part of its attraction. In the West, gay has now become "normalized" to the point of becoming mainstream: the stereotyped gay clowns you find in television soap operas; the yuppie gays that car advertisers and so-called 'lifestyle' marketers target; the model gays who magnetize Cape Town's booming rainbow tourist industry; the go-go cover boys found dancing on floats in gay pride marches the world over. But the gay village and the gay beach is only one highly visible, shared identity, one particular model of masculinity in which gay men can be publicly comfortable, assimilated, confident and aspirant. But it is a very narrow, globalizing, consumerist paradigm. No fats, no femmes. It also excludes bisexuals and the asexual. For another thing, it largely excludes older men, while offering them the purchase of happiness through some superficial, titillating, porn-imitating gay capitalist nirvana.

16

Is this really the best road to safeguard the rights of men who have sex with men?

The men I encountered outside the West forced me to question the very notion of the closet, the liberationist and peculiarly Western preconception that 'coming out' is the prerequisite to live authentically. I discovered the heterosexual/homosexual binary fails as a model for understanding human sexuality in many parts of the world including my own backyard.

Long before Europe had even been conceptualized, men who have sex with men have lived in almost every society that has ever existed, from ancient China and Egypt to the Americas. Socially accepted homosexual behavior is not only well documented in classical civilizations, but also in first nation traditional societies, and in such remote places as New Guinea and the Amazon rainforest, existing long before there was any contact with the white man.

The view that homosexuality is European and un-African is not only false, but a pernicious belief on my continent, spread by corrupt African politicians and white, North American evangelicals who preach their hatred in Africa. To say homosexuality is un-African is racist and patronizing to black homosexuals.

In so many countries – Russia, Ethiopia, Egypt, and India, to name a few – I found men who have sex with men trapped between political rivals, each trying to outdo the other in persecuting them.

And place after place, I found the wealthy and middle class can live and do as they wish, while the poorer are left to the mercy of intolerant communities.

It has been a journey of many discoveries, discoveries of what we already know but must learn to feel. If we think the mind is treacherous, the body is even more so.

I hope I have done justice to the boys and men I met along the way. These are a handful of their stories.

Cape Town, South Africa

Masree and Dahoud
BANANA ISLAND
Luxor, Egypt

In Cairo, on a sightseeing trip to the pyramids, entering one proved to be a vastly different experience from appreciating their famed exteriors. The pyramid I entered was pitch-black and there was a smell of dried fecal matter. There didn't appear to be anyone else present. I hesitantly moved forward, the floor uneven, not sure what I was meant to be looking at. Nearby was a strange rubbing noise, like an anorak against stone. I could see nothing. Then a hand touched my hip, and quickly felt its way to my groin. It was a large, rough ham of a hand with outgrown fingernails. I leapt back and bolted blindly for the exit, feeling every bit like Miss Quested fleeing the Marabar cave in E.M. Forster's *A Passage to India*.

Egypt has a rich homosexual history – from the transvestite khawalat dancers introduced by Muhammad Ali, the founding Pasha of Egypt, who banned women from performing, to the famed oasis of Siwa on the Nile that practiced boy marriages up until the 1930s, I must add to the disgust of the occupying bigots, the British colonials. Indeed, Anglo-Saxon travelers to Egypt in the eighteenth century often commented with horror on the prevalence of homosexual activity at all levels of society, from Sultans to fellahin.

At the time of writing, the oldest evidence of homosexuality is in Africa, in Egypt near Giza, in the 4390-year-old Saqqara tomb of Niankhkhnum and Khnumhotep, two men buried together for the afterlife. On the walls are several depictions of them in intimate embrace and nose kissing (the form of kissing also favored by heterosexuals in those ancient times).

Men who had sex with men used to be called *lotis*, rarer now, a word derived from the Prophet Luth ('Lot' in the Bible) who was sent to Sodom. Homosexual desire as an imprint from birth is acknowledged by Islam, but its practice is forbidden. According to some Islamic and Qur'anic scholars, the prophet Muhammad held that two men who loved each other and kept their love platonic were to be honored as martyrs for this sacrifice. And there is a wealth of literature since medieval times (today being suppressed) from passing references in the *Arabian Nights* to the Sufi poets penning odes to the Christian boys that poured them wine. The Sufis were a fine bunch it seems; the poets slept with their young men, and one can be sure their idealized poetic love often crossed into a more physically penetrative one, not unlike Plato's *Symposium*, which I first tracked down in the university library, with trembling hands, at last holding philosophical proof that I was not a freak. I wish such opportunities were available to Egyptian boys who suffer 'the love that dare not speak its name' and have for so long been written out of their classical history.

But Egypt is always in a state of constant tension between Islam and not only the pressures of the modern world, but also with its own proud history. Surprisingly, homosexuality wasn't technically illegal in Egypt. The police used other laws such as trumped up charges of public indecency or resorted to entrapment. The secret police cruised the internet chat rooms, targeting and detaining homosexuals.

A decade before the so-called Arab Spring, I was in Luxor, Egypt, taking a late afternoon stroll on the Corniche, Luxor's wide, rather boring promenade along the Nile. I'd heard it was a notorious strip for hustlers of all sorts. But it was deserted and eerily quiet. Perhaps the place had still not recovered from the massacre of fifty-eight tourists by Islamic fundamentalists on the west bank, in the city of the dead, in the shadows of the temple of the great female Pharaoh, Queen Hatshepsut. The tourists were gunned down with automatic weapons and their bodies mutilated with machetes. An Islamic pamphlet was left in the disemboweled cavity of one visitor.

A solitary boy on a bicycle nipped past me several times, his bicycle bell tinging over the bumps. Finally, he skidded to a stop, a fair distance ahead, and waited, arms folded, sizing me up circumspectly it seemed. I approached with a mixture of interest and dread, thinking, 'Please, not another damn beggar!'

When I reached him, he started walking alongside me, pushing his bicycle.

"Hey, mister! American?"

"African," I replied.

He laughed. His hair was a thick, tangled afro; his skin dark – concentrated by the Nile sun. His body and limbs were covered by a thin, off-white cotton galabiya, oil-stained from his bicycle chain. He looked black African, more Nubian than the people of the north. What made these Egyptian youths (and frankly some of the police too, in their immaculate white uniforms) so good looking? Was it the strength of their eyes – with their perfect contours, like the hieroglyphic eye of Ra, the whites large and pure, the irises deep brown – and their pearl-white teeth, offset against polished ebony skin?

"My name. Captain Masree."

"Captain," I said, making it sound impressive.

"I have boat. You want boat ride? Very cheap."

We were now approaching the pier.

"But it's late," I replied.

"Today, good wind. No pushing." He giggled at his joke. I laughed. "We back… two hours. Special rate for you. See – no business today." He indicated the almost empty expanse of the promenade.

My haggling lacked lustre and I gave in quickly. I felt he was asking a fair price, unfavorable market conditions aside.

"Boat very safe," he announced pointing to a tiny felucca, similar to the dhows I had been on in Madagascar, except it didn't have the extended outrigger. Another boy, slightly younger, was sitting in it, stripped to the waist, busy braiding twine into rope.

"That Dahoud," said Masree.

Dahoud gave me an enormous toothy grin. While I inspected the boat, his face stayed frozen in that position, as if I was the school dental examiner.

They got us underway within moments, and soon we were tacking out into the wide river, the white sail replete with a fresh Nile breeze. It was far cooler out on the water, but I'd caught the sun on my arms and neck that morning, and the gentle wind exaggerated the burn, a sensation like turpentine evaporating from lips.

The shore receded quickly, shrinking into a dusky line, though we could not have been that far out. I could probably swim to shore if we sank.

"Where you from?" asked Dahoud, working the rudder.

"Cape Town, South Africa."

"PAGAD," he said, to my astonishment. PAGAD was the acronym for a polarizing vigilante and largely Muslim organization called People Against Gangsterism and Drugs.

"What you do?" he asked.

"Journalist," I said.

"Take picture?"

He insisted. I took my camera out. Delighted, they screeched, and dropping the stays and rudder arm, jumped into the middle of the boat, arms around each other's shoulders. It was a charming image.

Then when we were further out, Masree asked, "Are you married?" He nodded knowingly, as if I had confirmed his suspicions, and licked his ripe lips, which shone now. His voice changed slightly, cautious but oddly bold. "You want to see Banana Island?"

"Where is it?"

He pointed vaguely.

"Perhaps." I'd heard there was such a place, apparently very pretty.

"Perhaps you like Banana Island very much."

"Why? What's there?"

The two boys giggled.

"Perhaps you like Egyptian bananas?" He turned to face the wind, his galabiya conforming to his body in the breeze. He smoothed his garment down with the palm of his hand so that I could clearly see the outline of his long, dangling fruit.

"Egyptian man good. One hundred and fifty pounds," Masree said.

I probably wasn't too hard to figure out: single, Western, male, one of those who returned the gaze.

"And me? You like me?" Dahoud suddenly spoke.

"He only hundred pounds," laughed Masree. "Not big banana like me."

Dahoud protested, banging himself on the chest.

Masree squealed, delighted. "You like to suck?"

But Dahoud said something sharply in Arabic, and Masree turned quickly. There was another felucca bearing towards us.

It was a much longer boat, in better shape, the wood varnished, and it had two lateen sails. In it sat a couple of Western women, I guessed in their early fifties. One had her hair sensibly tied up in a pink headscarf; the other had her face shielded by a slouch hat she kept pinned to her head with one hand. They wore badly fitting bikinis, the straps too tight, making their trussed up bodies bulge, their skin glaring white, the sun cream sweating out of it. The women's eyes were hidden behind large designer sunglasses.

There were three fetching young men sailing the boat, one in a striking, pale blue djellabah. On the deck were large wicker hampers, outsized bananas going black on top, and the distinct orange label of a French champagne. The looseness of the women's heads and their dangling arms suggested they were tipsy. We Westerners ignored each other, while the boys exchanged comments in Arabic, and guffawed loudly as the boat glided swiftly past us.

As soon as we parted, Masree said, "Now we go Banana Island."

"Mañana, no bananas today," I replied disinterestedly, staring out at the water, my tone hinting lightly at the famous song.

"Come! You will like! Two hundred pounds – Dahoud and me, special price. Two fuck!" He was rubbing himself avidly as if polishing metal.

Dahoud and Masree were both beautiful. I found it distressing, these two kids offering themselves to me this way.

"No, take me back to shore."

"Nice fucky. Look, big, very big." Masree was squeezing, both hands wrapped around his penis under the galabiya. "You can suck."

"No!" I snapped at him. "I said, no!"

I looked helplessly at the distant shoreline. They were giving me dirty, hostile looks. How ludicrous – I was stranded on a boat with two handsome teenage, street-smart hustlers, begging me to suck them off.

"To shore, now! Otherwise no pay for felucca ride. No pay for anything," I shouted angrily.

There was a long, stunned silence. Then at last, confounded, they turned the boat. It required both of them to revolve the yardarm.

I was thankful the sailing distracted them for a while. But I was raging inside. Sex has a habit of making unwanted intrusions.

My anger subsided with the rhythm of the boat, the gold sunlight, the muddy blue water, leaving me feeling more upset than anything else. I thought of boys on other trips. But those encounters had been different. There had been a semblance (however untrue) of equality, of payment as gift, of them being gay and trapped in their cultures, of me in some small way facilitating the exploration of their own sexual identity. But these two felucca boys were not gay; they were selling their bodies.

Who knows; maybe they enjoyed it. Perhaps they were just randy and liked getting their rocks off and being paid for it too. And there was that local belief that only the passive partner was actually homosexual. A Westerner's ass was just a rich, ugly hole, an ATM that took flesh.

There was no shortage of tourists eager to stick their heads under galabiyas, nor boys happy to feed the white monkeys their bananas. How long before this place went the way of sex-tourist Pattaya? Did these felucca boys keep condoms on-board? I doubted it. So the plague would soon reveal its true extent here too, as it had everywhere else in the world.

Did the punters care about these boys? Or were they no more than exotics, an adventure amongst the Arab studs harking back to Orientalist fantasies, a genre in an erotic gallery, to be sampled, tasted, and discarded.

In the end, we parted amicably. Dahoud and Masree gave me their names and addresses, and I promised to send them copies of the photos. It was hard to tell, if some part of them respected me more for having rebuffed them, or whether I disgusted them for rejecting their favors and wasting their afternoon. I paid them for the felucca ride, and then I gave them the two hundred pounds.

Back at my swanky tourist hotel, I crossed the plush carpeted dining room looking for a table that was quiet and had enough light to read my Cavafy. I recognized the two British women I'd seen on the classy felucca. They were now royally pissed; they'd obviously been at it since lunchtime. I overheard the one say, "Banana Island", followed by a dirty laugh. "I haven't been drilled like that for years," she tittered. Then they both guffawed.

So perhaps it was not only fat, old, homosexual white men that took their pleasures on the Nile.

William
PAGAN RITES
Damascus, Syria

The Syrian immigration officials simply refused to explain why I was being held. The captain pointed to a bench. "Sit there."

Of course, they didn't care if William had given up waiting for me. If he had, I was stranded. My last contact with him had been by email more than a month back. Since then, there had been no way to reach him out there in the sands on his archaeological dig near Ma'lula.

We were to have met here, in Damascus; in William's words, "to do as the Bedouin's do" – you agree on a time and a place, a year in advance, and then you simply show up; no mobile phones, no emails, no reconfirmations. While I waited, I silently amused myself by inventing words: 'officialdumb', 'impassport'.

A little pig-tailed Swiss girl, small fingers struggling with her camera, pointed it at me, and, flash, took my photograph. She gave me an impudent look. The chief official jumped up in his squeaky boots, shouting in Arabic, demanding to know who had taken a photograph. We all looked at the ground. I surreptitiously stuck my tongue out at the little girl, now sitting back down between her parents. She blushed with guilt. The official huffed and went back to his paperwork, giving all of us in the arrivals hall one long last look of loathing.

An official, perhaps the same one – they all had the same moustache, came over to bark questions at me with military courtesy.

How long are you staying in Syria? How much money do you have with you? Where will you be staying?

After each question he would disappear down a grim foreboding passage with its oil paint curling off the walls in leaves, his boots echoing down the corridor, followed by the chilling clank of a metal door firmly closing.

What is your profession?

After each of my answers, the police took up to ten minutes to deliberate. And each time I'd see my passport walked back to the immigration control box. Discussions in Arabic would follow. Maybe they were talking about sport or their in-laws. Again and again, I would watch my passport with its green cover returned to the police desk.

Where is your wife? Are you on holiday?

I knew that with bureaucracy, from Her Majesty's surly customs at Heathrow to the barefoot, gum-chewing immigration officer that stamped my passport in Zimbabwe (while gossiping and laughing on her mobile phone), it was crucial to be patient and outwardly calm.

Then on one round, I noticed my passport did not go back to the police kiosk. Instead, the official walked right past me without a word, slumped back into his seat and started writing in longhand.

The baggage carousel ground to a stop. In the stillness, the last passengers stood transfixed by disbelief, hoping the machinery would start up again. Of course it never does. They anxiously exchanged glances, and sighing deeply, strayed slowly across to the lost-luggage claims desk. It was closed. There were no more flights. Lights were being switched off, and there was the jingling of a large bundle of keys.

I waited humbly with my eyes fixed on the passport official filling out forms, his head bent low. Well over an hour had passed since I first presented my document. It was now minutes before 11 p.m., when William had said the last bus would leave for Damascus. I could wait no longer. I stalked over to the cubicle and demanded my passport.

Without the faintest hesitation, the official smiled, "Okay, okay, South Africa." He decorously handed it over. It was already stamped.

Flabbergasted, but grateful, I rushed to the exit. Approaching the barricades, I began to fret. Two minutes to 11 p.m.

Was William there? Had he come at all?

We had tricked in Cape Town and clicked with our computer mice ever since, but in truth we hardly knew each other. Many emails, but only two brief encounters – one in a leather bar, then a hasty afternoon exchange at my apartment a week later – constituted the sum of our romance.

I was staring up at the signage looking for the bus pictogram, when I heard William's American accent. "Hey! Dude!"

There he was, as promised, beaming. I threw my arms around him like a long-lost soul mate.

"I thought you'd have given up on me. Did you know the flight was delayed? And then the police held me. Luckily, the customs didn't stop me as well. Have we missed the bus?"

"Yeah, yeah, it's always like this." William spoke with a slight drawl. "Welcome to Damascus. It's normal, don't worry." I was grateful for his unshaken faith in me.

"But why hold me of all people?"

"Oh, just put it all down to Syrian incompetence. You'll learn. When our team arrived, we were also kept, because the clerk stapled our passport photos to the permits, not checking if they were the right picture with the right name – ten pictures, ten forms, staple. What's more, our names were clearly written on the backs of the pictures! Some things are hard to explain away through cultural differences. Some people are just stupid." He laughed. "So you came! I wasn't sure if you'd want to recognize me; look, I have this ugly eye. See?" And he pointed to his right eye; it was swollen, puffy and red. "I've so much to tell you, but quick, we've got to catch the bus. It's fifteen Syrian pounds, as opposed to a taxi which is fifteen times that!"

William grabbed one of my bags and we dashed for the exit.

The bus was still waiting. There were only a few seats; the rest was standing area. William spoke Arabic to the driver.

"It was only fifteen pounds when I came to the airport, now it's suddenly twenty. What the heck, it's fifty cents."

"I don't have any Syrian—" I started to say, but William pushed me to the back of the bus and started kissing my neck, my cheek, on the mouth. His teeth bit ever so slightly. I was wide-eyed, slightly terrified. This was the middle of the Middle East.

"Don't worry. We're brothers. We're foreigners." And he rubbed his crotch against my thigh. "We haven't seen each other in ages; we're long lost friends; we thought we'd *never* see each other again..."

I had to laugh. None of the handful of people on the bus were paying any attention. I noticed the women weren't veiled.

"Relax." He kissed me again and hugged me. I felt relieved, saved, taken up. I was ready to believe, perhaps like the strangers on the bus, that we were actually long lost friends, childhood buddies, kissing cousins. It was as if our semblance of a history had become real.

"It's quite acceptable for men to kiss here. You see it all the time." William chuckled impishly. "And I think the guys must be fucking each other too. They have to pay a dowry for a wife, and many of them cannot afford this before they're into their late thirties. They have to be getting their rocks off somehow, somewhere. Sex with women is out of the question, unless they go to brothels."

The libido is like any other appetite, the more sex you have the stronger it becomes, and it aches from inactivity, but if left unexercised, it shrinks. Perhaps, after a life of control, it ceased to be an issue for the Muslim boys. I thought of those images on television, of Arab militia poking their Kalashnikovs at the sky, firing off their sexual energy with a religious fervor.

"And how do archaeologists get their rocks off?" I grinned.

"By excavating!" William laughed. Then he added mischievously, "I'll demonstrate later."

William was an American and a hereditary Jew. But he worked for a

Polish university, and he put Episcopalian on his visa. Atheist would be accurate, but even worse in Syria than Jewish. Fortunately, he was swarthy with cropped black hair; I later found, sometimes people would spontaneously speak Arabic to him.

There was hardly any traffic on the road. The airport, for "security reasons", was located over thirty kilometers from the city. We lurched against each other in the back of the bus, which made good progress for a vehicle that felt as if it had been fitted with square wheels.

My first impression of downtown Damascus was one of neon. Liberal, if simple usage, was made of it across Martyrs' Square, the Arabic lettering spectacular in fluorescent orange and red. There was a heavy police presence on the streets. Even the country's two-star, three-striped flag looked like an epaulette.

This was in 2001, ten years before civil war would tear the country and its people to shreds. And in that conflict homosexuals would be targeted for killing, as they were in Iraq after the American invasion, where dozens were tortured to death with impunity in ways I simply cannot bear to describe here.

The 'hotel' in Damascus was a pleasant dump; a huge, three-story house renovated, but still crumbling, with collapsing beds. It was as if everything tilted precariously towards the stairwell, which spiraled like a great vortex in the center of the building. Arrangements were casual. You had to step over the great unwashed backpackers; Euro-grunge types on indivisible budgets, head to toe sleeping-bagged, covering every square inch of floor and verandah. There was little chance of William and me becoming intimate here. The five-star European hotel across the way charged two hundred dollars for a room, and then it still only had squat toilets.

"The whole team has been sick on the dig. Can't figure it out, the water, some bug, I don't know." William's eye looked pinched with pain. "I hope it's not pink eye or contagious. Hopefully, it won't spoil our fun."

I insisted on keeping our pillows strictly separate, and made William paranoid about touching his eye and afterwards touching me.

This was the very first time I'd traveled with a foreign companion. William possessed all the essential qualities of a good traveling mate: considerate, scrupulous, articulate, humorous, and most importantly, curious, even intrepid. Over the course of the next week, we explored the new territory of our relationship in a sort of saltarello way.

On the very first day, I placed my life in his hands. There is nothing in the world, including Cairo, that I'd come across that vaguely compares to the deranged netherworld of Syrian traffic. Rules are not enforced. The drivers are not mechanically inclined, and neither are their vehicles. You choose your destination and relinquish your destiny to Allah.

Most of the first day we spent trapped in our small Peugeot, hurtling through the flat landscape. It was a lengthy trip to Aleppo, in the far north of the country, about ninety kilometers from ancient Antioch and forty kilometers from the Turkish border. We took several detours for we could never establish for certain which road we were in fact traversing. Apparently, some Stalinists redrew Syria's roadmaps for "security reasons", deliberately obscuring the position of roads. Highways that did not exist were depicted, and roads that existed went unrecorded. I was to navigate armed only with this state fiction. Our dual carriage freeway regularly gave way to traffic in both directions. The first you knew about it was shortly before an impending head-on collision. Sometimes the highway itself would run out. If luck prevailed, you bounced onto a newly laid strip of sticky tar. A road sign placed outside almost every town, declared: "Make Light Speed! A place full of inhabitants". Syrian drivers took it as an invitation to travel at the speed of light.

William took it all in his comfortable stride. He was happy to be in charge. "We have time," he said. "And it's not like they have a lot of roads."

31

With the reflection in the windscreen glaring back at us from our Stalinist maps skating across the dashboard, we tore through the desert, sunglasses pinched down, and constantly nagging at us, the disturbing awareness that we did not have a spare tire.

We did reach Aleppo, and took rooms in Al Gedeideh, at reputedly the cleanest budget hotel in Syria. Everything was painted in pastel green enamel: the walls, the ceiling, the fan, the bed, the chairs, even a ball of paper that had been left stuffed in a vent. The enameled interior had been meticulously wiped clean. There was ample hot water and a flush toilet. You still however put the toilet paper in a bucket after use. But it was the décor – the curtains, lampshades, pillows and bedcovers – all in the same gaudy floral fabric (surely conceived by a designer suffering from deuteranopia) that made the room as conducive to sex as grandmama's flat. To add to one's nerves, we'd heard the proprietor made regular unannounced inspections, bursting in without knocking. Slobs, this included people who left the toothpaste cap off, were summarily evicted; any abandoned items, such as a pair of socks, a razor or toothbrush left on the basin, were permanently removed.

Aleppo, equidistant from the Mediterranean and the Euphrates River, had gathered to itself an eclectic population – mostly Sunni Muslim, but also Kurds, Orthodox Russian traders, Christian Armenian refugees from Anatolia, and even a few beleaguered Jewish families. The diversity was apparent when walking the streets; you saw red haired Syrians and blonde Ukrainians, unveiled Christian women and Muslim women in yashmaks. But what you saw mostly were men: men relaxing, men commuting, men working. A gay bar in the West will have more women in it than an ordinary street café in Syria. Men smoking hubbly-bubblies hung out together, playing cards, backgammon and dominoes or sometimes they sat and simply held hands – a seductive visual aesthetic of the old city. A generosity existed among these straight men, allowing them to enjoy physical freedom and intimacy with one another. Elderly men affectionately, unhurriedly, touched each other's skin.

I guessed, in this culture, their closest emotional ties were ordinarily with other men. Women were reserved for matters of honor, procreation, and family.

Even though the men all around us held hands, while touring the city, William and I did not risk it.

It was late afternoon, and William was on a mission for a loofah and Aleppo's famed handmade olive, bay and laurel soap. We were going to the hamam.

"It's the only way to get clean in Syria," said William. Yet there was a mischievous hint in his voice, and he slyly raised his eyebrows.

The hamam had been a major tourist attraction, but in that fateful year, with the United States manufacturing evidence for weapons of mass destruction and starting to beat its war drums in the Middle East, we found ourselves alone, and the staff respectfully absent.

In the hamam, men have always reposed together. In Syria, unlike Budapest or Finland, the social etiquette at a thermal bath is strictly to cover the genitals at all times.

After the searing heat of the sauna, we withdrew to one of the private alcoves leading off an octagonal center, each with its own fountain.

By turns, we lathered one another's limbs with the olive soap worked into a heady white cream. I turned onto my stomach, lying on the smooth, hard, ancient marble floor, William's loofah scraping, arousing each nerve across the soles of my feet, between the buttocks, between my fingers. I felt vulnerably clean, like albino skin kissing sunlight. One of my contact lenses swam away. The heat and mutual massage momentarily exhausted us.

When we finally retired, the supervisor unexpectedly ripped my towel off. I stood slightly embarrassed, somewhat proud of my detumescent cock. Taking no notice (as if he hadn't seen), he covered me with a light, stiffly starched, white percale robe, and wrapped my head up. I thought I must look like Lawrence of Arabia, but William said I looked more like Gloria Swanson.

We reclined on our benches, hearts still palpitating, propped-up on tasseled pillows, sipping mint tea. We were alone again.

Always the archaeologist, William was exploring the origins of the place, his long flickering eyelashes dusting away like an archaeologist's brush, scrutinizing the inscribed metal bowls, the wooden Arab chests with silver studs. I could hardly see a thing, having lost my contacts.

Just as we were about to leave, three women gingerly entered to inspect this male sanctuary. They hesitantly advanced a few steps, stared and pointed at various objects, speaking in hushed voices, while I, a stranger from another country, had permission to be naked and at home here. On rare occasions, according to William, women could hire the facility, but then exclusively for females.

We'd lost track of time. The souk would start closing around 8 p.m., so we decided to pass it over until the next day.

Aleppo's Al-Madina souk was one of the finest in the Middle East, all thirteen kilometers of it were well organized. Under a canopy of spectacular, lofty stone arches, it retained much of its fourteenth century feel.

Fortified with nickel pops, we were ready to elbow our way through its paved lanes. The stepped streets had narrow stone ramps in their center for barrows. We competed with a chaotic traffic of donkeys, vespers, wheelbarrows, and rails of fetid carcasses that careened past too close for comfort. You had to be cautious not to be caught under the wheels of brakeless, zigzagging carts overloaded with protruding wood and metal staves aimed at various parts of your body like medieval siege machines.

The quality or at least the authenticity of articles was almost assured; prices could be made good with firm bargaining, and traders, unlike those in the souks of Marrakesh and Fez, did not hound you. Until...

"Squeeze me!" said a merchant with a castrato pitch. I was genuinely confused. He was in his mid-20s, I guessed, but William insisted that the attrition of Syrian life meant you always subtracted seven years from people suspected to be in their twenties and five if they looked like they were in the thirties, making him eighteen.

"Squeeze me!" he repeated.

"You mean excuse me."

Without hesitating, he said cockily, "Show me the difference."

"Well, excuse me, means excuse me, and squeeze me ..." I squeezed his wrist gently. "Means this ..."

His voice dropped to husky camp. "I bet Oscar Wilde never said excuse me."

Taken off-guard, I felt transparently gay. Dumbstruck, I rushed after William who was walking on, quite oblivious.

A little further into the souk, we discovered that Oscar Wilde was alive and well and still posthumously facilitating homosexual introductions. A blondish boy, possibly of Russian stock, selling engraved silver bowls, volunteered in a mincing voice, "Oscar Wilde said you should always express yourself."

"He did, indeed, but that was in Paris," I replied.

"Do *you* enjoy exploring yourself?" he asked. At first, I wondered if the ambiguity was deliberate; did he mean exploring on one's own or playing with oneself?

"We'll manage," I replied, somewhat curtly.

"It's good to explore yourselves. At first, it will be hard, but soon you will be knocking at my door. I will be waiting patiently!" he predicted with great confidence. The poor boy's nose was mined by not one, but several, frighteningly prominent, white-headed pimples, each one about to explode any moment now. He had a viperish manner I did not like.

"I have a waiting list!" he yelled after us.

We stepped up our pace.

Here we were in a country where half the population believed homosexuals should be stoned to death, and yet we were ducking innumerable unwanted advances.

"We're being hit on by a bunch of queens!" I said to William.

He chuckled, and paused to peruse some woodblock print fabrics that had caught his eye.

Two young men manned the stall.

"How long are you and your *ex*-boyfriend staying here?" one of them asked.

"Let us discuss our future!" said the other.

"Very short," I replied.

"No, perchance you have a future with a Syrian man, ah, I mean woman." I gathered his clumsy technique was to sound us out by making idiotic mistakes in English. His voice had a peculiar singsong lilt. "Lady and gentleman," he started again.

But the other boy grabbed my arm, "You're acting like a big Sheila! Where are you from? Australia?"

"No, South Africa," I said triumphantly.

"Ah! Big scene in Cape Town, yes?"

"Lady? Did you call me lady?" I asked.

He turned to his friend, and said quite openly in English, "I want the dark one. I like him. You can have what's left."

But William and I were speeding away as fast as possible, convulsed with laughter.

"Come! Friends! Friends, let's break the ice, test the waters, and bury the hatchet!" he shouted after us.

Rounding a corner, I glimpsed the boy turning back to his stall, shoulders slanted, disconsolately shuffling to his station.

If I had been alone, the story would have ended differently. I would have been tempted to pursue a glimpse of their lives, where they lived, and how they survived under a state, which at that time, seemed more omnipotent and invulnerable than God. Everywhere portraits of the men of the Assad presidential family in military garb or flying jacket (the height of Syrian fashion) stared down at us. But these boys in the souk were uninhibited, at least in English, which like their sexuality, practically no one understood or wished to acknowledge.

Back at our hotel, William and I were still collapsed with laughter. With hindsight, it was cynical and arrogant of us. We were wealthy, transient, and free. I wonder now, whatever happened to the queens of Aleppo after the bombs fell?

I turned on the national television expecting a state propaganda broadcast, but was astounded by what I saw: a trailer for an upcoming 'documentary' about Christianity. It showed flashes of Christian fervor in fast succession: grotesque processions of Spanish flagellants and devotees hauling massive crosses up hills; believers having nails hammered through their hands in the Philippines; hysterical, weeping crowds of Brazilians falling at the feet of the Pope; priests kissing rings and icons; Goya's black paintings of the inquisition; American evangelical congregations heaping piles of dollars into collection boxes; the possessed writhing on the floor; holy water, stigmata and bleeding crucifixes. Without the Arabic commentary, it resembled a satanic music video. If I was a Muslim youth, and this is all I saw, I too might be tempted to martyrdom for Islam, if it would save the world from a crusading army with beliefs such as those depicted here.

On a rooftop restaurant that night, a small oasis on top of a crummy hotel, with pot plants and leafy greenery, I became deeply thankful for our urban Western freedoms. The queens of Aleppo reminded me of young men I'd come across in small rural towns in the United States and South Africa, where gay boys adopt the only aesthetic available to them. Some mistakenly believe being feminine will actually attract a male lover. They parody the female in a poorly styled version of high camp, so easily derided for its bad taste. It is a public front, a persona paraded on a precarious ramp of clichés, yet it is the only defensive space for a despised yet accepted identity, for the American sissy, fairy or flamer, the South African *moffie*, the Australian pooftah, the Scottish bufftie, the Cuban *maricone*, the Mexican *chulo*, the Brazilian *bicha*, the Thai *kathoey*, the Syrian and Egyptian *khawal*.

I looked around at the other patrons dining with us, all men. I began to wonder how many of the Muslim men were gay, walking hand in hand, enjoying a public freedom that would attract opprobrium in many a mid-West town. But then again, here, they were without any hope of life together as a couple.

I forget exactly which one he was or what he had said in the souk, but I recognized one of the boys at a table across the way. Catching my eye, he came over. We greeted him with the informal *marhaba*. Well-dressed and in the evening light, he made a far more seductive impression now than he had at the market.

"You are staying long?" he inquired, politely.

"We leave tomorrow I'm afraid."

"Ah, too bad," he sighed.

Then I felt the tip of his boot suggestively on my foot under the table, squeezing down, gently.

"I lived in Rome, you know? I had an Italian lover for many years."

"Rome is lovely, a favorite city of mine," I said.

He kept surreptitiously playing with my foot, while engaging in small talk with William, who knew his country so much better than I did. When our food arrived, he excused himself and returned to his friends who were already dining. The moment he sat down, their heads came together in conference.

The Aleppo kebab had arrived. It seemed that no matter what I ordered in Syria, it was my fate to be served the Aleppo kebab. This time I had ordered the one dish I thought could not be confused with it – couscous. I had even pointed to the couscous in the window display. But along came the same compressed, dried bit of lamb, like pemmican on a stick.

I looked up and smiled politely at the boys over at their table. They beamed back at me. As everywhere else in the world, including Iran, there was a subculture here of friends, intrigues, and lovers. The human enterprise cannot be suppressed, only persecuted.

A week later, in a public park in Damascus, William and I would watch the Syrian men cruise. Sitting on benches, alone, they would eye one another like stray cats. A round-faced boy with huge, revolving eyes and a lame leg, always smiling, distributed tea and nickel pops. I think he had some mental challenge. He kept forgetting where he had left bottles and trays of tea. His employer, which I hope was not his parent, would appear from time to time to chase him along impatiently like a beast ploughing a field. Apparently oblivious to the cruisy comings and goings, the boy would scurry along the paths searching for the empty cups and bottles, pulling his lame leg behind him, serving tea in glasses with wads of crushed mint from a kettle he boiled on a small gas stove. With the communion of tea, the single men would have an excuse to join up, form couples, sit together and exchange hushed conversation.

From where they sat, it was a short walk to the public latrine, where other men kept a lookout for the police and the uninformed in need of nothing more than bladder relief. What struck me was how ordinary the men looked. The gay aesthetic – gym bodies, designer clothes, and Western accoutrement – had not yet penetrated the culture.

The next morning we took breakfast at the legendary Baron Hotel, where Agatha Christie, Sir Lawrence of Arabia et al were rumored to have stayed. Were they alive today, they would probably not even consider it, for like an old actor that has fallen on hard times, it had nothing but goodwill and sentiment to trade on.

Breakfast over, we were about to depart, when a man, possibly the proprietor, came over to ask obliquely if all was well. William made some compliment about the hotel's charm, and not to be upstaged, the man decided it was time to exhibit his own charms.

"Wait one minute," he said.

He was slightly rotund, prosperous looking in an English tweed jacket. He returned with old magazine clippings of the hotel. Although decrepit, the elegance of its architectural design was undiminished with its tiled roof, the wooden shuttered lancet arch windows surrounded by decorative arabesque carvings, the simple cantilevered balconies with plain metal railings. I wondered if he saw his hotel through rose-tinted spectacles as reflected in the clippings, while daily familiarity inured him to its present dilapidated state.

There was a newspaper clipping from the *London Times* of him standing proudly in front of a Studebaker. Jokingly, he asked if we wanted to buy such a car. William was polite to a fault. Encouraged, he offered us a carpet. We told him we were not interested.

"What about beautiful silverware?" he ventured. "Brass? Gold?"

Again, we declined.

"I have very special – you won't find anywhere else – Cedar wood carvings?"

"No."

"Perfume?"

"No."

His eyes lit up. He produced from his pocket an old coin. "Very, very rare." William squinted at it, briefly intrigued.

It was a while before we extricated ourselves. William was laughing, "There you go," he said, "he's the real thing. The original, archetypal, Levantine entrepreneur. Commerce is in their veins. They're all survivors here."

We headed south, making excursions through the land of the dead cities, an expanse of the north-west, where lie scattered over 700 deserted cities dating back to 500 BCE. Ruins stretched to the horizon, where jagged shapes of dislocated edifices lingered solitarily. Imagine Warsaw after the blitzkrieg, never rebuilt, left to stand for a thousand years, baking in a hot desert sun. Keystones hung precariously in their arches. The once paved avenues were filled with the rubble of toppled columns, only the plinths remaining. Yet, these ruins were peaceful, the rusty brown patina of the weathered Byzantine stone relieved by a few green bushes, where birds twittered.

In Ebla, while walking down one rock strewn avenue, I came across a wooden door unexpectedly filling what otherwise looked like the disconnected facade of a ruined building. I saw the smoke of cooking, and seemingly out of nowhere children gathered, begging and offering to be guides. These families were caretakers, still living in amongst the ruins in villas two thousand years old, with makeshift lodgings screwed to the back of ruined facades.

Years later, during the devastating Syrian uprising, people would dig up the graves in these cities, rebury the bones, and entomb themselves, to live underground for safety.

Near Serjila, we came across an Italian team of archaeologists. They were celebrating a new find, a Byzantium city beneath another city. I wanted to take pictures, but they asked me not to. Apparently, archaeology is a cut-throat business; discoveries are sometimes stolen, and credit claimed by people who had nothing to do with it. It was a massive dig that included the reconstruction of a mid-Bronze Age settlement, an impressive complex that stood below ground level, where an old man the Italians called Maestro, was plastering.

Maestro wore a red keffiyeh, camouflage trousers, and a finely patterned cotton shirt. In the shade of the water truck, William and I sat with him as he generously shared a watermelon with us, the sticky cool juice dripping down our forearms. The dig was good money for him, about four US dollars a day, and the Italians also provided employment for three of his sons. He told me he had seventeen children. How many did I have at home?

William had to return to the dig in Ma'lula to check on the progress and the schedule ahead. As fascinating as it was to watch his team at work, I soon tired of the fine clouds of sifted dirt, the grit between the teeth, and the laborious recording of each discovery, most of which were no more than a millimeter in diameter, but each painstakingly labelled and positioned in three dimensions by laser theodolite.

After the early morning tea break, with its sardines, tomatoes and the ubiquitous bread and boiled eggs, William drew a rough map for me of the route to take back to town.

"It's easier the higher you walk," were his last words of wisdom as I set off.

I scrambled along the sloping loose earth, which casually yielded up more stone-aged implements, the forgotten fragments of tens of thousands of years of continuous human habitation. They were everywhere. I even found two stone arrowheads.

I shadowed the road, which was clearly visible below, but the deep wadis made the traverse difficult and kept forcing me to higher ground, until I was eventually hiking along the summit, with a precipice on either side. I began to have serious doubts as to whether I was on the correct route, but in blind faith, I trudged on hoping that at the end of the ridge there would be a way down.

In places, the rock formed a crest, and I descended under the overhang to explore several caves. The deepest were quite shallow, buried by thousands of years of debris and windblown sand. I crept into the back of one on my belly, and lay looking out over the arid landscape. Under me, there were probably Neanderthal remains, but the attrition to the rock here was so rapid, that no artefacts, like the stone arrowheads I found strewn on the summit, were visible.

If traveling between countries had not revealed the arbitrariness by which we decided good and bad, right and wrong, a journey through time was even more instructive. The stone arrowheads remained, but thousands of years of people living by successive customs and codes of behavior, laws, cultures, religions, ideas of acceptable and unacceptable practices, had passed with hardly a trace. And of all these civilizations that had come and gone, none had been predicated on anything as fragile as our own, as precarious as the computer microchip, the magnetic memory, the digital age, with its satellites, its viruses, its mechanisms only a small technocracy could fix and maintain, devices that became obsolete as soon as they were invented, and which could all be fried by one anomalous electromagnetic solar tsunami, maybe in ten thousand years, maybe by tomorrow morning.

As I thought of the solar apocalypse, the sun had reached its zenith, and there was no shadow on the ground. I scrambled back up to the ridge, and distracted for a moment by an eagle passing overhead, my boot came down into empty space. I toppled sideways and landed hard on my wrist. My foot was dangling into a perfectly round hole in the rock, almost large enough to swallow a man. I dropped a stone into it, and counted off the seconds: one, two, three, four, five, thud – so over a hundred meters deep. Had I by accident fallen in, I doubt my body would ever have been recovered, and my whereabouts would have remained a mystery.

William said it should take me no more than two hours, and sure enough, well within this limit, I arrived at the neon crosses that mark the apex of the precipice above Ma'lula. Below me were the unpainted dwellings of this small Christian settlement, bare concrete and cement plaster, dwellings punched like bunkers into the sheer rock face. People still spoke Aramaic here.

Strewn along the rocky crest where I stood, were the debris of rubber tires, burnt and rolled down the mountain for a night spectacle during certain celebrations. The good news was that there must therefore be a way down from here, unless they used ropes. However, from the promontory, all I could see were perpendicular cliffs, separating me from the town.

I started to backtrack in the hope that I had missed a way down, but to no avail. Surveying the area around me, I followed the highway to the south and spied a bridge crossing the rocky chasm to the tarred road. To get to it I would have to jump down from the ridge, at least four meters. But once down, there was no certain way back up again. Hanging to my fullest extent, I let go and dropped onto the boulders below.

From my new perspective, the treachery of the landscape became alarmingly apparent. Now I could see there was no direct connection.

The heat was searing. I was without water, without sunblock, stranded on the naked strata.

Beginning to feel weak from the physical exertion of clawing my way up and down the maze of boulders, I realized how it is that people get lost, panic and take foolish risks. At all costs, I kept telling myself, I had to keep calm and conserve my energy. One wrong step and I'd twist an ankle or put a knee out and that would be it.

My next attempt was to follow the electric cable that lighted the crosses, but this too proved impossible. It ended plumb over the edge.

I no longer knew what hour it was. The sun seemed to have hit noon and kept ascending.

I felt rising panic. On shaky legs, I eventually made it to the bridge. There were No Access signs, and it was clearly a condemned structure. Scrambling over the makeshift gate, the metal groaned in distress. Rust had eaten great holes in the foot walk, and it shook violently with each step, springing the loose scattered stones on its span into the canyon below. Gingerly, I took another step, unable to test my footing, for it was impossible to balance on one leg for long with the metal swaying and shrieking the way it did. Should the steel give way at any point, I would probably be tipped over with the entire structure.

By some miracle, I reached the far side; only to find the gate chained up and barbed wire cunningly strung across the top and both sides. The only attempt at health and safety considerations I ever found in Syria had me on the wrong side of it. I would have to jump from the bridge to a ledge below the lip of the road.

I vividly recall that leap: the bridge springing under me like a diving board, the barbed wire scratching my arm, the echo of the stones falling into the cavern below, and my knees connecting with the rock as I landed on the ledge.

Sunburned, dehydrated, I presented William with the outrage of his map. "This," I said, "this was a map to hell not Ma'lula."

He made amends by taking me to drink holy water from the natural spring at the Convent of St Tekla, established by the female saint within a generation of the crucifixion of Christ. The nuns had asked the archaeologists to date the radioactivity in the preserved remains of their saint, but the expedition had wisely refused such folly. Faith cannot be carbon dated.

There was a classic barbershop on the square, and William suggested I go for a haircut and some pampering. The barber, whose intense concentration on his work made him an appealing young man, kept bumping his crotch against my protruding elbows. Bump. The third time, I didn't withdraw my arm. He continued snipping. Bump again. I shifted my elbow. Snip, snip, snip... bump. He carried on cutting, as if unconscious of my elbow lightly rubbing against his groin.

When he finished, I said, "Very nice". He seemed ecstatic at the compliment. He led me to the basin for a shampoo and rinse. As he tilted the chair back I saw that pinned to the ceiling were semi-erotic photographs of European women, their copious breasts visible through filaments of white organza. He grinned and started massaging my scalp. I closed my eyes.

The next day, we were once more racing through the desert. Along the roadway, we passed what in South Africa are called koppies, flat-topped outcrops of rock. But these were tells, an archaeological term derived from the Arabic tal for hillock. They were abandoned towns and settlements, whole cities, silted up over the centuries. There were dozens of them. People had lived and died forever in Syria.

We stopped at a small, charming café, the only vertical in a long horizontal of desert, with no other human settlement within eyeshot. A painted sign proclaimed: Bagdad Café. We were on the main road to the Iraqi capital.

Tastefully decorated with an aesthetic sensitivity uncommon in Syria, it looked as if it had been readied for a photoshoot. Anywhere else in the world, I would have expected the queer eye for the straight guy at work. The only visible people were a number of good-looking men, who managed the place.

We sat on large pillows and drank mint tea. Tonight would be our last night together.

"You know I'm involved," William said, at last.

"Yes, I guessed."

"And that I love him very much."

"I'm not complicating anything, I hope."

"No," he said simply, his brow slightly furrowed with his characteristic quizzical frown; William, the perpetual inquirer.

By afternoon, we reached Palmyra.

We were trampling through the Valley of the Dead, watched over by its impressive Arab citadel. Ancient funerary towers – simple, square, stone turrets – littered this barren, ashen landscape. Inside them, the sarcophagi lay open, still full of nameless, shattered human bones.

When I think back of that time now, I mourn for Syria.

We walked in the heat to the ancient heart of Palmyra; the great colonnaded avenues where chariot wheels have rutted the stone; the arena where the downfallen were executed; the crumbling friezes on the portico, and the massive austere stone archways, precarious and unsupported, opening and closing onto nothing.

That evening we were allowed to stay in quarters specially reserved for visiting archaeologists. An ancient Arab caretaker let us in; clearly handsome in his day, now he was as toothless as the giant metal key he used to turn the rusty lock of the gates.

Sunset is a bewitching hour in Palmyra, when the colossal limestone ruins turn pink, and the last straggling tourists and their busses head home. We were alone in the temple.

As it grows darker, we slip out from our lodgings into the night air. With the help of my tiny flashlight, unsteady with anticipation, we negotiate our way across the fallen columns and between the giant hewn stones, scrambling over the treacherous masonry, erected at the time of Christ, the Temple of the supreme God of Palmyra, the God Bel. It is a massive, now roofless structure, sheltered from the desert wind yet open to the eternal sky of which Bel was the God.

Some local officials, who had a meeting earlier, have left behind a brier of red-hot coals. Next to it, William and I lie on our backs, side by side on the stone paving of the inner courtyard, holding hands, staring up at the emerging stars, until we can see each other only by their light and the glow of the embers.

This was once the inner sanctum. For two thousand years, people had come and gone, in the first millennia collapsing here in awe before their idols and ancestors, in the last century buying a postcard and listening to a guide's conjectures. Who knows what riotous ceremonies, prayers, vows, marriages and ritual sacrifices were performed on the spot where we now lay.

Inspired by our surroundings, finding ourselves alone and insignificant, shrouded by incomprehensible stone, we are overcome with an archetypal urge to nuzzle against each other, to establish ourselves, to consecrate our transgressive affection. Naked, we push each other against the warm, stone walls. William's nails scratch across my back like a steel brush; our body-hair pulls, chafes. I can feel the flinty stone etching itself on my skin. I teeter on the balls of my bare feet, my sacrificial sperm hissing in broad spurts on the coals, releasing sparks that float up effortlessly, and are then extinguished by the immortal sky.

Anonymous
I'M A BERLIN BOY, NOW
Berlin, Germany

The football star who must lie about his sexuality or leave the team; the rural lad who flees his family, his church or even his entire religion; the gay priest, living in terror of being lumped with paedophiles; the closeted man who visits rent boys on his way home to his wife and children; the labourer who loves men while his workmates only talk of sex with women and beating up queers; the executive who has no wife to take to company dinners; the homosexual immigrant who moves to a country that promises, then fails to protect him. If you are homosexual, it is unlikely you were born into acceptance.

"There are no homosexuals in Iran," said that country's president. We've heard it so many times: there are no homosexuals in our family, on our team, in our town, among our ranks. It is not in our blood. It is not in our culture.

It starts with the struggle to accept oneself. My black gay friends have to endure the constant refrain that their homosexuality is unAfrican. It is the argument of contamination – that homosexuality was introduced by the whites. The Senegalese blame the French; the Zimbabweans blame the British. Meanwhile, the British blame the Greeks, the Greeks blame the Turks, the Turks blame foreign infidels… But, we now know homosexuality was in fact invented by the Germans!

Of course, I don't mean the love of boys and men or sodomy, but the

Western conception of homosexuality as an identity, the recognition of homosexual orientation as an innate part of one's being.

The first instance of the word *Homosexualität* is in German. It appeared in a pamphlet of 1869 and the word has stuck. The first arguments for homosexual orientation as natural and blameless, not a wilful and perverse or criminal practice, come from Germany. The legal acceptance we have today in many parts of the world started with the brave and lonely struggle of German men such as Karl Heinrich Ulrichs – probably the world's first "gay" activist. He took the public podium in 1867 in a desperate struggle to convince the eminent jurists of his day to stop Prussian anti-sodomy laws spreading to the unifying states. It was a German doctor in Berlin in the 1850s who first articulated the biological argument for homosexuality. It was in Berlin that Dr Magnus Hirschfield founded the world's first homosexual rights organisation. It was in Berlin that thanks to sensible policing in the 1880s, homosexual life was allowed to thrive with the first gay bars and gay sex clubs proliferating. Police commissioner Meerscheidt-Hüllessem would take visitors on a Cook's tour of the gay nightspots for a titillating spectacle. Nollendorfplatz, Berlin, of the 1920s and 30s would eventually create the prototype for the gay village that would only flourish again in the 1970s, a continent away and two world wars later. Berlin was the first Western city to let gay people belong. If Western homosexuality were to choose a sacred capital, it must be Berlin.

But like all holy cities of creation it would be not only the wellspring, it would also be the site of the most terrible persecution and repression. Hirschfield's institute would be one of the Nazi's very first targets after Hitler came to power, probably because it knew exactly who among the Nazi party were homosexual.

Those who survived the Nazis would suffer unforgiveable treatment after the war; men of the pink triangle liberated from concentration camps finding themselves re-incarcerated to serve out their sentences as criminals and not acknowledged as the innocent victims of Nazi persecution and bigotry. "Gay rights" like most human rights was paid for with blood.

I do not wish to dwell on that dark period here, except to remind us that homosexuality remained illegal in Germany decades after the end of the war, during which period tens of thousands were prosecuted. The GDR was first to decriminalise homosexuality and to rid itself of paragraph 175 in 1968.

Even though many gay Berliners are quite unaware of the role their city played and think gay rights stem from the Stonewall riots on Christopher Street in New York, Berlin has now reclaimed its position as one of the most vibrant urban centres for gay life in the world, even acquiring an openly gay mayor for well over a decade. The city actively courts the international gay market.

One might go even further and say that in the face of rising immigration, especially from the Islamic world, "accepting homosexuality" has belatedly been thrust forward as a "German value". But we should be wary of acceptance when it comes with such a nationalistic agenda. It is a dangerous position – homosexuals once again pawns in a bigger political game.

When I first went to Berlin, my head was filled with notions of the Weimar Republic and the adventures of those notable homos Christopher Isherwood and W.H. Auden and the thousands of other gay foreigners who flocked to Berlin in the 1930s. I was also obsessed with Art Deco buildings, and Berlin architects were at the root of that obsession too.

Quite unexpectedly, coming from South Africa, I discovered I had far more in common with Berliners than I could have anticipated. South Africa had acquired democracy around about the same time and our own reunification process also got under way in 1990 (with the ironic twist that in South Africa we were unbanning communism and feeding it oxygen as opposed to watching it implode). One can see surprisingly many similarities between South Africa and Germany, especially in the microcosm of Berlin, in the social and economic process that has unfolded over the last two decades, right up to the same bizarre phenomenon of nostalgia among some in my country for the apartheid regime, like homesickness for the GDR. Under apartheid, we had a totalitarian state and our own form of the Stasi. I find that Berliners from the East have a much better understanding of my formative years than my counterparts in the rest of Europe.

But whereas Germany seems to be succeeding with the economic and social challenges around integration, South Africa is stumbling horribly. Often South Africa feels like a déjà vu of Berlin, not of Berlin in the 21st century, but the Berlin of the Weimar Republic – a progressive, liberal dispensation with great economic hardship, and with an Africanist National Socialism looming on the horizon. So, I have a sense of belonging in Berlin that surpasses sexuality. As a man who sleeps mostly with men, Berlin remains for me a beacon, the fountainhead for a shared identity and the historical birthplace for contesting my sexual orientation as our human right.

To my great delight, the Berlin I discovered in the 1990s felt distinctly different from the gay villages at that time in San Francisco and Toronto. The Berliners seemed energised, not dissipated by their sexual pursuits. Erotic sex was a rich and explorative part of their lives, not so much a ceaseless pursuit of addictive pleasure as I'd experienced in Sydney and New York. Or so it seemed to me. Perhaps it was purely an anecdotal impression, because of the great number of open couples I happened to meet, rather than the lone wolves in the darkroom basements of bars.

Like many gay visitors who had gone before me, my first week in Berlin was a rollercoaster alcoholic haze; out all night, snatching only three or four hours of sleep here and there. I was in my 20s and discovering that the Berlin boys were free and easy, promiscuous and uninhibited, sex and the cruising plentiful at all times of the day and night – from the nude boys stretching out on the sunny lawns of the

Tiergarten or with their pants around their ankles among the trees beside the Löwenbrücke, to the bone white bodies on the beach at Wannsee.

There was a professional young couple I'd met and slept with on occasion. They introduced me to others. At one Berlin dinner party there were three couples, all of whom it became apparent through conversation had relatively stable relationships that were the centre of their lives, but still had casual, no-strings-attached sexual contacts with other men from time to time, either as a couple or on their own. Extremely civilised, I thought.

The most attractive of the couples at the dinner party that night was a charming professor of something in the humanities, touching 70, with his 30-year-old Egyptian lover. The older man, Klaus, had a lean body, soft, affectionate grey eyes and skin freckled by many years spent far away in hot foreign climes. Hussein, though prematurely balding and slightly plump, was a handsome young man with a wide forehead, perfectly arched eyebrows and riveting almond-shaped eyes, the irises deep brown, the whites large and pure, and like his pearly white teeth, effectively off-set against polished, olive skin. His mouth too was broad and beautifully shaped with voluptuous lips that sipped red wine slowly.

When we finished dinner, Hussein announced he was going out clubbing. The professor politely asked to be dropped back at home. And then they kissed, there at table.

Years later, Hussein would be murdered by his family, apparently in collusion with law enforcement officers. Nothing came of it; the death of a homosexual hardly investigated by the Egyptian authorities and hardly to be grieved over by the disapproving family, especially when there was an apartment in Alexandria to be had out of it, a gift Klaus had bought Hussein the year before he was killed.

I had planned to set out independently that evening, tracking down some leads in my trusty Spartacus guide. Guidebooks going back as far as 1782, when Berlin was still a garrison city with soldiers pulling tricks for extra income, have described its "warm brothers". But instead, I set off with Hussein to some enormous monthly party near the river. However, I soon lost him in the dancing throng. There could have been a thousand people there. He must have decided to go his own way. I hope he lived that night to its fullest.

It was a raunchy crowd, stimulated by the summer air. The toilets seemed particularly active and there were plenty of sylvan darkrooms along the river. How strange to think of the number of bodies and faces one has entered in the most intimate way and yet one cannot recollect even their slightest detail. For all the intensity in the moment, after a day, most anonymous sex is no more memorable than the last fried egg.

When I finally left the carnival of free love, it was dead time on the U-Bahn. Entering the station, I could hear the train and I made a dash for it, only to arrive just in time to see a U9 miss me. Out of breath from too many stairs, I slumped down on the plastic wave of a resolutely utilitarian bench. The next train would be in ten minutes. The clock above the platform had started to laboriously count the wait. The station looked a bit like a big urinal with its floor to ceiling beige tiles. In the center of the single platform, which received trains in both directions, were a series of wide supporting columns, some with telephones and some with benches affixed to them.

I thought the platform deserted and I alone, until I heard a male clearing his throat. He must have been waiting for a train in the opposite direction. A young man stepped out from behind one of the concrete supports. I knew at once, I had immediately caught his eye. He was looking straight at me. We became self-consciously alone on the platform. He was rather non-descript on first sight – much shorter than me, stocky, stolid, in his twenties, Middle Eastern. Unlike so many others, I have never forgotten his face, the line of his aquiline nose. He wore bush camouflage fatigues with a bulging crotch and expensive black boots protruding from under the turn-ups. His gaze was definitely lingering on my fly. We approached each other, and as we gradually drew closer, we both burst into mischievous smiles; the spontaneous mutual recognition men who like men know so well. Speaking is always a risk; in an instant, it can break the spell.

But I asked, "Where are you going?"

"Home, to my boyfriend," he said in near perfect English.

So he'd been working a night shift. At a club perhaps? Did I detect a slight tremble in his voice? Was his boyfriend German, I wondered. It was not a question one could ask. Of course, he could just as likely have been born in Germany. Then before I could say another word, he moved forward and cocked his head to French kiss me. His chin chaffed against my neck, at least a day unshaven. I hadn't wanted to kiss any of the other boys that night, but him, I wanted to kiss, sensually, slowly. Did I taste of alcohol, of haram? I worried. He touched my crotch. He pulled my fly down and stuck his hand in.

"You don't wear underwear," he said chuckling.

We hastily checked up and down the platform, then withdrew behind one of the columns, out of view of the security camera, we thought. I could feel against my leg a tube of a flesh stretching down his inner thigh. I struggled with the buttons. He pushed my hands away, hastily undoing it himself. He had an extraordinarily thick cock, lined with veins, the head shaped like a wooden paddle. An ugly cock, I thought, but impressive.

He pursed up his lips like a French horn player preparing himself in the pit of the orchestra. Then he bent forward and started to suck on me frenetically, expertly, his hands helping themselves. I, listening out for footfalls descending into the subway, knew I would never come quickly enough this way. Three minutes and thirty seconds, the clock said. We were racing against time, but it was that very countdown to our imminent separation, him to his boyfriend, which made this sex possible.

I pulled him up and turned him around. I dragged his pants down just below the hips, stuck my cock between his hair-lined thighs, his long oval balls straddling its shaft. My hand was at once slick with his pre-cum. I felt I could have lifted him bodily with my cock it was so sexually charged. In an instant, I exploded between his sweat-moistened thighs, spraying white flecks across his boots. Trains for both directions were already in the tunnel, the wind blasting our faces, rushing over our sandwiched bodies. His cum splattered on the raw concrete with a groan that echoed down the vault of the station before it was obliterated by the metal ringing of brakes.

We hastily pulled up our pants. The trains slowed to a halt. Together, we stepped out from behind the pillar. I wanted to touch him, hold him. Someone at the end of the platform gave us an uncertain stare. They must have been there all along while we were having sex. Perhaps she'd heard that unmistakable groan. I could feel cum still dripping down my inside leg, my cock sticking to the denim. My warm brother was out of breath. He was giggling. I put my palm flat against his breast. I could sense his heart hadn't stopped racing. A first for both of us, I was sure. I smiled. He grinned impishly. What madness, I thought. But there was something exquisitely delicious about snatching that space for sex. And even if we had been caught, here in Berlin where we belonged, we would not have been stoned to death or publicly flogged for it.

I just had to know – "Are you German?" I asked.

He stepped into an empty coach. "My family is from Jordan," he said, facing me still on the platform. "But I am a Berlin boy, now," he said.

The doors misclosed and at once reopened. He laughed. Then the doors shut with a strange finality. I crossed the platform and stepped into my train. A second later, we were dispatched with a blur of faces in opposite directions.

Musa
BETWEEN TWO WORLDS
Paris, France

We were sitting together naked in lotus positions on a blue judo matt on the floor of the cubicle. Many of the cubbyholes were open at the top, and sometimes men would climb up to peer over at others having sex, only to be shooed away when spotted. But our cubicle was enclosed, though with such a low ceiling we could not stand up.

I had modestly, but casually, placed a white towel across my lap. Musa wasn't shy. He remained completely naked with his astonishingly long cock actually folding itself over his ankle. I'd brushed against it in the dark corridor outside, after skidding on a messy used condom on the floor. I always thought of bathhouses as refuges of desperation; or old age or sex addiction, which are kinds of desperation in themselves. They are grim, usually disappointing places. But occasionally, in foreign capitals of a certain scale, where barriers to enter the society are formidable, like here in Paris, in this gay sauna near the Gare du Nord, where anonymity is guaranteed, and class rules are broken, the bathhouse can offer one a tenuous foothold.

Musa was almost thirty, with a square face and fashionable, short, spiky dreadlocks. He'd wanted to fuck me. I'd refused. But it didn't seem he wanted to do much else sexually. So it ended up in interfemoral sex, more erotic and sensual than I'd ever imagined it could be. Afterwards, I asked him his name, and he asked me where I was from. We got to talking about Africa. I was flattered by how quickly he seemed to warm to me. I sensed he too was lonely on this grey afternoon. I had always felt Paris is a city best shared.

We decided to leave the bathhouse together. We found a small hole-in-the-wall Greek restaurant nearby where we ordered falafel. His English was quite good, but he did struggle for words now and again. I had a fair French vocabulary, but no grammar, certainly no tenses, and couldn't remember which nouns were masculine, which feminine.

Slowly, I learned his story. To my surprise, the more questions I asked, the more he spoke. I told him I planned to write a book one day about the different experiences of gay men around the world. He said, "But I am not *pede*".

Musa was born in France, making him a so-called 'second generation immigrant' (an oxymoron used by the jingoistic red-white-and-blue French) and one of France's *minorité visible*. From an early age, he had been straddling two contradictory worlds – Paris and Dakar.

He grew up in Dakar, where his parents still lived. They were Wolof, and from an even more elite minority within the Wolof. They were property developers. His parents were moneyed, socially well positioned, and respected by the community. And Muslim. To have *un pede* for a son would be a catastrophic disgrace. Not even his mother knew, not even in that 'not knowing' but knowing way mothers of gay children acquire. Besides, it was against the law of the land.

He went to a privileged boys-only school. But his childhood in Dakar was lonely. He had no shortage of playmates that would come to his parents' big house with its gadgets and its toys, but something in his behavior, perhaps the way he made physical contact with the other boys, aroused suspicion, sometimes a rebuke, even scorn, later ridicule and teasing. He learned to hide his feelings. He lived in terror of exposure. He was, he said, *un homme de noyade* – a drowning man.

"I felt I had a white man's disease," he explained. It was deeply wrong, woundingly shameful. And as everyone knew, there were no local cures for white men's diseases. Panic-stricken, Musa started having girlfriends. He told me with much laughter about the first time he slept with a girl, and how, all the next day, he had this ghostly sensation of feeling her wrapped around his cock like a bangle. His big, pure white teeth flashed when he said this. He said he became crazy for girls. For a time he stopped thinking about boys.

But the fantasies around men returned. He couldn't help feeling aroused, rubbing shoulders at sports, at football in the change rooms, noticing handsome strangers passing on the street, catching an eye here and there. He fell quietly in love with one of his uncles. He had erotic dreams at night.

Yet trying to actually picture himself physically with another boy was awkward. He couldn't figure out how exactly men could copulate. Thinking about it, frightened him. He put the idea away. Perhaps, he was cured.

After schooling, he came to Paris to complete his economic studies, attending the Sorbonne Nouvelle University.

At first, he found Paris unfriendly. This was in the mid-1990s.

"You should have been here in the 1980s," I told him. "Even the ice creams were in the tricolor."

I recalled my first trip to Paris; the thaw in Gaullism was invisible to me. Nobody spoke English, absolutely nobody. A gang of French ruffians late one night made threatening remarks and jeered, mistaking me and my friends for Americans. But today, there were little Union Jacks at the railway station, and if one started speaking in bad French, the clerks switched to English. In the eighties, Paris stood aloof – with its immense, sweeping boulevards, and the grand buildings that always seemed to be looking down on one.

I didn't mention to Musa how, when still a backpacker, I had been stuck in the corner of the Polly Maggoo with a drunk Algerian man, reeking of tobacco, his unshruggable arm slung around my shoulder. He told me the French were all "pigs and wankers". He'd seen his brother shot dead in *la guerre*. French women were not as good to fuck as donkeys. He said he was speaking from his personal experience. Looking at him, I believed him.

Now in the 21st century, at least in this area around my hotel, Paris had become in many ways an Arab city. There was a vibrancy to the street life that hadn't existed before. Paris had come a long way.

This was news to Musa. He said there were still "many problems".

One day, a classmate at the Paris university, a white French boy, made his sexuality public by giving a male friend a long, lingering, exhibitionist kiss in front of everyone in the canteen. At first, Musa shunned him. Then he became curious about the boy. The boy had always been very affectionate towards him and not at all racist. He furtively arranged to meet him for a drink. The boy guessed his secret. That night turned out to be the first time he had penetrative homosexual intercourse.

Musa had a habit when he spoke of giving a huge smile that revealed pink gum, while at the same time, closing his eyes.

Word got around about his freakily huge cock, he laughed, and although he didn't think of himself as particularly good looking, he was a hit in gay circles. Soon he was having a lot of sex with men, men that wouldn't normally have given him a second look. Some of them, he said, were hard to shake; they became obsessed with him.

I wondered, aloud, if some of that fixation wasn't racist stereotyping – big black dick?

He shrugged. "It is not important. I wasn't looking for love."

Through homosexual contacts, Musa met all kinds of people – the rich and the professional – people he was unlikely to have had access to in the normal course of French bourgeois society. "The gay mafia," he chuckled.

Today, he knew scores of gay people, also through his business, which brought him to Paris regularly. His parents exported African cloth to France. They kept a stall at Porte de Clignancourt market. He lived close to it in the eighteenth arrondissement, a colorful and cosmopolitan area that included Pigalle's Moulin Rouge and the red-light district. It was better than the slummy banlieues where many North Africans lived with their families and communities that were both nosey and religious. Homosexuality was still unquestionably haram in these observant neighborhoods.

Unknown to us then, in a few years' time, those suburbs would erupt across France into riots that raged for twenty nights.

I asked Musa if he had met other gay black Africans while in Paris. He said he had indeed, and it did make him feel better about himself. But many of them had opted for a completely gay lifestyle, and were what people called coconut queens. Some of the less educated even used Dax hair pomade, and he knew of at least two men that used Tenovate cream for skin lightening, though they claimed it was to hide blemishes.

Did he like, Paris?

So-so, he said.

One facet of gay Paris I particularly enjoyed was its sophistication, a gay intellectual life invisible in most gay villages. The gay bookshop in the Marais went far beyond picture books and pornographic novels. You found social theory, literature, philosophy, and art books dominating the shelves upstairs; an interest in cultural life and history beyond the ghetto.

Yes, he nodded, he'd been there.

Did he know the photos of Pierre Verger?

"No, but Pierre et Gilles, yes. Beautiful!"

Musa's life in Paris was irreconcilable with how he saw himself when living in Dakar. He knew of one or two closeted cafés in his home city where homosexual men went, but, he said, he'd never think of setting foot in such dens. He was not gay, he was *"un homme qui a le sexe avec les hommes*, you understand?" A man who has sex with men. Gay was some white thing; it wasn't even particularly French. I got the impression he looked slightly down on 'gays'.

We had finished our falafel. I hoped this wasn't good-bye.

"You know," he said, "I have never told my story before. Not like that, from how I came here."

I asked him if he wanted to meet up again that night; we could go to one of the big clubs on the Champs-Elysées – my treat.

"Only if I can fuck you, proper, *comme animal*." He chuckled wickedly.

In Dakar, he was straight; in Paris, he was homosexual. In both these worlds, I suspect he was as yet unfulfilled. As a successful, erudite young man with international connections, he'd become immune from family suspicion. I wondered, silently, if this double life fragmented his personality – made him Jekyll and Hyde. Was his straight life in Dakar more than an elaborate deception? Could it really in fairness be described as a lie? Or was it simply we who were confused?

As we left the restaurant, he said, "You know, I am thinking of going into politics." His family was well connected, and he had a good education with a university degree. Doubtless, he even knew some political people in Paris.

"But that means public life. Media scrutiny," I pointed out. "And enemies without principles."

Musa was smiling. "You know, you should come to Dakar, to my wedding. It is next month."

Jussef
THE OUTSIDER
Marrakesh, Morocco

Dusk, and the shadows of the minarets and the robed pedestrians are narrow and lengthening as I enter the square. A few living memories can still recall how the severed heads of robbers were once displayed here. It wasn't that long ago, and if certain fundamentalists had their way, it would be seen again.

Since the eleven hundreds, this infamous square, Djma'a el Fna in Marrakesh, has been a cornucopia of the seductive and the grotesque. Entertaining the crowds about me is a range of quacks and charlatans, traditional healers, clairvoyants, conjurors, musicians.

But I am seeking more princely thieves.

Without warning, a live cobra is draped across my shoulders by a toothless man. His cavity smiling broadly, he unexpectedly dumps another smaller serpent on my head. For a mere fifty dirhams, he says jovially, I can actually have them removed. I pay, quickly.

Rows of false teeth grimace at me; second-hand dentures all carefully displayed on a trestle table. Nearby, sits the dentist, waiting. The decayed teeth he has extracted that day, still with their bloodied black roots, are all neatly laid out, individually and evenly spaced, as a proud exhibition of an honest day's work. Some of the molars seem so rotten they might have simply fallen out. There are no signs of anaesthetic, only a range of jaw-dislocatingly large pliers. Alongside the dentist, seated on a wooden tomato box, a doctor wrapped in white linen, barks into a microphone fixed to his chin with masking tape. He demonstrates by pointing to a lurid green plastic skeleton and cardboard diagrams with gruesome, pop-up cut-outs of internal organs.

A mob of touts at once descends on me. Like a flock of shabby scavengers trying to get a predator to give up its bone, they ceaselessly pester me. Strangers pluck at my clothes, clutch my hand, try speaking to me in German, French and English.

"Where you staying?"

"*Vous voulez un guide?*"

"Come! Where are you from my friend?" asks a withered man, flashing gold teeth.

Spotting the tourist police, the touts speedily evanesce back into the crowd, but then hastily reappear once the law has brushed past.

"*Hotel? Deutsche? Ich habe gute Qualitätsteppiche.*"

"*Vous avez besoin quelqu'un?* I know good place"

"Hotel? Restaurant? Money change? Carpet?"

I try miserably to fend off their incessant advances; shaking my head; sharply changing the direction in which I am walking. Nevertheless, they hiss and dart around me. Perplexed, cornered, I seem to wrong at everything; I refuse to make eye contact; I walk away; I walk too fast; I say no, and, inexperienced, make my greatest mistake: I do not smile. It is a futile and a weak response; too flustered and they live in hope you will give them something just to get rid of them.

So they pursue, themselves exasperated, until one at last exclaims, "Ah, *non, monsieur*, you fucking tourist!"

I become equally angry, clumsy, like a juvenile predator heckled and badgered. I withdraw to the safety of the food stalls, with all the embarrassed awkwardness of a cat backing down a tree.

Amongst the food and drink stands roam water-carriers in elaborate evzone-like costumes with metal cups dangling from their necks, shaded by extraordinary hats resembling Mexican sombreros, but in peacock colors.

Before I left home, Anwar, my builder, a liberal Indian Muslim, warned me mischievously, "Those Arabs have a terrible sex instinct. They fuck everything! Any time! Anywhere! You have to watch out."

"But I'm counting on it, Anwar," I'd retorted.

I find myself now stalking the eyes in the crowd. I venture out again into the square. I enter a half-moon of overt, cock-teasing belly dancers, egged on by the frenzied drumming and the tireless flutes that compete on air paled by smoke. At least one of these girls, I believe, is a Berber boy.

But the Great Spirit that possesses the wild Gnaoua drummers eludes us foreigners. I am outside their magic circle, feeling only the elation of life. The rest is no more than the mythomania of the tourist brochure, perpetuating the oriental dream of nineteenth century Europeans, like the three whirling dervishes advertising a hotel show, but spinning as if in a trance.

Yet there is something seething here, an undercurrent of everything forbidden – narcotics, exposed women, sodomy. It seems ridiculous how in the anarchy of such a dusty carnival anything could be forbidden. But the homosexual freedom back in the days of Paul Bowles and Joe Orton has long since passed. And I am an outsider.

Yet the abundant homoeroticism of the Moroccan boys, who touch, almost kiss, and caress each other's necks with their arms, leaves me slightly trembling. This is the Viagra of the square. One has no need for the emaciated herbalist sitting at his stall, mixing his aphrodisiacs and pounding his mortar.

I find myself in a quandary: how do I seek out the gaze that I recognize in any culture (as I had in Peru, Madagascar, Estonia), find those receptive signals from a stranger, whether deliberate and intentional or inadvertent and natural, yet avoid the touts, the purveyors of tourist junk and the ceaselessly volunteering guides?

My approach so far had been feebly Western; my attempt to scent the gay spoor lost in the square's cacophony and madness. The carpet sellers continue to harass me.

I decide it is time to shift my approach, when a tout, who is pretty enough, presents himself. He takes hold of my sleeve, and offers me mint tea at his shop. I give him a direct, scandalous look, as if to say, 'I'm not shopping for carpets, darling, unless you care to wrap yourself in it and be delivered like Cleopatra to my hotel'.

I allow my fingertips cavalierly to touch his wrist. He returns my smile, seductively enough, but makes an efficient yet polite departure. Sex is not part of everyone's bargain, but there is no question he had understood the innuendo. More significantly, he had not taken offence. Not that I was in the least interested; it got rid of him pestering me. What if he had responded?

The spectacle of the square continues to offer up the beauteous and the monstrous. I come across a crowd standing around a screaming child. His eyes, separated by a fat, round face, are squint, and he has a deformed leg, bent like a hockey stick. A taller and older kid has prized away his bright red balloon. The victim's empty fists swipe impotently, out of focus. The parents howl with laughter at the mêlée of small boys that follows. It horrifies me – this uncaring, this indifferent mob of jeering relatives, laughing at the enraged, malformed child. The balloon rises in the sky, floats away out of reach.

It is in this moment of painful abstraction, that I first see him, a Moroccan boy, with a huge, black stare that leaves me winded. His gaze is intractable.

Have I just been outed as a sex tourist? Perhaps, he is only another tout. I cannot decipher with certainty the look he gives me. Is it flirtation or entrapment? But I have no references here.

I am apprehensive too; I am not sure what the sanction is for homosexuality in this country. Stoning as they do in Iran? Being crushed under a wall as is happening in Afghanistan? I do not think there is sharia law in Morocco, but I recall reading of the imprisonment recently of six boys for holding their own informal same-sex marriage ceremony. At best, if caught, it will mean the extraction of a very large bribe.

I have scarcely caught my breath when he turns, takes a few steps away from me, then looks back over his shoulder. He sees I am still watching. The dancers spin around me, veils trailing. As I walk away, my knees want to buckle. My face, I'm sure, has flushed blood red.

A blind man taps my leg with his stick. Another man bumps into my shoulder. I reach into the pocket of my jacket; put my finger on my wallet. It is still there.

I join the throng around a storyteller, seated in the middle of his blessed mystic circle. There are a few tourists, but the audience is mostly Moroccan, and the story is related in Arabic.

And then I see the boy again on the opposite side, laughing spontaneously, unselfconscious, showing off a full set of bright, near perfect white teeth.

Is it a coincidence? I imagine I am safe amongst the ring of credulous listeners. I can't understand a word of the story, a kind of Grand Guignol, but no doubt with a moral lesson.

My boy is wearing a Western style jacket, neatly keeping his hands in its pockets, and underneath a clean cotton pullover with Maghrebi script in blue. Unexpectedly, he shoots another arresting look at me. Obviously, he has been aware of exactly where I was in the crowd all this time. I cannot look away. Surely, he has guessed that I was eyeing him?

I retreat once more to one of the many orange-juice stalls, and gather my thoughts.

Business it seems is slow. The vendor first has to pull the ripcord to start his generator, like an outboard motor, before squeezing a few oranges through the machine. He hands me a full, relatively clean glass. The lukewarm juice spills over onto my chin. I glance around for the boy, but cannot see him.

After my first few sips, the merchant quickly tops up the glass without me asking. This extra bit is free, but he points to the number above his canopy. I understand. I am to remember his kindness and return only to him.

My quarry having vanished, I decide to buy a few bananas at the next stall, something safe and cowardly familiar. The bananas are measured out, with much smiling, perfunctorily placed on a crooked iron scale. The grocer uses an odd assortment of old rusty weights and scrap as counterbalances. I come away with two spark plugs worth of fruit.

I almost do not dare to look about again, in case the boy is near, but involuntarily, out of the corner of my eye, I see him hovering. He has been shadowing me. He is definitely not a tout, but what is his motive? He appears now to be less sure of himself and of me.

Then, the reality of being a tourist intrudes again. Yet another fellow, and this one conspicuously unattractive, is tugging at my arm, pleading with me to go to his carpet shop.

Now, my young man strikes. In a raised voice with sharp intonations, he hastily comes to my rescue, dismissing the tout. Perhaps he is merely defending his claim, according to the unwritten code of this market place. As the tout turns away, he hisses a curse at me, airborne with saliva.

"*As salaam alaykum,*" the boy greets.

The false courage lent by my Arabic phrasebook fails me, and before I can pluck the appropriate reply from memory, he says in English, "Come, this way", and he gently pulls my sleeve.

He steps up the pace and ducks into a doorway off the square. I follow him up flights and flights of narrow stone steps, worn down at their centers by centuries of climbing. I am breathing heavily, struggling as much with my own hesitancy as the exertion.

We emerge on a magnificent rooftop terrace, overlooking the town skyline, the smooth pink domes, the receding arches and the flesh-toned minarets – the perfect Oriental brochure. Directly below, rising towards us, the smoke of the Djma'a el Fna, a great melting cauldron, lived by the Marrakshis and merely gawked at by us tourists. Am I finally to delve beneath the surface, to be admitted into the subculture of the square?

"It's a lovely view," I say, mutedly, stooping to rest my arms on the cast iron railings.

"Yes, yes, Marrakesh, Marrakesh." He waves his hand indicating the obvious.

In that moment, I wish he'd take my hand, but instead he ushers me to a table, gesticulating excitedly. "Café?" he asks.

I nod at a waiter who is standing stiffly in the corner, aloof but aware of us.

"*Deux café si'l vous plait.*"

My new companion smiles, looks me in the eyes reassuringly, and waits for me to speak. He has one congenitally sleepy eye, the left lid drooping slightly, seductively, and a historical scar above the other, creating a small gap where the eyebrow has never grown back.

We eye each other. I hope we are both pleased.

"*Parlez-vous Français?*" he asks.

"*Un peu.*"

We sip the syrupy coffee from small cups.

"*Allemande?*"

"*Non, Afrique du Sud.*"

"Ah!" he exclaims excitedly.

"You speak English?"

"My English not good"

"My French *très mauvais.*"

"Jussef", he points to himself. His fingers are sturdy and sculpted. "*Et tu?*" I have to repeat my name. At first, he thinks it is "Prince".

He practises it a few times before getting it quaintly right.

We stick for conversation, smiling politely. I pull out my guidebook and unfold the map of Morocco from its back cover. I trace a path with my finger. I plan to hire a car and wish to go to Ouarzazate over the Tizi n'Tichka pass across the Atlas Mountains, to make my way down to the edge of the great Saharan erg. He bends over the map, using it as an excuse to draw his forehead close to mine, so nearly touching. He smells of olive soap. At Erfoud our fingers touch.

I am not sure whether he can read a map or understands its scale. Most people here just get on buses with no real idea of national geography. He knew distances by bus, time like sand, not in scaled millimeters. He isn't helpful at dividing my journey into stops. Haltingly, I attempt the names on the route. Jussef snickers. I give him a mortified look. He starts repeating the names after me, teaching me to pronounce them correctly – Taoussit, Timiright, Errachidia.

I ask if he has ever left Marrakesh, but he doesn't seem to understand the question. No, he loves Marrakesh and he does not want to go anywhere. Besides, this is where his family is, and where he grew up. A friend, *meilleur ami* – I think he is telling me that his close friend has died at sea trying to cross to Spain. They were *âmes sœurs*.

I watch his lip bulge against the rim of the cup.

I try a few quick phrases. He corrects me. My phrasebook puts things too formally. *Afwan* – excuse me. *Ma aaref* – I don't know.

Complicity is growing.

Momken – may I?

Men fadlak – I'd like to …

He explains in half-English and half-French that a *touriste* and a *garçon Marocain* cannot be seen going together on the square. Apparently, the police intervene. I guess this is to protect visitors from harm, and the tourist industry, rather than to police the morals of society. He continues, but in a café we might sit in peace together, and nobody will object.

The police in Morocco all seem to be of the same genetic stock – uniformly moustached and of formidable physical stature.

Jussef asks me at which hotel I am staying. I lie. I say I have friends with me sharing the room. He goes quiet.

Is he disappointed or is he not sure how to broach the next subject?

He lets me take a photograph of him.

Jussef insists on paying for the coffee. It is an old rent boy's trick, I think, sadly.

We descend to the square and cross to the gate of the great souk. The police watch these entrances closely to stop touts pursuing tourists. Touts don't usually follow, unless they can pass themselves off as your guest or guide. We separate in order to enter, Jussef walking slightly ahead.

Just inside, he is waiting for me. The souk is a maze of narrow alleys, like some termite nest that has been kicked open. My heart is sinking. Was Jussef going to drag me to a cousin's rug shop? Had all this been a salesman's ruse?

"*Où allez-vous?*" I plead.

He tries to explain. It has to do with a motorbike. I don't know what he is talking about. He beckons to me to follow him into the labyrinth. I hesitate. He smiles. I follow.

We meander through alluring alleys, against the crowds, like salmon fighting their way upstream driven by the urge to spawn. Jussef locks his hand firmly around my wrist. He drags me through the heat waves coming off open furnaces and ovens, the medieval sound of iron ringing under hammers, and spice burning my nose. Though it feels interminable, we cannot have gone far, yet I am already lost. Were he to leave me, I'd have to accost and hire a local to show me the way back out of this labyrinth.

Jussef disappears into a narrow, obscure shop, with no sign other than one unhelpful French word: *magasin*.

While I wait outside, I observe an elderly, white-haired Frenchman, standing head and shoulders above the crowd, looking up and inspecting the carpets hanging above the street. He points to several, poking the mats with a hardwood cane sporting a gilded swan head. He is something of an anachronism, with his cream linen suit and a striking black trilby. An old white queen, I think, unkindly. Beaming and jabbering Moroccan boys surround him, but he is clearly in charge of the situation.

"Shoof, shoof!" says the potbellied merchant and claps his hands. The boys roll out carpet after carpet for the Frenchman to inspect.

"Look, look!" The boys are trying to direct the Frenchman's gaze down from the other displays, but his eyes narrow with a connoisseur's hawkishness. He points at an exquisite runner, his jacket sleeve pulling back over a bulky, gold timepiece. This detail is important, as the vendors, I notice, estimate your wealth by the quality of your shoes and your watch. Both his are magnificent. He'll have to bargain twice as hard, but he looks like an old hand at it.

There is a commotion as the boys scramble to untie the carpet from the washing line, precariously clamoring up drainpipes, the merchant clapping his hands and shouting instructions. While he waits, poker-faced, the Frenchman notices me watching, and fixes me with a curious stare, as if I were an exotic objet d'arte.

At that moment, Jussef re-emerges and takes me by the hand. The Frenchman tips his hat, the corners of his mouth curling approvingly, with an ever-so-slight bow from the waist, as my garçon pulls me away. I suddenly have a dark thought, I hope the Frenchman will recall that glimpse of me, should I turn up missing.

As we near the exit to the bazaar, I smell blood in the air. A red jet spurts onto a butcher's white plastic apron. The neck of a chicken has been casually slashed and twisted open. The chicken, gurgling and jerking, is dropped into an empty metal paint drum, and covered with a lid. There is only the sound of dull scuffling, and a stench of collecting blood, as the butcher extracts from the cage the next bird for execution. The rest of the unfortunate bird's brethren stare uncomprehendingly from their cages at the slaughter, and continue fattening themselves up.

I am still staring in morbid fascination at the chicken stall, when Jussef drags me to the kerbside and pushes me into the back of a taxi. I hadn't even seen him hail it. Jussef climbs in front with the driver and the car pulls away. It has all happened so incredibly quickly. As we speed off, I spot two tourist police staring after us, arms folded, heads cocked back.

It is an old, French boxcar-thing with the exhaust bumping along the ground. The night is warm; there is no air-conditioner. It must be unbearable in this taxi during the day, and it is only autumn.

We are soon outside the central area of old Marrakesh. I look for signs of possible complicity between Jussef and the driver, but there is no evidence that they have ever met before.

We enter a conurbation of dense housing, seemingly endless regimented three-storied flats. The taxi winds its way through a tangle of narrow dirt roads. I am glad of this opportunity to see the Morocco where the majority of people live. But it is growing dark, and the details are obscure, the streetlights fewer and fewer, and the lights themselves grow dimmer.

A country on the doorstep of Europe's markets, rich in minerals, blessed in climate and agriculture, with an industrious people; it is incomprehensibly poor.

I wonder if Jussef realizes how completely I, the rich foreigner, has been delivered into his hands. He gives continual directions to the driver in Arabic. It is a relief to sense that they do not know each other, and this is not a set up. He keeps indicating with his hands where to go. Perhaps even the locals only know places by route and not address. There are no street signs. Hooded figures slouch against walls.

"*Arrête!*" says Jussef at last, pointing to a building. We have parked in some dark quarter in the outer-city.

Jussef turns around to me and in a hushed voice asks, "You have one hundred dirhams?" The taxi man pretends not to listen. I hesitate.

"Please … please …"

I pull out a few notes, careful not to let him see how much I am carrying. To make matters worse, this time I have broken my rule; the hotel I was staying at seemed dodgy, and didn't have a safe. I therefore have on my person, my air-ticket, passport, camera, credit cards, all my cash, my whole life.

Jussef takes the money and hastily disappears into a nondescript house. There are several men standing in the street outside the doorway, looking up and down the road. They are alert, I think as if on guard. Behind them shadowy figures and boys with their hands in their pockets lounge about.

Drugs, it occurs to me.

I am sweating into my socks. I wait. I feel safe in the taxi. There is no rational sense of malevolence, nothing sinister, only my creeping anxiety as I shift about on the seats, nervously picking at a split seam.

One of the hooded figures now takes a few steps towards the car, peers at us, and then turns back.

Jussef finally re-appears, looking hurried. This time he climbs into the back of the taxi with me, touching my knee with his warm palm. He is pleased about something, and smiling. I feel reassured.

The taxi takes us further into the suburb. I belatedly fumble for a seatbelt, but there is none.

My sense of direction obfuscated by the dark, the generic buildings, and the dust, I no longer have any idea where I am, how far we have traveled, or what time it is. To put off the hagglers, I had not worn a wristwatch.

We stop on the edge of an open common. He pays the taxi. I worry again; this is a deserted place. We set off on foot into the darkness. I can hardly see anything and have to feel the ground through my sandals. As we leave the road behind, without a word he slips his hand into mine. Had he sensed my fear?

Occasionally, strangers loom out of the blackness, traveling towards us on the same worn path. He disengages my hand each time they materialize. A bicycle bell rings out in sporadic percussion as the frameset jolts over bumps and potholes otherwise hidden in the dark, and a tiny white light, no brighter than a candle, overtakes us.

"Come! Come!" he says. Jussef pulls me up a low sandy dune, off the foot worn track. What is it he wants to show me?

We come to a small ruin on the abandoned lot. There is nothing obvious for me to see, only the debris of an old, mud brick building, with fingers of collapsing wall pointing skyward. They stand tenebrous and looming, in the silence, statues in their own right. The sight fills me with an intense aesthetic pleasure. Yet, I am afraid. The night is dead quiet. I can almost hear my heart beat. I am at his mercy.

Jussef unexpectedly clasps the back of my neck with his wide, open hand; like a kitten in an adult male's mouth, I await love or the coup de grace. Fear seems to freeze the air around me. Jussef caresses my neck, gently running the tips of his fingers beneath my hair and touching the back of my ears. He releases me.

I hear him pull down his fly zip, turn slightly away, and instantly a long jet of white piss arcs in the moonlight. I have to pee as well. I notice he is watching me over his shoulder. I feel it stiffening. My white stream sputters and stops, the erection cutting off the warm flow. I spread my legs so that the pungent rivulet runs down the sand between my sandals.

Without another word, we set off together again, traversing the nightscape. The silhouettes of the buildings have faded and sunk behind us, as if swallowed up by the earth.

Eventually we emerge on the far side of the common at another labyrinth of dusty streets, no lights, skulking shadows, children (always, at all hours in Morocco), and prowling stray cats.

He tells me again to wait for him. He enters a doorway with a lime green corridor; his heels disappear up some stairs. From outside, I can hear a woman's voice through the open window above. They are talking, and moving on wooden floors. Kids play soccer in the dust around me. Nobody stares. Nobody here seems to even question my presence.

Jussef soon re-appears, in his hand a gigantic, fairy tale of a brass key. He ushers me to an adjoining flatlet. We kick off our shoes at the threshold. He leaves the door slightly ajar.

His room has a mattress on the floor, the blanket covering it full of holes; a few folded clothes stacked in one corner; a schoolroom chair with a broken back and splayed legs. Only the floor with intricate mosaic tiles covered in patterns of dizzying arabesques and endless spirals relieves its grimness.

He pops a pirated cassette in to his small ghetto blaster.

Jussef strikes a match and lights two incense sticks. He wants to talk about music. The Western pop he puts on is at least ten years old. Excitedly, he shows me all eight of his music cassettes, one by one, each precious, handing them to me to examine.

"*Ataí?*" he asks. Without me answering, he slips out into the street.

Alone in the room, I take the opportunity to examine its contents. There are papers scattered next to the mattress on the floor. Possibly, he is studying. They are in Arabic.

How will this end? I am abrogating all responsibility for myself, and handing my fate to a complete stranger, like that drunken moment in which the condom is abandoned.

I hear a tap squeak open in the street and water gushing on metal, the telltale pitch flattening as the vessel fills. Then he is gone, back into the house across the street.

Jussef finally returns, holding a small, elegant copper teapot, steaming at the spout. He uses the rickety stool as a table. We sit on the floor. The way he neatly and carefully positions the glass tumblers suggests a ceremonial etiquette indecipherable to me. He pours the tea, drawing the pot away from the cup, creating a long pale arc; the smell of mint and perhaps tobacco leaf, suspended in the room. I feel my sinuses open. He is all smiles now, *laissez faire*. We sit opposite each other, cross-legged, not speaking, but now we are comfortable with silence.

There is nothing debauched, jaded or unsavory about this young man. I think of Cavafy, who wrote of the beautiful young men of Alexandria brutalized and ruined by 'the common men's debauches'. But Jussef seems to be the Moroccan version of the wholesome boy next door.

"*Sucre?*" he asks. He reacts with surprise. "*Non?*" and he laughs, spooning a third of his glass full of white sugar.

The hot liquid satisfies. I swallow the words, "*Shukran jazeelan.*"

Jussef unravels a page torn from a newspaper, and places on it a small compressed wad of leaves, unmistakably hashish. On the black and white press photograph of King Hassan II, he separates out the seeds and mixes what I take to be an opiate with it, and rolls a joint. He offers it to me first. I refuse. He smiles and starts smoking, inhaling deeply. He offers again. I shake my head; sip my tea.

I am disappointed. I have misgivings; maybe this whole episode was only to get him drugs. I fear he'll flag from drug-induced impotence and pass out stoned.

Jussef stretches back, supporting himself on his elbow, centerfold style. The vein on his bicep protrudes distractingly.

He tells me he turned twenty-one last month.

Was he not scared of the police?

He says his friend, before he set out for Spain, had been in jail. I wonder if Jussef has not been inside too. You have to be bought out he tells me. If you were sentenced to six months, you might be in for a year or out in a week, depending on the money. The system is corruption. Justice here is a fickle thing; laws arbitrary.

But tourists, he smiles, you are kings. He is inhaling deeply from the last coal of the joint, when the metal door cannons open. Oh God, here it is now, I think. But a soccer ball rolls into the room.

I am jerked back into the fear of discovery. But Jussef jumps up, sticks his head out the door, lobs the football into the night and shouts after it in Arabic. I hear a small boy's voice reply, sounding apologetic.

Jussef closes the outside door and goes into the bathroom. He pulls a chord, switching on a solitary light bulb hanging from the ceiling. He beckons to me.

I flinch as he unexpectedly rubs his hand across my jeans, and squeezes. Beneath the naked suspended bulb, he unbuckles his pants. Jussef is already hard, a thick cut cock standing straight up like a flagpole, pressing itself flush against the black hairs of his taut lower abdomen. He tugs at my pants, peering down at my white erection, looking enormous in the naked light. He slowly pulls up his top, but does not remove it; instead, he hooks it behind his neck. I touch his nipples. I pull him towards me, but he turns his head sideways offering his cheek. I desperately want to kiss him. No kissing on the lips, he makes it clear.

He is touching me, stroking. He licks his lips pleasurably, his head flung backwards. He begins to pull up my vest. Suddenly Jussef is pummeling my shoulder hard. He tells me, "Stop… stop!" I look up in alarm. Am I healthy? he asks. Am I sick? I realize he has seen the sunburnt skin peeling from my back.

"It is the sun, *le soleil, sur le plage!*" I plead. "It's okay. I'm not ill."

He wants to fuck me. No, I say.

As I straighten up, he shakes his head; he will not suck. His balls are shaven. I go down, press my tongue there, almost instantaneously, he draws but one sharp breath, then abruptly spurts across my clavicle; it streams down my shoulder blade, several rivers turning my skin to gooseflesh as they slowly trace the curvature of my back. Jussef doesn't make a sound. He spits thick and viscous in his hand and grabs my cock, not pausing for even a moment. It takes some time. As I come, he clasps my mouth shut with his sticky hand. I'm sucking the air between his fingers, my sound forming a vacuum in his hot palm. I taste salt and I hear a soft, low growl from the back of my throat.

"Sshhhhhhh," he quietens me, softly, "shooosh," his grip tightening my mouth. I cannot cry out. His other hand still squeezing me. I trust him completely; in that moment, like Desdemona, I have given myself absolutely to my General.

But there is no more ceremony or pause. We shower immediately afterwards. He scrupulously scours his hands with a stiff wire brush and lathering the soap into peaks of green foam scrubs his genitals until they blush darker.

I wonder if this is meticulous cleanliness, slight xenophobia or self-aversion at the hasty homosexual act we have just performed.

A great distance begins to open between us.

I realize he too has taken a great risk bringing me here.

I tell him it is late. I must go. Jussef smiles, cocks his head, and holds out his hand.

"*Un cadeau?*" A gift. Please, for his mother of course, not for him. This is how it is done here.

I pause. How much? I wonder to myself. I do not wish to insult or offend. I am satiated and complaisant. I hand him a hundred dirhams. I have already paid for the hash. He had paid for coffee and the taxi. He waves his hand, undemanding, but indicating that it is not enough. I give him another fifty. He accepts with a smile. Then he asks if I have a guide. No, I say.

However, we do not arrange to see each other again.

Together we set off through the streets, backtrack across the shadowy common, walking close, bumping hips occasionally, but no longer holding hands. The moon has risen directly above us. The sky is enormous.

When I see the road and buildings up ahead I say good night, but Jussef respectfully insists on coming with me to the roadside to make sure I am safe.

I am too polite to ask if he does this often, or if he'll do it again.

Courteous to a T, Jussef waits patiently with me until a taxi finally halts. They are few at this hour. He tells the driver where to take me and we say, "*Bonne nuit! Maa as-salaamah!*"

I feel rather silly as we head back into the city and I must correct the taxi driver. "No, not the Mousaffir, I'm at the Hôtel Tropicana."

The driver grins, nods knowingly.

Hakim, Asma and Julio
AFTER DARKROOM
Rio de Janeiro, Brazil

From the flight deck, the pilot came screaming through the loudspeakers, announcing our imminent arrival in Rio de Janeiro, "the most beautiful city in the whole wide world," he said. From the air, she appeared blessed with the natural tropical make-up of green hills and an aquamarine sea. We circled her twice, the pilot narrating in an exuberant, heavy South African accent, the beaches wide and white, the spectacular rock formations of Sugar Loaf and Corcovado, the paradisiacal sea... He actually sounded tearful, as if reunited with a long lost lover. Passengers glanced at one another with bemused smiles. Perhaps, we were all thinking, he has a mistress in this port.

It was my first time in Rio, long before the megalopolis started its remarkable recovery in the 21st century. It was post-carnival and the people of the city were dissipated and in recovery. At street level, Rio was a disappointing Latin American version of rundown Maputo in Mozambique. That Brazil had suffered several major economic catastrophes was patently evident. The buildings were falling apart. High-rises obscured the spectacular rock formations for which the city is famous. Glimpsed occasionally, these were more like the knees and elbows sticking out of an invalid's bed, scuffed with shantytowns that sprawled down to the beach. Corruption had built these informal settlements, an attempt to load the voters' roll with poor country folk, who subsequently could never afford to return home. It was hard for me to believe Rio was once the playground of Hollywood, of the rich and famous, from Lana Turner to Orson Welles and Eva Peron. Compared to pristine Cape Town, this was a slum. Circling in the polluted haze above the *favelas* were huge frigate birds, resembling giant pterodactyls.

I spent my first two days enjoying the rhythm of the beach, so much a part of life there. On the promenade, people were out jogging or exercising, men played volleyball, young lovers strolled hand-in-hand amongst elderly couples shuffling along for their evening constitutional. Locals were deeply engrossed with consulting soothsayers and tarot card readers.

Running the length of the beach were casinos, kitschy discos with young revelers, and markets selling souvenirs and "art" for the tourist trade. At Ipanema and Copacabana, with their unusual proximity to abject poverty, caught between the serenity of the ocean and a tidal wave of humanity, there were tin can collection points for the recycling hobos who patrolled the promenade; a practical, unselfconscious admission of social problems.

It was not long before I made hard contact with the notoriously ravenous libido of Rio. My first tourist destination was Pao de Açucar, the iconic Sugar Loaf. I had never been so hit upon by women as I was in this city. On the roller coaster bus ride, I sat with my leg pressed against the determined and prickly bare thigh of a woman, who had she not shaved I'm sure would have had more hair on her legs than I did.

The cable car operator singled me out from the crowd with his eyes and a salacious smile. He was a tall man, a few days unshaven, with powerful arms, skin like black varnish, green tattoos, a narrow waist and bubble butt – an updated Tom of Finland character if ever I had seen one come to life. He was wearing a T-shirt with horizontal stripes, almost identical to my own. Snap, I thought. I kept a poker face, staring at him from the back of the cable car over the heads of the tourists. Some Italians, all elbows and camera bags, were videotaping each other inside the cable car and completely missing the view.

The driver turned away from me to face forward for the docking. He rotated the ancient looking brake wheel and brought us to a jerky stop. I was disgorged with the crowd. We shuffled over to the railings. While everyone was pointing in a hundred foreign languages at the view, I was watching the cable car driver. He had completed his safety checks, hurriedly it seemed, and now, emerging from the car, looked for me, found me, and sure enough, he winked, cocking his head so as to indicate I should follow him.

He passed a small café, glancing over his shoulder, like a siren's call, to see if I was still following, before he disappeared into the men's toilet. Actually, I could do with a pee, I thought.

On entering, I found him standing at the urinal with his back to me. I heard him unzip. I moved forward, coming into sight of his dick, resting in the palm of his broad hand. I stood alongside and unbuttoned my fly. My face flushed red, my heart pounding. I couldn't pee.

In the cubicles behind us, doors closed, I could hear the occupants shifting on the plastic seats, tearing toilet paper, their shoes scuffling on bare cement. His top lip twitched slightly. Now he didn't smile. He kept showing off his richly veined cock, angling his pelvis upwards, thrusting with his calves, knees bent, holding it up for me to stare at, shaking it, watching intently to see how I reacted. Some pre-cum unexpectedly dribbled over his gold-ringed finger.

At that moment, the noisy Italian tourists, now having ticked off the view, burst in, almost pushing each other to get to the urinals.

He turned away to face the wall. From the corner of my eye, I saw him struggling to stuff his stiff cock back down his camouflage trousers.

I washed my hands and fled hurriedly, guiltily, without drying them. I escaped into the ticket queue for the helicopter ride, my heart still racing; ashamed, strangely flattered, slightly scared – all the thrills of misbehaving.

A chopper was landing, and the agent was hurriedly asking if there were any singles. As none of the couples wished to be split up, I was lucky enough to be jumped to the head of the line, and straight into the co-pilot seat.

From the ridiculous to the sublime, I was whisked away by helicopter. We sped off across Ipanema, before returning to circle the great Christ of Corcovado with its long queues of coaches and columns of tourists laying siege like the Roman army at Masada.

Below me, that great, stone Christian totem pole dominated the dirty white city with its ugly skyscrapers. Viewed from the statue's unseeing eyes, Rio is a Godly place.

I ticked off most of the obligatory tourist itinerary during my first week. I took to sleeping a large part of the day, and venturing out in the cooler nights, returning to my hotel with the newspaper round.

I started the weekend cracking open an expensive beer at the Rainbow kiosk, in front of the landmark Copacabana Palace Hotel on the gay strip of the *praia*. The twilight boys were out in strength, promenading in the warm air. I made a game of counting them as they passed, working out one in how many I thought sexually attractive. I forget the statistic now. But there were hustlers, chancers, effeminate boys (known derogatorily as *bichas*), men in drag, and heterosexual middle class folk. I'd met several of the lads already. There were the two skinny Danes with their alabaster skins; the three Germans – Mark, Klaus and the heart-stopping Joachim whose beauty made you ache; the suave César, who wanted me "to go" with him, but had a boyfriend at home and an appointment at seven; and the gorgeous Santiago with burnished eyes, who made arrangements as easily as he broke them.

But on this night, there was one boy I had never seen before. He was sitting at an angle facing away, his deeply tanned, thin limbs, poking out of a simple, loose, spotless white gym vest. He had a black bandanna tied around his head with a tassel that swished across the back of his lissom neck like a ponytail. His girlfriend kept eyeing me. She said something and he turned round to look at me. I was at once smitten.

When he stood up, I saw he was short, with faded jeans hanging low on his hips. He invited himself over and sat down in the empty chair next to me, resting his skinny, cinnamon toned forearms on the table. I felt slightly embarrassed; his girlfriend must have said I was staring.

"*Anglais, non?*" he asked.

"*Afrique du Sud. Français?*"

"*Oui*, 'oliday."

He was blessed with perfect symmetry; exquisite, almost painted eyebrows; sweeping eyelashes; dark eyes, like wet river stones; high, fragile cheekbones; expressive full lips. Even Joachim might be envious.

He held out his hand. "*Je m'appelle Hakim.*"

His voice transported me back to a childhood crush, ever since which I am defenseless against boys who possess the apparent contradiction of a slight physique but a resonant double-bass voice.

"*Enchanté,*" I said affectedly, blushing.

"We're from Paris," he said. He gestured to his girlfriend to join us.

She rose on her high-heeled shoes and strode over with the self-conscious poise of a ramp model, pointing her chin at the horizon and possibly an imaginary photographer. She wore a black denim bra-like top, and frayed jeans cut off as high as they could go on the thigh. Her lithe, but square build, and her solid face, surrounded by long, wild, red hair, were masculine. With more make-up, she could pass as transsexual. Asma, was her name.

She was French-Moroccan; Hakim was French-Algerian. They both worked in a nightclub belonging to a gay pied noir on the Champs-Elysées.

We made pleasant small talk about how long I was staying in Rio, when I had arrived, how I was enjoying it. They said they'd been many times and loved the city.

"But it's too hot," Asma complained, "thirty-seven! We watch videos all today with the aircon."

The longer I looked at Asma, the more unsure I became of her gender.

They said they would show me the best clubs and bars if I joined them for the evening ahead. We headed off to their hotel. I noticed Asma received many looks on the street, the unwanted macho kind. There was something delightfully seditious about the two of them. They spoke at the top of their voices, laughed loudly and often, made theatrical gestures, and stared back openly at people who noticed them.

Back at their hotel, right on the Avenida Atlantica, I noticed there was only one double bed, though sharing a *grand lit* was not uncommon with the French.

"I'm taking a shower, 'scuse me boys," said Asma.

Hakim switched on the television, protruding on a wall bracket into the tiny room. Then he sat down beside me on the bed. At last, I was alone with my infatuation. Without a word, Hakim leant over and started to kiss me, first on the neck, then on the lips, his long, spidery eyelashes tickling my cheek. I hesitated, though my body started to respond. He kissed me again. He tasted of mint. He didn't touch my body, stretching only his graceful neck towards me. He stopped. At once, I regretted my hesitation. He must think me a poor kisser. Or not particularly interested in him. I was about to take the initiative, to clasp him passionately with my lips, to seize him with overwhelming, irresistible desire, when I heard the taps being turned off in the shower. Hakim abruptly withdrew.

Was she his girlboyfriend?

"*Café?*" he asked me, coolly. Then he tapped on the bathroom door, "*Asma, chérie, café?*"

She rattled off something in French.

I had already finished my coffee by the time she finally emerged from the fogged up bathroom, battery operated blow drier in hand, teasing her frizzy hair. She had put on a black cocktail dress. Her eyes swept the room suspiciously. Was she only a friend? A friend with a possessive streak, prone to jealousy? She turned for Hakim to zip up her dress. I glimpsed her naked back – muscular, freckled.

Hakim swapped his sandals for boots, but kept on his jeans and vest. "Ready?" he asked.

"Yes," I said. I quizzically touched the hánzi character tattoo on his petite round shoulder.

"It means righteous," he explained, and smiled, which solicited a stifled cough from Asma.

We had, I thought, a perfectly good dinner of *filet mignon* and *batatas Portuguese*, in a small, attentive gay restaurant with clunky silver service. They insisted on paying for dinner, and typically Parisian, apologizing for the food not being up to their standard.

They complained about how Paris was too expensive. Both of them had French fathers and North African mothers. They were French citizens and rented in the Marais quarter. Occasionally, they would break into Arabic dialect; I suppose when they didn't want me to understand.

It was midnight already before we reached the nightclub in Leblon. We paid the *ingresso* of eight reals, while Asma – as a woman – though even the bouncer gave her a second look, had to pay nine reals.

While Hakim and Asma danced, I positioned myself at the bar next to a 'Barbie' – Hakim's nickname for any handsome, muscular poser. He did not speak English and we struggled with conversation, shouting above the deafening music. Finally, he asked the barman for a pen and scribbled on a serviette for me: 'I am taxi boy.' He looked me straight in the eyes. His rate was fifty dollars. I told him he was worth five hundred. He laughed.

Then Asma fetched me to dance. She had a nonchalant dancing style, while I revolved about her wildly with the other feral boys.

"These lights are very disappointing!" moaned Asma, airily, just to remind me she was the professional clubber.

Like most of the clubs I'd experienced in Rio, it had the same format. In a huge empty room adjacent to the bar and dance floor they screened films or music videos, which everyone watched until midnight. Tonight it was an American film about a woman and her children trying to escape a mass murderer by floating down the rapids on the Colorado River. The videotapes would often stop on the clock, even in the middle of the film's climax, the way the airlines once did, and then there would be a short, but ebullient lip-sync drag or strip show. On this night, three steroid junkies gyrated, did handstands, stretched, flipped, cartwheeled, stood on their heads, flexed and puffed, until they were divested of all their clothes, and were ready to parade on top of the bar counter with rather modest hard-ons. Everyone clapped encouragingly. The underground temple had opened.

Then a long black curtain was rapidly drawn across the room, dividing it in two. The lights went out. At first, I hadn't a clue what was going on. In a matter of minutes, splayed against the wall were men's bodies, and in front of them stooped figures, forming an arcade of shadowy limbs and ephemeral forms. Bodies arched as they were sucked, masturbating hands rattled jewellery, buttons broke, shooting across the floor, voices cried out orgasms. It was a great wailing wall of sex. The music now trance-like, a numbing beat, spiced with steel band sounds and carnival pipes whistling like prehistoric birds, and the DJ kept repeating, 'it's a dream … it's a dream … it's a dream'.

I stepped back on to the dance floor. I saw several couples, hand in hand, disappearing into the darkroom. Few people in Rio could afford their own apartments and many lived in the closet with their parents, so this was where couples came to make love.

The music was 'techno-house jungle fever', badly mixed by a local DJ, who was also selling his CD. I bought one as a souvenir. A sexy, topless boy, asked me if I'd buy him a copy as well. He said he was mad about the music. I said no, and ignored him, cute as he was. He shrugged and casually, ungrudgingly, tried his luck elsewhere. I later discovered that he was part of the band, boosting sales; ever resourceful is Rio.

Asma and I danced for a while longer on the disco side of the curtain, but I could see she was getting bored and her feet were tired. She was after all in stilettos.

"I think we're going home," said Asma. "But you should stay." Was she freeing me of obligation, or was she suggesting I do not follow?

"It's not great tonight," Hakim shrugged. "The music, the lights, I'm useless without snow ..." It took me a few seconds to realize he meant cocaine. I nodded, and we air-kissed, and said, *"Bon nuit, a demain."*

"If we don't see you, look us up in Paris," said Asma.

"But I don't ..."

They were already drifting away in the crowd. "At the club!" Hakim yelled as he was swept away.

A tall, lanky boy, topless, who had been watching us, sidled over to me the instant they'd left. I was slightly dazed, my mind still fixed on Hakim.

"I'm Julio," he said.

His intentions were quite clear. He made a few flattering comments, then dragged me by the wrist through the curtain.

Julio pinned me between two couples. He turned my face up to him. It was a rare pleasure to be stooped by a boy taller than me, and I lifted myself on tiptoes to kiss him. His nipples were unusually long and fleshy. They tasted of what I imagined to be the smack of adrenalin. I sucked in beads of his sweat. He pulled down his jeans. His thick black penis, looking almost prehensile, kinked like a boomerang, nodding as it throbbed. I had entered that space where the beast overtakes one.

The couples on either side had noticed our lanky, muscular shadows; their hands were now wrestling us, their mouths pressing in on either side. Two boys had started to suck his cock and balls, a third grabbing hold of mine with his lips, a fourth licking, caressing with his tongue Julio's firm, almost square buttocks. Julio and I only kissed, arms around one another's shoulders, leaving the boys to feast on us, succumbing to the rites of Rio after dark. The boy working on me was an expert. I could hardly hold out. "I'm close," I whispered to Julio.

His body jolted, his long, almost impossible-to-get-hard cock flexing. He kept on coming, and so did I. The boys were licking it up, like sharks at a feeding frenzy. I could see Julio's huge teeth smiling in the dark. His fingers were sticky as they slid between mine, and he pulled me away from the wall. The room was now crowded with boys having sex, no longer only against the walls, but standing everywhere, in twos and threes and groups. As we weaved our way through the throng, in the dim light I saw many were enjoying full penetration, fucking wildly, gasping with pain and pleasure. The boys on their knees clutched at our jeans, but Julio dragged me free towards the toilets at the back, still buttoning up my fly.

We stood next to each other at the basins in the bathroom, washing our hands with liquid soap. My white semen was smeared all over his rippling black body, even on his shoulder blades. How had it got there? Was it mine? He was laughing mirthfully, holding his arms up, turning for me as I wiped it off with reams of toilet paper.

Cleaned up, we went back to the bar. I looked nervously down at my clothes, afraid the UV would pick up blotches of stray white cum. Julio bought me an ice-cold beer.

He said he was a navy marine. Their ship was in for maintenance at Guanabara Bay. He was nineteen.

"Must be fun in the navy?" I suggested.

He shrugged. Actually, he said, his dad owned a gay club in Botafogo. He was not going to have sex there, he laughed.

We danced for a few songs, before he smiled and waved good-bye. He'd taken from me what he wanted. I had given gladly. I understood. Yet, part of me could not help feeling stranded. How I wished Hakim had stayed. And I watched, distantly, as I saw Julio slipping back into the darkroom, closely followed by another boy.

Abel / Isobel
SWAPPING SEX
Toronto, Canada

I kept thinking, what if she has become an unhappy woman? I was sitting on the front steps of my Toronto lodgings, which overlooked a small park, stretching my eyes for any signs of Isobel. I was mildly confident I would recognize her in whatever shape she now took.

The last time I saw her was when Isobel was still Abel. Abel, a 21-year-old Canadian boy I'd had a fling with back in South Africa. Isobel is; Abel is no more. He is she.

She. I had disciplined myself, with difficulty, not to say or think he or him or his or he's, especially when discussing *her* with mutual friends, who persisted in saying such things as we don't see *him* that often anymore.

To talk about he was to deny her, to betray her, and ultimately to betray what Abel had felt.

My handsome Abel; Abel, the old exterior of Isobel, with his taut, young, hard-edged body, but a trap in which *she* had been kept for 21 years. I kept thinking of Abel's nose; a beautiful, large aquiline nose that gave Abel's face such strength and virility. How had Isobel dealt with it? Had she sliced it off and thrown it out?

Two years back, Abel lived in Cape Town. Although exceedingly young, Abel displayed considerable and mature talent as a theatre director, skillfully coaxing astonishing performances out of his female actors. Perhaps it was my infatuation, but I had believed, then, he was destined to become one of the great directors of his generation.

Abel understood me. At the time, I was going through a stage of remembering my dreams in detail. Those mornings we woke up together, I would relate them to him. He had this uncanny ability to interpret, to make sense out of the jumble of my mind's nightly roamings, to soothe the recurring nightmares that terrorized me.

I did not know about Isobel for some time. She eventually revealed herself, on a romantic weekend away in the Cape Fold Mountains. Abel was sitting on the bed in our cabin, hugging his knees, his big bare feet planted on top of the sheet. He had finished telling me the story of his secret. "I've always known that this is not me," said Abel. "I am a woman. After sex, I feel… kinda dirty."

That hurt. We had just made love. Now I felt as though I had forced him. I felt a deep shame forcing tears to my eyes, a flood of tiny details, like death by a thousand cuts. It was all so clear now. The silence when he came. His squeamishness around penetration. His sexual reticence. His confusion around the act, which I had simply, insensitively, dismissed as virginal anxiety, as the precautions of one physically inexperienced. Had I forced myself into him? Into her? And why did that feel even worse?

Having someone break up with you is a moment of strange contradiction. In a way, it is when they finally take you into their confidence, enough to tell you the truth: I do not want this anymore. I do not want you.

I stopped seeing Abel. I felt as though whatever love there had been was entirely made-up in my head. I felt stupid and monstrous too.

The next time we met, it was accidental. I was at a party thrown by mutual friends. Abel was there, in drag, not showy, but in ordinary woman's clothes. The host didn't know I knew her. I was introduced to Isobel. I felt they were showing her off, a transvestite novelty to marvel at in their collection of acquaintances.

"So how are you?" Isobel asked, smiling, noticeably behaving more camp; the feminine parodied; or was she simply claiming herself? She led me to a corner of the lounge and sat me down. Almost immediately, we were deep in conversation, both of us ignoring the rest of the party.

I could see a red flush on her chest. She at once noticed I'd seen it. "It's from laser surgery, to kill the hairs," she said, covering it with her hand. "I had my face done too. I looked awful, for a bit. One comes up in a terrible rash the next day. It's much cheaper here than in Canada." Then she added triumphantly, "That hair will never grow back now."

It had begun. It was up to me to be supportive now. She'd need all the help she could get.

Abel told me he'd been going to counselling for years. His parents knew and understood, and they supported him in his decision. He had made that decision. He'd researched everything, down to the smallest details. She said she knew exactly what she was doing.

Abel was so bright, I was sure his research was thorough. But I had misgivings. As Isobel was in the process of being created out of Abel, she might start seeing him another way. By changing the observer, one changed the surrounding reality, shifting the perspective from which one understood the world and oneself in it. Awfully soon, all that research might start looking very different.

One thing I could predict with absolute certainty was that the rest of the world would start seeing and reacting to her very differently, perhaps to a point where it would become unrecognizable.

We agreed to see more of each other. Over the next few weeks, I played chauffeur, taking Isobel, vaguely dressed as a boy in loose fitting unisex styled clothes, to the laser clinic in Claremont. They had to zap each hair follicle several times, slowly killing off Abel.

Isobel's farewell party was held in a bistro in the gay ghetto. People came and went during the course of the evening. We hardly had space to talk, except for a few minutes at the bar counter. Isobel was bundled up in scarves like Mata Hari. This time, she was recovering from jaw surgery.

"All the things they can do here just as well as in Canada, I'm getting fixed now. It's much cheaper," she explained.

She gave me a gory and grueling account of the surgery that still lay ahead: facial reconstruction, which included brow bossing, a tracheal shave to reduce Abel's manly Adam's apple, further mandible reduction, rhinoplasty, ear pinning.

"Thank God my lips are okay!" she chuckled.

For how long, I wondered.

After the face, there was the bodywork. She listed the procedures. I could feel my sphincter constrict.

"They break all the bones in the hand and reset them to make them smaller, but before that I'll do the boob job. I can't wait for real titties." She giggled. "But I'm not going to do the radical stuff, like having the bottom rib removed, or my legs shortened. They kind of saw them off and then glue you back together!"

And I thought fondly of his sharp ribs that would dig into me when we held each other in the dead of night. I didn't ask about genitals.

That was two years ago. Now I saw her entering the other side of the park. I immediately recognized the shoulders, the overall silhouette, but there were breasts in the T-shirt. She was wearing a peak cap, with long blonde hair flowing down on either side.

Isobel came up the stairs smiling.

I was hugely relieved. "Oh thank God! You're not an ugly woman," I breathed.

She laughed loudly, and with a wet smack gave me a kiss. "So, let's hear. What do you think?" She did a twirl.

"You look pretty."

"Why thank you, sir," and she tittered coyly. I could hear she had been going for voice coaching, for the tone and pitch was dramatically altered from Abel's yet without sounding forced or constricted.

We set off down the street, entering Toronto's gay district, the section around Younge and Maitland, off Church, where almost everyone on the streets is gay. There were high-rise apartments, with rainbow towels drying on the balconies and rainbow flags in the windows, shops and gay emporia selling the usual gay crud, street cafés and restaurants packed with gay boys.

We had lunch at a busy Cantonese place, on the fringe of the ghetto. I noticed Isobel got a few second takes, mostly from other girls, not so often from the boys.

She was dressed simply. Feminine sandals, a white T-shirt, summer shorts. Her nails were a modest length and painted red. She looked like a gawky girl kid.

"It's all about passing you see. Can you pass for a woman – that's the test." She delicately picked up her spring roll. The movement of the fingers, the stiffness of the wrist, precise, practiced. She wiped her mouth with the serviette. She wasn't wearing lipstick or any make-up.

I couldn't figure out what had happened to the nose, or the chin, or the mouth. They were different, yet familiar. I could recognize the face, but it had altered in ways that I could not easily itemize. Like the pain of our relationship, although repaired, not completely faded for me.

"Are you doing any theatre? Any writing?"

"No, I can't concentrate on anything for long. I can't even read a book. It's all the female steroids, the hormone pills, the oestrogen."

"Well, when does that stop?"

"It doesn't. I have to take it for the rest of my life."

"What about your theater career? You're one of the best directors I have ever seen."

"It should settle, eventually, in a few years. It's not important to me right now."

I had made a commitment to myself to support her in her endeavor unconditionally. I was still feeling contrite about our past. I wondered what Isobel's relationship must be to Abel's memories. Did she embrace them or was she deliberately trying to erase that part of her life?

My three-cup pork ribs arrived. I tried not to think of her surgery as I chewed down on the bones.

Isobel said she wasn't hungry; the pot stickers and dim sum hors-d'oeuvres had been more than enough for her. Was she now weight conscious too?

She asked after the people she'd left behind in Cape Town, and we gossiped about our mutual friends in Toronto. The latter wanted to make a documentary film about her process of becoming a woman.

"But they've got it all wrong. I keep telling them – who gives a shit about yet another trannie having her sex-change ops? They need an angle. I am what's important. Me. What makes me unique. Not this stupid sensationalism."

We decided to meet up again for a light supper and a few drinks that night.

When Isobel arrived, she was dressed for the evening. Her hair was frizzed out; she had on a shiny, sexily cut dress that pushed up her cleavage; she wore high heels, make-up and jewelry.

On the street, men and women often looked twice; a few stared openly. She linked her arm in mine. I am sure it was simply affection, but it had the effect of reaching out for security, as if through me she was anchoring herself to a world she was no longer a part of anymore.

"This looks nice," she said. It was a cozy crêperie. We walked up the stairs and as we entered, the maître d' smiled and picked up two menus. But a short, plump, balding man (I suspect he was the owner) came rushing towards us shaking his outstretched hand, "Sorry, we're fully booked, fully booked. Full!"

But I could see open tables. Isobel had already turned on her heels, and with her nails digging into my forearm, was dragging me away.

"We're going, we're going, sorry, sorry!" she called over her shoulder to the blustering proprietor. "Don't worry about it. I'm used to it. Just go!"

I was appalled. And shocked; of all places, here, in the heart of one of the biggest gay villages on the planet, outright rejection. Or did they think we were a straight couple? Or I was bringing in a prostitute?

We tried another place; the same thing happened.

Further down the street, Isobel was greeted by another transsexual. This one had little hope of "passing". Isobel introduced me, telling her I was from South Africa. Isobel had to explain that it was in Africa, in the south of the continent. Very far away.

We walked on.

"Most of the trannies really aren't very bright." Isobel chortled. "They're like so in awe of me. Wow! Isobel's been to university and she's got like a degree and all." We laughed. "Did you notice her breasts?"

I hadn't. I glanced back, but phantom-like, she'd vanished.

"They're not right. Didn't you see? The one is lower than the other. Imagine that happening to one? I can't bear to tell her. I'm sure she must have realized by now. Some of these doctors are hopeless."

I asked her how she was paying for it all.

"The national health paid for all my counselling and everything up to my decision to have the operation. But Medicare won't pay for my surgery. And most of it I've had to do in the States."

Isobel was cashing in on internet porn. It was the early days of the industry. Men would enter a website on a pay per view basis with steep per second charges. There was a webcam. She'd then chat with them using text. Her job was to tease and to keep them on-line for as long as possible. She said she was really good at it.

"I type so quickly I can keep up several conversations at the same time, while the other trannies can only manage about one. I make four even five times what they do."

But all I could think of at that moment was a conversation I'd once had with a gay South African plastic surgeon who'd performed early sex-change operations. He said the weirdest thing he'd ever done in his life was his first penectomy, when he took most of a boy's penis in his hand, sawed it off and dropped it in a metal bin.

Isobel's patrons came from everywhere, from Abu Dhabi to Moscow. She had her regulars, mostly from Toronto itself, or the East Coast.

I asked if she had met any of them.

It was considered dangerous and against the rules, but it did happen. They'd start corresponding by email. Eventually, if it all worked out, they met.

"I've decided to keep my dick," Isobel unexpectedly blurted out. "It's been sweet of you not to ask, but I know you are dying to know."

Isobel was having sex with men. It was the only way she could make enough money quickly. She said she wasn't cheap; Isobel charged "thousands of dollars". Her punters, she said, lived as straight men. They did not think of themselves as gay, and they didn't feel or seem gay in any way to her. One other peculiar detail she mentioned, they were disproportionately politicians, arms-dealers and bankers. For the most part, she said, they were intelligent men who valued her, because with Isobel they had a trannie with a brain: sophisticated, urbane, somebody they could hold a conversation with about the world and economics, even if they'd never dare take her to a public restaurant. Instead, they went to select private clubs.

A series of these men had been caught up in her process of becoming. One of them paid for her breasts, a job done in California by reputedly one of the best and most expensive surgeons – Isobel's research again. Her surgeries ran into the tens of thousands of dollars.

"Men must pay!" she said imperially.

Eventually, we found a friendly café. We sat inside, off the street, at a quiet table. I was looking at the wine list.

"Go by the glass; I can't drink alcohol anymore," said Isobel.

"Well, good for you, but why?"

"My liver functions won't cope from all the steroids."

At that moment, the candle on our table sputtered and flared, casting up long shadows. Abel's nose had re-emerged. I thought that without the make-up, the dress, the heels, she actually passed much better during the daylight as a regular girl than at night with all her accessories.

"I'm leaving tomorrow," I said.

She smiled. I thought this might be a moment when she would say something about our past. But she didn't. "Travel is a new complication for me outside of North America. I suppose now there are countries I'll never be allowed to see."

I'd lost Abel for good. Isobel belonged to a new gender – not male, nor female, not straight, nor gay. Abel had not changed into a woman called Isobel; rather, it was an on-going project that would last for the rest of her life, requiring non-stop maintenance. To stop the hormones would immediately bring on unsightly physical regression.

What was her old age to be like? Age, with all its inevitable medical complications and degeneration, was bad enough even if you'd never spent a day in hospital in your life.

We were at the airport. We were saying good-bye outside the terminus. We kissed on both cheeks. She looked at my face. "What is it?" she asked.

I needed to know. "Are you really happier now?"

"Yes, I do feel less dirty."

"Dirty?"

"Yes, dirty. I feel more centered now. I'm happier than Abel ever was."

"And Isobel, is she happy?"

"I've never been happy, but this is better. And next week, I'm finally having that rib job. Adam is meant to have given up one of his to make Eve; I might have to give up two."

Chester
THE INVISIBLE GHETTO
New York, USA

Nowhere I know on earth gives you the same rush of energy than when after landing at JFK and checking into your hotel, you take your first hit of the pavements in downtown Manhattan. It is always good to be back. People walk with purpose and resolve; you don't have to march on the spot waiting for an opportunity to pass somebody idling along or constantly collide with ambling pedestrians as one does in European and Asian cities.

I'd find myself in New York every couple of years. As a youngster, it had been a revelation that anything as big as New York, and New York is exceedingly big, could transform itself so completely; that a whole city could metamorphose in its very soul.

All cities are in flux; they prosper and they decline; they are buffeted by economic cycles and political change; they shift with waves of migration and investment.

In one's hometown, it is less apparent thanks to daily familiarity, the way the growth of one's children suddenly takes one by surprise. How your city changes is also obscured by your own transitions as you pass through various stages of life. We grow up; we move neighborhoods; our social circles, friends and work alter over time. We mature to see the city from new angles, the way a child eventually sees the top of its parent's head.

New York is a city of astounding momentum, in comparison to the conservative inertia of a capital such as London. And nothing propels New York Inc. more than its voracious appetite for the acquisition of wealth and the celebration of success.

In the late 1980s and early 90s, when I made my first trips to the Big Apple, it was still seedy, dirty, more obviously corrupt, and if not actually dangerous, it definitely didn't feel safe. My friends neighbor had his throat slit in his apartment. You could easily be mugged on the subway. Coming from South Africa, one was however streetwise.

Back then, the gay ghetto was in full swing at the Christopher Street and Sheridan Square nexus; Greenwich Village was a hybrid of the Castro and to some extent Paris's Marais quarter.

Those were heady times. This was the place where, in my early twenties, I had semi-public sex for the first time, like so many South Africans, like so many people from all over the world, who found their freedom here. There was the gigantic warehouse-sized Roxy famous for its go-go boys. At the Splash bar, you could watch the boys shower. Places like the S&M Mineshaft with its slings for public fisting and notorious bath for men who liked golden showers had already been closed because of the AIDS pandemic. But as nights wore on, dance floors heaved with shirtless men and boys, sucking lips, hips grinding in simulated sexual couplings, forming daisy chains – snaking lines of skimpy shorts and black boots, hands on each other's hips, bum to crotch. Where the bodies became impenetrable, hands dived down each other's pants, teasing thickening flesh. It was the bacchanal, surrender to an irresistible primal thumping rhythm, a nightly sensory annihilation of meaning and the triumph of Dionysian love. Everyone loved everyone here, connecting through the noise of the music and the haze of drugs that made it impossible to speak.

My favorite was the Limelight, a club in a 150-year-old deconsecrated Gothic church, stain glass windows and all, with a gay and a straight entrance; those with a gay door stamp could cross to the straight dance floor, but not vice versa. There was one large room without music, only the thudding from the dance floor on the other side of the wall. It would be packed to standing-room-only capacity heaving with boys attempting various forms of sex. It was not a dark room but lit normally. Even more unusual, it had monitors vainly trying to keep activities safe, slapping people on the back of their heads. It was all rather comical.

Mayor Giuliani, you see, had arrived. On the tide of the great dot com bubble, he started the big clean up. Within a short space of time, if you didn't have a regular professional or corporate job, you soon found yourself unable to afford the rent in Manhattan. The Meatpacking District closed its last underground clubs and gave birth to new chic eateries. Even Brooklyn was gentrifying. Greenwich Village's famous gay Marlboro poster finally came down. My friends in New York, artists mostly, moved up to Harlem and Washington Heights, if they'd outgrown Alphabet City.

By the late 1990s, my diary entry on a visit read:

'Forget nouveau riche (that's West Coast), we're talking New World bourgeoisie here! New Yorkers now dress up, not down as they did up to the early 90s. Cosmetic surgery has tripled. The baby boomers are in for a body refit: $3000 for a buttock lift and $1900 per liposuction. They also pay $250 a head to eat at Alain Ducasse's latest restaurant. It is proof that zero unemployment is generally good, but affluence is a mixed blessing. Next to me are a few teenagers. I'm looking at a blond kid right now. If I add up his clothes labels, his designer rollerblades, his mobile phone and the other cyber-extensions to his being, he's wearing roughly what I earned in the last quarter in South Africa! It's somewhat disempowering."

Nobody was sincerely keen to return to the bad old days, but the city seemed to have lost part of its identity. It was true that in New York everything was now working, and you could at last walk unthreatened north of 125th Street and even Dumbo (Down Under Manhattan Bridge Overpass).

A defining moment on that trip was on the A-train around 145th street. A black woman entered the coach; with tangled hair, a cheap blouse that didn't fit properly, and her bra partly showing.

"My name is Cookie," she introduced herself. "I'd appreciate it if anyone here could please spare some change." She started to move through the coach and I remember her gnarled toes curling over her plastic flip-flops, while she repeated, "Spare some change?" No one other than a black woman with shopping bags clamped between her legs turned on her, and in a formidably loud voice, said, "Get a job! Get a job!"

The most recent transformation was obvious as I flew in early in the new millennium; New York was missing a couple of buildings. The elegant Empire State was once again the tallest structure in Manhattan. Life had imitated the Hollywood blockbusters that were forever blowing up New York. 9/11 was reverberating around the world. What would emerge was still not clear, but we knew the world was changed forever, and for the worse.

It was late June and summer was in full swing; rainless, temperatures day and night hovering in the high seventies and low eighties degrees Fahrenheit.

The siege mentality was ever so slowly loosening its grip on the city, but patriotism was still palpable. Along the streets, the Stars and Stripes hung from windows. Police cars parked in the middle of the wide avenues, blue lights turning. Law enforcement and military patrolled the pavements. They were armed like insane paranoiacs with ludicrously large semi-automatics, weapons that in the event of an actual incident could not possibly be discharged without killing a few innocent bystanders.

The old gay haunts had pretty much all gone. The denizens of Greenwich Village dispersed to Chelsea; the shops and gay bars that had once stood shoulder to shoulder were now spread out; and that cruisy energy on the streets had dissipated.

A new phenomenon had overtaken gay culture and New York was in its evolutionary lead. It was the internet. The gay village had essentially dissolved into cyberspace. The gay life you saw on the streets and in the bars of the Village, was now only a holographic depiction of a cyber-reality, an illusion generated by thousands of connections on the internet. People no longer made eye contact with you; they no longer cruised or followed each other with their hearts beating hard. When you saw what appeared to be strangers hooking up in a bar or at a Starbucks, they had already met in an internet chatroom, and swapped photographs and compared their physical statistics: age, height, weight, star sign, cock length and penis girth.

Sex was now something you shopped for and ordered on-line. We'd entered the world of post-modern psychosexual tribalism: rubber, polyurethane, medical uniforms, she-males, waders, bears, bikers, emos, chubbies, midget sex, puppies punished, uncut hooded cocks only, self-suck, web cam sex, felching, circumfetishists, sex magick, temporary piercings, flagellation, corseting and erotic asphyxiation, fisting, shaving, spanking, vacuum pumping, saline testicles, spitting, watersports, coprophilia, nonfatal (and later fatal) cannibalism, drug sex, bareback sex, gifting (where HIV is deliberately contracted). The Net never closed or had last rounds. It was a permanently dilated orifice. And this was ten years before the smart phone app revolution of GPS-enabled Grinder and the like allowed for quick hook-ups, dating and flash orgies.

"Why waste time hanging around in smoky bars?" a New York friend asked. "Only about one in forty contacts turn into a good connection. On the internet it's one in five or even better once you've learned to read between the lines." So he claimed.

The old bandannas and handkerchief color codes in back pockets signaling sexual practices – top, bottom, anal, oral, hustler, bondage, watersports, wanking, or "anything anywhere anytime", had gone, replaced by a whole new set of digitalized abbreviations: str8 looking, 23yo, 6'1", 145#, uc 11" BDSM looking for vanilla partner, must be btm under 40, with face pic otherwise FO!

Even the rent boys, more correctly called male escorts, had become sex entrepreneurs, with websites, videos to stream on-line, products such as silicone rubber replicas of their erect members and even loyalty cards with benefits for regular clients. Gay male porn stars were as big as mainstream movie stars, doing book and calendar signings at launches.

I was feeling nostalgic. The full moon had risen above the skyscrapers. I decided to head down to The Cock, a bar in the old style down on Avenue A, with a neon red rooster outside. I found it far more quickly than I expected and too early to go in. There was a police car parked squarely in front of its doors.

I carried on down memory lane: graffiti on the walls, Gothic kids selling bootlegged music; a few obvious derelict junkies and vagrants; I even hoped to see a car with its bonnet up. I had some greasy fast food for the second time that day. After a few weeks in the US, it was beginning to show. I was assimilating to the land of the fat.

Eventually, I considered it late enough to return. I hadn't however expected a cover charge at a place like The Cock.

"It's Foxy dollar night and we have a DJ too," said a reasonably polite young man on door duty. I could see the oversized turntables and a DJ smoking in defiance of the ban introduced by Giuliani.

Inside you felt you could touch the ceiling; the walls were painted black; the people basked in lurid red light. It was a varied crowd: youngsters, queens, old leather bears and their cubs, and a surprising number of women.

Foxy night was an informal talent show where the best act could win a hundred dollars. Predictably, most of the acts were bad drags and trannies, or fat people pulling faces with their bellies and other feeble party tricks. Then a woman in her forties hooked up her top behind her neck to show two prematurely saggy breasts; next, she took out a cigarette lighter and set fire to her nipples. It brought the house down.

But she didn't win.

About thirty minutes into the talent contest, the winner revealed herself. She was a short squat girl with a mini-skirt and no undies. She reached in and pulled out a giant turkey leg with basted skin. She then ate part of it to cheers and applause from the crowd. I couldn't stop wondering how long that turkey leg had been baking in there on the subway.

When the talent show was over, the DJ struck up the music. I started to dance, but the polite fellow with the big moustache from the door earlier came over.

"Please stop that," he said.

"Why?" I asked, bemused.

"No dancing allowed."

"I just paid ten dollars for the DJ."

"I'm sorry. The police were here earlier. We don't have a cabaret license."

"Cabaret license?"

"Yes, it's legislation from the prohibition period."

"Like 80 years ago?"

"They're using it now on us."

"But what's considered dancing? If I tap my feet, is that dancing? What if I just sway from the hips up? Like this…"

"Don't move," he said coldly, stepping closer. Clearly, I was beginning to try his patience.

"Great, I'd love to be arrested in New York for committing the offence of dancing. That would look good in the newspapers back home."

"You don't get arrested. We get closed down. So shut it!" He stalked off. *Sieg heil*, Amerika!

I ordered another beer. I was bored now. I sauntered over to the darkroom, separated by a black curtain that ran the width of the bar. The lights were turned up full. There was nobody inside. There was a television in the one corner mounted on a wall bracket playing 70s porn in malfunctioning color.

I went back to the bar.

"How ye?" asked a squeaky voice. It belonged to a blond boy in a denim shirt with an exposed white vest underneath. He was just over half my height, painfully young, and chewing gum.

"My name's Chester," he said, and flashed his teeth. He had a thick Southern accent. "I saw ye lookin' at me earlier."

I hadn't noticed him. "Where you from?" I asked, curious about his accent.

"I'm from Atlanta. I've come to New York city to be gay!"

"You're too late," I said.

Giovanni, José and Santos
SEXPLOITATION
Havana, Cuba

I thought Jürgen had been foolish. What had he expected from a relationship based on such disparity – a rich German from Hamburg and an urchin from Cuba?

"I have never met a people more keen to give themselves, you know, to sell themselves," he said. Jürgen spoke English with ease, but with a thick German accent, conflating 't' and 'd', and clipping his vowels. "No, it is true," he continued. "Men, women, boys, girls, they're all the same here in Cuba."

I assumed it had worked to his benefit though.

"You know, I found out my João was getting money from my friends, sleeping with them right under my nose! There is no excuse for that kind of betrayal."

What about the betrayal by Jürgen's friends? I thought that should have been of greater concern to him.

"It is a beautiful island. I used to visit every year. In all, I have probably five years here. But now, since João, I don't come so often."

We were huddled together beneath an umbrella, the subtropics drumming down around us, forcing us to sit closer than we would have normally. Our knees bumped. Bad weather friends, I thought.

Jürgen was thickset. He had a jowly face, but was not unattractive, except that his mop of black hair had an oily look to it. I had been aware of him for some time. I'd watched as three old Cuban men sat behind him, eagerly sharing a copy of *Rebel*. They had scraggly beards and wore berets, as if they were partisans just emerged from the woods, but fifty years after the revolution. Cuba has hoodwinked time for decades now. They didn't order food or drink, but shared between them one of those nine-inch Presidente-sized parejo cigars. From the way Jürgen had watched me, I'd thought all along he might be gay.

When the thunderstorm broke, I'd gallantly beckoned to Jürgen to come over to my table, the only one equipped with an umbrella. Huge drops were falling. Jürgen's plate filled with water; we watched the fish skeleton swim off the deserted table and into the patient jaws of a bedraggled grey kitty.

Jürgen told me he was a freelance journalist working mostly for a Catholic newspaper based in Hamburg.

"I found the Cathedral of San Christobel quite cruisy," I told him. I'd received more than one scabrous gaze when I entered. And from others a quick look-away – as strong a sign of gay recognition as any long stare. I was asked to remove my hat, but I thought it an odd mark of respect in a country with state-mandated atheism, and a big Cuban flag firmly perched on the altar. But Jürgen corrected me. "Not at all. Even the Pope has visited, and Fidel welcomed him."

Jürgen spoke Spanish and was knowledgeable about the island. Apparently, the Castro government had felt compelled to close the gay clubs, ostensibly for reasons of prostitution, not homophobia.

Homosexuality was illegal before the revolution. In the decadent days of Battista, a blind eye was turned for the elite who trafficked in boys. Homosexuality became associated with gangsters, the drug mafia and the worst American political corruption, like J. Edgar Hoover and the sinister debauched plotters behind Nixon. I suppose, for macho Fidel, it must have been a sort of national insult to have filthy-rich capitalist foreigners come over and screw your young socialist cadres for a few dollars. Yet times changed, and the Cuban Ministry for Arts even sponsored a gay film called *Strawberries and Chocolate*, which went on to international acclaim; a significant departure from the 1970s, when *maricones* (effeminate boys as opposed to machos) were denounced as imperialist perverts.

The irony of it: while McCarthy in the 50s destroyed the lives of homosexuals in America for suspected communism, the Castro government in the 70s was incarcerating homosexuals as capitalists and counter-revolutionary agents. Homosexuals seem always to be caught between political factions and religious leaders looking for scapegoats or competing for so-called moral high ground.

When I first visited Cuba, only public homosexuality (in theory at least) was illegal; "ostentatious displays" as they were called. But the discos were closed on various spurious grounds.

Jürgen said, on weekend nights, the boys pitched up outside the local cinema called Yara, and by word-of-mouth found their way to the gay party, always at a different location. Someone would remain behind each time to invite the next group, as individuals slowly straggled in to cruise the steps of the infamous movie house.

"Sometimes," he continued, "these *fiestas de diez pesos* are good, sometimes not. Last weekend's party was bad. The floor was concrete and full of holes. There was no light. You could not dance properly. You would twist your ankle. And the rum was some local brew – pure poison." Jürgen gulped down the last of his rosé, the red wine rescued too late from the rain. "But you must always be careful. It can be very dangerous to pick up boys here." And he dramatically made the gesture of a slit throat.

It seemed he was offering himself as my safe alternative.

"Yes, I got scammed by a young woman today. She had a baby in her arms and she begged me to buy milk for her. I knew better, but I thought, it was only some milk. Seventeen US dollars later for a half-pint!"

Jürgen laughed. "You were charitable at least."

"I was empathetic, the charitable bit was involuntary."

"Where are you staying?" He was popping the question.

"In Vedado," I replied vaguely.

"I always stay here, in Vieja, the old city." His tone turned nostalgic. "I love the beautiful colonial feel. It's the only restored section. We can share a taxi along Malecon, as far as Paseo Marti."

"I'm still waiting for my change."

Jürgen now laughed. "That waitress, she will not bring it. You must ask again. Tourists give up and the staff put it in their pocket. It's always the same. That's Cuba."

Eventually, I saw the waitress peeping from the window, probably checking to see if we'd gone yet. Jürgen hissed through his teeth, startlingly, like a note on a tin whistle.

"That is how you get people's attention here," he said. "Try it in a Latin club in Europe and all the faces that look round at you, they'll be Cubans!"

It worked. She came over. He spoke in Spanish to her. She clapped her forehead pretending she had forgotten, rushed off, and didn't come back.

The rain eased, but only until we reached the Malecon, the broad boulevard that follows the shoreline. There was no shelter and we were soaked in seconds, frantically waving at taxis that ploughed through the water, wheels submerged. A bus carriage drawn by a truck slowly rolled by, belching fumes like an oil fire, crammed to capacity with standing people, armpits pitted with sweat.

"I thought if you owned a private car in Cuba you were obliged by law to stop and give anyone a lift."

Jürgen laughed. "On the highways, not in Havana, and not for tourists. Even on the highways, people are reluctant to stop. That's why private cars have different number plates, and there are officials to stop cars. They wear yellow, or as they pronounce it here, the 'jello' people. You'll see groups of people waiting beneath the bridges on the national roads."

Eventually, a taxi did stop for us. The driver, an old man with a paco straw fedora and an extinguished cigar, calmly announced the fare;

triple the normal rate thanks to the rain. With my jeans sticking to my skin, and my wet clothes making me itch, we got him down to double the usual fare before we surrendered.

The taxi had a damp vegetable smell, as if he'd been boiling yams inside it. Its grubby windows quickly fogged up, obscuring any view of the seafront buildings. The windscreen wipers flicked frenetically from side to side like metronomes gone haywire, but didn't seem to connect with the windscreen. The driver could hardly see where he was going. He was hunched, peering forward, his face just millimeters from the windshield, helping to mist it up further. He kept wiping away with an old red handkerchief.

"I'll be at the Yara tonight, 11 p.m. Hope I see you there," Jürgen said as he climbed out. He meticulously paid fifty per cent of the fee to his stop.

The driver had by now chomped through half his dead cigar, yet I hadn't seen him spit or swallow. Maybe it was some act of wizardry. At least, he wasn't smoking it in the cab. He dropped me at the bottom of the Calzada de Infanta. The rain stopped and patches of blue appeared as I made my way up the hill, my back steaming as the sun peeped out.

A dance school was practicing in the street, undeterred by the threat of cloudbursts. I'm used to people in Africa spontaneously singing, whether at work or walking in the street; the Cuban equivalent seems to be to burst whimsically into dance, whether out of love, sadness or excitement. The class master, in his early 70s at the very least, but still dandy with a spring in his step, was tapping his leg and counting out aloud. The young students in leotards, their skins shining in the vapor-filtered sunlight, concentrated hard, working on poses for a *paso doble*, I think; the boys prancing gallantly in one long column, the girls enticing them from another.

Turning up Habana Libre, I stumbled upon a pleasant tourist class restaurant with a covered terrace, not far from my hotel. The waitress was voluptuous and scantily dressed, but unusually self-effacing for a

Havanan. It was as if she wanted to smile, but hadn't given herself permission.

What I hadn't noticed until I sat down was a reed partition that stood hip high and a young man on the other side of it brooding in the corner. He was staring intently at the waitress; in front of him, an empty glass in which some ice had all but melted.

I felt self-conscious, as one usually does opening a guidebook or a map in untouristed areas. I soon became aware of another two pairs of eyes staring at me. These belonged to two boys, both in their twenties, also on the other side of the reed partition. One wore a military green, cut-off T-shirt and his friend a tight-fitting, shiny, viscose top. They were eating drumsticks with their hands, grease all around their mouths, bits of chicken skin on their lips. Simultaneously, they both gave me huge, toothy grins.

I smiled. At once, they took this as a cue, gesticulating wildly for me to come over. I hesitated, not sure what they wanted from me; then I felt slightly disgusted by myself for being thankful for that little reed partition, the economic apartheid that separated me, the tourist, from them, the locals. Had they come to sit on my side of the terrace, they would have been shooed away by the management.

I went over and sat at a table against the partition, bringing my coffee with me. We shook hands over the reeds. The possessive young man smoldering away in the corner, debarred from even sitting in the restaurant where his girlfriend worked, now stared straight through me.

"Where you from?"

"South Africa."

They looked at each other, and laughed. They had obviously both guessed wrong. Their names were Giovanni, who spoke English, and José, who didn't.

"José's father fought you in Angola," said Giovanni.

It seemed now an incomprehensible scenario: that in the 1970s, South Africa was at war with Cuba. Over two thousand Cubans died in that conflict. It was heartening to hear that his dad survived.

Giovanni was a dancer and José a lifesaver. Both were proud to exhibit their muscular arms and shoulders, their skins like polished Zimbabwean soapstone.

"So what do you like to do in Cuba?" José asked.

"Meet the people."

"You like boys," he concluded.

I smiled. They both looked at each other briefly before turning their heads back to me, smirking openly. From the way they wordlessly communicated with each other, I guessed they had known one another for a while, which at their youthful age probably meant since childhood. I was sure they'd had this kind of encounter with foreigners before.

"What kind of boys you like? You're not racist? Black, white, you no worry?"

Was it because I was South African that they had asked?

"You're both very nice, both." I looked each of them in the eyes as I said it. They giggled.

At this point, the waitress stepped out on to the verandah. She shook her head disapprovingly at them, said something apathetically under her breath in Spanish, and went back inside.

One of Havana's many troubadour collectives sauntered over to our terrace, having spotted me – the European. They sang from the street. A group of schoolchildren with red revolutionary scarves around their necks passed by, winding their way around the band. The music was pleasant, with a güiro keeping rhythm. The boys started swaying in their seats. The ceiling fans also seemed to be wobbling to the tempo.

"Tonight we take you out," said Giovanni.

I took the precaution not to tell the boys my room number or my surname.

"I am at the hotel on the corner," I told them. "Meet me downstairs in the lobby at 10 p.m. If you're not there, I am going out. Si? I don't wait." I left a few dollars on the table and turned to leave.

"*Adios, amigo!*" they called after me.

I tipped the band and ended up buying a CD they thrust upon me. The only way to get by in Havana is to wear thick sunglasses; for the moment you make eye contact with a stranger, you will be engaged.

As I turned the corner, I looked back. José and Giovanni, smiling, waved exaggeratedly to me.

Not far from the hotel, I saw two men dressed up in sort of protest camp: tight fitting, see-through tops with effeminate sequins; jeans dyed bright purple, and tied with pink scarves instead of belts; colors and cultures clashing, it all hung together surprisingly well. It reminded me of the gay scene back in South Africa during the apartheid regime. Small, incestuous and underground, but generally allowed to carry-on, as the powers that were, disbelieving and ignorant, wondered: 'what do they do in bed?'

Back in my hotel room, sipping a disgusting blend of scummy instant coffee and insoluble powdered cream, I switched on the small black and white television. There were speeches giving lip service to revolutionary slogans: 'comrades in arms', 'the revolutionary masses', 'workers unite'. It was a developing world solidarity conference with the usual calls for justice, equality, condemnations of the rich nations' economic bullying, trying to preserve some dignity while having to beg and plead for food, debt relief and financial aid. Then the television blinked off and the air-conditioner wheezed its last. It was yet another power outage.

After ten minutes, the hotel generator kicked in. The conference came back on; the air-conditioner didn't. With all the rhetoric, I soon dozed off.

I awoke from my afternoon snooze feeling thick and heady. I opened the window for air. From my room, I looked out onto the squalid balcony living of Havana, where washing lines, bicycles, broken-down appliances, and families all vied for space. In that climate, a verandah acted as an extended living room. The spectacular Art Deco block of flats across the way had no glass. Makeshift shutters had been added. I could glimpse original light-fittings and furniture from the 1920s. On the exteriors, paint bubbled and peeled off in large sheets, while the railings and pipes dripped earthy shades of rust down the walls.

Across the street, a huge man with grossly enlarged, veined biceps, like phallic semaphores, was leaning on the railing, smoking a cigar, puffing out his broad chest with each inhalation, then expelling the fumes in a cloud around him.

The body beautiful cult was here too, and having half the country's men in uniform at any one time, didn't help ameliorate the macho culture.

I had to decide to either trust in Giovanni and José, or to head for Yara and the German. I decided that if the boys made the effort to meet me, I should pursue this for as long as I felt safe. After all, Jürgen had duly warned me.

I took the stairs to the lobby, in case there was another blackout and I'd end up spending the evening in the lift. The elevator was eccentric enough with electricity; stopping level with the floor depended on the number of people in it. On my floor, which was the third story of the building, the fourth floor light would go on, so whether you used the British or American system, counting or not counting the ground floor as one, it still didn't make sense. Somewhere between the ground and my bed was at least one ghost story. On the elevator was a sign: "No Use in Case of Fire".

There was no one waiting for me in the lobby.

"Any messages?" I asked at reception. The concierge shook his head from side to side, and ever so slightly shrugged his shoulders. As he made no effort to look in the actual pigeonholes, I began to wonder whether he had understood me.

Stepping out of the musty hotel, there was a refreshing gust of air. The earth had cooled down substantially, and it was a pleasant, inviting night.

I passed the restaurant where I had met the boys and was within sight of the Yara, when a beaming Giovanni blocked my path and threw his arms around me, laughing, as if I was his long-lost friend. There were three of them now. José introduced me to Santos, a student. He looked like a thirteen-year-old. His long blonde coif kept falling in his eyes, and he constantly flicked it back with thin, tapering fingers.

"I waited for you," I told Giovanni rather brusquely.

"The hotel security, they threw us out. The police want to know why I am waiting around," he explained.

I at once felt sorry. He however did not appear too upset by the experience, as if it never occurred to him how unjust it was. I felt a pang of guilt. There were rules for local people and special allowances for us rich capitalist foreigners. As a Cuban, you couldn't step into a Western hotel with dollar rates. On the streets, I'd met people clandestinely selling cigars for *divisas* (hard currency).

The four of us headed for a local *paladar*. These were small restaurants of up to eight tables run in private homes. The rules required them to be family run, and to cook only Cuban food, except lobster and chicken breast which were strictly reserved for tourist hotels.

The Cuban economy goes through waves of reforms and rescissions. When I returned a couple of years later, tourists couldn't use pesos and the *paladars* were all closed.

We went to one of the fancier of these eateries in an old colonial mansion. It had a romantic feel, but on closer inspection, the tablecloths were greasy and there was congealed dirt stuck to the salt and pepper pots. Not feeling terribly hungry, I ordered a bottle of beer. The waiter brought it already opened.

I'd been foolish. The food looked far superior to anything I'd seen in Cuba so far. The boys wolfed down a plate of spicy chicken wings, the meat falling off the bone. Then they ordered a platter of succulent chicken thighs, followed by yet more chicken, this time crispy drumsticks. I began to wonder how much chicken anybody could possibly eat in one day, when with a satisfied burp, José excused himself from the table. The feast was over. Between smacking their lips and stuffing down dinner, they had spoken mostly to one another and in Spanish. Although I was enjoying the spectacle and the overall ambiance, I had begun to feel somewhat spare. We don't speak about it, but whenever there is a new casual encounter, there is always a quick, silent financial computation.

Meanwhile, the waiter, a tall, pretty lad and the cleanest scrubbed thing in the restaurant, made little effort to hide his hostility. At first, I thought it was because of the usual misunderstanding service personnel have of their function in socialist countries, whether in old East Berlin or Shanghai, waiters and bank tellers behave like bureaucratic functionaries to which you are their supplicant. But then I realized he was homophobic, and he resented waiting on my decadent new friends who now had a foreign purse to dip into. We must have disgusted him. It didn't help that Giovanni and José kept making vulgar jokes about cocks and chickens, jokes the waiter clearly overheard.

"Some people are still too Catholic," said Giovanni.

With their hunger satiated, the boys at long last turned their attention to me. They wanted to know about South Africa, more specifically whether we were rich or not. I told them about all our Cuban doctors and trade exchanges. But conversation was a struggle. My Spanish was almost non-existent and their English was basic. Giovanni would keep translating what I said into Spanish for the others, but I increasingly felt he was misconstruing most of what I said.

Our surly waiter interrupted us by banging the bill, scribbled in childlike handwriting with red ink, on the table. As I'd anticipated, Giovanni, José and Santos folded their arms, and stared at me. I paid. The boys broke into great smiles and started to samba in their chairs once more. Throughout dinner, they had been constantly in motion from the hips up.

"We must take you to Fiat," Giovanni declared glancing at Santos's watch, which kept slipping halfway down his skinny arm. They conferred in machine-gun rapid Spanish.

As we were leaving, I saw José pocket the tip I had left. "Ah, fuck him!" he said, catching my eye.

Fiat was an old auto-showroom on Malecon converted into a bar. It still had floor to ceiling display windows and posted outside the old 60s' version of the four-cubed white on blue Fiat logo.

In the parking lot, a saggy transvestite was surrounded by a dozen boys. Some were drinking from paper cups, costume rings on their fingers glinting.

Inside were two haggard women serving drinks. We sat down at a small, round, white plastic table. There was a crush of patrons against the bar, flapping notes and shouting their orders at the two señoras. The music was playing at full volume and several boys were gyrating in a corner.

José motioned to me, opening and closing his hand. "Six dollars," he said.

I gave him the money and he headed off to the counter. Santos started to play with my feet under the table. Giovanni was contentedly dancing in his chair. I had noticed at dinner he didn't smoke or drink alcohol.

José returned with a bottle of white Club Havana rum, two cans of Coke and four cups. He decanted a round of rum, measured by placing the fingers next to the cup, as is customary, and pouring how many fingers' worth you wanted. We all had four fingers, topped up with cola, and we toasted each other by touching cups and drinking fast. José drank Giovanni's too.

The evening grew progressively rowdier, and the conversation in Spanish more volatile as José poured rum. I noticed he consistently filled his cup more than anybody else's. It was not long before we needed a second bottle; this time, we splashed out on the three-year-old Gold Club.

An argument and scuffling started at the neighboring table, training shoes squeaking on the showroom floor. Two local boys were arguing over the only other foreigner in the bar that evening. He was sitting with his shirt off, flaunting an underdeveloped chest, badly sunburned. His vest straps had left albino white stripes on his body and now he resembled a Union Jack. He looked plastered. Yet a third boy tried to engage him but was set upon by the two quarrelers.

As the rum held sway, I felt as if I was at some burlesque romp. Boys kept sitting down near me and trying to engage me in conversation, only to be shooed off by Santos and José, more possessive than protective.

Not a spirit drinker of habit, and combined with the humidity, the heat and not eating, I was soon intoxicated. Everyone was laughing. Santos had worked his way up from my feet and was now stroking my inner thigh under the table. I began to insist he show me his identity document, repeating drunkenly that he looked about thirteen years old. Finally, he produced his driver's license. He was on the cusp of eighteen. The legal age of consent he said was sixteen.

The bar was emptying out when José decanted the last of the second rum bottle into his cup. Looking blearily up from the table, I was confronted by a line of half a dozen boys leaning with their elbows on the bar, every one of them with their eyes fixed unwaveringly upon me. The minute I looked up, they sprang into action – prancing, posing, flexing in an erotic pas seul.

One of the boys winking at me clutched a wooden crutch with a bandaged hand, his leg in a plaster cast. Another one of these *pingueros* – hustlers – stripped off his shirt and puffed out his enormous pectorals, like a sage grouse in mating display.

In my inebriated condition, I found myself being dragged towards the quayside promenade. Everyone from the Fiat had gathered here, together with those too impecunious to enter the bar. The boys were singing, dancing the rumba, doing the lambada for themselves, getting steadily smashed on raw rum. My chaperones, while keeping a watch over me, were engaged in several energized conversations with their friends, who eyed me longingly. Everyone it seemed was speaking simultaneously. My head had started to spin. I was unsure which way lead back to the hotel.

It was in the small hours of the morning when we arrived at Giovanni's home, on the upper story of a suburban house. I noticed a shiny new SUV in the driveway, the first and only modern car I'd seen in Cuba.

"Politicians," José spat disparagingly.

The mistress of the house emerged in a luminous pink nightgown. From the way her hair stood, I could see she'd been sleeping on it. After some Spanish, she presented us with several huge bottles of beer and after lots of good nights in English and *buenas noches* we headed upstairs. I gave Giovanni some more dollars for the drinks.

Giovanni ushered us out onto the cement roof of the garage, which served as a large terrace. I remember us collapsing with laughter and behaving like schoolboys. Thanks to me buying them drinks, they had drunk substantially more than they were accustomed to. A brief altercation with José followed and I saw Giovanni defiantly down a large beer and angrily throw the empty bottle off the roof, landing with a dull thud on the lawn below.

Feeling unsteady, having drifted once too often to the edge of the flat roof, which had no railings, I sat myself down on the concrete. José was waving his shirt above his head and dancing licentiously for Giovanni's entertainment. They started sucking each other's nipples while Santos, standing behind me, began to play with my hair. We all linked hands and with Santos tugging, heaved ourselves into the bedroom. We were rocking together on the bed when Giovanni raised his hand over his mouth and made a dash for the bathroom.

"He doesn't drink," said Santos.

José followed and I could hear him soothing the retching Giovanni. I was disappointed. Santos kept yanking at my belt and clambering over me. I heard the hot water tap squeak open, the plumbing give a great groan and shudder, followed by an explosion. There was a stunned silence. Santos burst out laughing, like a kid astonished with a shred of popped balloon in its hand. After fumbling in the dark, the lights came back on. Giovanni reappeared, now wide-awake and awfully sober.

"It's never done that before."

José muttered something about the Miami Mafia and we crashed back in a heap on the enormous soft bed, flinging our shoes so that they cannoned off the walls.

Santos was still determined to get my pants off. My fingers could encompass any one of his thin limbs. From behind, he looked even more like a young boy, with his chicken thigh-shaped shoulder blades jutting out, his buttocks square edged, his narrow hips grinding under me. José had now stripped off as well and was begging Giovanni to screw him, parting his buttocks with his hands. Giovanni was groaning and saying no, teasing José with his glans, and without a condom; José all the time, watching Santos and me.

When I awoke from a series of confused and disturbing dreams, details of which I cannot remember, except the image of a child's limbs protruding from the rubble of an earthquake, Giovanni was conscientiously tidying up the room from our night's debauchery. Santos and José still lay in drunken torpor. I kissed their sleepy foreheads.

Half an hour later, Giovanni and I piled into the back of one of the old 1950s' Chevrolets, part of the retro-fleet of Buicks, Studebakers, Plymouths and Cadillacs that ply the streets of the Cuban capital, from the days when cars still had faces. Hooters often ring out the first bars of La Cucaracha. When I returned a few years later, they had all been given metallic paint jobs.

On our way back to Vedado, people climbed in and out of the car, dressed in casual summer clothes. We stopped every few kilometers, money changing hands with the driver.

Giovanni pushed my head down when we passed the police. I didn't ask why. The foam stuffing was escaping from the seats. Every time we pulled away, the car filled with fumes, and if the trip had been any longer, I feel sure I'd have died from plumbism.

As a courtesy, I invited Giovanni to breakfast. It consisted of grapefruit and spaghetti with ketchup – I am not kidding. It was served by a waiter with squeaky shoes; a young adult, who appeared to still have deciduous teeth. We discussed what I should see and do while I was in Havana, and I scribbled comments on my tourist map.

"I'm sorry I was so drunk, but I don't have alcohol," Giovanni explained forlornly.

"Do I owe you anything?" I asked.

"Here it is the custom. You go with boy, you make a gift. No, not prostitute, just polite, you understand?"

"For the taxi and the tour, then. And please give to Santos," I said, and slipped some folded dollars into his hand under the table.

We made plans to meet later in the day, but I never saw him again. Then I changed hotels. The food and service problems, and the fact that their credit card machine was never working, finally drove me out. I moved into the expensive Hotel Naçional, the 1930s palace where people like Churchill and Ava Gardner had stayed. In its heyday, it was the equivalent of Singapore's Raffles.

I decided to sequester myself for a few days, to read and relax, in an enormous, comfortable cane chair in the beautiful grand portico of the verandah.

Outside, Cuba was crumbling, and it would either carry on crumbling for another fifty years or change overnight. Peacocks and guineafowl strutted on the lawn; four tired-looking green parrots sat bedraggled in a light drizzle, protesting in mournful, almost human screeches, from their bamboo cage.

At the bar in the airport lounge, cherishing my last genuine Havanan cocktail while I waited for my flight to be called, I fell into conversation with a Swedish journalist.

"I feel sad that the revolution has failed so miserably," she said.

"Has it? Perhaps ultimately, but far from entirely. I'm afraid, I may have undermined the revolution too." It just slipped out.

She looked at me thoughtfully. "You mean you had sex with some poor girls I suppose."

"After all that bravery and sacrifice, everything and everyone is up for the dollar. Just as it was under Batista."

"Of course, a lot of tourists come here for the wrong reasons, to have cheap sex, but I don't think you undermined the revolution any more than Hemingway could be said to have delayed it."

"Sexploitation," I quipped. Or sexploration?

And we sat in silence, sipping our mojitos, staring at a giant, full color poster of an umbrella on a tropical beach, which hangs invitingly in the departure hall.

Sergio
MACHO
Cancun, Mexico

I could see my distorted reflection in their mirror sunglasses. That's how I must have appeared to them: painfully thin and white in the glaring light of barren beach sand.

"Why did you turn back?" the police officer demanded.

There were two of them. Both had those cliché teardrop mirror shades, shiny hair, and jet-black walrus moustaches. They were almost my height, which made them unusually tall and intimidating for people of the Yucatán.

"I was looking for a way to the beach," I stammered.

Unfortunately for me, hidden from sight from the road, I'd come across a battered, apparently deserted car. Parked next to it was a police vehicle. I had immediately done an about-turn, and headed back for the main drag. But just as I reached the highway, the police were shouting at me to stop, and these two officers came sliding down the dune.

"What were you looking for over there?"

"As I said, I wanted to get to the sea."

My imagination was galloping. Had I walked into a murder scene? Or a kidnapping? Had I happened upon a secret meeting between the police and an informant? Had I interrupted the police taking a bribe? Or was I being a drama queen?

"I think you must come with us," said the officer.

"But why?"

"Come now."

"But why? What for? What have I done?" I pleaded.

They paused for a moment, and made eye contact with each other over their sunglasses.

"Where are you from?"

"I'm on holiday."

"Where is your passport?"

"At my hotel."

"That's okay. We can go to your hotel."

"It's in Cancun town." That was half an hour's drive from where we stood.

"Do you have any identity on you?"

"No," I said. "I was warned not to bring anything to the beach because of thieves. I have everything locked away in the hotel safe."

Actually, everything was lying in the bottom of my cargo pants pocket: all my money, my passport, my hotel key.

"Come! We go to the patrol car." He gestured with a hairy thumb to the dunes down the track.

"Why?" I raised my hands. "You can search me here."

"Do you have any money on you?" asked the officer who had been silent until now.

"Nothing," I lied again.

Below the rim of his sunglasses, I could see the officer's eye tic.

There was no way I was getting into their car. They'd have to drag me kicking and screaming and resisting arrest. Every guidebook had warned me about the Mexican police and their bribes or *mordidas* (bites). Even the upmarket bourgeois guides cautioned against ever getting involved with the police, even if you were the victim of a crime. They only made things worse.

The quieter policeman raised his sunglasses onto his forehead. He looked so ordinary – flabby, benign, avuncular. There was no Hollywood gold or missing teeth, no signs of corruption. Instead, he smelt of cheap, strong eau de toilette. His hands were warm around my wrists as he turned my palms face up. Thick black hair sprouted from under his shirt cuffs. It was a strange intimacy, him touching me, one finger at a time.

"Needle marks," he explained as he scrutinized the skin under my fingernails.

The other officer snatched my bag. He made the most pathetic attempt at searching it: costume, suntan lotion, a poetry volume of Octavio Paz. I'd hoped that would impress them. Neither of them bothered to check my pants' pocket.

"You must come with us."

"Why? You just searched me. I'm here on holiday." Panic was setting in. It is the lone traveler's nightmare, to disappear without a trace.

The officer snapped his sunglasses back down, drew himself up in his shiny boots, hands on his hips. So my turn has come, I thought. After all my travels, my luck has run out.

"On vacation, eh?"

"You travel alone, hmm?"

This was not going to be good cop, bad cop; this was bad cop, and bad bad cop. I come from Africa and you're not going to crack me like some American kid, I thought. And then it occurred to me, the only macho vulnerability I could exploit. "I'm here because my mother just died of cancer," I heard myself say. They regarded me in silence. "Please," I importuned, and sniffed.

At that moment, a bus stopped, disgorging loud American tourists. A woman was pointing us out to her friend. Others stopped to stare from a distance, mouths slowly opening.

"Okay, he's clean," said the policeman abruptly, all his menacing maleness retreating. "But you understand, we have to protect you from the drugs?"

"Yes, officer. And thank you. I know you are only doing your job," I said, helping them to save face.

"Too many drugs in Cancun. We look out for you tourists," said the other cop.

The quiet officer patted me affectionately on the arm. They turned and headed back down to their car on the beach, back to whatever mischief I'd interrupted.

I started walking along the highway that ran the length of Cancun's twenty-two kilometers of American chain hotels. It had taken the bus longer to drive this stretch from the airport than my flight had taken from Havana. Still seriously rattled from my close brush with the *federales*, turning the incident over and over again in my mind, I lost all track of how far or for how long I had walked.

Eventually, I saw a sign for Delphines, purportedly a gay beach. But here were parents with children and the paraphernalia that accompanies families: cooler boxes, umbrellas, folding chairs, plastic buckets, reed mats, oranges, and 50+ suncream. There were however a few lone men, and also a handful of us blotchy gringo tourists.

A tall blonde woman strode topless into the ocean. Several podgy little local kids lying on their stomachs squealed excitedly, ogling her from the dunes, hips scooping into the sand.

Wrapping a towel around my waist, I changed into my surfer baggies and launched myself into the lapping Caribbean. There was a gentle swell, no breaking waves. The water was so warm I felt as if I was sweating in the sea. I kept close to the shoreline, a watchful eye on my bag and towel. But my gaze kept straying across to a motionless bronze body, stretched out on his back, his elbows resting in the sand. It seemed he was watching me too from under his red, peaked cap. After a few minutes, he stood up, his limbs dark against the white sand. He entered the sea, and swam towards me, until he was drifting nearby. We smiled at each other a couple of times, but didn't exchange any words. He circled me, floating on his back.

When I started to swim to shore, he followed. He was by my side as I waded up to the beach, the sunlight on the water lighting up his face. He was probably about my age, but with a much more powerfully built body. From his sizeable calf muscles, hairless legs and the effortless way he waded, he might have been a cyclist, while his streaky sun-bleached hair and pale blue eyes suggested a beach life.

"You live here?" I asked.

"Yes," he said. "But wait," he said eagerly. Then he sprinted off to fetch his towel, and came back to sit beside me. His well-filled bathers were impossible to ignore. I put my sunglasses on.

Unlike most beaches, the beach sand in Cancun is not silica, but made up from trillions of ground up coral skeletons. It is fluffy and soft and cool to the touch, even in the baking sun at the height of the day. It was as if we had landed with our bums in a bag of flour.

His name was Sergio. He was originally from Veracruz. He was a gym instructor at one of the giant hotels behind us. The money was not too bad, and the tips were in US dollars, which made it a good place to work. In the mornings, he flexed his muscles giving aerobic classes to overweight ladies on package tours. He said they could be quite predatory. He wasn't interested in women. He didn't have to say any more. In the afternoons, he supervised a parade of iron-pumping American frat boys admiring themselves in the pier glass at the gym. He said he found most of them offensively oafish.

We didn't stay long on the beach. We caught the bus to town together. On board, he surprised me by clandestinely slipping his hand into mine, down between our thighs. I looked around nervously. Mexico was the most homophobic place I'd ever been to. But he kept stroking me with his thumb all the while, playing with the hairs of my leg.

Our bus was invaded by a strong stench of spilt beer from a mob of boisterous, shirtless American youths, blaspheming and shouting profanities at each other. Sergio didn't remove his hand.

The stoic-faced Catholic locals suffered in silence. Fortunately, two stops later, after yelling at the driver, they realized they were going in the wrong direction and exited, pinching and slapping one another jocularly in male bonding.

"Fucken A-one bitch, man! Fucken A!"

Back in town, Sergio bought a couple of *cervejas* and we walked to his home. As we got to the door, he put his fingers to my lips and whispered, "You must not be seen."

I was smuggled through the hallway and past his housemates sitting in the lounge, glued to a horror movie.

Safely in his room, he closed the door, locking it carefully so as not to make a noise. He switched on the radio.

His clothes were stacked on the carpet; a couple of jackets and shirts hung on a rail suspended from the ceiling with yachting rope. The mattress was on the floor. At an old wooden desk, stood a copy of an ultra-modern designer chair, the single chic accent in the room. On the whitewashed walls, there were only a few fitness posters of young men, and women too, perhaps to throw his housemates off his scent. Tall windows opened wide onto a tree-canopied courtyard formed by the backs of other buildings. Flocks of noisy parrots screeched, making the room feel as if it were part of a giant aviary.

We were both sleepy from the beach, sun and beer, and we soon dozed off, lying under the high ceiling, enjoying a gentle breeze from the wooden paddle fan spinning above us.

It was dusk when I awoke. Sergio was already awake, propped up on his pillow. He took my hand, not saying a word, and we lay there silently, listening to the squawking birds as the twilight dimmed.

"I invite you for dinner tonight," he said.

We arranged to meet in a few hours' time at a street café next to my hotel, which he knew. We kissed good-bye, sea salt seasoning his lips. Then he also shook my hand, politely, somewhat formerly.

Returning to my hotel as dusk fell along the wide avenues of the little town, I passed several health and fitness stores, selling muscle supplements in massive buckets, like paint drums. There were penis enlargers on full display in the windows too.

Back home, my body-hugging ribbed vest, board shorts, and designer sandals would have been the *dernier cri* of the hetro surfer.

But here, for the first time in my life, I got a wolf whistle on the street from two smirking boys. I took it as a compliment. I did not feel in the least oppressed by their attentions. Machismo is less about impressing females than it is about intimidating other males.

Further along, a disheveled man approached me, offering marijuana and cocaine, speaking in English far too good I thought for a Mexican vagrant.

Back at the hotel, I shaved and took a shower. I gave myself a good scrub to get the sand off. As I soaped up, I thought achingly of my new friend's long, sturdy limbs.

Sergio was waiting for me at a table on the sidewalk. He leapt to his feet, graciously pulled out a chair, and seated me.

Sergio was wearing a freshly ironed linen shirt, and a lavish dose of citrusy cologne. Alongside him, I felt decidedly disheveled in my cotton top and chinos, crumpled from my backpack. I must have looked a disappointment. I'm thinking like a mistress, I thought.

It was a pleasant family-run restaurant. Every morning I enjoyed the thirty-nine-peso buffet here. As part of the breakfast ritual, Emiliano, the amicable owner, would – not altogether jokingly – offer me his daughters in marriage. They'd blush and carry on stirring the chafing dish of refried black beans. In such a macho culture, Emiliano fascinated me; gentle and warm, with hairy arms and thick black moustache; yet he glowed with an almost maternal charm. He did all the skilled cooking, dressed in an apron that was not only pink, but had a wide frilly border.

Our waiter was a short, rotund man, with the rounded features of the Maya, a less stylized moustache, and thick hair gelled flat.

Sergio asked me what I'd like to drink. I was parched from the heat and the sun. Even at this hour, it was still in the low thirty degrees Celsius. From the landscape, it would seem it had never rained in Cancun.

"Frozen margarita", I said, "and soda water separate, please."

The waiter understood me of course, but Sergio repeated the order, as if I were his señorita. What's more, he authoritatively added something in Spanish about the type of glass he expected my drink should be served in.

When we were alone again, I asked, "Does anyone know you are gay?"

"Only a few close friends."

"Your parents?"

"Never!"

"And at work?"

"That would be impossible." Under the cover of the tablecloth, he hooked his foot beneath my ankle. He was determined to make this a romantic evening. Suddenly implacably suspicious of men, I wondered how much it was about him proving to himself what a great romantic he was.

I wondered too where emotional fulfilment lay for a vigorous young gay man like Sergio, living here in this town, in a shared apartment where he had to smuggle me in, unable ever to show love openly. Hands held in deep bus seats; feet hooked behind tablecloths. If you could not be openly gay even in the hotel industry, there wasn't much hope, I thought to myself.

I proudly told him about the rights we now had in South Africa, and how gay couples were slowly becoming recognized for many legal matters, including marriage. My Cape Town friends were adopting children. As I talked, I could see his face transform with the vision of it, perhaps even with the thought of holding his own child. I was describing paradise and making him sad.

"Unthinkable here. I could never live with another man in Cancun. Maybe Mexico City, but there it can also be difficult, even dangerous. It's only okay if you're rich."

So it ever was. "The rich can always do as they please. It's the poor who must remain unfulfilled, even as people." That was as true for my country as it was of his.

I'd been to one Cancun gay bar, Karamba, the night I arrived. It was a small-town incestuous affair with a handful of queenish gays, muscle boys and tourists. A pretty waiter, Romano, gave me complimentary sangrias, pouring the tequila and mixing the drink directly in my mouth, cradling my head in the crook of his bare arm and deliberately rubbing his crotch against me.

Sergio went through the menu, explaining the items and dismissing each of my choices. "No, not the best here," he would declare, politely, but firmly. After discussing almost every item, I evidently ended up ordering his recommendations. We shared chicken and beef fajitas, which Sergio folded and fed to me. He seemed to take pleasure in watching me eat. It was spicy, but you could taste the individual ingredients – the chillies, the achiote, the sweet lime.

"Be careful, the green salsa is very hot," Sergio warned.

Dinner was a leisurely affair. We sipped on another round of frozen margaritas, the rock salt garnish reminding me of Sergio's sun-cracked lips that afternoon. It was a relief after a few weeks' travel to spend time with a local who also spoke fluent English. I had the impression that like many Mexicans, he loved his country passionately, but was not as proud of it in its modern state.

It could not have been a cheap night out for him, but it was clear that I was his date and he would not permit me to pay for anything. I would never have been at ease in a relationship like this, but here on holiday in a foreign country, I was happy to have Sergio treat me like a lady.

We took a meandering stroll, not touching, not holding hands, mostly in silence.

His immovable housemates were still fixated by the television, and we slipped in undercover of the sound of chainsaws and screaming women.

Sergio placed a thin scarf over the lamp to create mood lighting, and switched on the clock radio, a local station playing sentimental música ranchera. It hissed as he turned the volume dial gently down.

Sergio leant over and kissed me on the mouth, our bodies not touching. I felt his tongue between my lips. His hands dropped to my hips. He pulled my shirt off. I was to be undressed. His nimble fingers unbuttoned my fly. He pulled down my pants. I wasn't wearing under-wear. Sergio walked in a circle around me, blowing gently on my skin. I stood still as a statue in the warm air. I had never before been com-pletely naked with a clothed partner. I wasn't sure how. I didn't know what to do with my arms. I thought of the models at my life-drawing classes back home, of what they must feel. I resisted the urge to strike some pose, to escape into humor. Instead, I stood with my hands at my sides, feet slightly apart, erect, blushingly proud. Sergio took his time gazing at me. I felt unique, irreplaceable, strangely powerful; the beauty of being admired.

Then Sergio took off his pants, and the moment had evaporated. We were at once back in the almost comically clumsy world of sex. He had large, dangling balls with a dewlap of skin, his egg-shaped orbs peeping out even below his shirt line. His thick cock lifted itself surprisingly quickly. Sergio took a few paces away from me, removed his shirt, and flung it on the desk. He struck some body building poses, tensing his thighs and biceps, showing off his abdominals, his broad chest with its large, flat medallion-like nipples. It was my turn to admire. I enjoyed his macho dance, and he was undoubtedly beautiful, but I was grateful that before a giggle could escape me, he had pulled me down to kiss him. He hooked his bulbous legs around my waist. I could feel and hear the prickle of his shaved calves, rousing on my skin. He whispered in my ear, "Fuck me." I hadn't expected that.

"Condom?" I asked.

"No, just put it there … hold it there … just there." And he hooked his feet behind my neck, his hand guiding me. He was groaning, fingernails scraping on my back. Then he abruptly flexed his body, arching his back upwards. I had penetrated him. Without lubricant. I felt a coil of heat. I looked down in alarm. He whimpered in pain. But he held me there, his copious balls a pillow of flesh. I could feel him squeezing me. I stayed just inside. It took all my resolve not to start a natural rhythmic thrust and fuck him. I thought, if I don't move, it will be alright, I'll be safe.

I am built in such a way that I could reach him with my mouth. And he came fast. As I withdrew my lips, he spurted over his chest, viscous white pools flooding his bellybutton.

We uncorked. He lay on his back with his eyes closed, shivering with pleasure.

"It's been a very long time," he said.

We lay together in silence, as we had done earlier that day. After a while, he asked, without looking at me, "Do you want to come?"

I smiled gently and shook my head. How like a man, I laughed to myself. Gradually, I became conscious of the radio with its interminable announcements I couldn't understand interrupting the songs.

"How do I get to the toilet?"

Sergio got up, poked his head out the door, then signaled the all clear for me to zip through unnoticed. I tiptoed into the bathroom.

Over the basin I examined myself closely, especially the frenulum, anxious over any trace of blood or fluid. I breathed a sigh of relief; everything was remarkably clean.

When I sneaked back into the room, Sergio was fast asleep, snoring deeply. I picked up my clothes, and barefoot, slipped out into the hot night, like a ghostly, clandestine mistress.

Diego, Rico, Gregg, Scott and Kate
GOOD CITIZENS
Mérida, Mexico

There was no shade and the tropical sun baked down with a desiccative intensity, intolerable even for reptiles. Situated just south of the Tropic of Cancer, the great Mesoamerican pyramid of El Castillo was started around 800 CE, its architecture determined by Mayan astronomers. Its square top and the giant staircases on its sides have become the signature silhouette, a powerful geometric logo adopted for all Mexico's impressive archaeological sites.

The staircase is relatively easy to climb, though I did see some visitors scrambling up on all fours. At the time of the equinoxes, extraordinary shadows on the coquina stones of the staircase make it appear as though the giant serpent god is returning to earth slithering down the pyramid.

The descent for humans however is a precipitous sixty degrees with the stone steps treacherously irregular. Climbing the pyramid has been stopped now, but in those days, a column of tourists in their baggy outfits, their gaudy colors jarring against the sombre edifice, appearing as if someone had spun a washing line down the middle of the stones, could be seen descending on their bum cheeks. There were a few panic-stricken, overweight gringos, stranded with screaming children tugging at their hands. An ambulance on standby waited expectantly.

From the summit, I had a wide uninterrupted view of the various ruins in the immediate vicinity of the pyramid, beyond which the surrounding jungle stretched out, continuous to the horizon. This islet of ruins poignantly captures the timelessness of the natural process beyond man's control. That there are seven billion people alive today challenges comprehension, but think of the 100 billion people that have lived and died throughout time. Entire civilizations with their belief structures, their Gods and religions, their moralities, their ways of life – gone, disappeared on the inexorable death march of history.

The heads of a Dutch couple emerged over the rim of the stone platform, panting in their Polo tops, dark with sweat, stuck to their backs. The wonderful Dutch – you met them everywhere in the world, grown-ups with backpacks or on bicycles, trekking about the globe at age 70, tough old fowl climbing like spring chickens.

We said hello. They asked the standard questions tourists ask each other. Where are you from? How long in Mexico? Where to next? Did you like Mexico? Well, they loved Mexico. But, they complained, American tourists were spoiling the locals by overpaying on the craft markets. I couldn't be bothered to argue.

I gave them a cursory nod when I saw them again later, inside the huge modern air-conditioned tourist complex at the western gate, with its small museum.

In the tacky, over-priced cafeteria, I managed to grab the last available table, and gingerly keeping my elbows off the sticky plastic surface, settled down to some quesadillas. I had a long string of cheese stretching from my hand to my mouth, when a couple in their twenties, carrying trays, came up to the table and asked, in mild American accents, if I minded them joining me since everything else was taken.

Their names were Scott and Kate. They lived in Harlem, New York City. They'd moved there from the mid-States to go to Colombia University, and never returned home. Scott wore a green Ché Guevara T-shirt and Kate a comfortable flower-power blouse. It wasn't long before we were talking politics and speaking of George W. Bush.

"The blue states pay eighty per cent of taxes – in our capitalist country, wouldn't you think that should count for something?" Kate was railing against the elections. "And now we're going to go to WAR. You just watch the bastards. You'll see – it'll be another fucking Vietnam!" and she kicked the chair leg.

"I'm the converted," I said.

"Kate thinks she's pregnant," said Scott. "She's missed her period."

"Stop it, Scott." She slapped his shoulder. "Don't undermine me, mister. I'm serious."

"Personally, I think the whole world should vote for the American president. After all, we have to live with the guy too," I said.

"Cool," said Scott, lifting a dripping enchilada in his hands.

"The world has billions of people and something like 200 million American's vote for the guy? That's 35 to 1. Maybe each nation at the UN should have a vote for the American President that counts according to the number of people in their country, and since we believe in national self-determination, let's make the world constituency worth – I don't know – perhaps 15 per cent of the electorate. It would have been enough to keep Bush out."

They both stared at me for a minute. "The Republicans will rig the vote," said Scott. "Computers, gerrymandering, voters' rolls…"

Kate had an intense look on her face. "I like you!" she said. She pointed at my quesadillas. "Are those vegetarian?"

"Yip, cheese and corn."

She helped herself to my plate. "Hmm, these are good. We should have ordered this, Scott. So what are you doing for the rest of the day?"

"I'm staying in Piste."

"We're in Mérida. Scott found this really great hotel."

"I'm going to Mérida tomorrow."

"We must meet up. I mean it," Kate said between licking her fingers. "Here." She gave me the Mérida hotel's card.

"Be sure to call us," said Scott. "Room 108, right on the swimming pool." As they departed, he winked.

Everything went like clockwork the next day. No doubt, there was astrological magic left in those ruins after all. I woke up exactly one minute before the alarm went off. The early morning bus arrived bang on time.

After much effort, I finally found the hotel in Mérida where Kate and Scott were staying. They were out, so I left a note for them saying I didn't know where I would be staying as their place was full, but I'd send word sometime the next day and hoped to catch them in.

The owner, a decorous, elderly man in a linen suit, sporting a white panama hat and an ornate cane, referred me to the sister hotel, a few minutes' walk away.

It was a hotel that at once appealed to me. The lobby had comfortable wooden couches arranged in a long line that led to a patio filled with pot plants. There were tables and chairs along the arcade under the balcony, and everywhere, on all the walls, on the landings and, as I soon discovered, inside the bedrooms themselves, were artworks: modern Mexican paintings, small stone figures, sections of mezzo-relievo, colorful traditional Indian tapestries, and pieces of lacquered Art Deco furniture. No dreadful knock-offs of Frida Khalo here. The proprietor I discovered from a brochure also owned a contemporary art gallery.

As soon as I'd dropped my bulging backpack, that seemed to grow heavier by the day, I headed off to Uxmal, in the heat a more atmospheric experience than the austere Chichén Itzá. Here the jungle was clawing at the stones. There was less screeching from tourists and more shrieks from parrots.

Half a kilometer down the San Simon road was meant to be the Temple of the Phalli, something I naturally wanted to see. With its stone penises, some of which were waterspouts, it was unlike anything else yet discovered in the area. But it turned out you needed a guide to find it and visits were not encouraged. It was overgrown with jungle and only ever reluctantly shown to the most unrelenting of tourists.

Back in Mérida, evening descended quickly. I had however covered a lot of ground. The calendar Gods and celestial timekeepers were positively on my side.

Mérida had been a center of civilization for thousands of years for the Mayans, before it passed to the Spaniards, and now it was the wealthy capital of the Yucatán. It had ornate colonial buildings and a broad boulevard, but it was still in Mexico, where makeshift solutions abound: knotted balls of electrical wire, cables on the ground, and potholed roads. I'd also never before seen so many shops selling paint, yet looking at the buildings, there was no evidence of its use.

I positioned myself on a public bench under a laurel tree on the stately Plaza Mayor, listening to strolling mariachi bands, and watching the locals go by.

Two young men ambled past me several times. They were disguising their curiosity rather feebly. On their fourth sortie, I simply called them over. "Excuse me," I said, "is there a festival on?"

I'd been watching the snaking queues of people, the girls in white dresses with flowers, like bridesmaids, the boys and men in black suits and polished pointy shoes, their hair meticulously slicked down, waiting to go into the churches to visit the current god of Mexico.

The two boys laughed. "No, they're going for confession."

"Oh," I said. "Do you have anything to confess?"

They looked at each other, laughed and blushed. They sat down one on each side of me. They had round, friendly faces and rounded shoulders, and sat, hands together between their thighs, not sure what to do. They could have been sitting at church. Or school. It was obviously all going to be up to me.

Their names were Diego and Rico. They were students on Easter break. They came from conservative, wealthy families. Both were doing their bachelor's degrees in arts, majoring in English language and Spanish literature. Perhaps they were not great students, for their English was basic; surprising to me, considering Mexico's proximity to the United States. Perhaps the university struggled to get teachers, or teachers going to the US to improve did not return, finding more lucrative jobs teaching Spanish to the country transforming across the border.

"Did you really not know it was Sunday?" the one asked, frowning slightly and looking worried.

"Don't trouble yourself over my soul," I said, in a reassuring tone. "A hundred billion have gone before me."

I asked them if there was any kind of gay life. They'd collect me at my hotel at 10 p.m.

Diego and Rico arrived in a red Volkswagen beetle with black tinted windows; they liked tinted windows in Mexico. When I pushed my head in, I discovered three of their friends already inside. I wedged myself half-on half-between them on the back seat. There were another two friends in the front passenger seat. It was sauna temperature inside. The windows remained closed throughout what would have otherwise felt like a short drive.

Gasping for air, we arrived at the club. I bought a round of mescal shots and Corona beers for the seven of us. The barman offered me the maguey worm from the bottle. I dropped the sack of caterpillar into my mouth without a second thought and the boys unexpectedly cheered.

I was unlikely to have found this disco without local help. Mérida wasn't exactly Acapulco. There was no signage outside. I don't recall its name, but its advertising slogan, notably in English, was "a very nice place in the town". It was a low-key, parochial affair, deep in the closet. It was not particularly busy and the handful of boy patrons were all squeaky clean, neatly coiffed, dressed up in smart casual clothes, beaming with naivety and looking like they couldn't possibly have anything to confess except masturbation. If anything, I expected them to burst into a school anthem. They stood around like wallflowers, conversing stiffly, without much it seemed to say to one another. Everyone was waiting for something to happen.

I decided to buy the boys another round of mescal and Coronas. I was calculating the way gay men do. I wished to get the party going, but also to free myself; I did not want to be beholden to Diego and Rico for the rest of the evening. I was in the mood for a sexual adventure and I didn't see anyone appealing. Possibly my homoerotic aesthetics had not yet shifted with the geography, and I wasn't sufficiently appreciative of the cherub faces of the Yucatán.

Then a very tall, lanky blond boy dressed like a cowboy – deep-blue jeans, knee-high beige boots, large silver belt buckle, faded denim shirt, introduced himself as Gregg. Unbelievably, he was from Kansas. We stood alongside each other with our elbows resting on the bar counter, now gooey from slices of lime, spilt tequila and salt, staring at the empty dance floor; the only things moving on it were the little square reflections from a single, slow turning mirror-ball.

"Boonie, ain't it?" he said.

I was amused; he was the one from Kansas dressed up as a cowboy. The next thing I expected him to say was, "Daddy's got oil".

"Perhaps things get started late around here," I ventured.

"In Mérida?" He looked at his watch. "But I wanna get laid. I'm so darn horny. And not too late."

He gave me a direct look, raising his boot to my barstool so his thigh opened towards me.

It was on the stroke of midnight when we got back to my hotel. I asked for my room key at reception, and the clerk, who I had hardly noticed when I checked in earlier, cast an eye over the two of us, then pursed his lips campily, and said, "Your key, señor!" He dangled it in the air from a limp wrist, waiting for me to take it. "*Sueño bien!*" he called impishly after us.

The art, the camp staff member, the tasteful Art Deco furniture, the owner with a panama hat; I now realized I had by coincidence landed up in a gay hotel.

The minute Gregg stripped off I had my doubts. He may have smelt of sweet cheroot, but he wasn't anyone's cowboy fantasy. He was even skinnier than I'd thought, and his skin had never been touched by sun. All his body hair was shaved off, all of it, right down to the tender crevice of his butt crack. Above his pendulous balls, his fat-veined cock stood bent up like a saddle pommel. Once he'd got his pants off, he put his boots back on. Then, butt naked, he jumped onto the bed, splayed his legs, cocking his heels over the cast iron bedstead rail, and shouted, "Ah baby! Fuck me stupid!"

The following afternoon, I went to see if I could catch Scott and Kate at their hotel. I found them lounging on sunbeds around the dip pool under palm trees. Water spouted soothingly from the mouth of a stone gargoyle shaped like a serpent's head. There were no other guests about.

"*Buenos dias*," I greeted them.

"It's such a relief. We don't have to be tourists or go and see anything. We can just lie around the pool," said Kate.

She pulled up a sunbed for me, then disappeared. She returned with glasses, an ice bucket and a bottle of tequila.

"Whoopee! Cool!" said Scott, clapping his hands together. "You got to love my Kate."

He kissed her neck as she bent forward to pour the tequila, her perfect, replete, conical breasts dangling over the drinks. Scott was sitting in his bather and Kate had on a modest bikini. Neither of them had an ounce of body fat and they both modelled healthy tans.

"Better use ice, otherwise we'll be floating face down in that pool," she said. "So tell us, how was Uxmal for you?"

"I preferred it to Chichén Itzá."

She nodded.

"We love New York, but we've got to flee the city often. We try to hit the surf every weekend in summer," said Scott.

"Surfing in New York? I'd never thought…"

"Sure, we shoot out to the 'island'."

"We used to live in the East Village. But now Clinton's moved in to Harlem–"

"There goes the neighborhood."

"Yes, we'll have to move to Washington Heights next." Kate sighed.

"That's what you call creepy gentrification," I said.

Kate laughed.

"Kate's studying politics," said Scott.

"Three people in a room is politics," she said.

"Or around a swimming pool?" I smiled.

"Be warned, I'm an anarchist," said Kate playfully, and poured three more hefty tequilas.

I had the impression she was camping me up, but she was still unsure about who or what I was.

"Did you go to the temple of phalluses when you went to Uxmal?" I asked. Scott shook his head. "It's a little walk from the main pyramid, but there are these stone penises like mushrooms."

"Get out 'o here!" said Kate.

"Cool!" said Scott.

"I can't believe I missed that!" said Kate.

"You're meant to only go with a guide."

I could see the shadowy outline of Scott's cock in his speedo. I thought Kate might have noticed me peeping.

"Have you noticed", she said, "in all the art works – the paintings and the sculptures in Mexico – you never see a penis. That's unusual for native arts, isn't it?"

"It would certainly be unusual in modern art," said Scott.

I had also noticed this about Latin American art, especially coming from Africa, where the artists weren't shy. "But I think on the Yucatán peninsula, since ancient times, sex appears always to have been strictly regulated by the state; to this day."

"There's a cave in Guatemala with a Mayan rock painting of two guys with huge erections embracing each other," said Scott."

"The Naj Tunich cave." I nodded, unsure if I'd pronounced it correctly.

"We were in Guatemala last year," said Kate. "You never mentioned it then, Scott."

"We weren't near it," he said. "It's the only ancient depiction of male on male sex in South America."

"Maybe there were penises everywhere," said Kate, "but the Catholics and the missionaries smashed them."

"Some school teachers in South Africa, near a farm where I lived, rubbed the penises off the Bushmen rock paintings."

"Well, thank the gods we're not regulated!" Kate downed her tequila and plunged into the pool.

Scott and I followed. The water was cool and invigorating; my toes tingled, my skin alive with the erogenous sun. We felt so free and weightless in the water, floating in the fullness of time. It started with splashing and horseplay in the pool; then moved on to us drying ourselves in their hotel room, and more tequila, and ended, or started, with the three of us naked on the bed.

Later on, I wondered if they had spoken about it beforehand; hatched a plan. I'd been oblivious to any undercurrents. Usually, with couples, you can quickly tell which one is being dangled out as bait.

Kate initiated things. She positioned herself between us. I was surprised when she encouraged me to penetrate her, while she kept her husband in her lips. The sex was wild, and vigorous, and noisy, a strange kind of turn-on in itself.

Then, I finally succumbed to the heat, and drifted off to sleep, lying between them, but holding his hard body, while her soft curves hugged my sticky back.

I woke at dusk. Scott was sitting up in bed, reading Neruda's love poems. Kate was still sleeping off the tequila.

"Hey!" he whispered, seeing me stir. He stroked my nipple with his finger. "You've obviously slept with a woman before," he said.

"Several, and you've obviously slept with guys before."

"Yeah," he shrugged. "But not in a long time." He chuckled. Then slyly he took me in his mouth. Kate slept. Or pretended to sleep. I was surprised, even a bit alarmed, when he swallowed and didn't withdraw.

"Tasty!" he whispered, and licked his lips, smiling. "Must be all the Mexican you've been eating."

Chavez and Pepe
FOR A FEW DOLLARS MORE
Mexico City, Mexico

Chavez said, "We will show you around."

"We love our city, you see," said Pepe.

There was no prevarication, no awkward breaking of the ice or mundane questioning. They simply leapt straight to it. Pepe and Chavez; two hyperactive students.

I'd met them at a local fast-food chain on the Rio Praga. My hotel was in the Zona Rosa, the disco and club area of downtown Mexico City, where most of the streets are named after European capitals, though Oxford and Liverpool somehow made it in too. I was eating a hamburger. It wasn't yet eleven in the morning. The place was crammed with jovial youths I'd never have encountered if I hadn't broken more sensible eating habits.

Pepe and Chavez were on holiday from college, had time on their hands, and were looking for fun. Apparently, I qualified, even if I was a decade older than them.

Chavez was dressed casually, but conservatively – blue candy-striped shirt with button-down collar, black trousers, closed shoes – except for the beat-up khaki beach hat.

"I want to be an actress," he declared with sensual, full lips.

He never did stop performing. They were physical with each other, constantly squealing, pinching, teasing and slapping one another with youthful energy. Being around them felt recklessly full of possibility.

Pepe said he was studying accounting. He was quieter than Chavez, and more relaxed in his summer clothes – white jeans, open sandals that revealed small neat toes, and a thin T-shirt that showed his nipples. His most striking feature was his straight black eyebrows, like two lines drawn with a ruler.

They were shocked that I'd been a week in their city and still not been to see its origins, the Aztec ruins of Teotihuacán or "the place where the gods were created". They insisted we go. It was a promising start and a generous show of goodwill, I thought. It must surely be a bore for them; they must have been there a hundred times.

But walking around Teotihuacán, down the uncanny Avenue of the Dead on its approach to the great Pyramid of the Sun, I realized this was not a place one tired of after one visit, but a place whose eerie presence, had I lived in the city, would have drawn me too time and again.

"They would decapitate people here and cut out their hearts, still alive," Chavez said with almost schoolboy relish.

There is no doubt that the Aztecs and their contemporaries were a bloodthirsty lot with a great appetite for human sacrifice. Yet the archaeological evidence, at least as it had been presented to me at Chichén Itzá and Uxmal, seemed flimsy. I wondered if this aspect of the indigenous cultures had not been exaggerated to justify the geno-cide committed by the conquistadors, which was rather rich coming from Catholic invaders with a religion that had a human sacrifice, a man tortured to death, as its central symbol.

In a city said to have had 200 000 inhabitants, claims that on one day here 80 000 people were sacrificed, seem utterly implausible to me. I asked the boys what they thought of all this. They had no opinion, but understood that these ruins made their city exceptional. The vast majority of tourists here were Mexican.

We climbed up to the Pyramid of the Moon and took photographs of one another on the steps. Chavez was shouting in Spanish to Pepe, gesturing outrageously, without a care in the world. The locals glanced at my two new friends with faces subtly disapproving. Was it simply their boisterous behaviour? Or did they see something I couldn't? I was enjoying being with these two freewheeling boys. With them, I felt I had a certain social immunity, license to behave in a way I probably would not back home.

After our tour, we crammed into a minibus taxi heading back to the city center, fifty kilometers south-west of Teotihuacán. It was an informal taxi or *colectivo* on a local route that wound its way for almost an hour through one of the bleakest urban landscapes outside of the Ukraine. We passed seemingly endless single and two story dwellings with windows like missing teeth, made of bare unpainted cement, grim and grey, set in equally grey ground with not a single tree, bush or green blade for tens of kilometers. I thought of Octavio Paz: 'Earth tastes of rotten earth'. The great Aztec civilization had passed, swallowed by their own murderous death god, Mictlantecuhtli. There was a new god now in charge of the global world, the god of stock markets, commodities and hedge funds, this time fed with the sacrifice of souls not bodies.

I only saw what one could from a minibus window, but I saw no billboards, adverts or any signs for shops, nor any form of industry, nor any kind of entertainment facility; and yet there were children here and people, thousands of them, sitting, walking, and standing around. What could all these people possibly live on?

The taxi pulled off the road beneath a concrete overpass. Pepe said, "We must get out, here. See you tonight at your hotel."

With a shock, I realized, this ashen landscape was where Pepe and Chavez lived, and where no tourist ever went.

They paid the driver, and Chavez told him to see that I got off at the Camionera del Norte, from where I could take a public bus to my hotel.

That evening we checked our bags and jackets at the entrance of a glitzy club in Zona Rosa. Of course, I paid our cover charges. My new friends were determined to dance the night away with camp bravado, flaunting their fancy moves and footwork on the dance floor. They were jubilant, but I sensed a deep, desperate urgency for release, a need to escape into the thudding music of the big city.

The club followed the standard routine of most Mexican gay clubs: slow start, loitering at the bar, mescal shooters, a buffed couple dancing ostentatiously, then everyone rushing onto the dance floor at the first Shakira song. After that, a drag queen compère with a microphone and a series of striptease artists each ending with a split second flap of their cocks.

I couldn't keep pace with Pepe and Chavez on the dance floor. Instead, I fell into conversation at the bar counter. A young man in a summer suit said he was a lawyer, specializing in leases. He was exceptionally good-looking, in a sort of Jesus-gigolo way.

"Everything gay in Mexico City is a hustle," he said. I was watching Chavez and Pepe enjoying themselves. He was watching them too. "Boys here," he shook his head, "only after the foreigners. Always money, money. They embarrass me. It's disgusting."

Of course, it was only minutes before he had cadged a drink off me and at once drifted off to talk to someone else, drink in hand.

There were now several cute boys milling near me, clandestinely trying to catch my eye. A geeky-looking, pasty-faced, blue-eyed boy with short strawberry-blond hair said hello, and asked me where I was from. I soon gleaned he came from a staggeringly wealthy family, with a central European sounding surname. Sebastian was studying medicine. He had a grasp of English and a grasp of the world that was quite beyond Chavez and Pepe. "Before, it was never like this!" he said.

"Like what?"

"The government, it is changing towards gays. There are many more clubs. People are even coming out."

But it would still be a decade before Mexico City started the legalization of gay marriage.

Then Pepe and Chavez returned, topless, soaked with perspiration. I could see Sebastian's disappointment. I'd have liked to chat more to him, but I wasn't about to ditch the boys, even as the fickle traveler I was.

I'd had enough by 4 a.m. We collected our coats and bags from the *vestuario* and walked back to my hotel. The boys lived too far from the city to go home at this hour. Besides, it was already Sunday.

There was no one at reception and we slipped upstairs undetected. My room had twin beds. Pepe and Chavez collapsed together on one.

I was drifting off, almost asleep, when Chavez crawled into my bed. He wasn't there to cuddle. His hands, then his lips started exploring my body. I could hear Pepe shifting in the dark. After a time, he switched on the bedside light, took one look at my erection, and shouted, "*Ay caramba!*"

"I've never been fucked before," Chavez whispered in my ear. "Please me."

The doughy-white of Chavez's bubble butt with its pink crease rose toward me. I took him gently. Pepe watched silently, sitting in his boxer shorts, fascinated, his mouth open, shaking his head slowly. From the way Chavez's body quivered and his legs trembled from the strain, perhaps it really was his first time.

The next morning, Chavez did blush like a deflowered virgin. Something about his behavior, or perhaps I was reading into it, convinced me that the previous night had indeed been significant to him. He'd come without touching himself, while I was inside him. That had happened to me the first time too, and never again. But most strangely, I remember that, and the longing for it to happen again, but I have no recollection with whom it was. Several people present themselves vaguely to memory, but I cannot remember if it was any of them. Virgins are so self-involved.

And then, there was the way Pepe had sat and watched us, watched his friend.

I felt I now had a responsibility. Not the same responsibility one has as a man's first male lover, but answerable nonetheless. Or was I being sentimental? Chavez had chosen his moment.

I decided to avoid the hotel dining room, and take the boys out for a full breakfast with black-eyed beans, fried eggs, tomato salsa, spicy cheese, tortillas, sweet bizcocho cakes, ripe papaya, red guavas, and cactus fruits. They gorged themselves splendidly. Pepe kept ragging Chavez in rapid Spanish. Several times I caught the English words 'big cock', saw Pepe shake his head, then Chavez mumble something and both of them collapse laughing. I hardly said a word at breakfast. I enjoyed watching their jocular play.

When the bill arrived, Chavez started speaking in an urgent voice to Pepe. I said not to worry for I had invited them; it was my treat. But Chavez had turned pale, the virginal blush quite drained away. In a panic, he kept searching his bag.

"What's the matter?" I asked.

"My money – it's gone!" said Chavez. He again rummaged frantically through his bag. "They must have taken it out at the club."

"At the safe-keeping?"

"*Si!*" Pepe said angrily. "*Chingalo!*"

"And we still have to get home!" said Chavez, eyes watering.

I leant them thirty dollars. Pepe said they'd try the club, but it was probably useless. They dashed off, hardly saying goodbye.

I called their mobile phones several times that afternoon. They were always on message divert. Eventually it would ring, but they never answered.

Perhaps they had simply become caught up in their own lives again, and I had been a one-night stand. Perhaps they were afraid I'd want the money back and, as little as it was, they couldn't repay it. Perhaps they were never robbed at the club and it was all a petty scam. Or maybe Chavez had already forgotten me. I never did find out, but I missed them those next, my last, few days in Mexico City.

Michael
ARCHANGEL
Los Angeles, USA

I was doing a favor for an old friend in Cape Town. He had plunged into an all-consuming, passionate infatuation for a much younger boy, Michael, whom he described as his archangel.

Michael was a 22-year-old club kid from a dysfunctional home, troubled, recreationally addicted to MDMA, a drifter, or to put it more kindly, a dreamer. My friend still cherished a pathological Wildean weakness for cruel and thoughtless youth, whereas I had learned early on that young men with any ambitions to make their mark upon the world, pursue life with an aggressive self-centered interest, for which you will be sacrificed the moment a choice has to be made.

Perhaps then it was for the best that my friend, George, with an absolute belief in this protégé's genius, and blinded to all his patent faults by being made to feel young and loved again, had selflessly packed Michael off to faraway Los Angeles, all expenses paid, so the kid could make his dreams come true in Hollywood. George had absolute faith Michael would return a star. In an ethos of cynical, mutually exploitative love between moneyed men and pretty boys, which was so much a part of the gay club scene, my friend's *amour fou* for his Narcissus and his magnanimous act, seemed vaguely beautiful. For this reason alone, I agreed to check up on the boy while I was in transit from Tokyo, and to report back to his patron.

The utterly unreliable Michael, to my great surprise, was waiting for me at the airport exactly as arranged by email a week before.

He was tall, skinny as an Indonesian shadow puppet, with a bulging Adam's apple the size of his nose, a scrawny neck on top of which rotated a head with bulbous eyes and scraggly blond hair, thinning prematurely. Or as George saw him, a svelte physique, vast amethyst eyes swept with lashes, and a languorous smile.

As instructed, the first thing I did was to point my camera at him and take his picture. Michael, being an unashamed Footlight Fanny, immediately sprang into performance mode, professionally working the camera, swimming in his own reflection, and before I knew it, I had shot off a dozen pictures, the airport arrivals hall transformed into a photoshoot, and I into Paparazzo.

A little crowd had assembled around us, scratching their heads to figure out who this celebrity was; this was LA after all and Michael was saying loudly, "Sorry darlings, no autographs today, sorry, sorry."

On his high-heeled boots and stalk-like legs, he speedily made for the exit, me tripping behind him.

Michael was blessed with ample natural charm, ironically quite obscured by my good friend's amorist, often artificial and frilly theatrical praises. He was euphoric at seeing a face from home. "I thought I'd take you for a spin around the city. What time is your flight?" He spoke with a pronounced Eastern Cape accent, the genuine root sound of all South African English accents.

The flight was later that night, but I did not trust Michael to get me back on time. I told him it was early evening, and kept my boarding pass concealed. Luckily, they had already allowed me to check through my bags.

"Excuse the mess," he pleaded as we climbed into his car. On the outside, a wonderful red 1970s Chevy SS, but inside, a rubbish tip, covered in the detritus of his new American lifestyle: plastic bottles, fast food containers, squashed cans, miscellaneous filth, and strands of human hair glued to the headrests.

"It looks like you sleep here!" I said, gingerly sitting down.

"I do," he replied. "Sometimes."

We set off on the highways of Los Angeles, a vast system of ramps, concrete bridges and dual carriageways, standing over the city on pillars, enabled with dozens of exits, which seemingly never connect with the earth when you need them to. As always, even with eight lanes across, it was jammed with an endless stream of cars, circulating like little blood corpuscles in the veins of a concrete Frankenstein monster.

But Michael seemed to know his way around, and we were soon off the boulevards and on the 405 highway heading north. We were merging with another highway, and the traffic was edging forward now slowly, bumper to bumper.

He was desperate to speak Afrikaans.

"*Toe, was Japan lekker?*" (So, was Japan exciting?) He said Japan in English, not "yah-pun".

"*Ja, puik maar wildvreemd!*" (Yes, great but very strange.)

I was trying not to ask too many questions or distract him from driving. I kept the conversation superficial, thinking of topics he found interesting and easy to reciprocate.

"I suppose if you've moved to America you need a Chevy like this to complete the fantasy."

But he wasn't listening. He was chewing his bottom lip. "Somehow we've got to get off this bloody Ten and on to La Brea," said Michael, searching the great signs. He rolled down his window and flapped his skeletal wrist at the other motorists, calling out, "Excuse me, excuse me, auntie, hey! Auntie!"

Surprisingly people were responding.

"La Brea!" he yelled. "La Brea Avenue?"

A Hispanic man with an enormous bicep bulging over the window frame of his shiny new, black pick-up, indicated to him to keep going straight.

Michael sighed, in his mincing way. "It's never good, but this really is a terrible time to be on the roads."

"So how is the movie business? Any breaks yet?"

He fell silent for a while, and then said, dispiritedly, "It's really hard. I knew it would be difficult, but I did not know it was going to be this hard. I honestly thought at least one person would see my talent."

"Any auditions?"

"I'm always at castings. You cannot believe how many novels I've read. Funny that, I'd never read a book before."

"What about agents?"

"Ja, but none of them ever call you back. Oh! shit, shit, shit! I've missed the flippin' exit."

He was now rather unattractively biting his fingernail.

"Ag, sorry man, what time did you say your flight was again?"

I told him again, giving him the earlier time.

There was no working air-conditioner in his car and as the summer temperature rose above ninety degrees Fahrenheit, the remains of his Chinese takeaways were starting to stir themselves under my seat.

We took the next exit. We were on boulevards again, and he kept asking worrying questions, like, "What way's north?" and squinting at the sun. We were lost.

The pockets of urban decay we kept on passing through reminded me astonishingly of Johannesburg. Like Jozi, LA is also a horizontal city. As buildings are abandoned or fall into disrepair, or even when whole areas collapse and cease to function, the city simply keeps spreading laterally, like a splotchy melanoma.

Eventually Michael returned us to the freeway, and after an elaborate loop, we managed to get off at the correct exit. I had a hunch most of the driving we had done was pointless. I was irritated. I wanted to see the city and not spend my day circling above it on this concrete scaffolding.

At last, we landed and took a drive through Hollywood. It was unexpectedly bland. Even the people were nondescript. We stopped for pizza and Coke.

"I miss Cape Town. I'm really homesick, man."

"When do you think you'll come back?"

"Ag, I don't know, maybe for a holiday. I wonder how all my pals are at the club. I miss them." He held up the crystal he wore around his neck. "This is my good-luck charm. It will bring me all the success I need. The crystal can concentrate all good energy and it reflects all the bad. But you have to believe first."

"Deflect," I corrected, and nodded believingly.

"If you trust in the universe, it always gives back!"

As proof, I treated him to the lunch. It was clear he was living on air.

We set off again. The car had been standing in the sun; it now smelt like a galley on a Chinese junk; I was being carried inside the belly of American culture.

Triumphantly, he turned on to a wide avenue. "Look! This is the famous Sunset Boulevard. All the big studios are here. All of them! I've seen quite a few big stars since I got here." He mentioned a few names, none of whose faces I could picture, and several names I had never heard of before.

"What time is your flight again?"

I told him again.

"Look! Up there! We can go to Beverly Hills!" He pointed.

"So it's been hard?"

"Ja, jislaaik! But I owe it to Georgie," he sighed. "I won't give up, yet." But it seemed to me he'd already given up.

"I don't know, maybe I came here to find myself."

People often thought their difficulties were a matter of geography, until they moved and found they took their problems with them.

We passed a sign about number plates being checked; something to the effect that if your car was spotted passing more than twice in thirty minutes, you would be stopped.

"Are you having some fun in LA at least?" I asked.

"Oh yes!"

I immediately thought of drugs. Next, I thought of him living in the car. There was probably a stash of cannabis under my seat.

"No, let's not bother with Beverly Hills," I said.

"No, but Roxbury Drive – like Madonna's house is there!"

For some reason the homes of Hollywood stars either look like historical fantasies of the South or great big funeral parlors.

"Shit! Shit! Shit man! My watch has stopped! What time is it?"

I wasn't wearing a watch either. He switched on his mobile phone to check the time. "We'd better start getting back!"

I wondered how he could leave his phone off. If a casting agent called, I doubted they would ever bother leaving a message.

Somehow we found our way back to the on-ramp.

Since it had not occurred to Michael to ask in all this time, I finally volunteered. "George is very well, but he misses you terribly. He really pines for you."

"Oh," he said distantly.

"He has a new play on."

"Oh, kak!" Once more, we were snarled up in traffic.

"What now?" I asked.

"Petrol. We're almost out. I'll have to get off this highway."

I looked at the meter. It said empty and the red light was on. "You sure that's not broken too?" I asked irritated.

"No, I just had it fixed."

I could feel my anxiety rise as we slowly edged forward in the traffic, painstakingly working our way across the lanes like a crab, and running out of fuel. We didn't make it in time for the next exit, but eventually we did get off, Michael again stopping hooting motorists by extending his gangly arm out of the window.

Next, we had to find a gas station. By pure luck, when the car started to splutter and jerk, we were within sight of one.

I gave him cash to refuel and we refueled ourselves with ice-cold Cokes. I was nauseous from spending hours in the car, the rotten food, the heat, the traffic and the migraine-inducing tangle of roads. But soon we were once again hunting for the highway to get back to the airport.

We finally arrived at LAX. But thanks to 9/11, cars were not allowed within a mile of the airport building and we had to take a transfer bus. If I hadn't lied about the departure time, I would probably have missed the plane.

Michael stood in front next to the bus driver. "Can I try that?" he asked, pointing at the microphone.

The driver laughed. "Sure!"

In an instant Michael had the microphone in his hands and was announcing, "Welcome ladies and gentlemen to LAX on this beautiful sunny afternoon. Here's hoping you are going to have a wonderful trip wherever you are flying to. This bus is going … where we going?"

The bemused passengers on the bus were all laughing, enjoying the precociousness of his impromptu show. I could now see the charisma that had won George's heart. Months later, back in Cape Town, when I related this to George, it brought a tear to his eye, and he said, "Oh, I miss him so."

"That was fun," Michael said as we hopped off the bus.

"George sent you these," I said, and now I pulled out the little parcel I'd carried more than half way round the world in my hand luggage. George had begged me to take a carton of Gauloises cigarettes and a neatly folded pair of skinny, factory-frayed jeans.

"Well, good luck!" I said on my marks to scuttle through security, pretending to be in a hurried panic.

Michael suddenly threw his arms around me. He kissed me three times on the cheek.

"*Lekker* man, give that to George," he said.

When I reached the passengers-only entrance, I glanced back over my shoulder. He was still standing there, and he was holding his crystal. He waved. He looked quite abject; Michael, George's archangel, lost in the city of angels. And George has passed away.

Natasha had said. "Oh, you must come and stay; it's the gayest place on earth."

She was always up to date, trendy and fashionable, from the cute retro-looking home cappuccino machine to the latest Apple Mac laptop. She'd also recently purchased a gorgeous, three-story, bay-windowed, Victorian apartment in the heart of San Francisco's famous gay district, the Castro.

Natasha wasn't gay. She did however have a younger brother, and she had spent much of her time in his gay circles. Originally South African, she'd moved to America as a medical practitioner. Now, I was staying with her while I was in San Francisco. It is good to be gay and South African; you're sure to have a bed in any major Western city.

It was a quiet Sunday morning. I woke early. I'd slept well for the first night in a strange house, although I'd been aware of people arriving late, hushing each other, and pausing to peer at the unfamiliar lump on their foldout couch.

Natasha loved Frisco. She said it reminded her of Cape Town: the climate, relaxed atmosphere, the almost permanent holiday feel in the summer, the great bookshops and galleries and endless restaurants.

Her focus right now was her home, decorating it, furnishing it, smartening it up, investing in her new life. She wasn't going back to

South Africa. Her medical career was advancing well here. She earned a fortune in rand terms and there was no comparison in the working conditions. It wasn't simply about relieving suffering. People suffered and confronted mortality whether they were wealthy Americans or poor Africans, but a stint in a hospital back home, beset every day with advanced, undiagnosed, treatable diseases, knife and gunshot wounds, victims of violent gang rapes, could warp the way you saw humankind, damage the way you thought about people.

"And then there's AIDS of course and the lunacy of the president," she'd confessed. "Yes, I did feel guilty leaving. But I wasn't cut out for it. I think many health professionals in South Africa suffer post-traumatic stress disorder without knowing or admitting it. The things I saw…" She fell silent.

In SF she felt safe; she'd go for an early morning jog or take the dog for a walk on her own at any hour of night. "I could not do that back home. I love it here. Besides, I am a bit of a fag hag."

"Such an ugly term," I objected.

"There are lots of straight men about actually, and the good news is they're just as desperate as us."

I could hear someone moving about upstairs.

"Good morning!" Natasha called out.

A pair of sinewy bare feet, black with pink souls appeared on the landing. The stranger's body slowly descended – muscular calves and thighs, sleep shorts that also bulged, corrugated abdominals, a broad, bare, square chest with large flat nipples, and finally a round face with sleep-puffed eyes and a shaven head.

"This is my house mate, Adan," Natasha introduced us.

Adan sat down next to me at the breakfast table, put out his hand and gave me a township handshake.

"See, I know how!" he chuckled. "Xolelwa showed me." He had a clearly defined American accent, yet he pronounced the explosive, alveolar Xhosa 'x' perfectly.

"I still can't do that click!" said Natasha.

"Yeah well, you're a white South African." Adan laughed, then turned to me, "No offence."

"Xolelwa," I said passably.

"Is the child awake yet?" asked Natasha.

"He'll be down, eventually," replied Adan. "He takes almost as long as a straight boy to get ready."

Shirtless Adan gleamed in the morning sunlight. This was not the usual hamstrung, pumped-up, dumb-bell-trained gym body; his was supple, lithe, and elegant; physicality that makes one stutter.

Between coffee and chewing toast with marmalade I got the story. Adan was a dancer with a highly successful contemporary African American ballet company. He had won a prestigious solo award and his career was in rapid ascent. While he was describing his latest performance, a piece about Uncle Tom's Cabin, we were joined by Xolelwa, but he introduced himself as Zola. "They can't do the click here, you see," he explained. "So I chose Zola. Xolelwa is just for Adan." He gave Adan a lingering good morning kiss.

Zola was short, stocky, a slight stomach, at least ten years younger than Adan, with a smile and pure white teeth that lit up the breakfast room. He had a hot-potato English accent from one of the elite private schools back home. Zola's family were wealthy long before apartheid ended. "I don't want to know how my gran made all that money," was his only comment on the subject.

He'd come to live with Adan and he had been in San Francisco now for about six months. They had originally made contact using an internet-dating site advertised in the gay SF newspapers, which I was surprised to learn, specialized in finding eligible South African men. This was shortly before Adan was to tour to South Africa with the dance company. They met for the first time in person in Cape Town.

"I was tired of the black brothers," said Adan. I sensed he was only partly joking. "I wanted an African boyfriend, from Africa. I only date black men; that's just my aesthetic."

I smiled. "I have some white Afrikaans friends just like that back home."

"And that's how he found me," cooed Zola, his hand resting on Adan's taut thigh. "On the internet. Why does it still sound weird?"

"Don't be too cocky; there were only three black men on that site. The rest were Afrikaners."

I asked Adan what was the problem he had with the brothers.

"It's fucked up," he said, but the word sounded unfamiliar in his mouth, as if he only ever used it as a last resort. "I kept getting in trouble. It's hard meeting new gay black men, half of whom, if they're out, only like white guys. We're one of the few black couples living in the Castro."

"Frisco really is like Cape Town that way," said Zola. "I couldn't believe it when I first came here."

"The more I see of the USA," I said, "the more I think it is the closest country in the world to South Africa, with its ghettoes, inequality, systemic racism…"

"Look it's not apartheid, but, big but!" said Adan.

"Unlike in South Africa, blacks are a minority here," said Zola "And just like Cape Town, there's basically no African-American presence in the gay pride march. They do their own separate thing in East Bay, across the bridge. Can you believe it?"

"I get a bad vibe from the bouncers at some of the gay clubs. Probably think I'm there to deal drugs."

"And you wouldn't believe the suspicious looks I get when I pull out my gold Amex." Zola laughed. "The amazing thing is they are utterly unaware of themselves; they think they're doing their jobs well when they ask a black man for his ID. If you did that in SA… And they're absolutely unapologetic, here. Like, you're black, what do you expect me to do? Of course I must check that it's your credit card!"

"Anyway, I'd spend hours on the internet," Adan continued. "I'm not into quick hook-ups, anonymous sex, you know – the party-n-play crowd. I look after my body. Sure I smoke cigarettes, but that's all."

I laughed. "All dancers smoke and drink too much."

"I met one phony after another on the internet. Finally, I met a guy I took a real fancy to. He used to be a cop, but something awful happened, some shooting. I never got the real story, but he was in some hot mess. I felt he had a deep need to be loved, and I tried hard. I didn't know at the time how screwed up he really was. It wasn't long before I discovered he was on the down-low, like the rest of them."

"Down-low?" I interrupted.

"Black guys who won't admit they're gay. So they live with women, and sleep with men on the side. They see themselves as straight."

"And they treat you like their bitch," interjected Zola.

"Anyway, he seemed different. Men on the down-low it's usually because their support structure, their families and friends, which is hard to give up if you're African American, they just won't accept you.

"They also see gay as a white concept. I don't blame them. Look around the Castro. There is no black identity here. So even if homosexuality is not, gay is a white thing."

Natasha placed another plunger of coffee on the table. She had of course heard it all before, but I could tell from the tiny winces her face gave away, she felt for Adan's pain each time he told this story.

"I don't judge him now," Adan continued. "Possibly I failed him. There was a deep need to reach out, maybe even to admit to himself that he really was homosexual. But I couldn't stay the course; I couldn't put up with his bullshit." Adan sounded remorseful, then he said, in a voice almost ashamed, "When I found out about his fiancée, I knew what I was doing was wrong. But I thought I could change him."

How many gay men have lived that tale?

"Later, I discovered he was also cruising the clubs down at Tenderloin. I tried to forgive him, but my self-image was going down the plughole. I broke it off."

"There's nothing new about men sleeping around," said Natasha. "Straight, gay, black, white, married."

"Sure, there are lots of married white men picking up boys on the side. But this is America. We get the bad press – infecting our wives with HIV. And there's no strong black gay identity as a counterweight, like there is a white gay identity. Black community leaders are always saying that gay is unAfrican, a white perversion. It's easy for them. Who do we point to? Where is the example of black gay identity?"

Zola tapped the invisible watch on his wrist. "We'd better get ready, or we will be late for church."

Adan saw my lack of belief.

"Yeah, I'm Christian," he said.

"But …," I said, then thought better of it.

Zola was amused by my embarrassment.

"You're right," said Adan. "Because of the church's attitude, a lot of gay men also reject Jesus. I'm not some evangelist, but I believe in Jesus Christ, and the Church is important to me. It's a black thing if you like."

We set off in Adan's convertible, an old sports car. It was a sunny day and we drove with the top down. I couldn't remember when I last went to church. I had a vague childhood memory; silhouettes of a congregation, milky beams of light from Gothic windows; knee bones on stone; abandoned by my parents to Catholic neighbors. I can't remember what age I was. I never went back.

"When the white supremacists used Christianity to justify their slave owning," Adan was explaining to me, "you know – the curséd children of Ham and all that – that's when the black congregation broke away and formed their own denomination. There are churches, mostly white, who take people regardless of 'affectional orientation'. But I'd hate to see a black gay church forming. I want my church to change."

The more Adan spoke, the more I admired him. He had broken through so many pigeonholes. He was black, gay, out of the closet, asserting himself by living in the heart of the white Castro, doing volunteer work at the gay counselling service, building a successful artistic career. And endearing to me, he acted as though he was quite unconscious of his good looks. There was discipline to his physical beauty. It wasn't something he traded on, cheapened, or rented out the way so many gay boys did. As a dancer, it was an extension of himself, of his inner expressiveness, not a façade, not a means to manipulation. I wondered too if the fact that he was a committed Christian had not ironically given him the strength to stand up as a homosexual. Once he'd made peace with his God, what did he care what other sinners said or thought?

"At least I haven't been kicked out–"

"Yet," said Zola. "You are not yet out to the congregation."

"The reverend knows," said Adan brusquely. "There are churches where when the pastor finds out someone is gay, they kick them out. Or they deliver such a pointed, damning sermon, the dude just gets up and goes of his own accord."

Religious people are always so pleased when you tag along, but I sensed Adan was a little nervous about it too.

"Oh, and just so you know before we get there, any similarities drawn between gay rights and the struggle for civil liberties – don't be goin' saying anything."

"Have you ever been to a black church before?" asked Zola. "It's very different." And he gave me an impish smile.

"No, and it's also my first time to cross the Golden Gate." I cheered, staring up at the giant, red steel girders rising above me as we passed beneath.

Zola it turned out had not been particularly religious back home. He was a believer, but non-practicing, until he met Adan.

The church had a very long name, describing its lineage of affiliation and denomination. There were buses outside that had brought throngs of worshippers, even some tourists. The building had a colonnaded entrance and was about the height of three storys. It appeared to be a large mansion, but inside it was a single hall, cavernous and echoey. The walls were white with little ornamentation.

Zola and I went in together, but Adan said he was going to tell one of the church elders he'd brought a visitor; it was something they apparently liked to know.

"Don't worry," Zola said. "Relax."

Relax? I thought. I'm an atheist.

I noted the congregation was almost exclusively black, and largely female. People were clapping rhythmically and singing, a few soprano voices rising above the ensemble. We were sitting far back, close to the video cameras. For fifteen dollars, you could buy a DVD of the service afterwards. "God Our Father! Christ Our Redeemer! Man Our Brother!" began the preacher.

"Amen! Amen!" the congregation responded.

The preacher was a huge man, his size exaggerated by a posture so upright, he could have walked with a giant illustrated Bible balanced on his head.

"And I want to welcome our brothers here from all over the world." He stroked the grey filigree fringe of his beard while he paused to peruse his notes. "We welcome our brother from Canada." A hand waved in the air amongst cheers. "Our visitors all the way from Nigeria!" The Nigerian family – mother, father, two boys – stood up to applause. "Our brother from faraway South Africa." Thunderous applause and loud cheers, and heads looking around the room to see who it was. But I was silently praying: oh God, don't make me stand up. I doubted the congregation were at that precise moment picturing their South African brother as a lily-white boy. Zola was grinning. I'd never felt so white in my life. But God heard me and told the preacher, for the reverend passed on at once to the reading: 'The righteous shall live by faith'.

"I wish we'd had church like this at school," Zola whispered.

Sisters were called to give witness to the power of God; cheeks were stained with tears; around me, people were crying out with their arms outstretched in the air. Even I found the singing exhilarating, contagious.

"Praise the Lord! Praise Him!" a middle-aged woman with her

matronly moon-shaped face turned up to the heavens, the fleshy flaps of her great arms shaking. It was the fervor of her worship that caught my attention, and then I saw her one eye was cut and bruised. I couldn't help recalling the various grim scenarios Adan had described that plagued this neighborhood. But in church, she could come once a week, and scream her lungs out, and wail. I saw people fall to the floor that day. It was autochthonous, ingenious theatre; a release valve – transformative, cathartic, enriching.

"Pity we can't slaughter a chicken in here," Zola whispered mischievously in my ear.

According to Adan, ironically, the church was where many straight men cruised for girls, and sometimes other men too. At the time, America was yet again in cataleptic throws over the issue of gay marriage. It had been going on for decades. Adan wanted to marry Zola, and he wanted to do it more than anything else with the blessing of his church. He was also fighting to get Zola the right to stay in the USA. But almost all the African American churches and their affiliates had come out rabidly against gay marriage and found themselves in the unusual position of sharing platforms with white, fundamentalist Christian racists and the self-same Republican policy-makers long considered responsible for the implosion of black neighborhoods.

"Their argument is that the destruction of family values has done the most damage to black communities, and gay marriage is a further erosion," Adan explained later.

"You'll have to get married in South Africa," I said.

After church, we went for pasta in a trattoria that used to be a brothel. We were back in the Castro in the original streets that celebrated what passed for 'gay culture', dotted with rainbow flags, piercing emporia, porno shops, and adverts for discount lube and leather.

I asked Adan about his work at the community counselling center.

"HIV infections are on the rise again. The kids know nothing, and those who survived the AIDS plague in the eighties no longer seem to care." Adan always spoke compellingly, with passion and certainty. "The survivor generation is back to S&M and dangerous sex play. From what I see at the clinic, they're showing the biggest increase in positive testing."

I had no response. HIV/AIDS was decimating poverty-stricken sub-Saharan Africa, where people were desperate and dying for medication, while here, in the most affluent part of the world, in a tribe of high income earners, where a drink in a club cost what people earned for a day's hard labor back home, people were out carelessly destroying themselves. The old passive hippies had gone; now there were armored, sexual predators in a riot of hyper-sex. San Francisco had traded the flower in the hair for a steel ring through the penis.

Zola related an amusing incident with a guy who had come on to him one night at the bar. The man got angry when he was rebuffed; he thought he had not been given a chance. "This guy says: why you act like that? You don't know anything about me, you don't even know what I do, or what car I drive, or what kind of house I own. You're so superficial!"

"You joking?" I said.

"No," Zola squealed boyishly.

"You sure he wasn't joking?"

"Maybe he was being honest. Maybe there wasn't anything else to him," said Adan, a hint of possessiveness in his voice.

I asked Adan why infections were on the rise.

"I'll tell you a story," he said. "I met this guy, real cute, straight-looking and acting. He was twenty-one and unemployed. He seemed so unspoiled. Always fun, always laughing. Whenever we went out, we had such a good time. I had to pay for everything, not surprisingly, but I didn't mind. And because of his age, I was taking things real slow. I tried to encourage him to keep looking for jobs, giving him clippings from papers for career advisors or training courses, or a printout from job sites on the web. Anyway, I tried.

"I asked friends round here in the Castro if they could help him out, waiting or kitchen work, but none of them were too keen. Perhaps they were afraid it would mess with their relationship with me if things went wrong. I don't have an issue, but I do sometimes wonder if it would have been the same if he'd been a cute twenty-one-year-old white boy with a sexy ass.

"Anyhow, some time passed before I got physical. I immediately regretted it. He said he wasn't ready for that. But he was virtually living at my place by now. This is before I moved in with Natasha.

"One evening I'm out with friends at a bar, a decent kind of place, and I see him buying drinks, expensive drinks, cosmopolitans and champagne cocktails. Then I see that he's with this white guy in a suit. I didn't confront him, and he didn't see me.

"The next day I asked him what he did the night before, and he said he'd stayed at his mom's. He didn't look like he'd had much sleep. His eyes were all swollen. I lost my temper. If there is one thing I hate, it's a liar.

"He told me to f-off. Then he upped and left, crying and breaking things. He kicked holes in the kitchen cupboards.

"I called around and looked everywhere for him – for days. Nobody knew. Everyone said I was wasting my time.

"The next I heard was from a colleague at the clinic. He'd been in for counselling. He was addicted to crystal. Worse, he was using booty bumps."

I'd never heard of them.

Adan shifted a bit in his seat, then he spoke in a very matter of fact way. "It's meth taken anally. The other guy puts it on and even up his cock, so they both get the rush when he penetrates. Not exactly safe sex! But once guys get into crystal, they just can't imagine sex without it. It becomes sex. Straights do it too.

"He's now outta bounds, on the streets, having sex with anybody that will give him crystal. It's double bad, because he's so young. Whatever bastard gave it to him the first time, got him hooked …" Adan shook his head. "He has lost ownership of his life."

I thought of the woman crying in the church. Perhaps this boy's mother too had been there today.

"We see it in our communities. It's a return to slavery," said Zola. He squeezed Adan's hand.

Lee and Rex
THE EDGE OF THE WORLD
Auckland, New Zealand

I arrived in Auckland quite coincidentally on the day of the annual Hero Parade. A hundred thousand people had come out to watch. The small capital truly embraced its gay pride march.

The parade floats reflected the Kiwis' quaint obsession with clubs; there was a platform of gardening lesbians, one with synchronized lawnmowers, and another for do-it-yourself gay handymen. Even the Quakers had a float.

Like so much else in New Zealand, the event was one of moderation: sensible, rational and tolerant. Except for one group – a handful of Christians. Surprisingly, these were not old biddies. These were young evangelicals in Cistercian white and regulation haircuts. All the old folks I saw were clapping and cheering for the gays.

Being New Zealanders, these particular Christians were not calling for stonings or excommunication, nor warning us of fire and brimstone if we didn't change our wicked ways – a logical, even if irrational, fear – for if the Old Testament is to be believed and lessons learned from Sodom, God would burn them all to death for having turned the other cheek and allowed us homosexuals to parade in their midst.

Their complaint, however, appeared to be linguistic, and Sister Sledge and her 1979 hit song were to blame. "*They*", the Christians were protesting, "have stolen the word family from us."

I was guilty. After all, as a child, I had secretly stolen the word hero too, long before Auckland's Heroes' parade. My mother, an artist, will have to take responsibility. As part of my education, she'd sit me beside her while she paged through the Larousse *Encyclopaedia of Prehistoric and Ancient Art* filled with pictures of male nude sculpture – the Doryphorus, Hermes, Poseidon, plenty of Apollo. And elsewhere: a pair of potbellied dwarfs with enormous testicles – comic Greek actors; the discus thrower with his pointy uncut penis; the more invitingly reclined Barberini faun; Laocoön and his writhing sons; each held up to me like gay flashcards, and mommy saying repeatedly, "Aren't they beautiful, darling?" I was five.

My mom would read to me from an illustrated version of the Odyssey and the Iliad – my eyes lingering over a slim boy Achilles riding bareback on a hairy centaur, clutching his mane; young Achilles disguised in woman's robes; the warrior Achilles gazing intently into the eyes of a stricken golden-locked Tenedos; and finally, on the battlefield, cradling the neck of his dying "friend", naked Patroclus – so at a very early age, fixing in my mind handsome heroes and travel to exotic places. Thanks to the Greek sculptors, my solitary, erotic night-time fantasies revolved around one distinct part of the male anatomy – not the penis, but the heroic pelvic floor.

Now, standing in the crowd in Auckland, drinking from a plastic mug of beer, I watched the buffed lads in their satin shorts, thick blue pelvic veins plunging below non-existent tan lines, go rollicking by.

New Zealand's major gay pride event was suffering rumors of embezzlement. Little did we know then, the next year would be its last. Heroes do tend to make off with the golden loot.

As the last stragglers minced heroically past on Ponsonby Road, a fresh good-looking lad, ruby lips and shiny boy cheeks, latched on to me. "Parade was pretty half-pai this year, wasn't it?" he said.

I shrugged. "I'm visiting, never been before."

He said his name was Lee. He was part Maori. His granddad, so he said, had been a great warrior. And he had his granddad's build. He told me he'd only recently come out, at Auckland's coming-out picnic, when once a year a throng of families gathered in a park and picnicked together with their recently self-declared gay sons and daughters, to celebrate and rediscover one another. Parents invited by their kids to the picnic, knew what was coming. What a great way to tell them. Civilized, thoughtful New Zealand.

We ate slippery, foot-long hot dogs at a street stall. Then he suggested we go to a club, the one all of gay Auckland said was the club to go to that night. It was nearby.

But there was trouble at the door.

"He's blacklisted", was all that the bouncer would tell me, folding his scary arms in an emphatic you-will-not-pass.

"It's only when that fat bastard is on the door!" said Lee, making sure he was overheard. He suggested another club, and we were soon on some or other dance floor without a care in the world, Lee gyrating lasciviously with the stripped bare, oiled bodies of the Auckland dancing boys, their pelvic floors encircling us.

Lee was getting progressively drunker and becoming increasingly outlandish, toasting me and shouting, "*Kia ora!* You know what that means?" I didn't mind. I was too charged up from the long flight to this – the end of the world. It might have been 11 p.m. in New Zealand, but my brain was somewhere at lunch.

Lee wanted to kiss. He was a good kisser; a real little succubus.

"I've heard about rubbing noses with the Maoris, but this..." I said, as our lips at last parted.

He winked. It is only the innocent who show so much teeth when they smile, I thought.

I had to go to the toilet. Lee followed. At the urinals, he stood alongside, eyeing me while I peed. The moment I finished, he dragged me by the crook of my arm into a cubicle.

"Drop your gear," he said. It was that quick. "I just have to jump that stick now I seen it," he said.

In that bright, red interior, he attempted a blowjob. Maybe it was the booze, perhaps the traveling, but although my body started to unfurl and respond, I had to cut him short.

"Please, not here," I said.

I could hear other people entering the toilets. Lee was persisting on my part. There was a hammering on the door and an aggressive female voice shouted, "Oi! Get the fuck out o' there. I need to piss and the ladies' is flooded!"

Lee took no notice. The person kept banging the door. I smacked Lee hard on the back of the head.

"Christ!" the voice whined ever more urgently. "Rattle your dags! Get the fuck out. I need to gooooo!"

We sheepishly slunk out. The woman with the big voice was actually a skinny, diminutive girl in a hip helmet skirt. She hardly gave us a second look, but pushed past against my chest, saying, "If you bastards left cum on the seat…"

"Rark up!" shouted Lee.

We moved from one club to the next as the night progressed, ending up where the clientele were thickset, either shaven bald or grey-haired, the energy darker, and the men cruising conspicuously. It wasn't a leather-bar, but it smelt of leather on moist groins, and smoke.

I thought we might now have an opportunity to talk, as the music was softer, with more bass sounds and fewer vocals. I wanted his story. But all Lee wanted to do was suck face – his words not mine.

The club had an open courtyard. There were rusty poles, previously used for washing lines, a pile of building rubble pushed up against one wall, and a few chairs placed wherever the ground was a little even.

Lee lit a cannabis joint. There were several people smoking pot, openly, though Lee must have caught the expression on my face.

"No wucking furries," he said, and offered me a hit.

"Makes me vomit," I replied, ashamed of my straight-laced constitution.

"Want some crack?"

I recoiled.

"I can get us some good shit." Now I did feel queasy. But it was him, not the drugs that unsettled me.

"What the pigs say is bullshit to scare ya." He coughed. "I know people who've been using heroin for yonks, and they're doing alright."

I felt like a fist had been thrust into me, gripping my insides. I saw syringes and veins and blood and shared needles. I started to panic. Can you get AIDS from a blowjob?

Lee was looking at me expectantly. His eyes were already bloodshot from the grass.

Could such a healthily built specimen be a hard drug user? Had he latched on to me to buy drugs for him? Had the bouncer barred him from the club for dealing? I began to doubt everything; his story about coming out at the picnic, his warrior granddad, that was probably true. He'd targeted me at the parade. Lee was no innocent. And I was now gripped by what we called afrAIDS syndrome; the paralyzing fear of contracting HIV.

I noticed a man recognize Lee and nod. I guess in his early fifties, wearing military fatigue trousers and a green gym vest, his bare muscular arms and his face embossed with mokos – the distinctive traditional black Maori tattoos. He looked rough. He was going to come over, but Lee said hastily, "It's the guy I'm flatting with." Before he had taken two steps towards us, Lee sprinted to intercept him. They turned in such a way, the man alongside him, that they kept their backs to me. I couldn't see their expressions or their hands, nor hear what they were murmuring; it sounded like they might be speaking in Te Reo. Their temples almost touched.

Somehow, crack and heroin hadn't figured in my expectations of prosperous, sedate New Zealand. Nor AIDS.

I strolled towards the bar as if to buy a drink, but then quickly slipped through the exit.

I was staying in Auckland at the house of an old acquaintance, an ex-pat South African. He was away visiting in Chiang Rai with the family of his young Thai boyfriend, whom I'd never met. There was a photograph of them on the dresser, the boy looking serious, posing, standing stiffly next to his much older lover, in a suit jacket even though the photo was taken on a sunny beach. It was the type of picture you show the family back home; a strange choice, I thought, to have in their private bedroom. Maybe when holidaying, for fear of prejudice, they didn't often ask people to snap the two of them together, and this rare photo had to make do.

The boy looked intelligent. He was after all studying something impractical at university in Auckland. Education for wealthy Asians, who paid what to me sounded like astronomical fees, had become New Zealand's biggest foreign exchange earner.

Also staying at the house was another old friend of my acquaintance. His name was Rex. He was an art historian from Oklahoma, 16 hours and the International Date Line away. He had come south for the Sydney gay Mardi Gras and taken the opportunity to visit New Zealand. It was February, and he was happy to escape the American winter. We had breakfast together in the kitchen that morning.

Rex was in his forties. Once he had been tall, but now he stooped prematurely, giving him the appearance of possessing a paunch, even as he was wasting away. With his breakfast, he swallowed a regimen of tablets, which he meticulously picked up with shaking fingers, one at a time out of a plastic box, like a domestic toolkit with compartments for different sized screws.

"How d'ya like my personalized pharmaceutical Bento box?" he said. He had a thick Okie accent. Then he laughed, splattering some saliva with orange juice on the table. He had a thin ginger beard and an unkempt moustache, always a little wet. With his shaky hands, he was sprinkling cereal into a bowl for me.

"Thanks," I said. "Coffee?"

"Oh yes, coffee, coffee, coffee!" he said, his voice rising, in an unnerving way. "How long are you staying down under?" He spoke with his mouth full, dribbling milk. I couldn't watch him eat.

I poured myself coffee. "Don't know."

"You should get ya cute ass down to the Mardi Gras!" he said. He usually finished a sentence with a rising inflection in that Bible-belt way. He grasped the coffee mug with both freckled hands. "I was going to spend all my time here in Auckland, but I've been here for two days and fuck it, I thought I'd go to the coast, on the other side of the island, right to the very edge of the world, man." And he laughed again.

Rex, I soon learned, almost always gave the impression that he was on the point of erupting, a kind of hysteria brewing beneath the skin, the way he laughed with short, sharp intakes of breath through his mouth, then blowing the air out through his nose. Anger and rage at what had happened to him, and terror, painfully concentrated in that laugh of his.

"Sounds nice," I said.

"I'm glad you like the idea." He started to unfold a road map of New Zealand. "Because this is where you come in."

"I come in?"

"Look, we take the state motorway, the One to Hamilton, then Taupo, and then the Five to Napier. You drive. I don't think I should do this on my own and coach tours are for pussies."

I heard, incredulously, myself say, "Yes."

"Yes?"

"Yes," I heard myself repeating. "Let's go."

"Can we leave today?"

"Why not?"

"My *Lonely Planet* says it's just over four hundred kilometers."

"Four hundred seems to be pushing it a bit, don't you think?" I was considering his aching body cramped in the car for what I guessed would be at least six hours.

"Sure, after all you're going to be the driver. But I'm from Oklahoma. In miles, four hundred kilometers is nothing."

So it was, before noon, I found myself driving south in a hired station wagon down the state highway shadowing the Waikato River. We left Auckland behind in what seemed like no time at all, and we were soon in tame, evergreen farming country. It could have been Switzerland or the Cotswolds, anywhere in the world where modern agriculture has reshaped the land.

Rex pushed his seat as far back as it could go and slumped so low in it that I wondered if he could see the road over the dashboard. He spent most of his time resting the side of his head against the seatback, staring pensively out of the window. Rex's pants were all bunched up; from the worn holes in the belt, I could tell it had once tightened a few notches wider.

"So you got a boy at home?" he asked, still facing away from me.

"No. And you?"

"Dead." He said it in a way that made it clear he didn't want to talk more about it.

We arrived in Hamilton about an hour later. It was a neat, clean, somewhat anonymous city with white-fronted buildings and broad boulevards wide enough for an ox team to do a U-ie as they say in New Zealand. The river frontage leant it charm. We drove around awhile, but Rex said, "Nah, fuck it. Let's push on."

Along the highway, we kept seeing inviting signs to thermal springs, geysers, parks, adventure sports, but it was obvious that Rex wasn't going to be up for any of these activities. He had grown quieter in the car, calmer and less agitated, even if he kept drumming with his fingers on his thighs, and every so often, he would switch the radio on, search through a few channels, then say, "Fuck it", and switch the radio off again.

"Great pastures," Rex observed appreciatively with his eyes from the Great Plains. We'd been seeing more and more horses in the fields, and had past several tidy stud farms. A black stallion with a long dangling erection stood in profile by the roadside. Rex rubbernecked and whistled, followed by that edgy laugh of his again. I saw his hand slide, unconsciously, onto his lap and squeeze himself.

His neck suffered a bad case of razor burn, and elsewhere on his skin were the blemishes left from the battles he'd waged against opportunistic infections.

We branched off on to Motorway 5, passing through pine forests and a small town with a string of antique shops and funny corrugated-iron buildings the locals had fashioned into animal silhouettes. "Oh God," said Rex.

The landscape began to become more uneven and visibly volcanic, with numerous unmistakable conical forms. We were directly on top of the Pacific Ring of Fire.

I had turned the air-conditioner full up. I had noticed Rex was sweating profusely. "I think we should overnight here. We haven't booked ahead so we don't want to arrive too late on the other side," I suggested nonchalantly.

"No, not too late, not too late!" He chuckled, agitation again in his sing-song voice. Then more calmly: "Okay, let's find a place. I think I can get to sleep, even in this town."

Rotorua had a resort feel to it, situated as it was on a large lake. We passed a nondescript motel with a green billboard outside.

"Nope, let's not fuck around. We'll go there!" He indicated a neon sign for a five-star establishment.

"It'll be expensive," I said.

"Yeah, well, it's my treat, kiddo. And don't worry; I'll get us two rooms. I wheeze in the night, or so Rod used to tell me. I also snore. I don't know if I snore anymore, there's been nobody to tell me." He said it dryly. I assumed Rod was the dead boyfriend.

The motel was ultra-modern and a room was several hundred dollars.

"I have a small oil well on my property," he winked. "All we need now is a lovely war. Let's face it, ten dollars a barrel is nobody's friend."

There were spa facilities, a heated pool, a gym and sauna. We met downstairs in our Speedos. Besides the emaciation, there were no obvious signs of his disease, such as Kaposi's sarcoma, but it was clear to anyone looking at his naked notched spine and the rictus grin of his ribs that this was a very sick man.

We slipped into the small thermal pool. I noticed the other guests, strangers to each other as well, climbed out soon after we got in. Perhaps it was homophobia, maybe it was his obvious illness, or perhaps it was just Rex. He didn't seem to notice, and if he had, he hid it well.

We turned in early that night, tired and pink-skinned after the soporific heat of the sauna and jacuzzi. All the same, I lay on my empty, king-sized bed trying to take an interest in the New Zealand newspapers. There was almost no news about the world or anything of international consequence; it was mostly spectator sports results and sport hero worship. I watched television, skipping through the satellite channels in an obsessive-compulsive way, until I fell asleep on the bed, still in my lavish white hotel dressing gown, while Israel flattened Lebanon.

I didn't see Rex at the buffet breakfast, but when I had finished, I found him at reception, tucking his credit card away, having settled the account.

"Who needs a pension?" he snorted.

We left around mid-morning and made our first stop the famous thermal area of Waiotapu. The coach-tour buses lined up early here. The air had a distinctive and pungent odor, which was at once chemical, yet strangely earthy. There were misty fumaroles, bubbling mud and crystalline deposits in brilliant colors: cyan, sulfurous yellow, permanganate red. Watching the jets of steam escaping from the pitted ground, I wondered whether the New Zealanders weren't such a stable and steady bunch to compensate for this geologically volatile land they inhabited. On the surface at least. It might explain, too, their flipside, that crazy edge to them, their mania for suicidal sports.

We made only a brief excursion, before continuing on our journey, passing what is the islands' biggest tourist attraction, the Huka Falls.

Rex suggested we give it a miss, unable to resist repeating Oscar Wilde's witticism on seeing Niagara, "The wonder would be if the water didn't fall".

We arrived at Lake Taupo, the largest lake in New Zealand, shortly after 1 p.m. We parked overlooking the water. Rex pulled two miniature bottles of whisky out of his rucksack and offered me one. I shook my head.

He cracked open both and emptied their contents in two gulps. "Sometimes they add them on the credit card afterwards. Most times, you never hear a thing."

I asked Rex what an art historian in Oklahoma lived on.

"Oil." He chuckled. "Fund raising. I go to tea with these little ol' oil baronesses." He stretched his words satirically. "Their husbands have flatlined, and they sit on all this money, and they are bored and drink too much, and eat too much, and they get flabby and more bored, until eventually I help 'em metamorphose into beautiful, professional benefactresses."

I could easily see how with his dry, amusing patter, he made a caddish but charming old swindler.

"I take them to the hairdressers, and I introduce them to fashion designers. And we chat about art, and they get all juiced up about culture, and a sophisticated man that respects them, who sees them as mature women, not as wives or desperate widows, and then," he paused dramatically, "and then they give me a checkie for a million dollars or so for one or other museum or project I'm helpin' out." He drained another whisky, and gave a satisfied exhalation, leaving as always a few gleaming drops of moisture on his russet moustache.

"You make it sound easy."

"Oh, it's all about cultivating and networking. I do bump my head every now and again. Like when I tried to get funds for a Native American art exhibit to be staged in a museum not in a market. But the old duck's husband was still thrashing about, while we were sitting there, and from his sick couch under his blankies he was hollering, I ain't given a penny of my money for that damn nigger whittling!" Rex burst out laughing. "He's still not dead."

While he spoke, he'd taken out more miniatures, this time gin, and again offered me one.

"I'm driving," I said, starting the car.

It was a scenic trip to Napier. The geography grew more varied and changed constantly, with hills, and valleys and sweeping perspectives over a luxuriant landscape. Rex soon finished the gin and now produced two vodkas; he must have cleaned out the entire mini-bar in his room. I suspect he was an alcoholic, or at least a binge drinker. How that mixed with his drugs, goodness knew. Anyway, it was making him more amusing and less edgy.

Luckily for Rex, he had an academic position that covered his medical bills and his many sick days. He didn't like academia though, and described the head of his department as being to art what the Taliban was to Buddhist sculpture.

Finally, we arrived in Napier, a small town built up a steep hill overlooking Hawke Bay. According to Rex it started as a colonial seaside resort with Victorian and faux Edwardian architecture, but these ersatz structures were flattened by a massive earthquake in 1931. When the Crown reneged on promises to rebuild, offering instead loans with interest, Rex said the townsfolk turned to America for inspiration and that's how Napier ended up with the tourist slogan 'Art Deco capital of the world'.

The street frontage was on an accessible, human scale, like most of urban New Zealand. A local woman, a shopkeeper, told me later that day, "Art Deco was a style invented after the earthquake to build lovely buildings cheaply".

Napier had a village feel. I noticed people walking barefoot from their cars into the shops. The town's people were uniformly white and middle class and almost ye olde worldly polite. But coming from Africa, I found its homogeneity oppressive.

"What kind of a place doesn't even have Asians?" asked Rex, aghast.

There were no five-star resorts here. We took rooms at a creaky hotel in the main square.

"Siesta time," I voted.

When I awoke, it was already early evening. My jet lag had now caught up with me and was still working its way through. By the time I got downstairs, Rex was already in the snooker room with a beer. Clearly, he'd had a few.

"Hey!" he greeted loudly. "Ya'll meet my friend from South Africa!"

Rex had engaged four local lads playing a game of doubles.

"Another round of drinks for the boys!" he called out in his distinctive Southern twang. The boys had recently graduated from school and were the very image of health and innocence. They even addressed Rex and me politely with "sir", which made Rex giggle. Although they didn't seem to mind us, Rex was clearly for them some kind of bizarre life form from another planet. At first, he didn't make too much of a nuisance of himself, but hovered on the sidelines, calling out "good shot", or when they missed, "too bad". However, as the beer kept flowing, I could see his gimlet eyes developing a wicked intensity, and his gestures becoming more flamboyant.

"Ya'll so young. Youth, ah, youth! I used to have big hair once, like the Bee Gees!"

At which point one of the freshly scrubbed boys potted the black and the game was over.

"Ya'll have another round!" called out Rex, immediately placing coins on the pool table. Half the lads hadn't finished their beers and were soon holding bottles in both hands.

"What the fuck…" I could see the boy he was addressing start. Rex was asking, half perched on the edge of a low windowsill, "What the fuck are you going to do with your lives? Did ya'll learn anything at school here?"

"Yes, sir," replied the boy. It was obvious why Rex had picked on him. He wore a tight T-shirt that showed off his biceps to good effect. He was tall, but broad, thick thighed, handsome, with bushy blond hair neatly trimmed around cauliflower ears earned in the rugby scrum.

"Have you ever been outside of Napier?" asked Rex.

"Yes. We go to Hastings. Often. It's livelier than here." The boy was putting on his mature front, the way he held his drink and lifted his chin when he swallowed.

"Hastings! Well, fuck, it ain't Vegas. Have you been to Auckland?"

"No."

"Don't you want to go?"

He shook his head. "I want to go to the America, to San Francisco," came the very unexpected reply.

Rex shot me a glance and smirked. "Frisco." Rex grinned. "Why?"

"A friend of mine went last year. He's still there. He says he can get me a job as a barman. Good money, and I can see the world."

"Yeah, San Francisco will open more than your mind," drawled Rex, and again grinned at me.

"I'm sure you will do extremely well there," I chipped in to head off Rex. It was clear the boy had no clue as to the innuendo going on.

"But what do you want to become?" Rex asked, frowning.

The boy paused for a minute, then said proudly, "I'm going to join the police academy."

"My ex-boyfriend was a cop," drawled Rex, painfully slowly. "They're all liars and thieves."

There was a stunned silence; everything seemed to stop in the bar. The boy was blushing; they were all blushing. Then the boy said, politely, "I'm going to sign up next year," as if nothing had happened, as if Rex had farted at the opera.

"He's dead now," said Rex abstractly, looking at the air.

I bundled him out of the bar. I could see he was on the verge of tears. He didn't resist, but allowed himself to be led.

In the morning, we took a drive out to what was rumored to be the gay beach. It was deserted. Except, as we walked, we noticed, well-back from the shore and up on the dunes, a balding head with binoculars bobbing up like a meerkat, and then ducking down again when we turned to look. Three hundred meters further, there was another man, popping his head up with binoculars and vanishing seconds later.

"Gives gay Bob a new meaning," Rex said dryly. "Want to get you some prairie dog? I'll wait here."

"A gay cruising beach in Napier! We're everywhere, aren't we?"

Rex nodded.

We decided to drive round the bay. We stopped at a volcanic beach. The sand was black and blisteringly hot. Behind us was a line of evenly spaced American pine trees; it was unusual to see them so close to the ocean.

We sat watching the calm, flat white Pacific, like a sheet of aluminum, reflecting the thin layer of cloud, the sun burning through.

Rex stared silently, fixedly ahead of him.

"The Maoris call it the land of the long white cloud," I volunteered.

Except for the two of us, the beach was deserted. It was steep and descended quickly into the water. There were warning signs against swimming. We'd been told to keep a sharp eye on the ocean along this stretch of the island. Freak waves were common; they would come out of nowhere and sweep people out to sea. Apparently, almost every year there were incidents, when a rogue wave plucked a tourist from the beach.

Rex stood up and took a few steps towards the water. "Well, God, here I am. You've had your revenge." His voice was calm. "But I've made it, to the edge of the world. Here I am."

Daniel
OUT CLONING
Sydney, Australia

I was in default garb. I was dressed in beachwear, white Levi shorts and a black tank top, looking exactly like all the other gay boys who had flown into Sydney that week on the great gay pilgrimage. Quantas – also known by its reclaimed acronym, "queers and nancies trained as stewards" – had lost my bags.

Unlike religious pilgrimages, on this proud march to reverie sex is a prerequisite. It is this code of easy come, easy go, and greedy variety, that attracts the numbers. The annual Sydney Mardi Gras is where homosexuality has reached its capitalist zenith, where the Western gay lifestyle is today a globalized industry of magazines, travel and commerce, a fashion concept of whim and vanity, raking in billions of dollars a year.

As early as 2 p.m., people were camped out on the streets near the barriers to ensure a good view of the parade, which was only due to start at about eight.

Oxford Street was crammed with early evening revelers eating Asian street food, drinking beer from large plastic mugs or sipping cosmopolitans from martini glasses. They were out on rollerblades shopping for body jewelry or cruising for sex; celebrating the freedom of the streets and eagerly planning their drugs for the next 24 hours. I was grateful my hotel was on the other side of town, away from the frenzy of the crowds and the incessant round-the-clock noise of 20 000 of my tribe banging away within three city blocks.

The parade started the usual way, with a group of Christian protestors holding up two banners: one saying, 'GOD LOVES YOU, BUT NOT YOUR SIN' and the other, 'TURN TO JESUS OR BURN IN HELL!' The Christians marched for less than a hundred meters, boos and jeers from the crowd falling like divine manna upon their ears, elating them with a sense of martyrdom and self-righteousness. Nobody offered to pick up their crosses.

Next were the dykes on bikes, about a hundred lesbians, some topless with pierced nipples, some helmeted like Roman centurions, astride their blindingly chromed and deafening Harley-Davidsons.

A long procession of rather tacky floats covered the full range from the mundane to the definitively ridiculous: the bearded and sagging Sisters of Perpetual Indulgence, a truckload of Jewish Princesses, and a witty spoof on the film *Grease* titled Lube. To my surprise, there was also a group of black lesbians from Soweto.

As the parade petered out and pagan twilight ran its course, most of the crowds moved on to the orgiastic stadium party to watch the firework displays for which Sydney has built a world reputation.

Although there had been a brief downpour, it had hardly cooled the warm evening. One daren't enter a club wearing anything thicker than a vest. Already, long before midnight, the boys were shirtless on the dance floors, shiny with perspiration permeating amphetamines.

Waiting for a drink, a good-looking boy with a blond curl like Tintin, laughing with his friends, caught my eye. He smiled, nodded and gestured for me to join them.

"Have some lunatic soup," he said, offering me a beer.

"Haven't heard that one in a while," said one of his friends.

We made small talk about the parade. He was a perennial goer of the Mardi Gras and hailed from Cairns, where I'd just been scuba diving on the Barrier Reef. It quickly became clear he was trying to pick me up. I wasn't disinterested in him either (one doesn't exactly travel to find the love of one's life). But then he asked me where I was from. When I said South Africa, he instantly turned cold. He gave me a piercing stare with his clear-sky blue eyes, as if to say he now knew exactly what I was all about. He turned his back to me and started chatting with his friends.

I was speechless; stunned. I had not confronted this kind of prejudice for years, not since apartheid officially ended and Mandela became world president. I put the unfinished beer back on the bar counter, right in front of him so he could see, and I said loudly to the barman, "Can I get another. This one tastes like piss."

A good brawl is still not beneath dignity in Australia. But blue-eyes ignored me.

I stalked off to the lounge area on the mezzanine and dropped my humiliated self into an open corner of a leather couch. I had landed amongst a group of lesbians with crew cuts and dog tags. Until I hit that cushion, I hadn't realized how tired my legs were from walking and standing all day. Still smarting from the affront downstairs, and unpacking it in my mind, I began to brood. Ironically, it was in the belief that he was taking a principled stand against prejudiced white South Africans that blue-eyes had become guilty of bigotry himself.

"Move up," said a girl who looked like a pretty boy. I made room for her friend, a voluptuous, slightly plump, black woman, who flopped down alongside me.

"Hullo," she said, in what Australians refer to as a real Pommy accent. She had a roguish smile, short dreadlocks, a gold stud in her nose and dozens of bangles. She radiated warmth. But the very first question she asked me was the dreaded, "So where you from then?"

I said, full of trepidation, "South Africa."

"Great, at last a fellow African."

I nearly hugged her. It was my first time to be openly acknowledged as African by a black person. "I thought you were British," I said.

"I thought you were Australian!" She laughed loudly.

"God, no! Cape Town."

"I was born and schooled in London, but my mom's Gambian and my dad's from Sierra Leone. I try to get home as often as poss." She had that friendly disposition many British girls have, a smile in everything they say.

"I was just treated like I was a white supremacist because I'm South African."

She burst out laughing and squeezed my thigh above the knee. "Oh, they're so fucking ignorant here. I'll get us shooters and then tell you a story. Come on, girl, shot time," she yelled to her gamine friend, who obliged by volunteering to go to the bar. It was the vodka sours craze and we were all soon downing drinks in primary red, yellow and blue.

Her name was Vicky. She was co-editor of some or other glossy men's magazine.

"I took this coach tour, right, through the desert. All the stories you've ever heard are true, right down to the ones about the men's-only bars, where the bar counter also has a urinal with a gulley and they can stand and piss while drinking their next beer."

"That's a good idea for a leather bar," I chirped.

"Well, anyways," said Vicky, "I'm on this package tour for dummies. Oh and soon after we started, get this, right, they had to stop the coach. There were all these Chinese on the bus who didn't speak a word of English, and they were on the wrong tour. We had to wait for their bus to find us and transfer them!"

"Happens all the time," interjected her friend. "We call it Chinese 'confusionism'. It's spreading everywhere in Australia now."

"Of course, it's the Australian organizers' faults, not the Chinese," said Vicky, pointedly. "So anyways, we're in the middle of the outback and we come to an aboriginal reserve, and the guide, this stupid bitch whose been giving us this really boring voice-over, says something about how useless", and Vicky made a sign indicating inverted commas, "'the Abos' are, and how the government gives them land and taxpayers' money, but all they do is drink and fight and beat their wives. I was like, excuse me, let me off this fuckin' bus right now, I don't care if we're in the middle of the friggin desert!"

188

The Australian lesbians protested: "I can't believe that!" "How did she get a tour guide license?" "You should report it."

"What's more", Vicky continued, "there's like these Russians on the bus, and they were all sitting there nodding their heads in agreement. And I was thinking, how can this woman say these things, with me – this fat black woman – like sitting right in front of her?" Vicky then doubled up laughing.

"Because she obviously believes it's true," I said. "Australia was a great anti-apartheid supporter, but I always felt it a bit awkward given their backyard."

"So, don't you have a boyfriend, a pretty boy like you?" Vicky asked, shifting the subject.

"Why does everyone always ask that?"

"See anyone here you like then?"

"Sure, there lots of cuties, but this whole Mardi Gras thing, it's just too – how can I put it – too rapacious, perhaps?"

"Now there's a word you won't find in my magazine! But I know what you mean."

"It's like a feeding frenzy with everyone on the make. It's gluttonous. I don't find it erotic; there's no seduction, it's all a body cult."

"Yeah, it's all just hanging out there. Sells magazines though."

Vicky's friends were starting to get jealous of the attention she was giving me. It was into the small hours already, so I thought it a good idea to bow out. We exchanged email addresses and promised to hook up one day, maybe when I was in London again.

"Good luck," she said, and winked. "But be careful – there's been a syphilis outbreak this year."

I'd thought syphilis was stamped out, like polio or smallpox.

Out on the streets, the municipal workers were cleaning up the debris. There were still throngs of people about and some weird combinations, like Gothic hippies – long hair, Indian jewelry and floral shirts, but with black leather pants, coffin-kids' make-up and angry colored tattoos.

I had every intention of getting back to my hotel, until, as I crossed from Oxford Street to the Anzac Memorial in Hyde Park, I was cruised.

What made him attractive? Most likely it was because he simply didn't look as gay as the rest. His dress set him apart from us clones in our Calvin Klein. Perhaps it is simply an innate desire for the straight man's approval; the acme of homosexual desire bound to the straighter a gay man looks. He wore a red and black chequered lumberjack shirt with brand-new blue jeans and enormous tan boots. He had a large Roman nose, was exceptionally tall, with wide shoulders, his hair blond, but thinning, with a conservative side parting.

"You are walking this way?" he asked in a pronounced French accent.

"*Oui*," I replied.

He grinned.

"How was your evening?" I asked.

"Boring," he said matter-of-factly, softly dropping the 'g' and braying the 'r'.

"Aren't you enjoying the Mardi Gras?"

"The Australians all look like bulldog. We like bulldog, boxer in France, but for pet, for dog!" He laughed, showing dimples that ran the length of his handsome cheeks.

We had just crossed over the hillock in the park, when he said, "Come with me. I want to show you something."

I followed him to the Archibald Fountain. 'To commemorate the French and Australian allies in the first World War', the guidebook said.

I stepped with him, somewhat circumspectly, into the toilets nearby. A middle-aged, Asian man was standing to one side, alone, peering intently, his belt loose and his black suit trousers hitched around his knees. In the low light, I could see a line of men. Most of them older men, skins grey in the light. In the center, there were two 20-year-olds kissing and wanking one another. I was astonished; this was a public toilet in a busy park in central Sydney. You could hear the traffic roaring outside.

Nobody reacted to us. The chamber echoed with the rustling sound of clothes, the percussive scales of zips going down, the backs of leather jackets rhythmically scraping against walls, the creaking of boots, the whiplash of sleeves. The French boy grabbed me by the wrist and placed my palm on his groin. I could trace the outline of a tremendous cock. I shook my head.

"No, not here," I whispered in his ear. We slipped outside into the humid night. Behind us somebody cried as they ejaculated.

His name was Daniel and he was on holiday from Paris. His métier was wine retail; his family had been procurers for generations.

Daniel was a generous lover. His white neck and upper chest flushed scarlet – as it does with some boys when they approach climax. There was an idiosyncrasy to his lovemaking. He had one of those syphon-like foreskins, and as he came, he clamped his foot-long, curved dick tightly near the base, then, prolonging his toe-curling orgasm, he allowed his come to collect in the foreskin, like a condom. Then Daniel released it all at once. I can't say it wasn't fascinating.

I fell asleep with his sturdy arm resting across my back.

We woke to the bellhop at the door. The airline had finally found my luggage. I was grateful at last to get out of gay uniform. Daniel headed off to his hotel to freshen up.

We met up at lunchtime for dim sum in an overcrowded Asian-fusion restaurant.

"This is Kiet," Daniel said, unexpectedly slipping his arm around the waiter's slender waist, a short, slightly effeminate boy with the complexion of a buttery, wooded Chardonnay. "Kiet and I are going to his home in Thailand, and Kiet is going to show me around." He squeezed the boy. "Right, Kiet?"

Kiet smiled. He had one gold tooth.

"Are you serious?" I asked when Kiet had left with our order.

"*Mais naturellement!* I love him. And nice fucky-fucky too!"

Daniel grinned, his dimples like brackets around his mouth. I didn't know what to believe.

The restaurant was packed. My chair kept getting bumped by beefcake. They had come from all over the world. A decade ago, gay bodies didn't look like this, packaged and pumped up through weight training, anabolic steroids, ergogenic protein supplements, anti-catabolic hormones, and in extreme cases silicon calf and pectoral implants. It was a celebration of dysmorphia; the opposite of female anorexia: these men who could simply never be big enough, not until every muscle was tumescent, the veins visibly engorged, their bodies hard, until they looked like swollen cocks ready for phallic worship.

Some guys, already panicking about their age in their early forties and the onslaught of andropause, had their bodies waxed, nipped and tucked, cryolipo fat freezed, mesotherapied, carboxytherapied and Botoxed. They were left with wasp waists from popping metabolic lifters and thermogenic weight-loss supplements, the facial skin stretched against skulls, cheeks collapsed and veins protruding down foreheads. One overdeveloped older guy at the table next to us resembled a wooden écorché I'd seen in a dissecting museum in Bologna. He flashed a smile that said he'd just been on a gay teeth-whitening cruise to Alaska.

"I think they've been cloning people long before Dolly the sheep," I joked, gesturing to the room. Daniel laughed, but there was a cynical sneer in his amusement. "I suppose it's natural to want to be surrounded by beauty or at least fall in line with what is thought desirable."

"This – the *jeunesse dorée*?" Daniel scoffed. In his old-school clothes, he was still getting more looks than anyone else in the restaurant, and I had to admit I was basking in the envious stares he was getting.

"I don't know. I know it is treating people like objects, but anonymous sex is better when people get off on one another's bodies," I suggested.

"But it's too much now. Look at Kiet. So sweet, and not a muscle."

True, it was a great orgy spiraling into ever diminishing circles of narcissism, but, I asked Daniel, "Don't you suppose it's heaven for young boys who until they came to this city thought they were the only homosexual in the whole world?"

"Perhaps. For some, this is their realization," said Daniel. "To be gay à la mode. To be a gay thing. This is the beginning and the end. This is their ambition. To live gay, dress gay, talk gay, gay film, gay book, fuck gay." He shook his head. "*Non, non, non.*"

"It's better than living in a country where you get stoned to death or crushed under a wall or tortured or sent to a concentration camp…"

"*Et alors?* This is not freedom. It is ghetto."

I kept quiet. I was making peace with my own foolish youth of body fascism – Creatine, dumbbells, Gucci eau de Cologne, Tommy Hilfiger crotch, ribbed vests… I'd been so desperate to belong and to be loved. "At least we're in charge of this ghetto," I said. "Yes, we've gone from being a subversive subculture to becoming the cheerleaders for global capitalism, but without the 'pink dollar', gay lib would never have happened. And now we're getting the laws slowly changed elsewhere."

Daniel shrugged his shoulders. "*Chacun à son goût.*"

And Kiet brought us the overpriced bill.

Hiroshi, Hilton, and Jiro
AVATARS IN BED
Tokyo, Japan

Hilton was an Australian auditor with one of the big four global accountancy firms. Having experience, being a male, and still single at 40, his firm found him useful for relocations. We kept in touch by email, and every few years or so, we'd meet up in various parts of the world, depending on where he'd been transferred. I had an open invitation to stay with him in Tokyo, and I took him up on his offer.

That's when he told me his news, by email: I was most welcome of course, but I ought to know that he had a Japanese lover now with whom he lived.

In case I had any ideas about us, I suppose. I didn't, actually, and I thought it interesting he hadn't mentioned his lover before. His name was Hiroshi.

The apartment, in an ordinary concrete building in Shinjuku, was conveniently close to a major gay strip.

I should have predicted that my first impression of Hiroshi wasn't going to be what I was expecting. I thought high-status Hilton would have a flashy twink on his arm, but Hiroshi, who had a pleasant open face, was in his thirties, and like Hilton, a little chubby. Good for Hilton, I thought.

The apartment was on the fourth floor and from its open balcony, we looked over a treed park with greenhouses and a flower market. It was spring: the first cherry blossoms had sprung, the humidity was high, and the temperature hung around the low twenties Celsius.

Hilton and I caught up on gossip about people we had in common and made small talk about his work life. He'd been in Tokyo for two years already. The transfer was advantageous and the city fascinating. The alienness of its culture did not intimidate him. Hilton seemed to have acquired keen insights into the problems of modern Japanese society and the dreary lives of its urbanites: corporate power that had corrupted the entire country and its political system.

"I had always believed the Japanese lived like Scandinavians," I said.

"Yes, they have the highest standard of living in Asia if you look at literacy, health, welfare cover, but if you look at the people's daily lives, this isn't Norway."

Hiroshi had made a pot of green tea and was now sitting with us, smiling or laughing when we did, but I guess only following snippets of our conversation.

"The consumer here always gets screwed," said Hilton. "And many people only scrape by. They let in very few foreigners, mostly tall poppies like me, less than point two per cent of the population. So all the menial stuff is done by the bottom income Japanese. Even the Koreans here seem to be merchants, not workers."

"Still, it's not China," I said.

"More tea?" Hiroshi interrupted.

"Take this flat for instance," Hilton continued, "Hiroshi could never afford anything vaguely like this, and this is not spiffy by any Western standards. Three months' rent upfront, another month deposit, which you never get back, and another month as a gift to the landlord for allowing you out of the kindness of his heart to rent his apartment! Huh?"

In this tiny space, they had created work, living and leisure areas, even place for an exercise bicycle. But it was cramped. I was to sleep on a futon in the lounge area, partitioned off with traditional shoji paper screens. The bath, to save space, was dropped into the floor vertically, which meant you could have a bath, but standing, with the water filling up to your neck.

"Hiroshi has the week off, so he'll be able to chaperone you. I think we'll have tucker out tonight, but I can't have a late one."

Hiroshi smiled keenly.

That evening, before going to the restaurant, we went to a public onsen – a hot spa – one that also accepted foreigners.

"You don't have any tattoos on you do you? No little pink triangles or anything?" asked Hilton. "They won't let you in, even if it's minute."

I was looking forward to my first cultural test. I'd read up on the etiquette: wash thoroughly first with lots of soap, do not get soap in the bath, and foreigners, please do not fart or piss in the water.

We sat on little blue plastic seats in a row alongside a gutter, my long Western legs sticking my knees high in the air. Bathers lathered up thoroughly here first, until they were covered head to toe in white suds, before pouring the water over their heads. We checked each other's backs to make sure we had removed every speck of soap.

It was an ordinary place, old but clean, and busy with men of all ages and occupations, mostly city workers I guessed. There was something humane and sustaining about the declassification that came with nakedness, especially in such a rigorously ordered society. Hilton and I were the only foreigners.

There were two pools, one much larger than the other. Hiroshi was standing waiting for me, in that characteristic pose, the way Asian men tend to stand, as if permanently on those elevated clogs or *geta* with the split wooden soles, the upper body tilted forward, its weight sitting on the hips, the legs appearing bent, arms behind the back.

As nobody was in the smaller tub, I moved towards it, but Hiroshi reached out and grabbed my hand, "No, that one is too hot, not for … for you. First, you try this one."

"Yeah," said Hilton, "that one over there is Japanese temperature. You'll pass out, and that's definitely against the rules."

We slid into the pool. The water was far hotter than a normal bath. Hiroshi folded his modesty towel into a square and placed it on top of his head. "Stops you fainting," he explained.

Several of the Japanese men were bathing this way.

We relaxed, dozily. Nobody paid any particular attention to Hilton and I; people greeted with a stiff nod and that was all.

After a few minutes, I declared, "I'm going to try the other pool now."

"Too hot for Westerners," cautioned Hiroshi, shaking his head, and looking genuinely concerned.

"I don't think so," I replied.

I gingerly tested it with my toe. It was extremely hot, probably sixty degrees. I gave them a grin and slipped into the pool. Now, a rotund Japanese man immersed himself and started counting, "... *hachi* ... *kyu* ... *ju!*" His face unscrewed itself. He looked doubtfully at me. I smiled back, though I was feeling like a lobster cooking in a pot. Hiroshi laughed. Hilton looked puzzled.

"I give you thirty seconds max," he predicted.

"Very hot," said the Japanese bather, climbing out heavily, and giving me an approving final look.

Hiroshi joined me in the bath, giggling. I had passed my first cultural audition. Of course, my eyeballs and face remained flushed blood red throughout dinner at an *okonomiyaki* restaurant, where you cooked raw ingredients on a hot teppan.

"Is this my next cultural test?" I asked.

"We're *gaijin*, we're expected to make asses of ourselves. It is a great advantage. I've become quite blasé really. I break the rules all the time; it's all just arbitrary Japanese nonsense. No drama. But Hiroshi has a minor conniption every time. I try not to embarrass him. Naturally, nobody thinks badly of him.

"I suppose he doesn't want to see you as a flawed mortal before others," I suggested.

"Do you, Hiroshi?" asked Hilton.

I doubted Hiroshi had understood everything, but he had followed the gist of it, and nodded his head. "*Kampai!*" he toasted, holding up a pottery cup of warm sake.

Hilton turned to me. "And you are meant to say *itadakimasu.*"

Hiroshi happily did the cooking. The food was a bit stodgy, but it went a long way on novelty.

"You two been together for a while now?"

"Six months," said Hilton.

Hiroshi's manner was generally quiet, but upbeat. I could see how he'd settle in with Hilton's carefree way. The relationship seemed stable; to have achieved understanding, and Hiroshi was clearly a generous, kind and considerate person. Hilton was low-key, level-headed and laid-back. Perhaps their relationship involved no more than this emotional constancy, a desire for peace and order.

Did they discuss mutual friends? Did they talk about their pasts? Without fluency in a common language, I wondered how they did it; was there no compulsion to engage on an intellectual or philosophical level about life or art? Or was that not important to their bond?

Hiroshi had himself a kind and wealthy *gaijin*, who made him feel special, who needed and affirmed him. Hilton had a supportive boyfriend, and a bridge into the culture he was now living in. On some level, I am sure he desired greater intellectual stimulation from a relationship, but he had contented himself with Hiroshi's enigmatic charm. More engaging relationships were bound to come with more problems, and Hilton wasn't one for emotional trouble. Perhaps, Hilton simply needed a domestic partner, and Hiroshi had presented himself opportunely. Often male couples seem able to coexist happily in this casual way.

I was left wondering about their courtship. Had they slept together regularly? Had this become convenient and slowly drifted into what it was now? Had they talked about it and made a decision, and at some point said, "we are now a couple"?

I spent a few days with Hiroshi guiding me around the various notable districts of Tokyo and taking in the tourist sites, such as the Meiji Jingu shrine, the National Museum, a kabuki theatre, various gardens, and close to our apartment, the offices of the Tokyo Metropolitan Government from which one could see sacred Mount Fuji. Hiroshi was patient and went out of his way to show me the touristy bits. It must have been a bore for him.

Hiroshi was darker skinned than most of the Japanese I met on the streets of Tokyo, perhaps closer to the Ainu. I asked him about his family and his parents. He told me they lived in the countryside, a world away from Tokyo. Not being married at his age was a terrible worry to them. To avoid their constant opprobrium he had moved to Tokyo. Exogamy, never mind with another male, was out of the question, and a cause for great family shame.

Yes, he admitted he did feel shame about his homosexuality, but it was not shame for the love of men, but shame for the fact that he had not married. This is what flew in the face of family expectation.

"I'll swap your Shinto shame for my Judaeo-Catholic guilt, any time," I said jokingly.

"Tomorrow weekend," said Hiroshi. "Must sleep this afternoon. Late night tonight. We go out. Gay bars!"

I looked forward to a good afternoon sleep followed by an all-nighter. Tokyo, more so even than New York, really never did sleep. Besides, by now Hilton and Hiroshi must be dying to scream out their orgasms and have sex somewhere in the apartment other than hushed up in their bedroom with me behind a paper screen.

The three of us started the evening by going to Shibuya, the designer nirvana for Japan's super-affluent trendy youth. The department stores were buzzing with throngs of young girls, many in the company of men in suits.

"No, they're not shopping with their fathers." Hilton tittered. "Those middle-aged men are their sugar daddies. The girls can be as young as fourteen. They have sex with men who buy them anything they want. There is no shame or guilt in this. Nobody thinks anything of it."

Nor did anybody seem to mind the lingerie department's shop window display, which consisted of two pink mirror balls and three mannequins with different colored wigs – platinum, red and frizzy orange – dressed in nothing other than slinky, black lace underwear and fishnet stockings, American dollar bills spilling out of their panties and stuffed into their bras. The floor and the backdrop were covered in explicit erotic centerfolds of big-breasted Caucasian women, mostly blondes, several engaged in lesbian sex play.

"And there you see the *kogals*." Hilton pointed to a band of girls in their twenties, dressed up to look like they were still in school with pleated grey skirts and white shirts.

Then Hiroshi ducked into a shop.

"Oh, God," said Hilton. Hiroshi had spotted a rare Barbie doll and was having hysterics. It was for sale at an absurd price, a couple of hundred dollars, I think.

"Oh, no!" Hilton complained as Hiroshi emerged clutching a bag and smiling. "You didn't!"

After a cup of warm sake and Barbie in tow, we caught a bus back to Shinjuku Ni-Chome.

"I want to sing! I want to sing!" Hiroshi kept repeating.

"You've got to try a gay karaoke bar," said Hilton. He saw my skeptical look. He laughed. "There aren't any other kinds of bars! And it's a bit early for a mixed fetish box, don't you agree?"

I tried to imagine what that might be.

We followed Hiroshi. The bar was tiny, the size of my lounge back home. It had a serving counter, a television and karaoke machine. All patrons were Japanese, two women and about six men. The barman was portly, queenie, with long nails. Everyone there knew Hiroshi, and the barperson was admiring his new Barbie doll.

"There are over two hundred bars in these couple of city blocks, almost all of them this size," said Hilton.

Three small bowls of what looked like seaweed and rice, with what might have been pickled octopus tentacles, arrived.

"That'll be three hundred yen each," Hilton said.

I looked startled. "Did you order it?"

"No, just pulling your leg. That's the *otooshi*, you get it whether you like it or not, and you pay for it whether you like it or not. It's a big thing here; places can live or die by the quality of their *otooshi*."

"You see," Hiroshi chipped in, "that's why we have bar with no foreigner. Otherwise, always trouble."

"Many of these places have a small, loyal clientele, speaking Japanese. I think *gaijin* distorts the atmosphere for them, like having a woman in a gay steam bath," said Hilton.

"Bad to drink without food," said Hiroshi. He had already drunk most of his beer, and I could see his face blushing.

"Hiroshi, drink slower. Otherwise we'll be going home in a minute, and you'll be staring at trough lollies," Hilton opined. "It's the enzymes that break up alcohol; a lot of Asian people can't manufacture them and get stonkered in no time. Look how red you are already!"

But Hiroshi was frantically thumbing through the plastic folder of songs, looking for something to sing. In the end, he chose a Cole Porter standard, imitating Sinatra. There was no stage, instead a hand-held microphone was passed about, and patrons sang sitting where they were, at the bar or on one of the couches.

"I've got you under my skin..." Hiroshi began confidently enough. However, the words come thick and fast after that, and Hiroshi only truly managed the refrain. The videos hardly related to the songs; here were Vaseline smeared lenses of Bay-Watch type Australian couples walking on the beach. "I've got you under my ski-i-i-n," Hiroshi finished crooning.

There was polite applause.

"Another one! I want to sing again," he said, taking a second beer.

"No, my turn first." And Hilton was soon singing bad pop badly. Hiroshi sang once more, then paid for all of us.

"Okay, boys," Hilton announced, "time for a bar for foreigners with lots of *gaisen*."

Hiroshi feigned a look of disapproval. "Naughty, naughty."

"*Gaisen* are Japanese boys who only like foreigners. Sometimes they have match-making evenings; the thing to do in a town where nobody knows you." I didn't ask if that was how he met Hiroshi.

The bar had a large, rouge interior. It was closer to what I was used to, though the lights were turned up far brighter than in Western gay bars, the seats covered in a velvety fabric – the kind of material that wouldn't survive a week in Soho or Greenwich Village, and although it was nearly full, it was not particularly rowdy.

The Japanese boys stood in huddled groups of four and five, sipping drinks from glasses (not bottles), and chatting jovially, glancing out of the corners of their eyes, nonchalant yet clearly aware of any new arrivals. There were only two other *gaijin*.

I ordered European beer, which they had on tap. Hilton's eyes were cruising the room; Hiroshi, though not making a show of it, was keeping his eyes fixed on Hilton.

"To Japan!" said Hilton.

"Nippon!" said Hiroshi.

Although it was inevitable that I was in their way at times, I sensed I gave Hilton some cultural relief, a chance to chat within an easy frame of reference. Japan did not intimidate him; on the contrary, he was quite critical of the culture. He said he had little in common with his Japanese colleagues, and the other foreigners were all straight and married and experiencing a vastly different Japan from him.

Hiroshi and Hilton finished their drinks.

"Give me all your valuables," Hilton said.

I was baffled.

"No, just hand over everything: credit cards, passport, whatever crap you're carrying. So you don't lose it."

Bemused, I did as told.

"Okay, now you've got our address written down in Japanese on that card I gave you, right? And you have the keys? Okay. Now," and he pushed a bundle of notes into my hand. "My treat. I've enjoyed having you around. You can look after me when I get to South Africa. It's a deal you can't refuse! Go wild! See where it leads you. See you in one piece back at the ranch. Night! Night!" And with that, they sped off.

No sooner had they left than one of the Japanese boys sauntered over and said hello. His friends watched, giggling, then looked away, raising their eyebrows. I was the one left smiling. His eyebrows were refined, plucked thin, geisha like to my mind. He had exquisitely long eyelashes too, and eyes that naturally looked kohl edged. He wore a satiny tie, and grey flannels, and his long, thin neck, rose like a periscope from a white-collar shirt, the sleeves rolled up. His name was Ringo.

Hilton had said I would be expected to do most of the work. It was unusual to be approached by a Japanese man, unless you were a blonde European woman alone on the street late at night and you bumped into a drunken salaryman.

Ringo was at college studying to be a "knowledge worker", but he actually wanted to become a dancer. He wanted to travel the world and leave Japan. I had my doubts. I couldn't imagine what kind of choreography would suit his extremely thin body with its slender rectangular arms unvaried from wrist to shoulder.

"Why do you want to leave Japan?"

"Because I don't want to get married," he replied candidly. There it was – the brutal reality in our midst.

Conversation turned out to be an effort. He seemed to be struggling to hear me or was it the fault of my accent? I kept having to repeat myself, even though I was projecting straight into his ear, my lips occasionally touching their neat mouse-like perimeter.

After an awkward silence, he asked, "May I call my friends?"

It was obvious they had been watching us.

"Of course," I said.

He looked relieved. He waved to them. Although some way off, they were still within bowing distance, so I tilted slightly forward at the waist and bowed my head.

"Let's go over," I suggested.

There were four of them. They all looked about twelve, with downy bumfluff on their Cupids' bows, slight puppy fat under large eyes, glossy raspberry lips, immaculately smooth skins … like children. I was getting stage fright. I couldn't imagine myself taking any of them to bed. I'd feel like a pedophile. And the alcohol was starting to go to my head. I excused myself, saying I was going to the toilet, but instead I headed straight for the exit.

As I stepped out, I collided with a Japanese youth in faded jungle camouflage.

"Sorry," I said.

"*Iiyo!*," he said. He smiled, holding me by the arms, my elbows suddenly cupped in his hands. He was stockily built, well kempt, if slightly roguish looking. "Where are you from?" he asked.

"Africa."

"*Hee!*" He looked surprised. "Really! Where are you going? Why you leaving? The night is early." His eyes seemed to twinkle.

"I thought I'd try a few other places."

"Are you alone?" He was still holding my elbows in his warm hands.

"Yes."

"Don't leave now, come!" He pulled me towards the door.

"No, not here," I said firmly.

Around his muscular neck hung a decorative silver chain; he had one black pearl earring, maybe Tahitian, which suited his eyes, and a single black bangle on his right wrist.

"You like Japan?"

"Well it is fascinating for us *gaijin*."

He puckered his lips, amused. "I am born in Tokyo, but I live now in Singapore."

"Holidays in Sydney?" I gave him a complicit smile.

"Ah, yes!" He nodded his head, laughing.

"Do you know of any other good gay bars?"

"Sure, I'll show you a nice place. Come." I could see something had occurred to him. "But I need a snack, first. You like pizza?"

I was pretty hungry after the alcohol.

A hundred meters down the road, we found a cheap and starkly utilitarian fast food joint.

Jiro – that's what he said his name was – passed me a menu. It had English on it, but I thought they must have had a rotten translator; the mixture of toppings was so bizarre.

"What's *shimeji*?" I asked.

"A type of mushroom."

"Okay, *shimeji*, with beef, bacon and shrimp? And sweetcorn?"

Some of the pizzas had spaghetti on them, and mayonnaise, and lettuce leaves; I could not imagine how you cooked that.

"It's American pizza, Japanese style."

"Pizza is Italian."

Jiro's energy was contagious. He said everything at the top of his voice, as if he was inside a disco, and everything it seemed excited him. I played along as the offhand foil.

I selected a pizza that didn't cross too many Linnaean lines. "Can you tell them to hold the sweetcorn?"

"No. Don't try it. It comes as it comes. This is Japan *gaijin*! You can't make changes."

Jiro was now fiddling and texting with his mobile, and laughing, while talking to me. I didn't mind, it took the pressure off making conversation for a bit.

Jiro's pizza was a shock; it looked almost normal, with giant shelled shrimps neatly curled on top, threads of red bell pepper, and cubes of white fish, but it was pitch black.

"They use squid ink instead of tomato," he explained.

"Why, is it better than tomato?

"No, I like the color."

Jiro said he was a graphic artist working as part of a conveyor belt of creative people that produced erotic anime or hentai. This was long before 3D animated and avatar porn took the adult industry by storm.

He said he loved Singapore. As such a free spirit bon vivant, I wondered how he coped with all the restrictions there.

"They think I'm crazy. The crazy Japanese guy. But they wish they could be like me. I am also rich in Singapore. Tokyo is too expensive."

I asked him about gay life in a city where homosexuality was still illegal.

"Lots of gays. And there are good gay bars. The police look away. But I go to the straight discos. Better music."

He described examples of his work, including *shounen-ai*, which were illustrated depictions of romantic love between young boys. It was an alluring fantasy world for not only men but apparently young Japanese women too.

Jiro finished his pizza, and tucked away part of mine too.

Back on the street, he soon dragged me into a large building, and into an elevator. Alongside the buttons there were names containing words like 'freak', 'Satan' and 'baby' – and explicit ones – like 'Hotel Nuts' and 'Just Dick'. He pressed for the 11th floor.

The lift doors opened onto a wide, carpeted corridor that looked like it belonged in an office block, but with a long line of doors to apartments. Stumbling towards us was a row of very drunk, besuited salarymen, arms around each other's shoulders, at any given moment the line supporting at least one of its collapsing members. They were singing. We pressed against the wall to let them stagger past. I don't think they even saw us.

I eventually lost count of how many bars Jiro dragged me into that night. We went from one door to the next. At some we stayed for a beer. At several, after one glance, we closed the door and fled.

The bars were all about the same size, like the karaoke bar Hiroshi had taken me to earlier. Sometimes a shimmering, sequined, transgender host would come towards us, palms open, madly theatrical; at other times it was clear that neither Jiro nor I were welcome, and we were given hard, narrow stares. In one bar, everyone wore uniforms, in another, everyone had facial hair and exposed nipples. We went in and out of apartments and up and down buildings. Then at some point, he dragged me onto the fire escape in the light well of a building.

"Show me," he said.

He wanted to look at my cock. I took it out. I don't remember, but there was a noise, or a window opened, or a light went on above us in an apartment.

"We fix you later," he chuckled, clearly pleased.

We eventually landed up in some underground café, like a Parisian boîte. It had a darkroom with nobody in it, and a packed lounge with people, all of whom I think were on one or two mind-altering substances. The air was thick with noisy improvised jazz and cigarette smoke. With hindsight, I think it must have been then and there that Jiro scored the drugs.

"Now we go for fun," he declared.

As we came out of the club, I noticed a large American-style sedan with tinted black windows, and leaning against it several men in dark suits with pinstripes and black shirts, their hair pomaded, neon lights dancing in their wrap-around mirrored sunglasses.

"Yakuza," whispered Jiro.

Why did they try so hard to look like gangsters? I wondered. "What do they want?" I asked Jiro.

He shrugged. "Waiting – pimps, protection money from the club, loans, the boss's girlfriend."

They had their arms folded, sunglasses making it impossible to tell if they were looking at us. One had a bandaged hand, perhaps he'd just lost the tip of his finger, chopped off for an offence as is the yakuza way.

"They're so obvious, I don't get it."

Jiro laughed, "Japan my friend. Yakuza have their own magazines, all about them, with nice pictures. You can buy. It gives the history of the gangs, and how to sign up!"

Jiro flagged down a taxi. In the back, we slumped together on the leather seats, my one leg straddled over his thigh. I heard a disembodied woman's voice speaking English and welcoming us.

"I'm really, really, really drunk now." I chucked my other leg over his. The pre-recorded voice was reading us our rights as passengers.

After a short interval, Jiro was waving his hand and speaking Japanese to the driver. When the taxi stopped, it looked like I was back in party-town Shibuya, but to this day I don't really know where it was. The driver reversed into a parking space, and in another voice, the car started telling us we were reversing. My head was spinning.

"A hotel?" I asked, seeing the entrance.

"Yes – l o v e hotel." He breathily drew out the word love.

Check-in involved no personal contact. There was a lighted board of photographs, similar to a takeaway display. All the writing was in kanji characters. Some of the pictures were dark, the backlights switched off. I guessed those were the rooms already occupied. Jiro seemed to be having fun looking at the options. He selected one, pressing a button.

"My favorite is free!" he said excitedly.

A slender hand emerged from out of a grey curtain holding out a card with the room number on it.

A few minutes later Jiro was undressing me on a satin-like waterbed bathed in indigo light; above me, an open-petal shaped ceiling mirror.

"Best love hotel in town. I helped them. Look, I have a membership card." He'd stripped down to his black jockstrap.

A row of enormous teddy bears sat on a shelf above the headboard staring down at me with their big black button orbs. The walls on either side were large color murals of skimpily dressed Japanese manga heroes descending towards the divan. A television was on, running 70s' Gonzo porn, the sound as if it was recorded from inside a glove; the camera shaky (he must have been on the bed with them); the image green like old video; two women were giving one small cock fellatio.

Jiro tied a kind of silk tourniquet around my genitals. All I could see was the back of his punkish hair in the ceiling mirror, and his powerful, muscular back ending in his smooth buttocks while he operated.

Jiro looked up, and held a small bottle, probably amyl nitrite under my nose, and lifting his thumb I sniffed. Instantly my heart started palpitating, and everything throbbed. I saw Jiro take me in his charcoal black lips and mouth, licking with his black tongue, stained with squid ink. The light suddenly went into strobe mode. Jiro popped something into my mouth, like a sticky sweet ball.

The strobe is getting faster, the teddy bears seem to be drifting, the manga heroes are smiling, following me with their eyes. I look down and see my wrists are tied tightly together with a soft silk scarf; it doesn't hurt, but I don't think I can wriggle loose.

Jiro lights a candle; it softens the strobe effect. He is softly stroking my sides with a synthetic quill; I feel a sense of great calm, as if I'm floating, back in that rainforest in Malaysia, floating down the Tembling River. Jiro is watching my reactions closely. He produces a small joint, like a butt end; he manages to drag out of it a few puffs. I can hear the crackle of its burning end and his deep inhalations. I can hear skin flinch.

Jiro faces me, grinning, sitting on his knees next to me on the bed. The strobe light stops. I see now that familiar movement of his hand in the shadow between his thighs. He lifts the candle and drips wax on to the tips of his nipples. He laughs ecstatically, caresses his stomach. I feel it burn, but there is no pain.

"I hope you haven't read too much Mishima," I hear myself say.

Jiro pulls out a small ribbed dildo.

"I'm a top," I protest. "I don't…"

"I'll use lubricant." He grins.

The room seems to be expanding, it grows cavernous; whatever he has popped in my mouth is moving into a new phase; the walls are filling with light; the faintest variations of shadow and flicker are visible; the manga figures appear to move. Staring at my naked body in the mirror above, I feel as if I am falling backwards into space.

Then I explode. And again a few minutes later.

At some point, I must have passed out.

Images from my dream have stayed with me ever since. I do not recollect the whole sequence, but there are flashbacks as vivid as if I were opening a picture book and looking at them. The ethereal nymph-like manga heroes, with their attenuated bodies, floated down from the walls and gathered around me, their movements making no sound. They gently touched my skin with their cold fingertips. Their cobalt eyes were shiny, lit from within, and they were talking to each other in Japanese children's voices. My body gently lifted, rose a few inches above the bed, levitating. The room and everything in it, every detail, was now a drawing, shadowless, the dimensions illusory. Jiro had disappeared. I had entered his world of animation. A beautiful boy with red hair was smiling at me, and holding my hand by his elongated fingertips.

I awoke to a disorientating noise of cars. I could not have been asleep for long though, as we only had booked the room for three hours. Jiro was sitting at the bottom of the bed, still shirtless, still wide-awake, with a console on his lap playing Nintendo on the TV, and shouting at himself.

"Jesus!" I said, "I've still got a hard-on! What was in that sweet?"

"Ha-ha! Make you dream good things." On the screen, Jiro was doing 200 kilometers an hour at the Grand Prix.

"Yes, these figures … your creatures, came down off the wall and took me to their world."

"Now you know," he laughed. "And that one there," said Jiro, gesturing towards the slim male figure with a vampire bat holding onto his arm, "he is gay. See his red hair, his name is Hiroshi – my avatar."

I stared at him in disbelief; the drugs must still be at work.

"Game over!" exclaimed Jiro, punching the air as his vehicle rolled and burst into flames.

Lao Ping Lee
THE CUT SLEEVE
Shanghai, China

I arrived in China on a balmy summer day at the turn of the 21st century. The Giant Panda flexed its muscles nowhere more strikingly than here in Shanghai. On the taxi ride in from the airport, after we past 70 construction cranes, I stopped counting. There were endless skyscrapers and smart German motor vehicles cramming the roads; Bill Gates and President Jiang Zemin smiled down from billboards; posters advertised luxury goods like Rémy Martin cognac. Yes, the French were back, filling shop windows with beauty brands and extravagant lingerie. There were imported computers and digital merchandise; no more little stalls with glass cases selling rusted submarine parts, machine cogs or inscrutable bits of wire as had been the case just a few years before.

China's juggernaut state capitalism was in full throttle, freed of democracy, virtually free of irritating dissent, workers' rights and environmental lobbyists. As Western capital greedily poured billions into investments and the ruling elite siphoned it off into deposits in their Hong Kong bank accounts, the state could steamroll through forced removals, bulldoze homes for developments, fill mineshafts and sweatshops with docile labor in conditions not seen since the Industrial Revolution. China, that great "dollar opportunity", was now poised to eat that paper tiger of the West – the dollar.

I had arrived with rather different notions about China; romantic ones, inspired by the historical legend of Emperor Ai of the Han Dynasty, from back in the first century BCE. A beautiful male concubine called Dong Xian was his constant companion. (Emperor Ai never had children.) Awakening one morning, so as not to disturb his adored bedfellow sleeping on his arm, Ai cut off his sleeve, and slipped out of the bed. Homosexual relationships became poetically known as "the passions of the cut sleeve" (断袖之癖). Upon the emperor's death, his lover committed suicide.

I set off with a list of addresses for gay establishments from the internet. My reconnaissance went speedily, as the roads, by Chinese standards, were not particularly crowded. People on bicycles, chatting on their mobile phones while peddling, zipped past me. None of the places listed seemed to still be in existence however, and after ranging up and down endless side streets, I eventually gave up trying to find a gay bar in this city of twelve million.

The only demonstrations I saw of China's famed "people power" were the tidal waves of populace that stopped cars by their sheer numbers, with no regard for the traffic signals. Men and woman with little red flags patrolled crucial intersections, barking at the stoical front line of ever-mounting pedestrians. Then I saw an old woman, with long, unkempt, grey streaked hair hanging down to her shoulders, stepping down into the street. The traffic controllers waved their small flags and blew their whistles furiously. A martial advanced and just a foot away from her face, bellowed at her; I presume telling her to get back in line on the pavement. Perhaps she was a peasant from the rural areas. The rest of the pedestrians stared ahead – poker faced, determined not to be involved. Perhaps she was the sane one. It reminded me of the giant goldfish tanks at the Dongtai Lu market, where thousands of densely packed bulging fish eyes stare glassily at you. She stood, stony-faced, as if deaf, obstinately refusing to budge. It seemed a striking scene for China; one individual literally standing out, ignored by a disapproving multitude. Even the marshals gave up, and ignored her. When the lights changed, she was swept away at the head of the wave of crossing pedestrians. How many obedient homosexuals were among them? I wondered.

On Donglu Nanjing, I came across a throng of people reading newspapers displayed page for page in glass billboards on the outside of a building, stretching the length of a city block. The vast crowd of worn faces pointed in the same direction, reading, while others standing further away, with failing eyesight or poor literacy, listened to people paid to read the newspapers aloud to them.

I do not know how to respond to this mass of people, not united by an event, like a sport's game, but going about ordinary humdrum daily pursuits, united alone in common humanity. Each stood, their expressions transparent, natural, unaware of me watching them, responding to the latest developments, to death notices and sport results, to news of natural disasters and wars, to propaganda and commodity prices, to events back home and events in places they had never heard of, listening to all that wondrous churning mess we are making of the world; a sea of humanity rippling with mirth, awe, disbelief. Each face, a reflection of a family and a history behind it, each with its quirks and foibles, their personal struggles, the bottomless pits of pain and sometimes love. Taken together it produced a deep, inexpressible emotion that slowly overcame me. I found myself brought to the brink of tears. Tears – neither sad, nor joyful – simply the physical manifestation of my body going into shock, like a city person overwhelmed upon seeing the night sky in the countryside for the first time, and realizing that the stars go on and on forever, that each holds unfathomable and immeasurable mysteries, so the faces of a billion people, each a spec of light, becomes ungraspable.

That evening, I promenaded along the elegant colonial Bund, slowing my pace across from the distinctive green pyramid roof of the Peace Hotel. This strip of the Bund is meant to be notoriously cruisy. I longed for some company, for somebody to show me their great city. One of the advantages of being polymorphous perverse is that you are never short of friends to show you about. Nevertheless, Shanghai, as yet, had not opened that door for me.

A mist was coming in. The new city across the dark waters resembled the ugly shelves of a wholesaler or bulk supermarket. AMWAY, PHILLIPS, EPSON – three-story-high neon signs, bright but casting no practical light were stacked up on the opposite riverbank. Behind them rose the weird sci-fi movie architecture of modern China's Pudong skyscrapers, daunted only by their shadows thrown up like black searchlights against the fog. The word 'royal' was commonly used in advertising. Rather odd for communists, I thought. And there were other signs of naked capitalist ambition, like the retailer called 'Three Guns Monopoly Shop'.

It was the weekend and the Bund was crammed with people in rather drab Western suits, posing for photographs. Many stood far too far from the instamatic cameras with their fixed wide-angle lenses, clutched in shaking, arthritic hands by elderly relatives. I imagine hardly any of the people snapped would be recognizable to anyone outside of their immediate family, but it seemed culturally important to get the whole person in.

People were polite here, sauntering on the riverside, exercising restraint, and with great patience negotiating their way between the many camera lenses generously framing their targets. This was not my experience elsewhere. On the subway people in perpetual motion spat, pushed and shoved as if in a stampede; all purpose without logic. I would quietly stand to the side of the doors until the shoving was over. I'd then calmly step into the coach. Not only was there usually a comfortable space still left, but several motionless seconds before the doors closed. There was always time, and no train left without me. But nobody registered my silent example. Nobody was looking at what I was physically doing; they saw a foreign face, one that irritatingly, weirdly, took its time getting on the train.

But here on the Bund, people shuffled along for the most part, calmly taking the river air. Except for the spoilt progeny of China's one child policy, which were everywhere throwing tantrums and screaming at their doting parents and their four doting grandparents.

Generally, I was ignored in Shanghai, but occasionally girls would call, "Hullo *laowai!*" Foreigners, though still not commonplace back then, were no longer exotic. The old people liked to practice their French or English and I had several eccentric interchanges. A wizened man called out to me, "Hello, come sit down!" and when I declined, he curtly asked, "Why not? Why not?"

While strolling the streets of the old French concession, a distinguished looking man with a walking stick approached.

"Good-morning-sir-nice-to-meet-you-and-how-are-you?" he sang, and without pausing for an answer, walked straight past me and continued with a benevolent, "Good-bye", neither stopping nor looking back.

Once, sitting on a park bench, a man passed me walking backwards. Then a bandy-legged octogenarian drifted over from where his friends were shouting and arguing over a game of checkers. "You sit all alone. Don't worry, I will talk to you." He sat down, not alongside me, but on another bench, next to mine. "That man is walking backwards to bring him good luck you know," he said, pointing with his malacca. "These trees, you know, are over fifty-years old. Yes. The new parks don't have that, you know. You cannot manufacture a fifty-year old tree, you know. You must wait for it to grow. No factory can make such a thing, not tomorrow, not ever. This is the best park in all Shanghai!"

Back on the Bund, teenagers desiring to be hip, modern and Western, would smile and look me up and down in a complimentary fashion. I took photos for a young yuppie couple, in their leather jackets, posing near the bridge, where the Bund crosses the Wusong tributary. Next, they insisted on taking a picture of me with their camera. I politely agreed and they happily clicked away, before disappearing hand-in-hand into the crowd.

Was I ever going to find a homosexual in China?

The Chinese abhor a vacuum even more than nature. You can't stand on your own for long. People soon gather nearby, even if they make no contact.

"Excuse me, I speak English," a physically slight man, even by Chinese standards, was addressing me. He tilted his head to one side, quizzically, and smiled, smoke escaping from between his brown lips. He doffed his traditional blue Communist Party cap. "Good English. You are on your own?"

"Yes."

"Are you married?"

"No."

His smile widened. He was missing a few teeth. "You like me?" he asked patting his chest. "Tongzhi." By which he could have meant comrade, but I knew it was also slang for being gay. I suppose it was easy to spot single gay tourists by their inquisitive and flirtatious stares.

Now an attractive young man, I guessed in his early twenties, came and stood at his shoulder.

"And who is your friend?" I asked. The boy laughed.

"Not my friend," the man objected, shaking his head vigorously.

The boy laughed again, but held eye contact with me. The man smiled, his eyes moving back and forth between the boy and me, and then he burst into a chuckle exposing the yellowed teeth astride the gaps. He sucked on his cigarette butt.

"People are quite forward here," I said.

We all laughed, but I don't know if they understood; the man's eyes, like a pinball, again bouncing between the boy and myself.

The boy and I moved towards the railing on the quayside, ignoring the man. His English was more fluent. He said his name was Lao Ping Lee, but he asked me to call him Aiden. And he said he had a French lover from Toulouse, who was currently away on business.

The short man hovered for a while, before giving us a clearly derisive smile, and skulked off.

"Hard luck, ugly man!" Aiden shouted after him. "In what hotel are you staying?"

"Perhaps we should have a drink first, don't you think? Do you know any gay bars?"

"No, all closed, closed!"

I knew the authorities monitored the cybercafés and were busy clamping down on gay chatrooms on the internet. But there is always a club somewhere. Yet Aidan seemed clearly unwilling.

He had a triangular face with a delicate bone structure, flawless skin, thick jet-black eyebrows, and voluptuous ruby lips. His eyes were a magnificent, deep shiny black, and he seemed to radiate a clear intelligence.

Was this the start of a great holiday romance? I wondered.

"We go to your hotel, much better."

I had to admit, I was feeling rather tired and somewhat punch-drunk from the crowds.

We walked to my modern, soulless hotel, which was not far away, just on the very edge of the old town, where the laundry still dripped onto the sidewalks, and the roofs had clay tiles. Typical of the erupting skin of this city, brand new, glass and metal buildings were going up only days after the quaint, old brick houses were demolished, their elderly tenants evicted by local authorities hand in glove with developers.

Aiden walked close to me, almost on top of me, as it seems was the Chinese habit, getting under my feet like a cat. We kept bumping elbows and hips.

From my room, situated across from the ferry terminals, we had a command post view over the Bund. It was approaching full moon, and there was a ghostly light on the river. We stood at the window watching the constant activity of the black, low-slung barges, half-submerged in the dark waters of the Huangpu, occasionally sounding their foghorns, the deep chugging drone of the diesel engines almost drowned by a rushing sound of the traffic on the freeway, and the mopeds incessantly croaking their burnt out hooters like hoarse donkeys.

"Perhaps I shall need a guide these next few days while I am in Shanghai," I suggested.

He gave me his mobile number and said that he worked in a restaurant near Renmin Square, but he was free during the days.

Then he started to unbutton my shirt, and nuzzled against my neck, his lips pinching my skin. I flinched.

"Don't make a mark," I warned.

Then he bit my nipple, hard.

"Stop it!" I slapped his head gently. "What's this? Chinese torture?"

Aiden giggled. "Come, we must shower first."

He liked the water hotter than I could comfortably take. He was tall, almost my height. He stood facing me, with his strong, solid feet, like a Rodin sculpture, planted on either side of mine. We lathered the soap on each other in the Asian way; beneath my palms, his muscular neck, his narrow waist.

I was besotted by his looks, and started making plans ahead to spend more time with him.

Before I had even properly toweled off, he dragged me back into the bedroom. It started as a sort of tango. He kept biting my nipples and neck; then my cock, strangling it between his teeth, a rough teasing that my body found confusing. I kept flinching, withdrawing, feeling sure the bites were going to leave bruises. At times, I was more aroused than ever, then suddenly uncertain and retracting.

He leapt off the bed and crossed to the wardrobe, flung it open, and carefully positioned the full-length mirrors on its inside doors so that they faced the bed.

"Suck me," he said. He grabbed me roughly by a tuft of my hair. He was watching himself in the mirror. His scrotum was shaved smooth, and a much darker color than the rest of his body, almost bluish, the raised seam down the middle shiny; the rest of him hairless too, except for a fuzz of dense, curly, black hair.

I wanted to switch off the booming television; some dreadful game show was on, but he seemed oblivious to it.

"Suck!" he snapped. Then he demanded, "Fuck me, fuck me now."

He turned over onto his stomach, lying spread-eagled, looking back over his shoulder at the mirror, pushing his cock down so that it stretched out, visible between his thighs.

I was rummaging in my bag.

"What?"

"Condom …"

"Oh! Westerner! Westerner!" He writhed on the bed.

He didn't let me fuck him for very long.

"Now you," he said, forcing me onto my back, turning me so that we faced the mirror sideways.

"I don't—" I started to say, but he moved fast and violently. It hurt; I thought skin tore. He was thrusting hard. "Stop! Stop!"

"Turn over then, turn over". He pinched my buttocks with fingers like vice-grips. We both ended up on the floor, backs propped up against the bed.

Then he jerked off, throwing the condom onto the floor, staring at himself in the mirror, not at me.

I went to the bathroom to clean up.

When I returned, he was fully dressed and looked ready to go.

"Will I see you tomorrow?" I asked, disappointed, but cool.

"Yes, text me on my mobile." He kissed me, quite gently on the cheek, and then asked, "Can you help me with the taxi please?"

"But of course."

I went over to the small hotel safe.

He sat down beside me on the bed, our thighs against each other again. I gave him fifty Yuan from my wallet. He said, "Thank you." Then he asked, "Tell me, what does the money in your country look like?"

I opened my wallet and as quick as a flash he had snatched the US dollar notes and leapt to his feet. He was stuffing them in his back pocket. I grabbed him by the wrist. "Hey, give that back, that's actually a lot of money," I said naively, confused.

He started to wriggle loose, protesting, "No, no, I for you! I for you! I for you!" Suddenly his English had become very poor.

"Look, Aiden, that's too much money. I am not a rich tourist. I'll give you money, if that is what you came for, but let's agree on it."

He sneered contemptuously, and made for the door. I grabbed hold of him by the shoulder.

"Aiden!"

When I'd soaped myself in the shower, there'd been blood. Things got out of hand fast.

"But I for you! I for you!" he squealed.

I was suddenly enraged. Before giving him another moment, I pounced on him, bashing him hard against the wall. I think I must have winded him. He reached for my throat, with those strong bony fingers of his. I punched him in the stomach, blindly. He doubled up and crumpled sideways on to the bed; maybe I'd hit him right on the solar plexus. I couldn't tell if he was acting. Partly, I didn't care. I threw myself on top of him and turned him upside down, pulling the money out of his tight back pocket, skinning my fingers. He reached up for my throat, snarling. I struck him on the ears with my hands cupped and he let go.

"Get out! Get out!" I shouted.

I dragged him across the room by a clump of his hair, unlocking the front door with my other hand.

He looked to me on the point of tears, saying, "But I for you! For you!"

Then he snatched my hotel key.

"Give it back," I screamed.

He was standing in the hotel corridor now, laughing crazily.

"You're a thief. Give it back!"

He hesitated, and in that moment, I snatched the keys, and brought my other hand down like an axe, as hard as I could on his collarbone. He buckled. I slammed the door in his face, and double locked it in a flash.

I pushed my eye up against the peephole. I could see him getting up from the floor. He laughed, his breath misting up the lens. Then cockily, he strode off, from the back, looking as if nothing had happened.

Shaking, I sat down on the bed. Was he going to come back? Had he gone to report me? Gone to the police? I was a Westerner, a foreigner in China and homosexuality was illegal. So was prostitution. Had he gone to the reception desk? There were CCTV cameras in the corridors; my ejecting him from the hotel room and hitting him would be recorded on those.

I fell into a panic. My first thought was to get rid of any evidence. He had tried to rob me, but how did I prove it? Any evidence of sex had to go. He hadn't showered before he left. He still had me on him. I combed the sheets, like a criminal at the scene of his crime. I hastily wrapped the spent condoms in bundles of paper and luckily, there was one window not hermetically sealed. It was at a funny angle. I was on the fourth floor. Below me, I could see children throwing Chinese crackers. In the street, people filed past a burning brazier, each cocking a leg over the smoke for good luck. I awkwardly lobbed the paper missile out of the window. It landed on a tiled roof below, disappearing in a collection of filth.

Above the bed, Aiden's shoes had left wide black welt marks all down the wall. The paint was silky enamel, and with a lot of scrubbing, the scuffmarks slowly started to come off. I felt as if I was doing some form of penance. My fist throbbed and a contusion had started to spread on the side of my hand. Twenty minutes must have passed before I was done, during which I went through waves of anger, then tears, then fear.

After a while, I decided he was probably not returning. I was about to put my wallet back in the safe and lock it, when something made me check. Sure enough, there was at least a hundred dollars still missing. He must have shoved that in his other pocket. How expertly he had moved. My whole body ached with an overawing feeling of wretchedness, of betrayal. I felt raped.

On my last night in Shanghai, I was out walking the Bund again, when, as I approached the ferry terminal, I recognized, coming towards me, the man who had first introduced himself on the night I had met Aiden.

He smirked, and then, just as we passed each other, I heard him say, "A bad, bad boy that one."

Jason
ADDRESS LOST
Bangkok, Thailand

I was at a gentlemen's dinner party in Toronto, when I asked if anyone among this somewhat older gay set had recently been to Thailand. I was planning a trip. I received knowing winks and salacious smirks. At the mere mention of Bangkok, this otherwise erudite soirée soon descended into ghoulish tales about savoring snake blood in back alleys. The creature was hung on a meat hook and stripped alive of its skin, writhing before one's eyes, its blood collected in a glass, its still-beating heart offered to you like a cherry in your Kir Royale. And then inevitably there was the apocryphal story of live monkeys with their necks clamped through a circular hole in a specially designed table, the top of the skull removed, and the brains exposed for eating.

An elderly man sitting beside me said that it was utter nonsense. Thailand was a beautiful country and he was planning to retire to Chiang Mai. His pension could go ten times further there.

"The boys in the clubs and at the gym here in Toronto would as soon as spit on me as talk to me. But not the Thai boys," he said.

The conversation swept on to the thousands of pornographic sites, gay and straight, innocently labelled tourist information, but actually punting what they call 'Asian pages' with offers to download erotic photo-sets of skinny nude teens, and DVDs with titles like 'Masturbasian', 'Fortune Nookie', 'Sticky Rice Dream' along with 'Poontang in

Patpong' and 'Enter the Fist'. Thailand it seemed was the geriatric's rite of passage to sexual Elysium.

So it was no surprise when as a male traveling alone, I was confronted with sex tourism throughout South-East Asia. Pimps constantly accosted you. They'd follow you on the street, persisting with offers of "Asian babes", "very young" and "lucky-fucky". When I resolutely refused, they would shake their heads with feigned incomprehension, as if I were unnatural.

In the course of an asexual week, I worked my way from the border of Malaysia up the coast to the idyllic beauty of Kho Phi Phi, cliché of the ubiquitous tourist brochure but with beauty undiminished. I planned to avoid the more depressing and dissipated fleshpots, like Pattaya, in those days the prototype for sexual exploitation in the developing world.

I arrived early at Phuket's busy airport, with several hours to kill before my flight to Bangkok. There was no restaurant in the departure lounge, so I waited at arrivals at a bar on the first floor.

"You heading for Bangkok?" asked a bulky, sweaty man with an American accent, breathing audibly through a nose visibly clogged with hair. He'd been watching me keenly.

"Yes," I replied, rather coldly. But he was not discouraged.

"If the flights weren't so godamn full, I coulda been outta here already. Wanna beer?"

It would pass the time.

"I came in from Singapore," he volunteered. "Not much to see there, not like Phi Phi."

There's an adage in the East that goes, when Westerners arrive they instantly move "from dud to stud". He wore what looked like loose – really female – slacks, and a loud, daffodil shirt exaggerating his considerable size still further. Unbuttoned at the top, it revealed a clunky gold chain. Perched on the crown of his head was a straw pork pie hat, too small for him. His pink feet and knobbly toes spread over his white plastic open sandals.

"There are lots of great bars in Bangkok." Then plucking up his courage, he leaned towards me, "Gay bars, you know?"

I could have ended the conversation at that moment quite easily by pretending that he'd mistaken my sexual orientation.

"Yeah, I figured," he said.

An exporter of sunglasses and other plastic junk, he traveled several times a year around Indonesia connecting through Bangkok, where he was a hit with the local lads.

He took my silence as an invitation to relate with relish his experiences of boys in Thailand. In one bar, the dancing boys were suspended in cages from the ceiling and "just sweet sixteen"; they were lowered down to foreigners waving dollar bills. "Mostly Germans," he said. "All you have to do is point."

He'd heard stories of men emerging from their sexual dalliance in the backroom to be greeted by applause in the bar; the entire act having been screened live on close-circuit television.

"I like Asians," he added. "But small cocks," he laughed, sneaking a glance at my crotch. He at once snorted into his beer, and the froth splashed onto the red, spidery arteries that crisscrossed the tip of his nose. I had an involuntary visual of his cock submerged in some boy on a big screen TV in bar.

Fortunately, as it turned out, he was on a different airline.

On the flight, I was seated between a Thai woman and a squat London cockney in a conventional double-breasted blue blazer with naval buttons. Discovering this was my first trip to Bangkok, he told me I was in for a great time thanks to the "fuckin' incredible Bangkok birds". They shot ping-pong balls and feathered darts, could even smoke a cigarette "from down there". But, he chuckled, as the night wore on, their muscles fatigued and they started to miss the balloons. For the first time in my life, I felt I was getting airsick.

He was a toy exporter. "I come over at least three times a year," he said boastfully. "The missus and I first came out in the seventies, but the trouble and strife 'as never been back." And he guffawed, slapping his thigh; on his finger a thick gold wedding band.

"One tart 'ad this long, beaded necklace, you see, she threads it up your rusty bullet hole and then pulls it out as you cumming. Wicked! Phwoar! Class act." He didn't stop talking, loudly, not even when the air hostess politely twisted open two more gin miniatures; both for him. I was sure my ears had turned quite pink.

"Mind you, a lot of them these days are sex changes. They get everything fixed: silicon tits, hair implants, it's incredible. You have to look twice!"

Then for the first time, he lowered his voice, though only slightly, and leaning towards me said confidentially, as if nobody could hear him, "But some of 'em, well, they keep their cocks, don't they. Fanatics!"

From what I had gathered, almost half the sex-workers in a place like Pattaya were in sex transition. The boys were masters at teasing out the encounters with their punters and jacking them off one way or another before they got wise. Other foreigners slept readily with them, either too drunk to notice, or they didn't care; despite their protestations, they were curious and wanted a kinky experience they wouldn't try back home. These sex workers were the *kathoey* or 'ladyboys'. Rumors abounded that some sprayed Rohypnol on their nipples, a date-rape drug, allowing them to strip the john of his money.

I tried ignoring him, and paged through my glossy in-flight magazine, page after page covered in photographs depicting Thailand as a paradise of pagodas, pristine corals, saintly monks, and unspoiled beaches.

"She likes you, I think," he said, and nudged me, his eyes darting to the quiet Thai woman beside me. To my relief, throughout his tour d'horizon of Thai prostitution, she stared blankly at the clouds from her window seat, not once glancing our way, except replying to the stewardess that she wanted a still mineral water. I prayed she didn't understand English.

But now, she turned to me and asked clearly, in humiliatingly well pronounced English, "Are the two of you traveling together?"

"No!" I burst out, blushing brightly at the very implication.

"So you are traveling alone?"

"Yes!" I exclaimed, the lewd cockney's remarks reverberating in my head. I wanted her to know I had nothing to do with the Londoner in the blue blazer. If only I had acted with some nobility earlier and put the oaf in his place. I felt I needed to somehow apologize to her, to show her I was not some horrid, sex-pig tourist.

"Told you so," chirped the toy sales rep, smugly adjusting his paisley cravat and grinning.

She was attractively clad in a striking, deep purple dress with a halter neck, and a single strand of large white pearls; her hair cut in a 1920s' pageboy bob as perfect as any mannequin's.

"And where are you from?" she asked, ignoring him.

"Cape Town."

She frowned. I don't think she knew where it was. Then she asked, "Are you married?"

"No."

"You have a girlfriend?"

"No, I don't," I replied, awkwardly.

"Your first time in Bangkok?"

"He's never been before!" the Brit, unabashed, butted in, swirling his extra G&T like mouthwash.

"Where will you be staying while in Bangkok?" she asked, smoothing down her silk dress.

The Brit dug me in the ribs with all of a voyeur's excitement.

"You must be very rich to travel so young." Her red fingernail dug into my forearm on the armrest between us; casually she let it stay there, a subtle solicitation.

She had not been squirming all this time in her seat. On the contrary, the vulgar Englishman had encouraged her to make a move on me!

Fortunately, it is a short flight from Phuket.

We did meet again. I noticed she pushed her trolley with great effort, tilting forward in her high heels, all the way around the baggage carousel to where I was waiting for my backpack.

"Do you know Patpong?" she asked.

I knew that it was an infamous fleshpot in Bangkok. I shook my head, and with great relief saw that my bag was among the first to appear on the belt. She looked at my backpack with disappointment.

"Have fun, mate!" the cockney said, slapping me on the backpack. "Let me help with your bags, Miss," he said sweetly, turning to the Thai woman.

As it happened, my hotel was fairly close to the red lights. And Patpong was exactly where I ended up on my first night in Bangkok.

The brothels had first sprung up here for priapic, combat-fatigued, gung-ho American GIs during the Second Indochina War, known as the 'Vietnam War' in the West and the 'Resistance War Against the Americans to Save the Nation' in Vietnam; both titles ignoring the civil war nature of the conflict, and the many other countries drawn into its devastation.

As the weather was threatening rain, though it didn't seem imminent, and as Bangkok's notorious smog had unexpectedly lightened, I went by motorcycle taxi. This was long before the city was at last rescued by its subway system. Red vested motorcyclists hopped around the city like fleas. It's an effective method for zipping through the snarled up traffic with the added benefit of wrapping one's arms around a well-built Thai lad with a rugged set of abdominals, though it was speed that he seemed to get off on. I imagined from the way my man diced with the cars that he lived life as if it were in a fantasy video game, dodging trucks and shooting through the gaps that briefly opened in the cross-traffic. If I had not kept my legs tightly squeezed against his, I would have lost my kneecaps.

On that first trip, Bangkok had no real appeal or distinct identity; it was yet another vast Asian metropolis congested with humanity, the filth and blight of rapid, inexorable urban growth.

A few novelties gave Bangkok its local color, like the flocks of monks that glided past in their saffron robes; the occasional elephant on the city pavement, usually a wretched creature ambling next to its rustic owner, who on catching a tourist's eye, beat it with a stick to perform trunk lifting, and then they both begged for a handout.

The traffic never dwindled, not even at night. In the dark, the city took on a psychedelic quality, the hot tropical air electric with pink and rutilant neon, the humidity enough to wrinkle your fingertips.

Walking through Silom, I saw boxing rings with perspiration-shiny Thai boys in silk joggers, viciously bashing blood from each other's faces; the onlookers, many women, many European, shrieking with delight.

As a traveler, I have figured out signs written in the Greek or Cyrillic alphabets after a few days, but the syllabic Thai script was impregnable. There are no spaces between words, thus: »มาเถิด ให้พวกเราลง ไปและทำให้ภาษาของพวกเขาสับสนที่นั่น เพื่อไม่ให้พวกเขาพูดเข้าใจกันได้« (Genesis 11: 7). Developed by a succession of Thai kings, the most recent by King Narai in 1680, it left me, for the first time in my life, experiencing the world as an illiterate.

Few people know the full Thai ceremonial name of the city, Krungthepmahanakhon Amonrattanakosin Mahintharayutthaya Mahadilokphop Noppharatratchathaniburirom Udomratchaniwet-mahasathan Amonphimanawatansathit Sakkathattiyawitsanukamprasit, which is why we call it Bangkok.

My guidebook listed several gay clubs in the vicinity. I canvassed them, barefacedly ignoring the numerous pimps. In one bar, skinny Thai boys were parading on the stage in wet-look, ciré jockstraps, with numbers handwritten in felt pen on their backs. In another, I caught a glimpse of a bizarre Boy Scout pantomime, a naked master with a pith helmet, a submissive cub, and Kipling's Mowgli watching from behind a cut-out palm tree while fiddling with his crotch. I moved on when challenged to pay a cover charge.

From the descriptions, the most promising bar was at the end of a cul-de-sac, off Soi Surawong. I hesitated to go down the narrow alley. But some pimps had started to harass me. Exasperated, they were no longer offering me men and women, but children under their breath. I fled.

The bar was laid-back, and at least not conspicuous in its sleaziness. Everything inside, including the leather, was pink. I sat on a barstool near the entrance, watching the foreigners, mostly German and French, come and go with their Thai boys in tow. These invariably older Europeans, sometimes American, caroused together, anchored to their beers, drunkenly enjoying each other's company, while their Thai escorts stood out on the pavement chatting, smoking and waiting patiently. Several of them winked and smiled secretively at me.

Other free agents appeared from time to time, asking arbitrary questions. Their approach was simple: "Hello, you like me?"

They came and went between street and bar, working the room, trying to engage anyone who reacted. They were mostly ignored. Many of these boys looked poorly: sulky, yet agitated, raccoon eyes, dark blotched skin from acne, unkempt hair. I guess they were strung out, waiting for some foreign trick to cover their drug habits.

In this Bangkok bar, there were once telephones on every table, enabling you to call other patrons.

Here I met Jason.

We'd been eyeing each other for a while. "I'm sorry to ask," I started off, awkwardly. "I'm new in Bangkok, so forgive me – you're not a sex-worker are you?" I could feel myself blushing as the words came out. I hid in my beer, gulping sheepishly.

But Jason laughed, lips rising on perfect, pearly teeth. By way of apology, I told him about the woman who hit on me on the flight in.

Jason was quite unoffended. On the contrary, he was at pains to convince me of his credibility. He said he was on vacation visiting his family; he was enrolled in his second year of economics at a university in Perth. He was soft spoken, yet energetic. He regarded me silently for a minute. He had one congenitally sleepy eye, the left lid drooping slightly, adorably. Then he said, "I can't believe I am doing this!"

"What do you mean?"

"I have only met you. I do not do this."

He giggled; I was willing to believe him.

"Well, I'm flattered," I said, perhaps somewhat manipulatively. "I'll buy you another beer."

He'd learned to drink in Australia.

"I can't believe I'm doing this … And you're from Afrika!" He gazed at me, marveling.

"To Africa!" I toasted.

"Do you like black men?"

"Yes," I replied. "Do you like black men?"

"No. I do not think so. Like aborigine. Oh! The hair!" He gasped, queenily, then added, "No, Thai like *farang*. *Farang* like Thai. Perfect." He smiled, crossing his fingers.

"So you have a thing for Europeans."

"Yes, me – potato queen!" He had a boyish laugh.

"Now you're an African-potato queen."

"Ah, this is my lucky day. And it's not even Thursday."

We finished our drinks and Jason volunteered to show me the night markets. Outside the air-conditioned bar, a tremendous thunderstorm was building, the neon lights whited out by intense flashes of lightning.

We walked together around the tourist night bazaar, where I steadily negotiated away all the cash I was carrying. Haggling was a form of relatively cheap entertainment. I bought three fake brand name watches and a small collection of bright Thai boxing shorts. Jason didn't intercede between the sellers and me, but every time I did strike a deal, he'd say, "You got a good price!" or "You good bargainer!"

And he looked at me approvingly, I hoped with some fondness.

A massive cloudburst ended our night on the Sukhumvit markets.

Jason waved down a cab to take us to my two-star hotel in a small soi off the Phaya Thai.

Bangkok wasn't the modern city it is today. We ploughed through the fast-rising waters; a dead dog buoyed up on the flood floated past. Any more rain and it would be coming through the doors of the taxi. But the downpour was short-lived and, by Bangkok standards, negligible; only, Jason said, all the drains were blocked, since it hadn't rained for weeks.

I wasn't sure what to expect from the concierge at reception when she saw me with a local boy in tow. But when we arrived, she was, thankfully, fast asleep next to the telephones, her head resting on her arms. I found that common in Thailand: people doing several jobs, exhausted and bored to sleep by at least one of them. We tiptoed past her and up the carpeted stairs.

I'd hardly closed the door and Jason had already linked his arms around my neck and started to kiss me. Startled, I unclasped his skinny arms by the wrists and physically sat him down on the bed.

"Tea?" I offered, and without thinking, ruffled his hair. "Oh shit! I'm not supposed to do that, am I? Touch a Thai person on the head?"

"No, don't worry. Yes, it's true, but it depends on the context." He laughed, and took my hand and placed it firmly back on the crown of his head.

I made green tea, boiling the water on my handy camping gas stove. We spoke about his university courses. He said he was the only Thai student in his economics' class. He had one close friend, a Thai girl, who was studying industrial psychology. It was clear that his parents were wealthy, but as a young gay man, he felt freer in Australia.

I was sipping my tea when he took the cup out of my hand and began to kiss me again, pulling me down onto the thin foam mattress, too wide for the narrow metal bed.

"Ah! You *farangs*, you have big big cock."

He lay on his back; his hard, slender, hairless body pinned beneath my ribs. We didn't stop, even when the precarious bed finally tipped us over onto the floor, his heels digging into my back, and I could feel the cool draft along my spine from the air-conditioner humming under the windowsill.

I was close, but he kept saying, "No, wait, wait. Not now, not yet, please, not yet." Jason moaned, his balls swelling into one big, shiny globe the way some boys' do, his lower abdomen like a drum, taut and tensing with each jet. He splattered the floor well above his head, and burst out laughing.

We lay next to each other on our backs, spent, wet with perspiration, my skin sticking to the floorboards.

"How long are you staying in Bangkok?" he asked, taking hold of my hand. But it wasn't simply that he held it, it was the way he looked at it too, studied it as something precious.

I explained that I wanted to go to Vietnam, and it depended on the time the visa would take to organize; there was no consulate in South Africa.

"But you have to see the royal palace," he said.

I pulled out my guidebook and we looked at the pictures of Thailand. I turned to the preface, which had a section on decorum in the East. It pleaded with tourists to behave respectfully, since, it said, the Thais had come to regard Westerners as "wealthy, decadent and promiscuous".

"But we are!" I laughed.

Jason giggled. "You guys from the West, I think you are very brave. You never get Thai people traveling alone like that."

He was quiet for a while. Then he asked, pensively, "But why did you come to Thailand? Was it for boys?"

"No," I said, which was partly untrue. "Not only. I've been many places, but I wanted to see the East. It's so beautiful. And it's interesting. For the first time in my life, I am in a society where I am illiterate. But Thailand is without question the friendliest country I've ever been to."

"So, we meet," he said, bestowing us with the inevitability of romance.

In the morning, when Jason left the hotel, the concierge – still the same unfortunate young woman on duty – didn't betray any expression. She presented me only with my laundry and the bill. Jason spoke a few words to her in Thai, and they both smiled, and laughed amicably. He was a charmer, alright.

We spent several days together sight-seeing. He took me to the Damnern Saduak floating market with its visually appetizing colorful produce sitting incongruously on a stinking canal; the magnificent Royal Palace complex of which Jason was clearly very proud; the Wat Arun on the river; the giant reclining Buddha of the Old City; the house of the mysteriously disappeared Mr Jim Thompson. We had a picnic in a leafy green park, as unexpected in Bangkok as our short, intense affair.

My holiday romance with Jason was the very last thing I had expected to find in notorious Bangkok. Sex, yes, but not this. We sat eating our duck spring rolls from Tupperware, watching youngsters fly kites, while others sang for one another, and a handful of old people practiced their graceful, solitary Tai Chi. Nearby, a few novice couples learning ballroom dancing in the open air kept standing on each other's toes.

In no time at all we found ourselves at a hole in the wall restaurant near Siam Square – a lunch to say good-bye. Jason was flying back to Perth that afternoon. I was grateful he would be leaving first, as opposed to the usual scenario where the traveler rolls on, able to distance himself quickly as he faces new challenges, leaving the people he has touched behind. This time I was the one to be abandoned, and I was glad for Jason.

Around us, a few mangy, tailless cats mewed for our attention. The minute a patron stood up, the cats were licking the plates.

We settled the bill, and Jason as always was scrupulous about paying his own way.

"For you," he said, and with both hands outstretched, he offered me two black and white passport-size photographs of himself: one of him as a schoolboy, bareheaded but in a sombre elite-looking cadet uniform with lapels and badges; the other, more recently taken at university enrolment, in a white shirt, looking serious about his economic studies. I was to keep these in my wallet, he said.

"I wish I had something with me in return. We should have gone to one of those passport photo booths, the way they do in Hollywood love stories."

Jason smiled softly. He promised to email me when he got back to Perth. We even made plans to try to meet up in Mauritius the following year on his family vacation. On Siam Square, we wished each other well, and in a rare display of public affection for a Thai, he hugged me. After that, slowly, waiving, we each walked away, vulnerable with that melancholy combination of freshly discovered attachment and raw sentiment.

This was before Facebook and social media, before mobile and smart phones made it so easy to keep in touch without seeing one another for years; before the digital age created wormholes through time and space and shrunk a vast world to fit into the human mind held in a human hand.

I never heard from Jason again. I hope, that like many boys his age, it was simply only my address that he had lost.

Muhammad and Terrence
SINGABORE
Singapore

I hadn't slept in over 24 hours. As I climbed into the airport bus, the morning chorus of raucous tropical birds screeched from their camouflage of matted, soggy green vegetation. At one degree north of the equator, my head had fogged up like a closed bathroom after a hot shower. I could only take in ghostly impressions, the way traces left by fingers reveal themselves on a misted mirror. I do not remember much of the trip into the city, except that the coach was packed, and I stood the whole way, hanging onto a metal hoop, balancing my backpack with my legs perspiring against the canvas. My body was in combat with this radical new environment; trying to breathe, stay cool, defend itself against bursts of harsh sunlight breaking through the trees.

I alighted in the general vicinity of the budget hotels and started going door to door, peering through squinched up eyes at one backpacker lodge after the next, each one a disappointment. Everything I could afford was fully booked.

Eventually, I was directed to some derelict accommodations that would just have to do. At least everything was clean, if broken: the wrecked Venetian blinds dust free; the Medusoid wires that hung loose from the ceiling wiped clean; even the cracks in the plaster vacuumed. The bedspread had several smokers' holes in it, but smelt of fresh synthetic apples. The enamel bath was flaking, and a clean, bleached rag substituted for a bath plug. There was no hot water for shaving. This was not the Singapore you read about in travel magazines.

After sleeping off my jetlag, I was keen to explore the city streets. My new neighborhood was far from the super modern city I had been expecting. You definitely would not attempt to eat off these pavements. Every now and again, a nauseating stench of fish sauce burning in cooking oil that had turned black wafted across my path. Contrary to what friends had said, Singaporeans did jaywalk, did smoke in the streets, and did litter, but they resolutely did not spit on the pavements the way people did in China or chew gum like Americans.

I wandered the streets for hours. I worked my way down Little India and through the Arab district, passing temples and mosques, acupuncture centers, foot doctors and stalls with quacks of various self-description, endless rolls of densely patterned fabrics, innumerable gold shops, 'wet markets' of fresh produce, and an overabundance of eating stalls.

Eventually, I reached the legendary Raffles Hotel with its iconic doorman, a seven-foot Sikh in gold livery with an impressive turban. A travel-writer friend had once done a piece on a specialized restaurant at Raffles run by an apothecary-chef who, on asking after your ailments, produced a customized menu which might include *lu bian*, a deer penis and ginseng bouillon, or Japanese fugu, the deadly, toxic puffer fish, its milt carefully extracted as a delicacy. There were sautéed praying mantises, deep-fried scorpions, and chocolate covered scarab beetles too.

I continued west along the famed Orchard Road with its uninspired modernity that came closest to Singapore's export image. It was an eerie sensation waiting at the traffic lights amongst a vast mass of people, none of whom said a word.

Outside one of the glass and concrete banks, sitting at a desk on the pavement, were three good-looking young men in spotless white shirts with thin blue ties. A small sign on the table read: Public Share Offer.

Nobody was paying any attention. It seemed very odd, even in commerce-mad Singapore.

At the Christianity Supermarket, piles of books, racks of Evangelical CDs, and shelves of kitschy plastic religious paraphernalia took up a block-long window display with offers of special 'lunar discount' prices. Lunar New Year seemed to be an extended affair, as big a marketing idea as Christmas. You could even get a MacLunar Burger.

Earlier, I'd seen a toy, battery-operated, foot-high Father Christmas in his red suit and white beard, gyrating a hula-hoop to Elvis Presley's 'Rock around the clock'. This fervor for religious consumerism did not always translate well across cultures, like a Father Christmas nailed to a crucifix.

I sat down at a corner pavement café. It was rush hour for pedestrians. A seemingly endless stream of faces floated past me in virtual silence. I was clearly no longer in Africa, where we like to make a lot of noise. The demure mood, the constrained expressions, the quiet orderliness created an impression of undifferentiated humanity. From the waist down however, they were much like New Yorkers, pounding the pavements, briskly getting between home and work.

Watching the concourse, I wondered whether I'd be able to identify any gay people. Obviously, there were gay people here as everywhere in the world, whether you're among the Salt Lake City's Mormons or the Pashtun Taliban, but would I recognize one of my own in this culture, a culture utterly foreign to me?

Back home, I can make an educated, usually accurate, guess about a stranger. The kids picked on and bullied at school for being gay were more often than not straight. I would bring gay friends home, and my parents and brother were utterly clueless to what was going on. Our kind knew who we were. Entering life, I thought I possessed some secret psychic power. Then I found it beautifully articulated by Proust in his magnum opus, in *The Cities of the Plain*, how gay people can identify each other, while straight people cannot tell, a mystery that led to comparisons between vampirism and homosexuality.

Vampires too can identify one another, but appear normal to strangers, until they transform after dark and go about their corrupting in the secret of the night. Like homosexuals, they are depicted as heretics and seducers – immoral and predatory. Once they have sucked on you, you are in danger of becoming one; a popular prejudice long held about homosexuality too. The thin, elegant, wealthy, aristocrat Count Dracula in his tailcoat calls to mind the artistic, dissipated, stylish, decadent 'invert' of the nineteenth century. Moreover, like the homosexual, the vampire, neither living nor dead, belongs to an ambiguous in-between category – neither entirely male nor female, the undead. Homosexuality, despite the best attempts of religion, is stubbornly immortal.

In my own culture, I am seldom wrong about someone's sexuality, or their vampirism for that matter, unless wishful thinking overtakes my better judgement, or if the person has not quite figured out for himself his sexual idiom and sends mixed signals. "But how can you be so sure he is?" straight girlfriends always asked, mystified and disappointed. The phenomenon has been dubbed gaydar.

I scanned the pedestrians. At once, so soon that I had to doubt myself, I noticed two boys walking towards me. They were some way off still, but I instantly took them to be gay. They were laughing and chatting animatedly for Singaporeans; so they were definitely gay in that sense. They were also immaculately dressed and groomed. The taller boy appeared to me ever so slightly camp. Effeminate camp seems to be universal, but is – more often than people tend to think – not coincidental with homosexuality. Perhaps he became aware of me watching him. He adjusted his tie, though it needed no adjustment, and ran his fingers through his perfectly straight black hair.

The two of them slowed as they walked past. I waited for the moment of truth. Yes, they did look back over their shoulders.

Realizing that I was still following them with my eyes, they paused, turned in my direction, and backtracked towards the restaurant where I was sitting. At that moment their courage failed them; they both changed direction, bumped into one another, and slightly confused about what to do next, sat down at the neighboring café. They ordered soft drinks, but kept glancing across at me. I felt awkward and fidgeted in my seat, my heart quickening. Did I really want to speak to them? I looked away, my courage failing too.

The waiter interrupted with slippery *phad thai*. Being left-handed, I'd probably appear an uncouth foreigner to them. When I looked up from my plate, the boys' eyes were fixed on me, and the three of us became ensnared by an instinctual recognition. They had identified me too as one of them, though I was probably more conspicuous here in Singapore.

They laughed, and signaled to me to join them. I pointed to the food that had just arrived, and raised my eyebrows as if helpless, but they called out, "No ploblem! Come."

The waiter – jowly faced, expressionless, peeping over his puffed cheeks – made no move to stop me migrating with my plate to the other restaurant.

"Where are you from?"

"South Africa."

"Af'ica! But you not black?"

I told them there were many whites in South Africa. The biggest problem when traveling was to explain to people abroad, firstly, how you could be from Africa and not black, and secondly, how you could be white, from Africa, and not terribly rich.

Terence sold sports' shoes and Muhammad was an air-conditioner technician. During our conversation, Muhammad kept mentioning that his grandfather was Irish. I wondered why he felt it important to insist on this. He had very dark skin, and luxuriant black hair; to me he looked as if his progenitor may have been Indian.

It wasn't long before they started to complain about how restrictive Singaporean society was; a refrain I was often to hear.

"Too much control. It is no good for young people. Singa-bore we call it!"

I pointed out how little crime Singapore had. There would be even less crime, they laughed, if ordinary people, like homosexuals, were not made criminals, and where so many trivialities, as petty as chewing gum or failing to flush the public latrine were not illegal and punishable with imprisonment (an urban legend, surely).

The gay scene, they said, was still underground. People cruised more than clubbed. I suppose the city fathers, at that time still guided by the grip of that legendary authoritarian Lee Kuan Yew since the 1950s, faced with a declining population, could not bear to see any sperm wasted. In fact, trying to coax sperm out of their population had been an unsung obsession of the government for years, at various stages involving state subsidized pleasure boats for youthful lovers, and even a eugenics program with free housing for beautiful young newlyweds. Until, that is, foreign observers pointed out that a similar plan had been devised in central Europe during the 1930s by someone called Adolf Hitler.

Money and wealth were national obsessions; Muhammad and Terence, peppered their conversation with economic jargon, talking about equity, the consumer price index, the country's liquidity, and GDP, and voiced their concerns over another currency crash in the East. This is not usually how gay boys chat one another up.

The boys said they had to get away from Singapore twice a year, but had no interest whatsoever in visiting me in Africa. It was all gay catamaran cruises on the Great Barrier Reef and beach parties in Cairns for them. I wondered how they could afford it.

"Sydney, A-one!" Terence kept saying, giving a stumpy thumbs up. He was the camp one, with high cheekbones, the ramp model Asian features that had only recently started to find favor with the European fashion industry. I noticed how power-dressed women passing us gave him a second glance.

It was overcast, the light grown crepuscular, and it was comfortable to sit in the tropical outdoors. But I could sense they were getting ready to make a move. The boys were still in their work clothes. They both gave me the numbers for their pagers, which they wore proudly on their belts.

"Where are you staying?" Terence asked.

I named the lodge and held up my key ring with its purple, glass evil eye. It was a malevolent-looking thing clearly designed to deter guests from making off with the room keys. I still use it to this day.

Obviously, the boys had never heard of my hostel. Muhammad offered to walk me back, but Terence said goodnight, shaking hands. I was a little disappointed, he being the prettier one.

As we climbed the stairs to my room, Muhammad grew quiet. I was struggling to make conversation. It felt as though we had created a tacit obligation from which both of us were too courteous to extract ourselves now. I thought him handsome, but it was now more about the expectation of sex than any real physical attraction to him.

My room was hot and humid. I switched on the fan, which hummed for several minutes before it started to turn. The air-conditioner was hopeless. There was no room for preliminaries here. No tea or coffee or drinks to offer. Without a word, Muhammad stripped off his shirt. His skin was hairless. I felt increasingly self-conscious, especially about my sweaty socks, from all the walking. I excused myself and went into the bathroom before I dared to take my boots off. I washed my feet under the cold tap.

When I returned, Muhammad's clothes were folded up tidily on the chair. I watched him take his wristwatch off, check the time, then neatly place it on the bedside table, standing up like a clock. He lay on his back, straight as a plank, naked, his cock flipped up on his tummy, so rigid it could hardly be lifted. A kiss seemed out of the question. I took off my clothes. His silence was total. As I approached him, he unexpectedly switched off the light.

Within hours of landing, here I was naked with a stranger I'd met two hours ago, in a foreign culture and country I had never been to before, having somewhat mechanical sex. I presumed it was the same for straight people, only easier.

AIDS crossed my mind, because of the ignorance surrounding it in this city-state. I need not have worried; Muhammad was sexually reticent. At first, I thought there might be some or other etiquette at work of which I was ignorant. But his short, ecstatic breaths, and the force with which he came, within moments, suggested instead a combination of sexual inexperience and pent-up desire. The light from the bathroom door fell across the bed, and I could see his shiny come start to run like tears down his side. He leapt up and dashed to the toilet. I could hear him rubbing himself with a sponge, followed by the sound of the shower.

He returned with a towel modestly wrapped around his slim hips. He patted the bed to check if there was a wet patch. Satisfied, he lay down next to me, and took me in his hand delicately with his fingertips. I thought, given our huge difference in size, he might have made more of it. I felt hopelessly self-conscious with him lying there, waiting patiently, politely for his barbarian lover.

EPILOGUE
India

Our flight came in over the subcontinent shortly after midnight. I was entering India through the great gateway of Mumbai (formerly known as Bombay). Already from the air, there were clues as to what awaited me.

In the blackness below, mapped out in yellow lights was a great question mark, itself a puzzle, possibly a giant bridge or a causeway. Where the city should be, there were only vast areas of dim lights, and vaster areas of darkness and mystery beyond. Out there in the suburbs below, leopards still made a habit of emerging from the jungle and eating people who thought they were living in the 21st century.

Chhatrapati Shivaji International was itself half dark, unlike our wasteful Western airports where immense areas of empty tarmac are always illuminated.

If Mesopotamia represents the cradle of civilization, then India is our umbilical cord stretching back to prehistory, a living past that is simultaneously as industriously engaged with computing, genetic engineering and space exploration as it is with worshipping a pantheon of one million ancient deities. Imagine arriving in Egypt today and finding people still worshipping the gods of the pharaohs and writing in hieroglyphics. India has taxes first levied in the time of Buddha that remain collected by the modern state today, as there are still two-thousand-year-old laws and millennium-old irrigation systems in daily use.

India and its customs are bottomless and unfathomable. There might be a wise old man or a guru who has a theory, but nobody has an absolute claim to the truth, since there is no single canonical text, such as the Bible or Qur'an. India simply does as centuries of practice have taught and as the community sanctions. The Western tradition with its keenness to dissect and find 'the bottom line' to everything, will usually leave India defeated.

During my time in India, it felt as if a million fairy tales could come true each day, but never did. India is sublime and wretched. India personifies for me the human enterprise.

As we came in to land, for some reason, I don't know why, I suddenly recalled a terrifying story of modern neo-cannibalism. Years ago, a syndicate had made a business of hunting down and killing children abandoned on the streets of Calcutta. Their organs were harvested for transplants in the West; a few of their small, perfect skulls turned up in undergraduate anatomy classes in the United States. I learned later, that the gruesome trafficking and sale of kidneys to raise money for a daughter's dowry, pay back an indenture, or stand as collateral for a loan to study at university, was not that uncommon. A swathe of rural southern India has even been dubbed macabrely the "kidney-belt".

However, for all its misery, India has never suffered any of the great ideological and religious purges of the last two millennia. No Mao, no Stalin, no Charlemagne. The society has never been revolutionized in those murderous ways. Neither conquistador nor inquisition nor Reformation. The old Gods remain. And it is a much happier place for this.

There were brutal rulers and conquerors, but they were absorbed into the society. Except the British, who seem to have existed in a parallel universe. Even the Mahatma, whose mass passive resistance delivered the subcontinent its independence, has otherwise failed; his grand ideas for social engineering mostly shrugged off by India. He is a tourist monument, now.

"India's greatest, most important, historical figure," says my very informal guide in Delhi.

"Why? What did his life teach you?"

Shrug. "Many tourists come, also Indian tourists." He smiles.

The new conquerors – globalization, urbanization, capitalism – are being absorbed too, and altered, metamorphosed beyond recognition by India. The notion of gay rights is one such area.

Flying may be far more convenient, but the use of trains is for many of us visitors the blood transfusion on entering India. The best part of it are the porters with their distinctive monochrome dust jackets – red, pink or yellow, depending on the station – and plain turbans, under which they keep a stabilizing ring to help carry bags on their heads. At train stations, I would cautiously watch the comings and goings of porters, and then choose one that I decided was the most competent, polite, and trustworthy. He was invariably the most handsome. None I encountered ever spoke English. We'd agree on a price, maybe ten rupees a bag or some such negligible amount. From the moment you engage the fellow, he will do everything, lifting your bags on to his head, glancing at your rail ticket and walking directly and smartly to the platform.

Once, when I did not yet have a confirmed sleeping bunk, my porter disappeared to find the stationmaster and returned shortly afterwards with a carriage and bed number. If other passengers placed their luggage in such a way that there was no room for my bags, which happened frequently, the porter would simply remove their bags and make sure that mine had priority. No passenger ever dared to interfere with the activities of a strapping young porter.

Sometimes a platform number is changed at the last minute. I would never have heard these announcements, but my porter would and immediately transfer me to the correct platform. As we pulled out of the station, I'd watch with great satisfaction little clumps of tourists staring perplexedly down the railway line for a train that never came.

Tourists in India are a wonderful source of cruel amusement. Unwilling to part with a few cents, paranoid and suspicious, unwilling to hand over their belongings to an Indian stranger, I would watch them struggling up stairs, dragging their bags, wandering around stations, lost and panic stricken in the chaos that always ensued as a train pulled up to a platform.

Now, a porter will jump on to the train before it has even come to a halt, block the door, fight his way down the aisle and in the pushing and kicking, sometimes I swear even biting, wedge himself into a seat and secure it. He will not move until you slip into it from under him.

Yet the instant the train pulls away, passengers that had been at each other's throats moments before are opening food and offering each other ladoo sweets.

On the overnight sleepers, people generally settled down to slumber quite soon after departure. In second class, there are three sleeping berths opposite each other in the length of the subdivision, and across the aisle from these, in the length of the coach, another two berths. I usually reserved the top bunk, but not the one directly opposite the ventilation shaft, which in the north in winter can be terribly cold. Indians did not like the top bunk, whereas I preferred to be above the boisterous games and pecking orders of the gangs of free-ranging children below.

One night, I was on the bottom birth, turning over in the small hours. In the gloom, half asleep, through partially closed eyes, I discerned the silhouette of a bearded Sikh with a large turban sitting on my bed, his lower back touching my shins. It was strangely comforting, almost a romantic nocturne.

Conversations with my fellow travelers invariably began with, "From what country are you?" Next, "What work do you do?" And often, "How much do you earn?" This last question was tricky. Looking in the local newspapers, I was shocked at how little people were paid for highly qualified jobs, even university professors. I avoided a direct answer by saying that as a writer I got paid ten rupees per word even if I wrote 'the'. They seldom persisted beyond that, but looked impressed.

A gentle way for Westerners to ease themselves into India is to first acclimatize in Goa, a former Portuguese colony only relinquished by the fascist junta in Lisbon after their administrator was driven out by Indian military forces on the eve of 1962, nearly fifteen years after the British had left.

As we left the airport, I noticed my taxi driver was only pretending to be wearing his seat belt. For the entire ride, I struggled to appreciate the beautiful washed-out colors, the pale paddy fields, the dark hulks of water buffaloes ambling along the roadside, the smells that alternated between freshly turned fecund earth and sea and salt. Instead, I was in fear of my life.

My cab driver obviously trusted entirely in his Catholic paraphernalia spread across the dashboard: pictures of the Virgin and Jesus, crosses and rosaries hanging like talismans. We hurtled around blind corners, through unmarked intersections, and at one point, we narrowly avoided a head-on collision with a four-by-four. At nail-biting speed, he swerved around (or more often simply pushed from the road) pigs rooting through rubbish, bleating goats with their chops visible, homeless dhobi dogs with bent spines, cows with enormous horns, and tourists on motorbikes without helmets. Ignorance is bliss though; I later learned Goa officially has six hundred road accidents a year with a fifty per cent fatality rate.

I settled down in a small, piscatorial village well south of the main tourist beaches, which are patrolled by hawkers and decorated cows, with bombed-out, tattooed British hippies and bare breasted German women offending the locals.

The village I chose was the type of place that has no post office and where in the evenings you are welcome to help the men launch their boats from the beach for night fishing. I noticed the fishermen made the sign of the cross as they pushed their boats out to sea.

Miraculously, the village also had a hotel. A wealthy dentist, who had retired from practice early, owned and ran the place.

My spacious room had the essentials, and a squat toilet with a bucket for flushing. The room was clean, except for where mosquitoes had been swatted on the walls. There was even a swimming pool, and hot water – a scarcity in India. A daily invasion of tiny black ants swarmed over any form of moisture, even carrying away spilt toothpaste. The electricity was volatile; my ceiling fan would rotate faster as the light bulbs suddenly glowed brighter, then decelerate as the room grew dim again.

On my first morning, the coconut gatherers arrived. With deep insteps and feet shaped like the zygodactyl toes of chameleons, they shinned up the palms surrounding the pool, and made great whooping sounds to warn us below that enormous coconuts and giant dead fronds were to come crashing down upon us. Two French couples quickly fled indoors, while an Indian couple (they spoke English and I think they were from the diaspora) didn't stir from their sunbeds. Then one greenish looking coconut landed with a plop in the water. With great interest, we all watched the coconut bobbing in the swimming pool. The pool boy, with his net, continued sifting leaves, and made no move towards the coconut. Two of the women (the men climbed the trees with their machetes, the women gathered the fruits in reed baskets below) stood helplessly on the side of the pool staring at the nodding fruit. After several minutes of this impasse, I couldn't take it anymore. I dived into the water and rescued the floating coconut, handing it to one of the women. The pool boy gave me a panic-stricken look. I suddenly realized I might have committed a terrible faux pas and disgraced him and his proprietor.

I was aware of how intricately defined the division of labor was here in India, and this coconut had upset the status quo. The crones were helpless, since collecting the coconut might have meant defiling the swimming pool and having the entire thing drained. Clearly, the pool boy did not believe it was his responsibility to gather coconuts, only to clean the pool, removing leaves and frogs. To remove the coconut might also be to gather it, and that was not his duty. And now, a guest, whose duty it was to laze around the pool, had embarrassed the staff by collecting coconuts and cleaning the pool. I decided if there was going to be trouble, I would simply say that I was swimming and I found a coconut in my way, I removed it from my path, and the woman collected it.

No sooner had I returned to my position, than I heard twigs snapping and a fire crackling behind me. Several thin laborers, with ribcages and clavicles clearly defined, and hair disheveled, had started burning rubbish on the neighboring property. The smoke drove the Indian couple to the far side of the pool. The laborers rested with their arms on the fence, neighborly-like, pointing and casually discussing us tourists in our enclosure. A pasty British boy and his girlfriend, both with colorful tattoos, apparently fascinated them. The swimming pool was soon covered in a flotsam of half burnt paper and ashes blown by the wind.

I headed off for the beach. The sand was scalding, baking under the midday sun; I felt like a fakir crossing a bed of coals before extinguishing my soles in the cool of the Arabian Sea.

I made a long amble along the water line in the direction of the tourist resorts. The shore had numerous baby crabs scurrying into their holes, hermit crabs with barnacles attached to their shells, dead cuttlefish with opaque eyes staring up, and washed up starfish – some still alive. A man with an ancient paddle-ski made out of two planks tied together with rope was rowing out to sea using what looked like a road sign. Wooden fishing boats stood in rows hauled up on the beach; one was christened, *Lovely Jesus*. Sitting in separate groups were men and women, picking out dead fish that had stuck in the nets, and throwing their glistening bodies to the black crows to fight over.

There was a chubby awkward kid making gurgling noises, in khaki shorts, barefoot, building sand castles on the water's edge. Straddling him was his mother. He was wearing sunglasses; I realized later, to hide his appearance; he had Down's syndrome.

As I neared the tourist resorts, albino white Europeans, many of them Russians, began to dot the beach like ghost crabs.

By late afternoon, I took shelter in one of the cafés that lined the beach with their lean-to patios, a few poles in the sand and a reed roof, with a kitchen and bar shack at the back.

A pack of half a dozen male dogs was pursuing a mangy bitch on heat. She could not move fast; she only had three legs. While the alpha male was chasing away rival after rival, the others mounted her, yelping, one after the other, taking their opportunity. An American woman tried to intervene and was nearly bitten.

"She is on threes and they get on twos," laughed the waiter. "And what will you be drinking, sir?"

I ordered an Ugni blanc from the Sahyadri Valley. It was surprisingly good, made from Trebbiano grapes, with an unusual Riesling nose. Somehow, they managed to get it ice-cold to me.

Closer to the water a small boy was playing with a starfish, hopefully dead. As tourist couples walked past, he would run up to them, hug and kiss the women, after which he'd hold out his hand and beg. None had the heart to refuse. He ran up to the restaurant, threw his thin arms around a middle-aged European woman at the table next to me, and kissed her shoulder. She actually looked flattered, even though she had seen him do this indiscriminately half a dozen times already.

"*Hebt u een paar rupees?*" she asked her husband, in Dutch. He shook his head. Smiling, she then gave the boy a litre bottle of mineral water that she'd been keeping next to her table. She gingerly ruffled his hair. He squealed, delighted, took a great mouthful of water, then spat it out in a clear jet, three feet into the sand, the last foot sputtering as he burst into impudent laughter.

"Oh dear, dear," muttered an English lady behind me.

What was left in the bottle the boy proceeded to toss into the air in great celebratory fountains, dancing down the beach. The Dutch woman looked mortified, then furtively confused; her husband was annoyed; both felt humiliated. I had to laugh. What had she expected? The water had stood half the day in the sun; it must have been as luke-warm as piss. I would spit it out too. The empty bottle was probably more valuable. I noticed restaurants crushed them after use, an instruction to that effect printed on every label, either for reasons of landfill pollution or so that they were not reused with contaminated water, which was a regular scandal in Goa.

As the sky began to color, I ordered a red snapper and 'pommefrit', expecting French fries, but 'pommefrit' turned out to be a misspelling of pommefret, a delicious type of flat fish.

A young chef, with bulging triceps, cooked them on an open fire nearby. He nodded courteously to me. He scarred the sides of the fish into strips, I presume to make it easier to eat by hand, though I was given cutlery, this being a tourist café.

I returned almost every night, and slowly built up a friendly, but superficial rapport with the chef. He was shy. As pretty as he was, I expected he had many single male tourists taking to him, and he had learned to be cautious. And so, I established a routine for the next week: swimming pool in the mornings, walk the shoreline from noon, dinner cooked on the beach at sunset by the pretty chef.

Life was easier here in Goa than Delhi. I could sip wine on the beach for a couple of dollars; the food was fresh and plentiful; the youngsters, like the chef, were in hip jeans and T-shirts.

I'd seen several churches in the vicinity, but also small Hindu shrines by the roadsides. Judging by the number of pigs and piglets running the streets, I was in a Christian neighborhood. Although the lusophone generation are at an end, Catholicism is still the major religion. So no condoms I guessed. I wondered if AIDS would eventually flush sex in general (and maybe homosexuality too) out of the closet here.

However, in the newspaper the next day I came across a small article. A British tourist had been arrested, after staff at a hotel tipped them off. He was up on charges of homosexuality and 'pedophilia'; though the local boys he had been caught in bed with were, it said, aged 20 and 21.

It was only towards the end of my stay that I understood the hysteria and significance of this report. In this magnificent coastal paradise, there was a sinister underbelly.

Some of the channawalla or ice cream sellers on the beach also acted as pimps for child prostitution. The girls were brought in from impoverished debt-bonded families of the nomadic Lamani, and from villages in northern Karnataka. The boys were often orphans, as young as seven. Some of the children's mothers sold tribal crafts and cloth on the beaches, where their children were exposed to Western pedophiles. But most of the children came from broken homes with violent and abusive parents. These children were either bought or lured by European tourists, apparently mostly British men, to specific hotels, sometimes two or three children living with them, and at their sexual disposal during their holiday. The problem had reached such awful proportions that Goa, no longer Thailand, had become the world center for pedophilia. Afraid to jeopardize their tourist industry, the authorities were dragging their feet, trying to downplay the truth, while some police were taking their cut of the profits.

The problem for Indian men who had sex with men was that pedophilia and homosexuality were conflated. The word pederast was splashed about and used synonymously with pedophile. Yet in a land of child brides, there is no equivalent heterosexual term employed for men who have sex with little girls.

I left Goa for Rajasthan, renowned land of desert forts and lake palaces. Our bus crossed many dry riverbeds, and passed through dusty towns with lines of men lying in the shade on their string-beds. In the white city of Udaipur, a sense of desperation hung in the air. The normally friendly Marawari men with their burnished skins, luxuriant jet-black hair, British military style moustaches, ruby and gold studs in their earlobes, and seductive deep brown eyes, seemed somewhat more hardened here.

My hotel was rumored to have five stars, but I could smell the drains through the basin plughole; in the windows fat lethargic horseflies flew so slowly you could catch them with a pair of chopsticks; and an oversized rat peeped at us from behind the drapes in the dining room.

At the Chittor palace my guide proudly told me of a great johar, when thirteen thousand Rajput women and the Rani Padmini followed their husbands who had died in battle, by burning themselves to death in a massive bonfire within the courtyard walls where we now stood.

"It was not like today," he explained. "They were honorable, and they did it willingly."

Yeah, right, I thought.

He was an irritating man, who had a repertoire of corny jokes, and no sense of editing his endless and boring narration, hardly a word of which I could hear; his already heavy accent distorted still further, because he spoke far louder than necessary and the hallway echoed. I cupped my hand around my ear to reduce the reverberation, but he took this as a sign that I was hard of hearing, and began saying his lines louder, until he was actually shouting. The echoes kept amplifying. Soon everyone in the palace was staring at me, as I stood there flinching, cupping my ears, bombarded by nonsense and historical trivia from a guide standing two feet away.

This was not the first time I came across defensive postures and justifications for *sati* (bride burning). Like everything in India, the reality remains obscure. It can be suicide from despair, from a lack of options and extreme vulnerability for the widow amongst hostile in-laws; it may be plain villainy or a dowry scam. There were instances where the bride was killed because the dowry was disappointing. In one notorious criminal case, a black and white television set instead of a color one. Some claim the practice is discontinued and no longer happens; others that today it is made to look like an accident – a nylon sari and a gas stove explosion. But if exposed by the bride's family or activists, murder is today murder, and not accepted as a custom by the courts.

There was another unrelated puzzle on my tour of the city palace. When looking at the great ornamental cities and the art works of Europe, for instance in Florence, Venice or Rome, the artist is usually credited. It is Bellini's altar, Michelangelo's *pietà*, Da Vinci's portraits.

It is not the Medicis or the Borgias that are glorified alone. But I observed in India, the artists were never mentioned. It was always instead the celebration of the great and wondrous maharaja, the rajput, the nawab, the sultan, many of which didn't possess an ounce of artistic talent.

Then there are the persistent stories that the Mughal emperor upon the completion of the Taj Mahal, had most of his stonemasons' hands chopped off to prevent them repeating their work, and that the architects' eyes were put out and his tongue cut off. This could simply be a pernicious ethnographic slander by the British. However, when I mentioned this story to my guide, his reply was remarkable.

"Yes, but the villain [the architect] was planning to make a copy!" he protested.

How absurd, I thought, to think there must have been another emperor with twenty thousand laborers and twelve years' patience waiting to copy just such a project! But in my guide's mind, one of the finest designers to have ever lived was a villain whose creativity and talent was the copyright of an emperor.

The cruelty of these emperors, both in the East and the West, is not disputable. We have just come out of a hundred year period in which 37 million people perished in wars, but in which governments had deliberately exterminated 170 million of their own citizens. Clearly, one's own rulers are to be feared most.

The night before I was to see the Taj Mahal in Agra, I slept badly; like Amanda in Noël Coward's *Private Lives*, I feared that the building might be a disappointment, like a biscuit box. Could anything live up to such a reputation? I feared for the scale of it, either far smaller than imagined or disappointingly grandiose. How I wondered would it compare to that spiritual misadventure – St Peter's Basilica in the Vatican, a place of such intimidating design and dimension it was contrived to browbeat the soul into submission, to instill fear and awe, to bring the simple peasant to his knees in supplicant worship. It is of course actually a great testament to the genius of man, not God.

The Taj, however, has none of that architectural bullying. Rather it employs seduction. It remains the most beautiful building I have ever seen. All the clichés are true: perfect in its symmetry, it can only be taken as a whole, its subtle whiteness delicate, ethereal. Humane in scale, sublime in conception, the entire structure does indeed appear to levitate.

It seemed impossible to believe that anyone could consider destroying it. But British officers of the Raj had proposed just that – to quarry its white marble. Then again, I'd seen what the Indians had done to many of their own palaces, what the British have done to many of the artistic treasures in their own country, what the Taliban had done when they blew up the third century Buddhas of Bamiyan, and what the Americans were busy doing to Iraq.

The only ugliness here was a stain, like a dirty bath ring around the Taj. As I approached, I saw it was a never-ending parade of tourists. Perhaps, as on the Sydney Bridge, all tourists should be required to wear a monochrome pullover the same shade as the structure.

I asked a young Indian man if he wouldn't mind taking my picture with the Taj Mahal in the background. He immediately offered me his comb to neaten my hair. It was such an unexpected and kind gesture, I accepted. It was typical of the hospitality of the people of India; open, engaging, giving of themselves, always wanting your affection. Often volatile and excitable, sometimes quick to argue, the people of India were equally quick to bounce back from a disagreement, to forget and instantly forgive any misunderstanding or affront.

Back in Udaipur, I was dining at a restaurant across from the lake palace. Normally surrounded by a spectacular lake, it stood high and dry, its cracked foundations exposed, the green algae turning black, a fleet of gondoliers stranded at its foot. The bed of the lake was now a pasture for roaming cows and a track of road cut through it for jeeps and mopeds. The beauty of Udaipur had been drained into the sands by drought and corruption in the capital.

To freshen up I ordered a lassi, a delicious yoghurt drink mixed with spices. I'd learnt to refuse the bhang or 'special' lassi – which contains a liquid distilled from cannabis. One of those and you can easily misplace a day of your life.

The restaurant did not have a liquor license, but they brought the tourist a quart of beer. The key to enjoying India is to avoid water in any form – drinking, washing, cooling or swimming. After pouring half of it in a glass, the waiter placed the bottle out of sight against a low wall, with the comment, "It is disrespectful to show it to the palace." It would later appear on the bill as 'tandoori: one hundred rupees'.

In a quaint reversal of the way Westerners look at the exotic regions of the world, in 1901, when Maharaja Madho Singh II went for the coronation of Edward VII, he took his own water in the world's largest silver vessels, holding nine thousand liters each. It wasn't because "the water in London was not safe to drink" as my guide amusingly told me in the City Palace Museum of Jaipur, but actually (and boringly) a matter of purity and some religious injunction against crossing the ocean. The water the Maharaja took was from the holy Ganges, and it was essential to maintain his purity. I preferred the guide's explanation.

Asian travelers to Imperial London also kept journals, and wrote their own accounts of the "Lands of the Hat Wearers", the peculiar habits of native Europeans, and what they claimed was the easy sexual availability of white women.

I wonder how many homosexual love affairs went unrecorded too.

In one of the smaller, more rural towns of Rajasthan, I overnighted at a sort of Indian hacienda, more small fort than mansion.

The bellhop, like all the staff, wore a military style uniform and a beret. After he had shown me every detail in the room, right down to how to flush the toilet, he seemed reluctant to go. So I tipped him, modestly. He asked a few mundane questions, then told me what he earned in rupees. It was about fifty US dollars a month.

"Sir, are you married?" he asked suddenly.

I told him I was not.

He was twenty-four, he informed me. He had a wife and a child. His son was two years old. Would I like to try the massage service downstairs?

I shrugged, maybe.

He kept standing, not saying anything, looking down at his shiny black shoes, lifting their tips from inside with his toes. I wasn't sure what he wanted: was this an attempt to camp me up, to avoid doing other work, to satisfy his curiosity, to be hospitable, to find some other service he could perform for me for a tip?

"I do not have a good future," he said gloomily, turned, and left the room.

As it happened, I discovered the Ayurvedic masseur was rather keen to have me on his table.

That evening, the proprietors, members of India's million member royal family, came down to socialize and have a drink with their guests. They were three married couples and one young man, representing a total of four generations, the generations bunching together towards the eldest – the grandparents of those running the hotel – in their seventies, their children in their sixties, their grandchildren only entering forty, and the great grandchild having recently matriculated.

The British had gone about promoting many minor rajas to maharaja status, which is why for instance the sovereign of Udaipur was particular that he was 'maharana' to differentiate himself from the rest, for his family had never capitulated.

They were courteous, if slightly stiff and formal hosts, yet urbane and worldly. The men ordered single malt whiskies and the women sipped good red wine. I was offered a sherry.

The husbands dressed in smart dark blue jackets, cut for a former period; the wives were costumed in traditional saris. The great grandson was nondescript and awkward in his suit, as if he'd been forced to dress up for dinner. The managing generation was more colorful; she was power dressed in a heavily embroidered traditional skirt with a modern jacket that combined well; he had a middle-aged playboy look: white shoes, cotton trousers, a khaki shirt unbuttoned to the midriff, gold necklace, bushy but fine hair with an untidy side-parting, and a buffed up physique. He looked like he had recently put on weight; his ripening paunch didn't yet seem to fit with the rest of his figure.

The lounge walls were filled with historical portraits of the family, their ancestors and dead relatives. All, I observed, were hanging exactly straight; they must have kept a servant dedicated to this task alone. Very few of the family in the photographs wore Western dress, and when they did, it was usually combined with a puggaree. Most of them were noticeably deft at posing. Many of the photographs were of young boys, one particularly striking, possibly a yuvaraja, in his shiny fine brocade and leopard skin slippers. I noticed there were no solo pictures of women.

There were several pictures of hunting trips, shooting leopard and deer in the 1930s. In the hunting lodge bar, animal heads were mounted above a billiard table. It looked rather British Raj, except for some of the decorations, as elsewhere in India they used shiny Christmas baubles – blue, red, and gold – as arbitrary decorations, hanging inside archways or in the corners of rooms.

Wandering around the town earlier that day, it was obvious that the towns' people knew I was a guest here, and their courtesy was different from elsewhere in India; it contained a certain deference. An almost feudal lord and serf relationship still existed between the town and this house. They were the patrons. The town was dependent on their beneficence for good works.

I was staring at a strange object in a glass cabinet, when the playboy member of the family came up behind me and asked, "Do you know what that is?"

It was ball shaped, with about a twenty centimeter diameter, perhaps silver filigree tarnished black.

"No," I replied.

"It is a ball with a gyroscope for playing polo at night. They would put lamps in it. Do you play polo?" he asked casually, as if it was the most natural thing to do in the world.

"Unfortunately, I've never learned," I said and smiled.

"Game of the gods I tell you, and maharajas." He sniffed proudly. Then he offered to show me around his family's hotel.

"You must see our most fantastic room," he said.

It was the royal suite: an enormous four-poster bed with gold fili-gree, a bathroom with mosaic mirrors, a lounge crammed with large, ornate lacquered furniture, an Art Deco bar, an office with a wooden bureau, its own telephone and fax; the décor as fine as palaces such as Jodphur's Mehrangarh or Udaipur's turret of glass, the Kanch Burj, with gilded walls and partitioning screens with stained glass.

"Nobody is allowed to ever stay here; only the king. One day he will come. We must keep a room for him or he will just take everything away!" He laughed. "It would be beautiful to sleep in such a bed, would it not?" His eyes gleamed.

We returned to the family and the other guests. "Polo, game of the gods," the playboy announced as we entered, as if that was what we had been talking about all the while.

The conversation was strained; the voices subdued. The tourists were asking the obvious. How long has your family been here? What a lovely skirt, is that real gold thread? Where is it from? What do you call that? Pointing.

I empathized with my hosts. The old ladies ran through a potted history of the lineage, something they probably had to recite every night they had guests.

"This drought is terrible," I said.

"Yes, and you think the people would care. But I see the taps drip-ping in the houses and outside the water running down the gutters," said the playboy's wife, her heavily ringed fingers clacking on the wooden arms of her chair. She had a smoker's voice. "What will they do by March?" she lamented.

"The government is giving them six kilograms of grain for a few days' work on the roads," added her husband. "I think that is very fair."

"This sherry is excellent," interrupted one of the tourists.

"It is a cause of mosquitoes," chipped in the grandfather.

"Of course the ditches they dig collapse overnight, and they spend the next day digging them again," said the playboy.

"But at least it is work," his wife sighed; an afterthought.

I visualized a thousand copies of Sisyphus in Indian garments, digging trenches in a long line by the roadside, as if reflected in a set of infinite mirrors.

"The town must be a big responsibility," I ventured.

"Not ours, the government's now," said the playboy. "But we do our best; each in his place. You cannot just ignore them, and the government cannot control the weather."

Each of the big cities of Rajasthan has a distinctive color: the pink city of Jaipur, ever since it was painted for a historical visit by the Prince of Wales in 1876, ostensibly as a tactful apology for calling him "a pink-faced monkey", although some say the Raja's contractor was simply unable to acquire quantities of any other color paint in time; the blue city of Jodpur, after the pale blue paint the Brahmins apply to their houses, both as a mark of caste, for coolness and apparently as an insect deterrent; and then there is Jaisalmeer, a yellow fairy-tale city.

I entered in good tourist style – by camel. My particular camel was not only a gawky, garrulous, male adolescent with an evil-smelling stomach complaint, but he was in musth too. Which meant that when he didn't want to bite me, he wanted to fuck me. We'd trekked for four days through a corner of the Thar Desert, close to the Pakistan border. Patrolling fighter-jets roared low over our heads.

The main tourist attraction at Jaisalmeer is the fort city, built in the first part of the twelfth century. It is a complex of temples, palaces, winding roads, shops and homes. The outer-fort area is like all Indian settlements – a chaotic embarrassment of poverty and riches. Climbing up the cobbled streets, with their thin polished patina of cow, dog and human shit, smoothed out by tires, hoofs, boots and wagon wheels, people asked ceaselessly, "Your country?"

The street kids called, "Tata, Tata, baksheesh, baksheesh, Tata!"

Vendors made their best pitch: "Come, delight your eye!" "Looking is no problem!" "This will be most fascinating on you!" "Come back, come back! Don't break my heart, please!"

A young boy put me to shame by reciting the names of the entire South African cricket team, when I could not even remember the name of our captain.

I found respite in a charming café inside the fortress. It was almost too tastefully decorated, as if it were awaiting the lens of an interiors magazine, with floor cushions, single flowers in elegant vases, a refined choice of wall hangings, and tranquil lighting. As my eyes adjusted to the dark, a young man, with slightly East Asian features, loomed towards me, saying in a friendly well-pronounced voice, "Would you like to use the internet, sir?"

I tried logging into my email, but it was unusably slow. He placed a cup of tea on the desk and stood behind me.

"This is not a good time. I'm sorry, perhaps later."

"Well, I'm not paying for the time unless I can get my email."

"That is no problem," and he leant over my shoulder, putting his hand over mine on the mouse. I was unsure as to whether this was not simply the usual comfortable physicality of Indian men. He opened another browser window to check if the Yahoo server loaded any faster. It did not.

He placed his crotch, I thought quite deliberately, against my shoulder. I laughed, and caught his eye in the mirror above us.

"You're not married, are you?" he said.

I smiled.

"You can come back later, I will not charge you." And placing his hands on my shoulders, he started to massage them, then affectionately patted my back. "Come," he said, and led me by the hand to the lounge area, where we sat down on the floor cushions. He put on soft sitar music and lit an incense stick.

His name was Ajit.

The uses or abuses of English by non-native speakers are part of the texture of a place, and a dimension of the traveler's enjoyment. However, this is not stenography, and I would not want to recreate cruelly the awkwardness of Ajit's English, purely for the reader's amusement.

This is Ajit's story as related to me over many cups of fortifying masala tea. It was still early in the morning, and we were not interrupted by customers for quite a time; India habitually starting late.

Ajit was originally from Assam in the far east of the country, near Burma. He had all his belongings stolen while he slept on the train. Everything, he said. Until then, he had not believed that such things really happened.

Now, he was stranded in Jaisalmeer. Why he had come here in the first place, I never asked. It is several nights' journey by train from Assam. But this was no hard luck story; he was proud that he was doing okay. Slowly he was saving up enough to return home. He had refused his mother's offer of financial help. He'd hooked up with a gay New Zealander and was working for him. This explained why the décor of the café was such contemporary chic.

His family was a military family. His dad had been in the artillery for thirty years and Ajit was planning to join, although he also wanted to study political science. A political career seemed much lauded as a profession in India.

I asked him about gay life in India. There was no such thing, he said. But I knew of shrines even in conservative Pakistan where men gathered in drumming circles and had sexual orgies, and foreigners were not allowed.

Ajit knew of nothing like that.

And what of the gay movement in India? What of gay rights activists? That, he said, was only in the big cities, like Mumbai, of which he had no experience.

And what of himself?

He explained that men and boys fooled around – neighbors, friends, sometimes brothers. He had his first sexual experiences with two other male relatives, one an uncle not much older than himself. They had been sharing four to a room at one stage, and sex just happened. It was called masti, meaning mischief, frolicking or fun. It sometimes strayed into sex – mutual masturbation, very rarely penetrative. Everyone did it, Ajit claimed, but nobody talked about it. He'd even done it on the train. Some liked to get up to it more than others did, but they were usually also married, with children, leading regular lives.

I had heard of married men in south Asia giving massages and having homosexual sex for money with the full knowledge of their wives.

But was he, Ajit, more sexually interested in boys than girls? Would he sleep with a woman?

He was unsure how to answer at first. Girls were completely out of reach. I sensed that performance with a woman was a cause of anxiety for him.

Marriage was the big problem. Although homosexuality was taboo, the real transgression would be to refuse to marry, to break with the family. This was unthinkable.

Perhaps, I laughed, one day gay marriage would also become legal in India, as it had started to be recognized in the West, and children could be conceived with surrogate mothers. He shook his head, smiling. That would create a headache for the astrologists, he laughed.

He knew about Western gay life from what his Kiwi friend had told him, but it was a concept his mind could not assimilate. Not only was such a life impossible, it was not even a dream. To him it would be bizarre how some gay Westerners placed so much of their identity on their sexual preference, some to the exclusion of almost anything that was not gay related or endorsed by the so-called gay lifestyle.

Whereas in the West a hateful parent is often rejected and ostracized by the child, in India, care, respect, weekly financial contributions are usually maintained even to the most beastly parent. I'd been told that for the vast majority of Indians their definition of themselves was inseparable from their family. To build an identity based on one's sexual orientation would be something utterly absurd, even freakish.

How could it be healthy for gay Westerners to invest so much of their identity in something defined by societal prejudice?

And yet, here Ajit was; living away from his family, with a semblance of a relationship with his New Zealander, and occasionally picking up foreign tourists like me. He invited me for a session of mutual masturbation in the back room, saying he could close up the café for a few minutes. I said, no.

Was this then all just masti? Could it be said, as many Western gay activists would claim, that by marrying, having children, and spending his life with a woman, he was hiding in the closet, denying his true nature and living a lie? I do not believe so. By getting married, Ajit would be remaining true to an essential and integral part of himself, not only his identity, but his sense of personal worth. There was no other being trapped inside him waiting to get out. To break with his family and community, to go off on his own and lead this thing called a gay life would be psychological surgery as radical as performing a sex change operation in the quest for self-authentication.

India contains the world. All the patterns and lifestyles I had met on my journey around the globe were here in India. There were undercover gay bars and out of the closet gay activists. There was even a thirty-person, three-float "rainbow pride march". There were (though few and far between) men living together as couples. There were gays among the returned Indian diaspora, in the Bollywood film industry, in high-rise offices; people with wealth and private space, persons with the ability, the means and the desire to live their lives as individuals. There were well-cruised parks and toilets for homosexual encounters where men of all classes and social standing would go, and where as a Westerner you were not welcome.

The wealthier men looking for sex with other men were increasingly using the internet. As were the youth. At one internet café in a Himalayan hill station, I heard three boys giggling in the cubicle alongside me. I couldn't resist, and I leaned around the divider, lifting the screening curtain. The boys were gathered, with lumps in their pants, around an image of a big, bare-titted white woman: 'erotic site hosted by Suzy'. I smiled at them, and they kept on giggling.

As in all scriptures, including the Bible, positive references to homosexual love can also be found. Even in Islam, there are promises, not only of *houris*, but also beautiful boys for the faithful. And the influence of sensuous Sufism still colors Indian Muslim life. There is a history of explicit homosexual erotica in Mughal miniature paintings. On Hindu temples, not only in Konark and Khajaraho, there are tantric carvings, including homosexual acts, though I was told Nehru and the somewhat repressive Gandhi had set about having these effaced.

Unlike Christianity, Hinduism sees sexual pleasure as part of the human project. In the Bhagavad Gita itself, Arjuna is sexually aroused by Krishna, including mention of his penis. Hindu myths include Shiva sexually pursuing Vishnu, dressed as a woman and one of his sons is born after the fire god Agni swallows Shiva's hot semen.

Although heavily codified and regulated, sex is not sinful, nor is it an obstacle to salvation, nor a hurdle to personal enlightenment.

At various times there were laws against homosexuality, but the laws that have remained on the books making homosexuality a criminal offence were actually drawn up by the British Raj with their sanctimonious Victorian morality. Indian activists point out that there is not a single anti-homosexual pronouncement in the Hindu religious texts, unlike the controversial interpretation given to references to Sodom in the Old Testament and the Qur'an. And yet, in 2013, the Indian Supreme Court reaffirmed the British anti-sodomy law (whereas Britain itself had abandoned such laws long ago as nonsensical).

The politics remain complicated. Whereas in America and Europe, the fight for gay rights and the decriminalizing of homosexual behavior are firmly a cause of those on the left, in India the socialist left sees homosexuality as a decadent capitalist perversion, even as they are pitted against the equally condemnatory conservative religious Hindu nationalists who declare homosexuality a colonial sin.

Stranger still was my encounter with India's "third gender".

I first caught a glimpse of members of this "secret society" in the holy city of Pushkar. I had met up with an English woman from the BBC. She was shortly to go to Pakistan, but she asked me not to mention it to anyone as there was a real fear of kidnapping. Tall, blonde, and busty, in India she was constantly hit upon by men. She now covered herself well, including the top of her head with a faille scarf she would draw across her face at times of unwanted attention.

She was taking a short vacation before heading out to Islamabad. She had just come from a budget airline office to reconfirm her flight. The clerk had methodically copied the numbers from her air-ticket, typing on a computer. She could tell from the colors and typeface that letters and numbers had been replaced from several different keyboards, in a few cases the top of the keys had been blancoed and its function scratched in pen on the surface. This made her somewhat cautious for it seemed that the keys were not always the correct replacements, and that the clerk had learned by rote that for example the second 'a' on the left hand side was in fact an 's', and so forth. She therefore leant over and subtly checked the screen. There was nothing there. The clerk finished tapping away, hit the enter key, and smiled triumphantly. She pointed to the screen in alarm.

"Yes, the computer is broken. They have not fixed it for three days now."

It seems it was simply his function to type the numbers religiously into the computer. Whether this had any result and what happened thereafter was not his responsibility, but nobody could accuse him of shirking his duty or not doing his job.

"I am sorry, it is not my fault." She took back her ticket.

We were walking along the road behind the ghats. She was trying to find a pundit to perform a ritual *puja* for her, when she pointed and exclaimed, "What the heck is that?"

Squatting on the pavement were what at first appeared to be three disheveled women. A second glance at them revealed an unmistakable masculinity creeping through the whorish rouge on their black skins and their smudged red lipstick. Their faces were hard and shriveled; dangling from their ears and around their necks, cheap imitation gold jewelry. One extended her hand in a begging gesture. We pulled away, and hurried down the street.

I came across such folk again in a smallish village, also in Rajasthan. While exploring the steep dusty back lanes on foot, a man invited me to a wedding. It was one of those weekends deemed auspicious by the astrologers, and there must have been at least a dozen weddings that day. By this point, I think they were inviting anybody at all.

Musicians were playing in amongst a crowd of well-wishers all standing outside the house. The newlyweds were in the doorway; the young groom perched on a small horse and the bride standing alongside, finely decked out in sumptuous gold and red cloth. Neither looked happy; their eyes glazed and trance-like, as if they didn't quite believe in reality. Every now and again, the groom would smile, revealing beautiful white teeth, and then his face would return to a deadpan expression.

I'd only been there a few minutes when a group of five transvestites appeared in the street and started hurling what were plainly insults and jibes at the groom and his family. I asked the man who had invited me, one of the few who spoke English in the town, what was happening.

"It is the hijra," he replied. "They are he-shes." He was laughing; evidently, their jibes were very amusing.

One hijra had a thin, narrow face, with refined features, yet with horsy teeth pushed forward, black triangles visible against the gum. She had dense eyebrows plucked into elegant lines and her long, shiny black hair was swept back, pulled tightly against the head, with curls for sideburns. She had the red forehead bindi mark and a large round black beauty spot on her cheekbone. Gold earrings were clasped on her lobes and a single strand of white beads hung around her neck. Her dress was made from a diaphanous, dappled fabric.

Another hijra was less boyish. She had a rounder, more feminine face, but with a slight moustache. She wore a small black tika and a light blue sari.

The hijras were getting rowdier, and more belligerent, and seemed to be making vulgar gestures and taunts about the groom's sexual prowess. I thought a faint smile crossed the face of the bride.

"They seem to be causing trouble," I commented.

"No, it is good luck to have hijra bless a wedding, also a birth."

"Are they hired for the ceremony?" I asked.

"No, they were not invited. But they are always welcome. And they will be given money."

The wild bunch had started singing and one was drumming expertly on a dholak. They were dancing licentiously, until the plumper hijra broke into a funny, exaggerated walk, as if showing the bride how she will soon look – pregnant – an entertaining mix of amateur clowning, ribaldry and camp burlesque. The audience was enjoying it, women clasping hands shyly over their smiles.

"What are they singing?" I asked.

"Verses," is all he replied, then he said, quite jovially, "The hijra steal babies and castrate the young boys you know."

Back in New Delhi, I asked a recent acquaintance, Jeetu, who was working on an HIV/AIDS project, about the hijra and what I had heard. We were sheltering in the marble inner sanctum of the Imperial, a hotel in that grand tradition of Singapore's Raffles, Havana's Naçional, Rio's Copacabana Palace, Marrakesh's La Mamounia, Cape Town's Mount Nelson.

"The British thought they were eunuchs and tried to outlaw them, but the stupid English never understood anything," replied Jeetu.

He was in his early fifties; grey had started to pepper his thick wavy black hair. He wore a boldly patterned shirt, unbuttoned to the middle, chest hair visible. I had realised the moment he sat down, that I had sent him the wrong signal, that by inviting him for a drink he thought I was interested in him. The waiter – a tall thin, quite pale boy – with enormous liquorice eyes, kept darting Jeetu mistrustful looks.

"In the past, yes it is true; they would kidnap young boys and castrate them. How else were they to replenish their ranks?" Jeetu felt he was stating the obvious. "Castration is illegal. But like all customs that are made illegal it still goes on! Like caste rules. Or sodomy for the matter. India is a big country with over a billion of humanity."

I liked the phrase.

"But most hijra are keeping their testicles now. If a baby was born hermaphrodite, a he-she or a she-he, depending on which organs are most normal. If the sex organs that were there are not complete or do not develop, then when the hijras would come to bless the child, and if they see this, they would claim it as one of their kin. In cases, perhaps, just as well, you know." Then, unexpectedly, "Do you have a boyfriend and all?" Jeetu sneaked in the question.

"No," I replied. "But tell me, what would then become of the child?'

"The head hijra will raise it. She acts as a kind of motherly brothel madam. She would be entitled to part of the earnings when the child started to work. Hijra also prostitute you know. But, you are so nice-looking and clever, how is it you do not have a boyfriend?"

"Surely, the hijra are outcasts. Can they work as anything other than prostitutes?"

Jeetu had oversized, square, slightly tinted, black-framed spectacles, which he kept pushing up the bridge of his nose, every time he started to answer a question. I was attempting to steer the conversation towards more of an interview. It was quite clear from his physicality that he was more than just interested in giving me the low-down on Indian gay life.

"Yes, they do struggle to get jobs. But many do have other work. I heard that a hijra was elected to the council in Hissar and that another was even elected mayor in a town in Utar Pradesh. When it was discovered that she was a he-she in a sari, she was disqualified, since the mayoral position was reserved for a female only. But then, after a petition by the community, the hijra was re-instated!"

"Is this homophobia?"

"Yes and no. If you told a hijra that they were gay, I think you'd get your face slapped."

There was no question that Jeetu considered himself gay. He was quite camp, somewhat queenie. The waiter I thought had clearly marked him as such.

"But what do men who have sex with men call themselves, if not gay?"

"People talk about kothis here. But kothis are usually effeminate, out-there queens, you know, that type who only have passive sex. Most of them also end up big prostitutes. But they even have beauty pageants these days. They are what you call pushy bottoms." He burst out laughing.

"But then what about the men who fuck the kothis? How do they see themselves?"

"They are called giriya. They don't really see kothis as men. It is a terrible struggle to educate these people about HIV. They are almost all married themselves. And you get all sorts. Giriyas and panthis are usually tops."

I interrupted him. "In Cuba with its macho culture I found the same rigid separation, there the active males are called bugarrones."

"The world over, exactly. But in India, you also get men that like to be fucked and who also like to suck. You get men who want semen inside their bodies. These assorted characters think the sperm makes them stronger, manlier, all the better to pleasure their wives when they get home!"

"Like that tribe in New Guinea, the Asmat?"

"Exactly, and here in India we have the Ho in Jharkhand who have always allowed homosexual acts."

"Do you think of yourself as gay?"

"Yes, this is a fact. I don't think India is really all that different from America around the time of the Stonewall riots. The gay identity was not at that time defined either. Everyone was in the closet with a few role models, Noël Coward and Quentin Crisp or what have you. I know gay was invented by the Americans to get away from all the other nasty words. But for many Indian men who have sex with men that gay word is so contaminated. It is like faggot. Imagine I say to you, are you a faggot? Won't you please join our faggot pride march on Saturday? We need faggot rights."

I understood his point. It was for the same reason many Muslim women's rights campaigners abjured the label feminist.

He laughed loudly now, his two gold fillings clearly visible. "You can only get away with gay in parts of Mumbai and Delhi. But everywhere else you are a pervert."

I made a point of paying for our expensive five-star tea and over-tipping the handsome waiter. Hopefully, he would be less homophobic next time. I used the excuse of another appointment to end the interview, promising I'd pop in at the clinic to see his work.

From my discussion with Jeetu, it was clear that his funding from the West enabled him to run his HIV clinic and supported him in his gay lifestyle. But it seemed to me, that it was not ultimately up to Western activists, but up to the hijras, kothis, panthis of India, men like Jeetu and Ajit, the lotis of Syria, the tóngxìnglìan zhě of China, to change attitudes. As politicians viewed fundamental Islam as needing appeasement and it developed into the religion of the underdog, liberal changes were increasingly unlikely. Singapore would not want to anger Malaysia, Syria and Egypt would not want to stir up further hatred against their oppressive regimes. And trapped in this mess were men who simply wanted to, if not always, sometimes sleep with other men.

Gay rights should not be about preserving the rights of a gay identity. The dream should be about making man's inhumanity to other men illegal. It should firstly be about decriminalizing sodomy and homosexual sex, outlawing hate crimes, and changing the judgmental behavior against the sexual side of the human enterprise. Western gay culture and lifestyle, pandering to every faddism in the whole pantheon of false gay gods, is a spiritual dead end, like much of our materialist culture. And with it come too many cultural presumptions about identity and personality. Some Western gay activists, ignorant and condescending, foist their narrow preconceptions on other cultures. It's a fundamental misunderstanding. Gay rights are not the same as the right for a man to have sex with another man. The concept of a gay identity has allowed activism to make great strides in the West, but outside of this paradigm, in Africa and the Middle East, it may be counterproductive; the political and religious backlash might not be quite as dramatic if homosexuality was not ostentatiously packaged as if it were a marketing concept. Sex between men is not the sole preserve of those who see themselves as 'gay'.

Homosexuality has existed in every culture, and every culture has had extraordinary homosexuals – whether artists, rulers, warriors, or religious leaders. The better route is to reclaim the rich but suppressed histories of same sex love in the world's cultures, whether Muslim, Hindu, Jewish, Christian, Japanese or communist Chinese. Theology might be used to fight theology in the non-secular world.

I spent another day in Delhi, but after months of India, I felt a need to escape the pressure of the populace for a while. Despite daily reports of heavy snowfalls with plummeting temperatures that iced in the residents and closed down roads and railways, I decided to go to the Himalayas. On television, a group of European tourists were shown after being stranded several days without electricity, having to melt ice for drinking water.

I headed for the Kumaon Hills where I settled into a ramshackle hotel, with long wooden floorboards that creaked all the way into the neighboring room. Fortunately, I was the only guest. The season was over. It rained solidly for three days and I decided to take to bed, reading Indian history, watching Bollywood films, and sleeping during the frequent power outages. The accommodating staff served me in bed, but invariably left the door wide open to a freezing draft from the unheated passageways.

When the rain passed, I set off into the small town. It didn't exhibit the squalor and filth of the cities on the plains. Nor did I see any other fair-skinned tourists. People were not as friendly as elsewhere in India; here they seemed far more reticent, if not faintly morose, yet no more so than Salzburgers or Genevans. There were Tibetan and Kashmiri traders and groups of peasants with skins the texture of beef jerky, squatting on their hindquarters on top of the public benches.

I hired a car and driver for three days. His name was Raju. He had a luxurious moustache and woolly hair, and was probably in his late thirties. He was squatly built, though it was hard to tell, since he appeared to be wearing at least half a dozen layers of old clothes. Visible were a turtleneck sweater, over it a button shirt, and on top of this a V-neck jersey and a loose jacket.

Like many Indian drivers, he had transferred a lack of personal space at home to his driving, and it was as if he tried to miss everything else on the road – cars, bikes, people, cows – by a hair's breadth even when there was plenty of room to pass. There were also times when my heart stopped as our wheels reached the brink of the road edge, which plummeted away for a thousand meters below.

We passed lines of Tata trucks sounding their musical horns, festooned as brides by their drivers, every inch covered in an intricate and dense decorative calligraphy of pictures and designs, using flamboyant colors, garlands, flags and slogans in Hinglish. Magpies with long tails flew alongside us, and white crested laughing thrushes with their plumed headgear fluttered up into the trees. We often came up behind what at first looked like moving haystacks – women carrying impossibly large loads of wood, some with whole tree trunks on their heads. Some had children on their shoulders and while they staggered under their burdens, they stitched wool with large pink plastic knitting needles.

There were again several wedding parties. We stopped at one and they blessed us, making yellow *tilaka* marks on our foreheads and giving us a hard, white sugary sweet. We gave a donation of a few rupees.

Farther on, we got trapped behind a truck towing a white jeep, crushed like an empty can. It must have rolled off the road. It was a chilling sight, stuck in front of our eyes for so long, facing us.

Stretching down for at least five hundred meters were steep terraces of tea, and at the bottom of the valley a patchwork quilt of luminous green rice-paddy fields, laced together by threads of white river stones, with the occasional black rumps of water buffalo moving slowly, and the red flecks of women in their bright saris; a man-made world as blessed-looking as nature.

Raju hit the breaks, the tires squealed, my camera and binoculars flew from the seat and hit the exposed metal floor with a distressing thud. There was a man in the middle of the road waving at us to stop. Raju pulled over to the rock face side.

A cow had been hit on a blind corner. It was lying on its side across the lane, its right hock sliced open, blood spluttering from its mouth. A four-by-four with a dented bonnet and a windscreen covered in shaved off hide, stood in the road. A group of people were gathered. They were relatively quiet, not the consternation I had been led to expect with calls for retribution and mob anger. It looked like it had been a healthy beast, unlike the city cows feeding on garbage, with threadbare joints, needles of bone about to break through the skin, and guts twisted with polythene containers. The crowd was sombre, sorrowful and pensive. The beast kicked and bellowed in obvious pain, blood spraying from its nostrils. I told Raju we should leave. To preserve their souls, nobody was going to put the beast out of its misery. The cow would be left to bleed to death, however long that took.

As we drove past, I noticed a few of the men had gone to sit next to the beast, as if to comfort it.

It was an omen of sorts, for from here on, the road deteriorated rapidly. The car shuddered as if on some torturous testing block. Once or twice, we were nearly stuck in thick black mud.

Eventually we stopped.

"Baijnath," said Raju.

I was expecting a magnificent temple, from the eleventh century dedicated to Siva in the form of Vaidyanatha, Lord of Physicians. But this was a small complex, with a modest temple surrounded by memorial stones, themselves aesthetically pleasing, but all only a couple of meters high, like giant funereal urns, each with a tiny door. They were made of flat stacked volcanic stones set around a courtyard. The caretaker, sitting near a small fireplace, was clearly stunned to see me. The place had that feeling of a reception to which invitations had been accepted but everyone failed to turn up. He gave me a pleasant smile, but did not approach me or say anything.

"Eighth century," said Raju, pointing.

Surrounding us were the magnificent snow-capped Himalaya peaks, five and six thousand meters high. It was a lonely, yet peaceful place. It did feel like a place of healing, a spiritual waiting room.

Inside the temple were shrines and I think a lingam (a stone phallus), but it was hard to discern in the gloom. I wholeheartedly approved of a pilgrimage to a phallus. Nevertheless, this was not the enormous lingam I had expected. There was also meant to be a cave with an ice lingam, the focus of an annual yatra.

Raju shrugged when I asked him.

Had he understood me? "Lingam, ice, cave."

He shrugged again.

This place didn't appear to be anything like what I had expected. It was eloquent in its own right, and felt ancient, but where were the magnificent pillars, the stone carvings, the nine architraves of the ceiling I had read about?

A wide set of steps led to what I took to be the Gomti River. Nearby was a stone pond, with two little boys catching tadpoles. It would all look quite different in summer, I thought.

As I turned to go, an old man, sitting quietly on a low, stone wall, startled me. I hadn't been aware of him until that moment. It seemed he had been watching me all this time. He laughed at my small fright, and said something, I think in Hindi. I looked at Raju, and asked what he had said. Raju smiled and looked doubtful.

The old man had grey hair and was wearing a type of anorak, with a British aviator style fur collar, and a pair of suit flannels, quite unusual for the region. He had a grey beard like a hugely extended goatee, and a thin line of grey stubble on his upper lip. It was a polite and smiling face, but with stern eyes.

It sounded like he was repeating himself now.

I asked again, "What did he say?"

"He asked you where you are going." Raju said at last, reluctantly I thought.

"I haven't decided yet," I replied. Raju translated.

"But how is it you do not know?" the old man had asked, frowning.

"I'm traveling."

"But you are too young."

I supposed he was referring to what all Hindu men were meant to strive to attain. After performing their duties as fathers, providing for the family, educating the sons, marrying off the daughters, a man should enter the world as an aesthete and embark on a journey in search of spiritual enlightenment.

"I decide each day where next."

"But how can you know?"

"I have a general plan, but it doesn't matter for I am on holiday."

"On holiday. But where is your family. How can you be on holiday alone? Not holiday."

"I'm traveling."

"But you are not sadhu. Sadhu wonders the world but only looks inside himself."

"I want to see the world."

"What world? What do you mean? Why?"

Raju's translation might have been going seriously wrong; "world", how had he translated that? But, I had to admit, I had run out of answers. I politely excused us as we left. Then he shouted something. I glanced at Raju.

"He said may God find you."

It was still early and I wanted to push on to the Pindari Glacier or as close as we could get to it by car, that is if we were actually on the road we were meant to be on. Raju shook his head.

"It is too dangerous," he said.

I took him to be unwilling, that it was too much trouble, and that he was not sincere. After all the blind corners, narrow roads, rock falls, and the dying cow, he was suddenly concerned about danger? As it was, it was hard to imagine what could be more dangerous than just having Raju as a chauffeur.

I took out my map. "It's not far. Look, Raju." I traced the thin dotted line of road with my fingertip. He shook his head again and said no. I was by this time suspicious of Raju. I began to wonder if he had taken me to the wrong place and that now he was afraid I would uncover his deception. There had not been an English road sign for miles.

This is when I made my near fatal mistake. I offered him more money. He remained recalcitrant, but then I took several notes out of my wallet and held them up. He looked at them broodingly, then smiled and, glancing at his wristwatch, said, "Okay, we go now."

I felt smug, triumphant.

We backtracked through the vertebrae chipping stretch of road, and the treacherous mud, before we took a turn to the right and headed up a steep narrow track. Eventually we joined up once more with the winding mountain pass. The road continued ever higher, and I could feel the chill in the air intensify. Raju had pulled his polo neck up covering his mouth. Rocks had fallen in numerous places, and as we were on the mountainside lane, we repeatedly had to swerve around them, inching on to the edge of the cliff face.

It was during one of these evasive maneuvers that Raju lost control of the vehicle. It happened appallingly fast. As he turned the wheel to get back on to the left side of the road, the steering stopped responding. We glided sideways, paralyzed, unable to alter our destiny, our engine shrieking hysterically. We slid for almost fifteen meters, spinning completely around, eventually colliding against the rock face with the back of the vehicle.

We were thrice lucky. Ironically, it was the rock fall that had saved us, for had we not been directing the car back to the left lane we would have skidded over a three-hundred-meter drop. Secondly, we had reduced speed because of the rocks in the road, and thirdly we lessened the damage to ourselves by crashing in reverse, being thrown into rather than out of our seats. Neither of us had been wearing our seat belts.

I climbed out, hands trembling, legs shaking. Raju was inspecting the damage, hand pressed against the back window. The road was slippery with ice; we'd hit a patch and aquaplaned.

Raju restarted the vehicle, and miraculously, although the impact had smashed out all the backlights, it had not dented the hubs in any way that impeded the wheels.

"We must go back," Raju said. I was relieved he didn't rebuke me. But I knew that it was my fault. He'd warned me. I had seduced him with his greed, when he had known better. Then we both started laughing, until Raju was crying tears.

I hope Raju is well.

Much later, I realized that I had confused this Baijnath with the Baijnath also in the Himalaya, but in the Kangra Valley. No wonder there was no temple or ice lingam. Stupid tourist.

Three people are a crowd in the desert. In the Himalaya no matter how many people were about, it still seemed deserted. Much is made of the great pressure of innumerable people in India, and it is evident. Nevertheless, throughout my two months on the subcontinent, rarely did I feel crowded or claustrophobic, far less so than in many a European capital, Westerners seem to occupy so much more space than is their due.

The greatest density of humankind I experienced in India was at the holy Hindu city of Varanasi, formerly named Banares by the British, also known as the city of bathing and burials, of fire and water, of burning and learning. To die in this, the city of Shiva, situated on the sacred Ganges, is the dream of Hindus all over the world. Many retired, old and terminally sick people move to live out their last few years in Varanasi. If they can afford it.

To get to the river I take a bicycle rickshaw. A car has no chance at this hour in the traffic. My rickshaw driver is an old man used up as a beast of burden. I had not wanted to hire him, but he had beseeched me most pathetically. If we refused to use him any longer, what would become of him? My misgivings are not helped when another young rickshaw, possibly one of his sons, gives a running push to get us started. The old man has thin bowed legs, that seem incapable of propelling this vehicle, and yet they do. His diet is possibly too poor in protein to build mass; instead, the muscle tissues twine together ever denser, his calves like the fibers of a shipping cable. He has a white cataract over one eye, teeth stained from chewing red paan to keep him going, and a tubercular cough.

Almost everyone I meet in India seems to have some or other kind of respiratory problem. I have to clamp a handkerchief across my nose and mouth; the smog and exhaust fumes feel lethal, and to add to it there are open fires smoking on the pavements.

The road is implausibly crowded with every conceivable means of land transport known to man, including the Ambassador Car. And in between it all, cows – not one or two, but dozens of imperturbable bovines, dividing traffic, calmly chewing and shitting. It's a kind of madness that is exhilarating.

As we get closer, the traffic converges, until the directions of flow are no longer clear and soon we are all like salmon struggling up a waterfall. In front of us, a bicycle is hit by a car. Both cyclist and driver apologize profusely to one another. Tempers do not fly, emotions are muted; there is no road rage here.

At the Ganges, the major crowds have already left. I hire a small boat, and we row gently down river, passing the sacred ghats. People are doing their morning yoga asanas. There is a balletic beauty to it, groups of young men, with egg-shaped bum cheeks visible through their wet sarongs, lathering themselves with soap, white and creamy on their dark bodies. There are fake tourist sadhus dressed too perfectly in carotene robes with long white guru beards, too obviously signaling to me. Old men in homespun khaddar dhotis sit in lotus positions conversing. A blond Korean takes photographs. Indian widows in white robes with their heads shaven bow.

A giant piece of graffiti catches my eye – "End the Caste Rules!"

As we approach the cremation ghat, unmistakable with its huge piles of timber and billowing smoke, there are yellow petals floating on the black water. My boatman, who has a speech impediment that allows him only to make strangled sounds, drops me off.

The cremations are performed in the open. It is a privilege and only for the moneyed. Good timber that burns at a high temperature is expensive and massive amounts are required to dispose of a wealthy human body. Other corpses are burnt in the massive electric crematorium; still others are simply (and illegally) dumped in the river, as are the bloated carcasses of sacred cows.

Earlier, I had seen bodies on bamboo briars on their way to the ghats, wrapped in gaudy colored cloth. In front of me there was a somewhat obese man's body burning on a giant smoky, wooden pyre, the flames licking about it, a bubbling fatty sound, a barbecue stench, a fatty white ooze like sun cream. Children sat nearby playing a game of ludo.

Purified by fire and a final wash in the holy waters, where his ashes will eventually be scattered, this man it is believed has attained enlightenment; cleansed of his sins and failings, his soul will be relieved from the otherwise eternal cycle of reincarnation. Finally, peace has come for one, one less of India's ever burgeoning population, as if this nation were perpetually attracting the souls of all those who died on the rest of the planet.

I walked up the stairs and into a narrow alleyway. In a small square some way behind the ghat, a gnarled old woman, covered in a blue cloth, standing against the corner of a building, completely alone, caught sight of me. She was so bent over by age that she was shaped like a capsized L. She beckoned to me with a bony, witch-like finger.

"Come, come!" she rasped.

I glanced over my shoulder to see if anyone else was following, in case this was a mugger's trap.

She led me through a small inner courtyard. Women were sitting on the ground, stitching white shrouds.

"Come, come," she said, disappearing into a room through a low doorway. I stooped to enter. It was pitch dark and my eyes struggled to adjust. I could hear her moving about, mumbling in Hindi, and repeating "Kali-ma, Kali-ma, Kali-maaaa".

She struck a match. The deity was dark blue, almost black, an oversized bright red tongue hung out like a dog's, panting at me. She had four arms, one holding up a broad sword, beads of blood on the edge of the blade. From her lower arm, dangling by its hair, a decapitated man's head; in her opposite hand, she held a human heart. Her fourth hand was lost in shadow. Around her waist was a girdle of severed hands, and she stood on what looked like a corpse, depicted with a mortician's accuracy. From under the body ran dark stains, like congealed blood, from libations and offerings of fruit.

I recognized her: Kali, God of Death.

The old woman was now nudging me in the ribs with a metal plate. I was expected to make an offering. I placed ten rupees in it, but she nudged again, shaking her head while Kali looked on, sticking her tongue out at me. I placed ten more rupees on the dish. The crone looked pleased and smiled. Kali seemed to smile too, with her fixed doll-like eyes. Extending an arthritic forefinger, the nail jagged and broken, the old woman blessed me, scratching a tika mark on my forehead, cold and wet, the liquid ran into the corner of my eye. Now she hung a marigold garland around my neck.

Kali is also a liberator; she bestows knowledge, completing the cycle of rebirth as much as death. She is creation in destruction. It is not a corpse at her feet, but Shiva, her husband. And for me, she represented India more than any other god.

I was happy to have been blessed by her in this vast country where people were born and died on the streets, where birth and death were visible as in no other, where people loved, talked, cried, laughed, ate, squatted and excreted in full view – the grandeur and misery of the human condition, beauty and dereliction on an shattering scale; the irrepressible human enterprise.